# The Catch

A roommates to lovers sports romance

Leonor Soliz

# Contents

# Author's Note

My books always end in a Happily Ever After. My stories are generally fluffy, with a good mix of humor and low-level conflict. Nevertheless, I believe it's important to give readers every chance to consent to reading my book. Although I write generally happy romance, if you'd like to access content warnings for these stories, check leonorsoliz.com/the-catch.

Did you know you can get other free short stories by signing up for my newsletter? There's art too! Some of it spicy...

Sign up to always be in the know! visit leonorsoliz.com/newsletter

For anyone who's ever thought they needed to change to deserve love.
You don't. You're lovable as you are.

# Chapter 1

## Saint

After three dates, it's time to end things with my current situationship and move on. As soon as Rebecca leaves the bed and goes to the bathroom, I jump out of the nest of sheets we slept in and put my underwear back on. Wearing only boxer briefs, my diamond earring, and my chain, I trot to my semi-professional kitchen. The elaborate fruit tart I made for her waits in the fridge, and I place it carefully on the white stone of the kitchen island.

A maximum of five dates or one week, whatever comes first— that's my dating style. Secretly, I ask subtle questions about what type of flavors they like on our first night together, then design desserts inspired by them. I have this process down to an art. If I make something special with their favorite treats in mind, I can guarantee they have at least one good thing that day. Even if it's the pleasure of stuffing it in a trash can.

I'm adding the last swirl of fresh cream when Rebecca appears.

"So the legends are true," she says. "You never date for long, and you always end it with pie."

She wears the same impeccable black dress she wore last night, and stands by my marble island with a cocked hip. Her arms crossed, she stares at me with a raised eyebrow.

Her eyes take a long gaze down my body. My underwear is a dark navy with a gold, geometric pattern. It's bold enough that I don't feel underdressed.

Technically, a tart and a pie are not the same, but I don't correct her.

I smile. "Baking for others is a gesture of goodwill. Is there anything cozier than dessert?"

The precise art of flour, sugar, and fat calms my mind. My mom taught me as a teen, and I never gave it up. Muffins, cookies, pastries, and baked bars are for friends. Cakes and pies are for break ups. It's the lore.

The way Rebecca reacts, she's not taking my gesture as a sweet one.

"Yeah, cuddling," Rebecca says.

I place the tart in a carry-out container and close it. "I'm sorry. I'm not the kind to cuddle."

I casually re-arrange my gold chain around my neck. I'm on a schedule. The first order of business is to let Rebecca down gently. Next, run to training. We're in the middle of an important football season. We almost got to the biggest sports event in the country last year. This time, we want to not only make it, but win.

Ah, getting the ultimate trophy. The reason for all of my and my parents' sacrifices. The one thing that will prove that the devotion they had to my career since elementary school— and their support since— was worth it.

"Right." Resignation shows on her face. "I should have known... but you've been so sweet with me... I thought maybe..."

I push the container to the edge of the kitchen island, where she can take it easily. She doesn't.

I step closer to her and give her a kiss on the cheek. "I told you this was casual. That it wouldn't last."

"Doesn't mean I didn't have hope."

I let my smile intensify. I know my dimples will help my case. "Look— you're gorgeous. Your laugh is brilliant. Going out with you was lovely and fun... you're quite the catch."

"*You* are the catch, Saint."

It's funny. I'm a wide receiver. *Catcher* is a baseball term, but it has followed me around anyway. I think one of my many exes came up with the term and it stuck. Catching the catcher has a nicer ring to it, they say.

"That's kind, but what I'm trying to say is— You'll find someone. It just won't be me. I'm not looking for anything long term."

Rebecca is nice to hangout with, but there's no spark. That's okay. Sparks are hard to come by. In fact, in my twenty-nine years of life, I've only felt them once.

So I call a car for Rebecca. Soon she takes the tart and steps into the hallway, sighs, and waves goodbye. The door closes behind her and I lean on it. I release a sigh of my own.

When I felt those sparks all those years ago, I couldn't follow them. Not without testing myself first. No way I would mess things up with *her*.

The best solution I could come up with in college was finding someone else to try— really try— to go steady with. *She* was in a relationship, anyway, and I couldn't get in the way of that. Could I get to the sparks with someone else, if I gave it time? Could I make it work? All I needed to do was take a break from dating half the girls on campus. Pick someone I liked, and give it a real chance.

The person I tried to date, Kylie... I gave her everything I thought would make me a good boyfriend. Dates, flowers, and cooking for her. I ran her a bubble bath with candles, wine, and sprinkled rose petals. Only to have her flat-out laugh at me. She said not to ruin it with promises I couldn't keep. I had always been a playboy, so why pretend that I suddenly wanted something else? Playing make-believe would only hurt people. Everyone knew I would never be Mister Right.

She wasn't wrong. Kylie had known me for nearly two years at the time. She knew what I had to offer. I'm a guaranteed nice time, not the subject of happily ever afters. When people like Rebecca tell me I am a catch, I know what that means. It's all the external stuff. Success? Check. Fame? Double check. Money? Triple it. But those aren't the things that keep a couple together and in love.

Now I'm stuck breaking up with people I feel no sparks for, because without those there's no future. Just like no one seeks real love with a man they don't believe is truly relationship material.

It's fine. Fun flings are what I'm good for. I'm a great time. I let my dates charm me, and I show them interest. We flirt. We take that to bed, and have mind-blowing sex. Do the same once or twice more. Then I let them go, before they think they will be the ones to tame the receiver. After a week it will only hurt them a little. Much better than breaking it off after years in an empty, unhappy relationship that leads nowhere.

Pretending I can go long-term makes me a selfish asshole who doesn't care if things go wrong and people get harmed. I can't imagine anything worse than wounding someone because of it.

My watch reminds me it's time to get ready and go to the Thunderdome, the team's training facility. I sigh again and push myself off the door. Coach Clark won't tolerate any of us being late when the ultimate trophy is at stake.

Right as I take a single step, the doorbell rings.

Fuck. I thought Rebecca had left graciously. It's always awkward when I have to break up with them twice.

I don't have time for this. I flip through tactics to send her on her way gently—and fast. My mouth already sets in a half smile, ready to be conciliatory and ask Rebecca to go.

Except Ames stands across from me when I open the door.

My heart stops.

Ames, who taught me what a spark was. Who has a thing for artist types and is a serial monogamist. The one that inspired me, once upon a time, to test if I could ever offer a long-term relationship.

She's my friend Pablo's sister. She went to college at the same place he and I got a football scholarship. While Pablo and I hit it off from the start, two Latinos dreaming of rings and championships, I didn't meet Ames until the start of my third year. Pablo and I shared an apartment at the time, and she joined us for dinner one evening.

*My sister is dropping by tonight,* was his text to announce her first visit. *Her name is Amelia, but call her 'Ames', said like* aims. *Don't get it wrong, or she'll put you on her blacklist.*

I didn't get it wrong. In exchange, she gave me a look that ambushed me. Her smile burrowed into my chest. Her vivid brown eyes lit a fire in my belly.

Shit. Today there's no smile. A suitcase waits behind her in the hallway. Her wavy hair is messy, wind-blown and down to her shoulders, and her eyes are rimmed in red. Ames' beauty shines through, but I don't let myself think about it. Her gaze is heavy on me.

"What's wrong?" I ask.

Her lips press together, like she's holding back tears.

"Ames—" I take a step forward but she doesn't move.

It took me years to silence my heart when it asked me to follow that spark and see where it led us. I had to be cruel with myself at times, and pay close attention whenever she met someone else and fell for them.

The tallies were clear. She melted for the English majors. There was a philosopher once. Never an athlete, and never did I get her eyes on me. Eventually, I learned I'm simply not her type. Considering my reputation and what people made of it, and the fact she was in search of her forever, I couldn't say I blamed her. No way she would look at me and say, *him. I want him.* And if she couldn't, and if I tried anyway, all I would do is cause her pain. I never knew if I had what it takes to give her what she sought, anyway.

She firms up and swallows the tears that never make it down her face.

"I didn't know where else to go," she says.

Her words sucker punch me. I'm breathless. Those feelings I learned to suppress shake at the core of my foundations, because she's here. Whatever is going on, I'm the answer.

Belatedly I move away to let her in. All at once, I'm hyperaware that I'm only wearing my jewelry, my watch, and my boxers.

She moves slowly but comes in. "I'm sorry I showed up like this. You're probably busy—"

"Are you okay?" I take her suitcase and guide her to the guestroom. "What happened?"

Pablo didn't make it to the big leagues. He's off in Canada now, after playing in the CFL for a couple of years, and then transitioning to coaching special teams for his team. When he left, I promised I'd keep an eye on Ames. I have— sometimes more than I should have. Yet she shows up unannounced to my condo, and stands in front of me crying.

We face each other in the middle of the room. The walls are the most subtle vanilla cream color, to complement the off-white of the bedding, the warm wood tones of the furniture, and the rust-colored blanket and cushions on the king-sized bed. It has its own bathroom, too. It's well kept even if no one has ever used it before.

She stares at me and bites her lip, not telling me anything. My watch vibrates again. I should be out of the shower now.

"Fuck. Sorry." I silence my alarm. "I have training but— forget it. I'll pretend I got food poisoning."

Coach will kill me for it. I'll get an epic talk-to for the ages. A fine isn't out of the question, either, but I couldn't care less at the moment. I can't stand seeing Ames like this. I can't leave now.

I tap at my boxers like they've suddenly grown pockets and my phone hides in one of them.

"I just need to call them— never mind." I shake my head. "Are you okay?"

"No, Saint. I should be apologizing. I know it's a big season for you guys. Everything's gone wrong today. I can't be responsible for getting you in trouble, too."

"Ames. I can't leave you like this."

"Please. Go. Don't worry about me." She lifts her hands like there's nothing to worry about. *Nothing to see here*, they tell me. "I shouldn't have shown up like this, only that I don't think my friend Jo can't take me in and I just... I'm crashing hard. I need a nap. Can we talk later?"

I hesitate.

"Please," she says. "I'll be fine. I don't mean to get in the way of your life."

"Are you sure? Do you want me to call..."

I don't know what stops me. Maybe it's the way her brow pulls up at the center, like there's a pain she can't face yet, but I don't mention Aidan, her long-term boyfriend.

"... Someone?" I finally say.

Tears fill her eyes, but she squeezes them shut and wipes the one tear that falls with force. Anger cloaks anything else she might be feeling.

It stabs me. Right in the breastbone.

She shakes her head again. "A nap will help."

My heart aches for her already. Not with the angst of my old unreciprocated feelings, but out of worry for whatever happened to her.

"Are you okay?" I ask again. "Will you be okay? Who's ass do I need to kick? I'll sic the whole team on them."

She snorts. "Aidan."

She only needs to say the name for my whole system to match her anger. That knife in my breastbone— it twists.

My watch vibrates again.

"Shit," I mutter and I stop the alarm.

"Go," she insists. "I'll be okay."

"Nope. Can I get you water, maybe?"

7

"No, please. Really. You can go."

"You can sleep. I will stay right outside..." I make a vague gesture behind me toward the living room.

"I won't be able to sleep if you're out there. I know you're supposed to be in training. Don't let me get you in trouble."

I suck my bottom lip and search her eyes for a couple of beats.

I sigh. "Fine, but I'll call you later. I'll check in on you after work. You can—"

Who did I know that wouldn't be busy with training?

Evie. She is a Senior PR exec for the team, our quarterback's girlfriend, and a personal friend. As far as I know, Evie and Ames have mostly interacted professionally, and only occasionally met in social situations, but I know Evie will help.

"I'll give you Evie's number in case you need anything," I add.

"Thank you, Saint. It means so much to me."

"Of course. There's food in the fridge and you're welcome to snoop around for anything you need."

She nods. I turn to leave, but she stops me.

"Did I see that right?" she asks. "Did a beautiful someone go into the elevator with a pie?"

I study her. Anger still tightens her lips, and her shoulders remain weighted down by her sadness, but she's masking it well. A hint of humor brightens her eyes.

"Rebecca," I explain. "I told her we're over."

"She got the Bake and Bye treatment, then."

I raise an eyebrow. "Bake and Bye?"

"It's the breakup pies striking again. That's what Pablo calls them."

I snort. "You know me. Short flings only."

"Thank you for letting me stay," she says again in a small voice.

I hesitate one last time. I'm torn. I want to touch her somehow. A simple caress on her face, or a hand on her shoulder— anything that may be comforting to her. To us.

I shake my head. "Of course. We'll talk later. Rest, okay?"

I close her door, run to my closet, and grab the first set of joggers and hoodie I can find.

Jesus.

I dictate a text to Evie.

> **Saint**: Super big major favor. Ames is at my place. Something to do with Aidan. That's all I know. Can I give her your number in case she needs anything? I can't have my phone with me while in training. Please??

Just as I grab my bag on the way out, I get Evie's response.

> **Evie**: Sure, give her my personal number, but I'll have to interrogate you about this!! Be ready, Gael Santiago!

I leave her number on the kitchen island with a note.

My lungs seem to have grown ragged edges, and I rub my chest on the way down to the elevator. As soon as I am in my car, a feminine, slightly robotic voice announces I have an unread text from Pablo.

> **Pablo**: Ames broke up with Aidan. It was ugly. She has nowhere else to go. She's on her way. Can you let her stay with you for a bit? Only until she gets her feet back under her. I owe you big time.

The text arrived forty five minutes ago. If I had seen it, things would have made a lot more sense.

The jagged edges in my chest roughen up, making it hard to breathe for a second, two.

It wasn't just a big fight. Ames is single—

*And probably heartbroken, you asshole.*

It's not the time to think about what it means for that old spark I had to trample away.

I dictate a text back at the first red light.

**Saint**: She can stay as long as she needs. You don't owe me a thing.

And neither does she.

# Chapter 2

## Ames

I wake up confused. I'm sprawled on a bed, but the scent on the comforter is different from what I'm used to.

It smells like Saint's clothes. We don't hug often, but somehow my brain has made sure I remember. It hits me hard how badly I need a hug— or for Saint to hug me? Still confused. I need to be held, regardless, because...

Two blinks later, it all comes back to me at once.

How Aidan got a promo segment on the most watched morning show to talk about his new album. As the singer for the late night show on the same network, it only made sense for him to spend the night in the office. The couch in the green room was a perfectly good place to catch a few hours of sleep, he said, since he would have to be back so early.

Like a good girlfriend, I was excited for him. A true cheerleader, ready to invest in the relationship and his career in every way. Trying a hundred ideas to show him my support. Getting up at the crack of dawn to show up at the TV network building where we met a few years ago, when I got a catering contract for the popular late show he sings for. Surprising him before his promo segment with his favorite sandwich and veggie-fruit juice.

How I froze in SBN's Hello Seattle's hallway, my smile disappearing as I flinched, when Aidan came out of the green room. Giggling with a beautiful blonde. Holding her hand.

Giving her a quick kiss. On the lips.

The memory is a shard of glass boring through my heart. I close my eyes again as if it will erase everything from my mind. It doesn't work— I can still remember how I followed them to the studio and everything that happened after. The spectacle I orchestrated without any plan or fear of the consequences.

Fuck, I should have spared a thought for the consequences.

I cringe and reach for my phone, abandoned on the bedside table before I hid from the world via sleep.

**Jo**: what the fuck happened? Ames, this is bad

**Jo**: AMES. Tell me you're okay.

**Jo**: Amelia Guerrero! Where are you? The only reason I'm not sending a search and rescue team to find you is because I know you're a badass woman who will come out of whatever this is victorious, but I'm so fucking worried that I AM STRESS EATING ALL OF OUR CLIENT'S CUPCAKES

**Jo**: If I don't hear from you by 4pm, I'm sending the rescue team. Don't test me

I snort. Tears threaten to come out at the multiple texts from my coworker-slash-friend, but I hold them back. I'm not sure if I'm grateful for her, or if it's because I discovered the man I thought I'd be with forever had been cheating on me. Until I know, no crying for me. I'll count the times I cry for Aidan, so I never forget what he did to me.

Because, shit, we were buying a house together. I did what I swore I would never do. I moved into my boyfriend's house without a place to come back to, or without enough money to get away if I needed to. All because I believed him when he said we would be together forever.

It made sense, he reasoned. We slept together most nights. I had things in his place. We would be living together soon enough, so why postpone the inevitable?

Then he wrote a song and called it *Settled*. How romantic, I thought. It was settled— we were settled. Surely it was a sign we were meant to be together forever.

Cracks rip through my heart. Sandpaper fills my throat. My eyes get blurry again, and I stop it once more. Later, I'll let myself cry. Now I need to answer Jo. She's worried and, as my right hand in my personal chef and catering business, I need her help.

> **Ames**: I'm okay. I found a place to crash (I know you don't have the room). I'll explain everything as soon as I can but this is what we need to focus on right now: 1- don't cater to the show tonight. We were fired. 2- Can you please keep the ship afloat? There's a lot I need to figure out. 3- Aidan is an asshole and was cheating on me

I don't wait for Jo's response and get up instead. I note the private bathroom in the room, and open my suitcase on the floor for now. I only grabbed essentials before leaving what had been Aidan's bachelor pad. I take a couple of pills for the headache threatening my skull, and make it to the kitchen with downtrodden steps.

After gulping some water down, I open the fridge and peruse the food. It's the prepped meals I send for Saint and, though it feels strange somehow to eat food I made for him for work, I go ahead and take a chicken and veggie meal and pop it in the microwave.

I lean on the kitchen island, the hum of the microwave the only sound. My posture is awful, with my shoulders curved inwards and my chin down to my chest, but I don't have the energy to fix it. What a mess. The TV network was my single largest client. I can only keep the catering business afloat for a short time, unless I find another big contract.

As much as I enjoy making food and smoothies for Saint and his friends, and as much as they pay well, it's simply not enough to cover the salaries for every person I employ. The sheer size of the late show meant I doubled my team to keep up. Without that client, half of my employees will become redundant at the business level. At the ethical level? I can't imagine firing them.

I need a new big client, stat. A team of ten people depend on me. Hell, *I* depend on getting a new contract. I don't know what will happen to my career if I can't salvage my business.

All because the man who promised me forever and wrote songs about it couldn't keep it in his pants.

Now I'm back at square one, wondering how something so *settled* had gone so wrong.

If only I had ever seen a long-term relationship that worked, I might have known what forever love looks like. As it was, I never learned. My parents divorced before I was ten, only to start on a journey of a hundred one-year-long relationships. All I got out of it was my mom's *'be free, Amelia,'* and my dad's *'relationships are a trap.'* Only I decided to use my freedom to be different from them. I would find a relationship that would be good to me. I would never make the mistakes they did.

Except I did. I missed the signs with Aidan. Somewhere, somehow, I failed at making the relationship work, and I have no idea how. Now I'm in the dark again, not knowing what I did wrong or how to make it right one day with someone else.

Who knows. With my history, maybe I never had a chance at a happily ever after. My love story with Aidan had checked all the boxes, and followed every beat of the script. And yet here I am, in my brother's friend's fancy condo, crying over a man who didn't think that was enough.

I allow myself a few tears. Okay, fine, it's many of them. They run down my face and drip down my chin when I glance up at the ceiling. It makes this the second time I cry about Aidan. The first was right after I confronted him in plain view of producers and morning news anchors and other guests. At least, the way I reacted, with everyone looking at us in shock, I'm one hundred percent confident he hated it. Because I said my piece at the top of my lungs, not caring who heard— wanting everyone to listen to every word. I gave him his sandwich and smoothie in a dramatic fashion, and left. Bawled on the way out.

The embarrassment must have killed him inside.

Good. He deserved it.

With that thought, I dry my face and take the food out of the microwave. It's only when I place the container on the kitchen island that I see the note.

*Ames-*

*I'm sorry I have to go. Anything you need, this is Evie's number. I didn't want to text you now so you can sleep. I didn't know if your notifications were on. Please check in with Evie later. She'll let me know.*

*In any case, I will let the concierge know you're staying here. Below are the codes you can use if you need to go out— the code Pablo gave you will get you up the elevator, but the new one will get you in here. I'll make a key for you asap.*

*We'll talk later.*

*- Saint*

15

*PS: I'm glad you came here.*

Saint's kindness has me crying again, but I can accept these tears. They fall softly, leaving cold trails that dry up fast.

When my brother left Seattle for work, the two friends agreed that Saint would be there for me. He has been in a hundred small ways, but I had never needed him like this. Not to this degree, at least.

I make myself eat the food. It's a damn good easy dish, if I do say so myself. Despite my loss of appetite and my grayed out senses, I can still make out the depth of flavor that butter and spices added to the food.

My relationship with Saint is a bit strange. When I met him back in college, he was already the popular athlete dating his way through the school. Friendly and self-assured, confident and unassumingly hot, all he had to do was flash those dimples and he got whatever he wanted.

If he had ever directed that smile at me and suggested he wanted something more, I would have given him anything he wanted, too.

But he didn't, and he dated ten times as many people as I did. Which, good for him, I suppose. It never made sense to be jealous. Not that I was. Even back then it was clear we weren't compatible that way. At some point in college, I heard him say he wasn't looking for commitment. Meanwhile, commitment is all I ever wanted. All we could have was a quick something that might have been spectacular, but not what I was looking for.

Besides, I'm pretty sure he sees me more like his friend's little sister, rather than someone he could have fun with then bake something for. He's never made a move, and has seemed happy to quietly help me out when I need it.

The least I can do is do as he asked. I sit at the kitchen island, the food in front of me, and I check in with Evie.

**Ames**: Hey Evie, this is Ames. Saint gave me your number and asked to check in. I'm okay, but I'm sorry for getting you involved in this

**Evie**: It's all good! I'm glad Saint involved me. I know you and I have barely spent time together so far, but I'm happy to help with this.

**Ames**: I'll be okay. I swear Saint thinks he's my big brother, the way he worries about me.

Except my secret is, I couldn't ever see him like a sibling. Especially not when, only a few hours ago, I saw him wearing nothing but boxers and his jewelry. Even through the fog of my catastrophic early morning, that image is seared into my brain. The chain, the glint of his earring, the long, muscled lines of his body. One day soon, I'll get to delight in the memory. But not today.

**Evie**: Mhh, well, I'll let him know you're okay. He'll be happy to hear it. Oh, and anything you need, even if it's just a chat, let me know. I may have seen a clip going around about you this morning.

Shit! Did someone record everything? At least they can't fire me twice.

**Ames**: Thank you, Evie. I appreciate it.

I don't make it far into my search on social media when I get the link from Jo.

**Jo**: YOU THREW A SMOOTHIE ON HIS HEAD RIGHT BEFORE HE WENT ON THE MORNING SHOW?

Uhm, yes. When I said I had given him the smoothie and the sandwich? I may have underplayed it.

**Ames**: in my defense, I wasn't thinking they'd fire me for it

It seemed completely worth it at the time. Rage ran in my veins, and I moved without making a conscious decision. With one hand, I dumped the large smoothie on his head and shoulders, like it was an ice bucket and I wanted him to freeze and shiver. Cower in response, maybe. With the other, I pushed the sandwich onto his shirt and *smeared* it. Mustard, it turns out, stands out against blue fabric. Artistic moves, really.

I finish eating and decide a shower will help. The rain showerhead I peeked at earlier will wash my hurt away. If a new set of tears escapes me, at least I won't notice.

With morose movements, I aim for the guestroom. Saint's door, right next to mine, is ajar. It tempts me, winks at me, while I'm on my way back to the guestroom. He may have said I'm welcome to snoop if I need anything, but this feels wrong. I may be curious about him and the kind of things he gets up to in there, but the devil on my shoulder gets heard only once a day. I ruined Aidan's gorgeous curls with a wet-and-sticky mix of oatmeal, berries, and almond milk, after all. Right before he joined the show to promote his latest album. It's plenty to satisfy the red little rascal.

Even now, a part of me delights in how it dripped down his amazing hair, streaming down his torso and plopping down on the floor. The hundred eyes staring at us in shock. The gasps. The anger electrifying my nerves.

I turn into what will be my space for an undetermined amount of time and go straight into the bathroom. Despite the emotional nicks and bruises weighing me down, nothing can erase the satisfaction of ruining Aidan's promo segment.

It probably says a lot about me and the things I didn't really feel for him, that a moment of rebellion puts a small smile on my face.

As the water cascades down my body, I cross my fingers that it will be enough to keep me composed. I have too much I need to figure out to crumble.

# Chapter 3

## Saint

It's a conditioning day for the team. I'm doing sprints, which serves me well today. When I'm running, I have less of a chance to talk to people. It lets me keep thinking of Ames non-stop.

She broke up with Aidan. She's moved in with me— temporarily. That's all I know, and it's enough to make my heart strain.

Fuck, the pain on her face. The barely-subdued anger.

I run until my lungs feel like they might explode from the effort. One of the trainers insists I need to take a break, and I sit on the grass to recover.

Evie appears through the large glass doors out of the building, and waits at the edge of the field. I'm about to stand and go to her, just in case she's here to tell me Ames texted and something is amiss, but she calls Logan. Their conversation looks serious, so I make myself wait. A few minutes later, the quarterback gives her a quick kiss, turns, and runs to me. I meet him half way.

His frown is severe. "Evie wants to talk with you. It's going to be rough, but it's going to be okay in the end."

"Is Ames okay?"

"As far as I know. But this— we'll talk about this later."

My stomach turns into a knot.

"I thought you'd want to know what's going on," Logan adds, "but if I was mistaken, you can berate me later."

"Cryptic much?" I add a smile to soften the question.

Logan slaps my shoulder and goes back to training. I jog to Evie.

"What's up?" I ask.

Worry mars her brow. It's not quite the killer frown her boyfriend typically sports but, with all the time they spend together, maybe she has started to adopt some of his quirks.

She purses her lips. "I heard something in the front office. It's not good. Can you come find me after training?"

"You have to tell me what it's about or my concentration is shot." I smile because my dimples will help convince her.

"I think they're talking about trading you, Saint. I'm so sorry."

All sweat from sprinting cools down at once. I freeze. My smile falters.

"It's about the salary cap and other stuff," she adds. "I'll tell you more later."

I'm glad she doesn't try to explain, because the way blood rushes in my ears, I can barely make sense of what she says.

I take a few deep breaths.

"Is it certain?" Is all I think to ask.

I swallow through the vise taking hold of my throat. I can't get traded. This team means everything to me.

Now I'm as serious as her. Football is what I'm best at. I could do it elsewhere, too, but I wouldn't find friends like this in another town. Or fans that stayed with me through difficult times, and a beautiful city to make my home.

These are my people. They are the ones who know who I am, even when I can't see it clearly. Finding people to be so effortlessly close to is a miracle, and not one I take for granted.

"I don't think so." Evie puts a hand on my arm. "From what I hear, they're watching you but have not decided. I put some subtle feelers out. I'll tell you everything after training— I almost didn't want to say anything, but Logan thought you'd want to know."

The Strike has never been as strong as this year. We've won every game this season. We're playing as one. Winning the biggest game in the sport for the first time in history is within our reach.

I'm a really good player, but even so I don't really have a say in what happens in the front office. All we hear gets filtered through friends like Evie, our agents, and the general rumor mill. I don't know where this thought of a trade is coming from, but one thing is sure. This is awful news.

I sigh. "He was right. Thanks, Evie. I'll go to your office afterwards." I shake my head. "Any word from Ames?"

"She texted me and said she's doing okay. I'll keep an eye on her for you, too."

"Thank you. You're the best. Talk later."

I give her a quick hug and go back to training, so I can think some more.

This is the year I get what everyone in this industry dreams of. It's when I get to look at my friends at the end of the season and say we managed what seemed impossible three years ago. I'll get to look at my parents and my little sisters and thank them for believing in me all these years.

Getting traded would ruin everything. I can't let all this work go down the drain. I have to up my chances of staying. A ring and something just as big. Going for the MVP isn't out of the question. I knew I was already in the conversation for that.

Having to leave the people I care the most about is my personal nightmare. And just as Ames lands in my condo single for the first time in years, the team's front office has served me a bitter meal.

# Chapter 4

## Ames

At first, I don't notice that Saint has come home. I'm too busy watching videos of me going viral. When I've memorized the shot someone recorded, I find another one. So far, I've seen three versions from different angles. A few edits.

If nothing else, the rage I see on my face makes me feel better.

Until I find the videos made by Aidan's fans. As a suave Irish musician and all around artist, with his impeccable looks and charismatic presence, he has plenty of those. He's a fixture of the late night show and, when his deep blue eyes stare into the camera, sighs come to life all over the country.

I know, because I used to be one of those fans. When I got the contract catering for the network and I got to meet him, I was absolutely starstruck. When he smiled at me and invited me out, I felt special. When he said he couldn't think of anyone else, I thought my dreams were coming true.

Fuck him.

I get up and, as soon as I'm out of the room, the sweet smell of baking and chocolate greets me.

And fuck *me*, Saint looks amazing in simple jeans and an embroidered blue hoodie, with tigers and lotus leafs and flowers in silver thread. He bends to the top oven— he has one of those double baking compartment sets— as he pushes a tray of cookies in. Those jeans must be custom-made, because his ass is perfectly round in tight-fit denim.

Ugh. Thoughts like that don't serve me well, especially not when I'm at the mercy of an emotional rollercoaster.

Angry and hurt over Aidan? Makes sense. Suddenly remembering how easy it is to lust over Saint? Reproachable.

A long time ago, Pablo was the typical misguided older brother and warned me off Saint. Pablo insisted that's not what he was trying to do, but what was I supposed to think? My brother reminded me that Saint dates at the same pace that he breathes, and that we would probably not work out. Like I needed the warning at the time. I may need it now that we're living together, but it's an entirely too-premature thought. It's just the shock of having Saint closer than I have in years, and more accessible to my senses than I've been used to.

I push all those notions away and sit at the kitchen island.

He faces me. A hint of worry lines his brow. "Did I wake you up? I'm sorry."

He wears his diamond earring tonight as well, and the look is effortlessly sexy.

*Tsk, tsk, Ames. You shouldn't think about these things.*

It's okay. I'm only acknowledging it as a fact. It's an obvious, irrefutable statement. I've always known Saint is extremely attractive, with his hair and the way he styles it pushed back, giving him the just-out-of-the-shower look, no matter the time of the day. His light brown skin is tan from working outside so often, in a sun-kissed way that is truly alluring. He's tall and full of thick, long muscles, which he tends to dress in bold clothes. It doesn't end there. His face is gorgeous. The lines of it reflect the long history of mixing genetics in Latin America. His dimples are delicious. His smile is always playful. It's no surprise he has his own big fan club.

"I was awake," I respond. My tone is casual. Friendly. "I was doomscrolling."

I add airquotes to the last word.

"Mhh." He arches an eyebrow. "Were you watching the video from this morning? Evie showed it to me."

I cringe. "You saw that?"

"It was epic. That righteous fury on your face— you really honored your last name, Amelia Guerrero."

I purse my lips not to show a full smile. It's wrong to be proud of that description. And the way he pronounced my name in perfect Spanish and with a Colombian accent...

"You probably want an explanation," I say instead, "before I ask to stay with you for a bit."

He leans on the stone surface of the island and studies me, arms crossed. "It would satiate a question or two, but you don't have to explain or ask to stay. I'm already saying yes. And I'll be pissed at Aidan regardless. I don't need to know what he did to enlist my team and go give him a bit of a fright."

"That's... very generous. But if I'm to invade your home for some time, I should at least explain why."

I hate that I have to ask Saint for refuge. The idea that I might be a burden to him weighs me down with guilt. Someone who has made the right choices would have their life together, and wouldn't need rescuing. Now I'm asking my brother's friend to give me shelter, like he has any responsibility over me.

He gives me a long, serious look. I hold his gaze. He's the first to pull away. With a gentle nod— like he's made a decision— he sighs and turns to the oven.

After a quick glance at the timer, he puts his attention on the pot on the stove. "What did Aidan do?"

"How do you know it was him? I could have gone ballistic on him for no reason."

"Doubtful." His dimples are nowhere to be seen, but he smirks. "I don't really know him, but I know *you* enough to know you wouldn't waste good food on someone, unless they did something to earn it."

His response would have gotten a grin from me any other day, because it's true, and I like that he knows this. Today, it gets a weak smile.

I'm putting on a brave face but, inside, my foundation is still cracked and sinkholes have appeared all around. Aidan and I were so good, I thought. We made so much sense. He was who I had been looking for. So why did he cheat?

No answer makes itself known. Confusion and pain is all I find when I look for the response. I have to tread carefully, or I'll fall into one of those holes and who knows what would happen next. All I can afford is to recoup, and figure out how to prevent the same thing from happening in the future. One day, when I'm ready to try again.

Saint doesn't add more and waits for my reply. I take a deep breath before admitting the truth. Somehow, I feel like I'm revealing something shameful about myself. How embarrassing, that I couldn't make things work with Aidan. Worse, that it ended the way it did.

My breath comes out shaky.

"I caught him with someone this morning," I say. "He was cheating on me. But my little rage show cost me the largest client I had."

"Ouch." His nose wrinkles. "Asshole."

"And since I lived with him while we shopped for a place of our own, I had nowhere to go."

"Incorrect." He lifts an eyebrow. "You have this place."

He checks the timer and the pot again, before taking a plate with cheese out of the fridge and placing it near me.

I rub my lips. "I appreciate you've always been around, no matter how busy you are. But you didn't sign up for a roommate. I don't want to get in the way of your life."

"I'm not concerned about that."

"Please, no need to pretend— I saw someone leave this morning as I came in— I'm pretty sure you *invite* people over often."

He doesn't say anything, but grabs two mugs and two spoons, and fills them up with what appears to be hot chocolate from the pot.

"Never mind that," he finally says. "I'm glad you don't have to worry about a place to stay. You can call this your home for as long as you need."

He pushes one of the mugs to me, and the other to the place next to me. I sniff the chocolate in my cup and detect a few spices. Cacao, cinnamon, and cloves are the strongest notes.

"I'm making you chocolate chip cookies and chocolate con queso." His Spanish is just as clear as when he said my name. He adds a few paper napkins to the arrangement. "I thought you'd enjoy a sweet treat tonight."

The timer goes off and he takes the tray out of the oven with swift moves. It looks graceful, just like when he's maneuvering to catch the ball in the middle of a game, or when he dances after a touchdown.

I may have watched the Strike play once or twice out of curiosity through the years. It's never been a big deal. I've always known I have to be careful with my feelings around Saint. Not because of what Pablo said years ago, but because I've always known Saint and I look for different things. My brother just happened to have the same take as me. And a secret part of me, one I keep hidden and away from sight, has always known I could easily let things get complicated with my brother's friend.

Soon there's a plate of cookies between the two spots, and he sits next to me. He throws a few cubes of cheese into my mug, and then some into his own.

"Cheese in chocolate?" I ask.

"Colombian treat. My mom made it for me often." He puts a teaspoon in each cup. "You scoop it out and let it amaze your palate."

I copy him and try the mix of spiced chocolate and melty white cheese together... and moan.

"Wow," I say. "Salty, sweet, flavorful..."

"Right?" He smiles.

Finally. Those dimples make an appearance.

27

"This is very nice of you, Saint. Thank you."

"Hey— I can be nice." He offers his mug for a clink, like we're toasting something. "In fact, *nice* is my brand. Until I'm not nice, if you get my meaning."

He winks, his dimples dangerous as ever.

I laugh. "I'm sure that's right."

"Try a cookie. I can't wait to hear what a trained chef has to say about them."

They're as good as the hot chocolate he made.

"This is wonderful, Saint."

"Thank you." He leans back on the barstool. With an elbow over the back of the leather seat, he watches me thoughtfully.

It's a gesture that shouts his openness to me, to life, or to both. It's a way of living that has always seemed so far away from me. So different from how I've been feeling all day.

It heightens the crushing feeling in my chest, that my life could be falling apart. A break up, my business at risk, no home to call mine. With most of my things still at Aidan's condo, it feels like my life is what I carry in my suitcase and nothing else is certain.

His eyes narrow, as if he can sense the thoughts running through my head. It's like he's tracking if the weight in my chest shifts and softens... like he wants it to. Almost as if opening the door to me, baking me cookies and making me a comforting drink from his childhood were only a small part of what he'd like to do.

The wide receiver, ready to catch— me.

My heartbeats drum at a faster pace, to have his attention on me that way. I'm too raw, and reading too much into it. If I grab onto reality, it's more likely he's doing this because he's friends with my older brother. That's always been the way between us.

I cast my eyes to the chocolate in my hands and sigh. "Can I stay with you, Saint? I'll leave as soon as I can. I'll figure out my business, find my own place, and get out of your hair, I promise."

I'll try to fix the pain and doubt this morning caused me, too, but I don't mention that part.

"Of course you can stay," he says. "Make this your homebase as long as you need to. There's no rush."

"You have to let me know if I'm overstaying... or overstepping in any way. Please. I can't take advantage of your generosity. That would be wrong."

"You won't."

"But if I do—"

"Ames. It's fine."

"And you have to let me pay rent."

He laughs.

"Saint. I'm serious."

"Sure. I'll ask my assistant to find a fair price." His lips curl into a placating line.

"Why do you look so suspicious? Like I shouldn't believe you?"

He raises an eyebrow, and busies himself scooping more cheese from his drink. "Not at all. I'll invoice you at some point."

"Saint..."

"I need to research a fair price, right? It will be a one-time fee. Negotiable." He eats the cheese, chasing it with hot chocolate. "Give me three months."

I frown. "What? Why three months?"

"A lot of things can happen in three months."

Something in his tone changes. It turns... heavier.

I cock my head. "Hey— everything okay?"

He sips from his drink again and avoids my eyes. "I got some pretty bad news today. My GM and the team are considering trading me."

"What?" I place the mug on the counter with more force than I intended. Some of the chocolate spills, and I dab at it with the paper napkin at my side. "But— last year— you guys almost won! They can't be thinking of splitting up the team now?"

"Evie connected the dots. Between a couple of emails she got and something she heard while waiting for a meeting— well— some fans think my contract was bad because, when you take the amount of years into consideration, we haven't been winning enough and I'm not worth the cost. Not until Logan. So they think Logan, as the quarterback, should stay and try with a new receiver. Someone who's cheaper and will free up the money for other players."

He still doesn't look at me. His next bite takes two thirds of the cookie in his hand.

I shake my head. "I don't know enough about football to say this with total confidence, but I'm pretty sure that's bullshit."

"Apparently, that really depends who you ask. Williamson— that's the GM— he's pushing for it. I don't know why, as we don't really get told these things directly, but I think he wants me gone. He's latching onto the argument and suggesting I should be the sacrificial lamb if we lose. In short, he's decided I'm replaceable, even if I'm having my best season to date."

He stared into his cup, a rare frown at the top of his nose.

I frown, too. "What does Evie think? Logan? The guys?"

"They all think it's bullshit, too."

"Validated!"

He snorts and gazes at me again. "We're in the running for the big game this year. It's almost certain that they'll wait to see if we win. If I get the MVP on top of it, it would really help my case. I'm a pretty damn good player and quite expensive to other teams, especially with an MVP-style season, but there's a non-zero chance they'd trade me. More so if they need a fall guy. We'll see what happens when the season ends in three months."

"That's a lot of pressure, Saint."

He nods. "Looks like the next little while is pretty high stakes for both of us."

"You have to be the best at what you do this year, which, no biggie. And I have to find a replacement for my biggest client. Easy peasy!"

He clinks his mug with mine again and smiles. "Maybe that's why it makes sense we're shacking up together for a while."

"So we can cheer each other on?"

"I live for a good cheer." He smiles. "Can't wait to see you in a mini skirt, jumping up and down and singing my name."

I snort. "And how will you cheer me on?"

"I'll wear a mini skirt too, if you like."

"And sing my name?"

"I'll dance to it, too."

"Should we get pom-poms?"

"In your favorite color."

"Purple."

"As long as it's a deep, saturated purple. Lilac tones wash me out."

I laugh and he gives me a self-satisfied smile.

"Thank you," I say again.

The weight in my chest still craters between my lungs, but it doesn't wreck me like I might have guessed before this horrible morning.

At least in part, I owe it to Saint and how he's handled this evening. Now all I need to do is figure out how to salvage my life and my business... and do it all as soon as possible.

# Chapter 5

## Saint

Another win for the books, and I can breathe a little easier. Nothing is settled yet. To win the championship, we need to play with near perfection. For me to be the MVP, I need to break records. Still, getting a great score that I helped with in an away game, means I'm on the right track.

Finally in the parkade under my building, I turn off my car. I sigh and check my phone.

> **Dom**: Dammit that was a long flight back. Everyone made it home?

> **Damián**: Yeah. At least we won again.

> **Bear**: Recovery tomorrow will be hell. My whole body is a bruise. You ok, Logan? You got sacked pretty hard too

**Logan**: I'll be fine. I'm in the hot tub right now. Let's rest tonight and deal with everything in the morning

**Bear**: Let's go out tomorrow night. Relax at the club, plan ways to make sure the GM doesn't play with Saint's contract

**Saint**: Yeah, let's plan, but I can't go to the club tomorrow.

**Dom**: Wait. No club tomorrow?

**Saint**: You're all welcome to go to the club without me this time. I won't be too offended

**Damián**: The fomo will kill you, Santiago.

**Saint**: I'll live. Staying home for once might be good for me. Maybe

**Logan**: Is Ames still at your place?

**Dom**: I guess that means you won't be alone at least

**Saint**: I'm not allergic to being alone, guys. I've never found a reason for it, that's all. AND I won't be alone.

**Bear**: How long has it been since Ames has been with you?

**Saint**: It's been a bit over a week and yeah, she's staying with me at the moment

**Logan**: Interesting.

**Bear**: How is she doing?

**Saint**: Better than I thought tbh, but with ups and downs as far as I can see. Stays in her room a lot.

**Damián**: Is she eating enough?

**Saint**: I make sure she does. But we were gone for the weekend, so I want to check on her

**Bear**: Makes sense. If anyone asks at the club, we'll tell them you're alive and healthy, and no need to send the search and rescue team

**Dom**: Nobody has to panic that you're not there to take someone home. We promise he's alive and he'll come back as soon as he can

**Logan**: Brunch on Tuesday may be a good idea. It will be proof of life for those concerned

**Saint**: Now you're making jokes, funny guy?

**Logan**: Good night, everyone

**Saint**: Brunch on Tuesday it is.

When I make it home, Ames is nowhere to be seen, and her door is closed. I leave early on Monday for a long day at the TD, where we spend our time in recovery and reviewing tape.

Finally home again, I take a shower under cool water. After, in my loose pajama pants and a shirt, I make my way to the kitchen, then to Ames' door.

I usually only wear my boxers to sleep. Even if Ames has seen me in those now, some modesty is called for.

Light shines from under her door, and I knock. She calls me in.

I open the door and lean on the frame. "Want a drink?"

I'm carrying two glasses with vodka, soda, and lime.

She's on the bed, a book closed next to her. Her smile is subdued, and the curve of her shoulders tell me she's tired.

This isn't the same vibe I've come to know and... enjoy about her.

Pablo and Ames seemed to get really close after their parents divorced. When he and I lived together, Ames stayed in the dorms but visited us often. I got many chances to watch Ames do her thing through the years.

Ever since I met her, she's had this way to fill a room with her presence. She's quick to join a conversation with a tease or with an argument— whatever the situation calls. She has a deeply thoughtful side but, when she gets sarcastic? Damn, it makes me want to sit back, smile, and watch the show.

An immediate pull took over my chest whenever she was around— something I had never felt before. It was her beauty, too, of course. The gentle waves of her hair, those dark eyelashes, and those large, pretty brown eyes. The confident dips and curves of her generous body. Ah, to feel the weight of her on me as she rides m—

I shake one of the glasses in my hand, until the ice clinks in an inviting manner. Like jingling keys to distract a baby, only I'm trying to distract myself from the image of Ames naked on top of m—

Shit.

She nods and sits up. I gulp and give her one of the drinks. Sitting at one corner of the bed, I gaze at her.

Today she's still beautiful, of course, but her humor is muted.

"How are you doing?" I ask.

She gives me a despondent shrug. "It's like I can't make up my mind about what to feel."

"What if that's not something you decide? I think feeling is something you... do."

"Then I would be feeling a lot of different things, all at once."

"How long were you and Aidan together?"

"Four years."

I nod. It scared me, back when we met. What I felt for her. I was no one yet, except her brother's friend. She had a boyfriend. Fuck, she's always had a boyfriend. Even when she didn't, I knew she wouldn't look at me that way.

I had already been a serial casual dater back then. It was easy to keep going as usual. Let it help me forget, that the one person I felt a true spark for felt nothing of the sort for me.

"Then it makes sense you're feeling a lot after moving out," I say.

It hits me again. She's single and, for now, living with me. It's a scenario I would have dreamed of back in college.

I sip a sobering taste of my drink. None of this changes the story between us.

"He'd been cheating, Saint, and I don't understand it. I thought we were good. He went to work the night before with an 'I love you' and a kiss like every day. When I caught him— he was too busy trying to keep me quiet so his friends and coworkers didn't notice the *spectacle*. That's what he called it. He couldn't even deny it!"

Now I gulp again for a different reason. Shame on me, for thinking about my old feelings and her being in my condo, and not why she ended up here in the first place.

She shakes her head. "When I first found out, I grabbed onto my anger. It felt better, you know? But now that I've had time to think about it, well... I'm unraveling. Not going to lie— my confidence is pretty low at the moment. If I at least knew why he did it, I'd know where I messed up."

"You didn't mess up. He's the one who wrecked things."

"I just want to learn where we went wrong, so I don't have to go through this again. There *has* to be a way to get my happily ever after with someone, right?"

37

My heart crumbles somewhat, but I manage a small smile. "For sure. You'll have it, Ames. I have no doubt. You may not be confident enough to believe it right now, but I am positive. Borrow from my conviction all you want."

That gets me a small smile back from her. "I'll try."

"Has he reached out?" I ask.

"No. Most of my things are still in his condo. I think he's waiting to see what I do."

"That cowar— well. I shouldn't..."

I gaze away and around the room. She's been settling into it. A couple shirts are folded on top of the dresser, and her suitcase is nowhere to be found. The bathroom door is ajar. Through the shadowed door, the shapes of a few bottles line up on the counter.

It gives me warm feelings I don't focus too much on.

"Were you going to say he's a coward?" she asks.

I press my lips together. "Yeah, sorry."

"Don't apologize."

"I don't know what's okay to say about him. What if you're getting back together and I called him names?"

She gives me an incredulous look. "Would you go back to someone who cheated on you?"

"I don't think so. But it's not like I understand what it's like to be with someone for a long time."

"Maybe I don't, either, because it still failed somehow. We had a routine, we were comfortable— or so I thought. We didn't fight. Ever! We were so... *soft*, together. Smiles and gentle touches all around. And we had plans. We were buying a house. We'd have a music room for him and an amazing kitchen for me. Maybe in a few years, we'd elope. We were too busy so one thing at a time made sense. We barely had time to sit and chat these days, but I thought that was just the stage of life we're in. He's always got something going on for the late show he plays for, and his album, and the poetry book he was writing—"

She sighs and shakes her head. She sips from her drink and I mirror her.

Confusion and anger rest heavy on her. Her eyes have lost their shine. And yet, she doesn't seem too sad. Curious.

As far as I could gather through the years, Aidan was exactly what she looked for. An artist through and through, elegant and smooth. Always polished and unruffled, and utterly charming. I could never imagine him wearing joggers and a hoodie and cackling with his friends. In my mind, he can only wear tailored suits, and every word he says is measured and effective.

Not that I thought of it often, but I imagined he would read poetry to Ames at night. Stanzas he wrote about her beauty and his undying love for her. And she would sigh because, right after he made tender love to her, they'd philosophize about love and life deep into the night.

Ever since college— she always went for guys like him, never for the jock. And Aidan had fame and money to back it up, too.

"What I'm hearing is that I can call him names," I say.

She chuckles, but doesn't take me up on my offer. Pity. I would have enjoyed it.

"I was busy, too," she adds instead. "Catering for the network was a big chunk of my day. It kept the business running, so I could get creative instead and try new recipes to keep you guys happy. It was great. I was finally getting close to doing what I like to do best and *cook*—but I have to stop that again. I can barely make it into *your* kitchen these days, I'm so frustrated."

I put a hand on her knee and rub in a comforting pattern. No wonder she looks worried. There's no time to be sad.

She sighs. "I should be busy trying to find a new client. Go back to my business and reassure everyone that I'll do everything I can to keep things afloat. Instead, I'm spending most of my time in your bed, trying to figure out what went wrong."

"If you'd spent any time in my bed, we'd both know it, Ames."

The words escape me before I know what I'm saying. I freeze. She does, too.

I watch her, carefully tracking for any signs. Why the hell would I say that at this time? Damn my flirtatious nature.

She lifts her eyes at me. The line of her lips stretches slowly, so slowly into a smile. It pushes a button inside, and I let myself grin. Friendly dimples to the rescue. Playing them up to claim innocence has always worked well for me.

"I mean *this* bed, Gael." She laughs. "Your *guest* bed."

My first name on her lips is a tease, because she knows I prefer my nickname. It's her version of scolding me.

Fuck. Do I want her to scold me?

Double fuck, because I shouldn't be thinking about that.

I should be supporting her as she figures out what comes next. I should be thinking of a way to make sure I stay with the Strike. All of my focus should be on winning and being named the MVP.

And yet, I make a small offer.

"We'll find a way to get you out of this trouble, Ames."

I know what I'm good at. I'm good at football. I'm the receiver they call the catcher, cheekily pointing out at my fame and my dating habits. I'm the easy-going guy who you call in case of an emergency. To my dates, I'm a fun time and a wonderful lay. It's not a long list, but it's plenty for my friends.

She nods. "I'll start by going back to the office. Look at the numbers. Draft an initial plan."

"You got this, Amelia."

Ames is heartbroken and seeks something I don't have. All I can offer is friendship. I will be good to her anyway.

# Chapter 6

## Ames

It's eight in the morning. The professional kitchen that houses my business is dark when I arrive. Without the tight schedule to supply food to the network, most people won't be needed until ten, when prep for the Thunderdome delivery starts.

Damn. I only have eight clients. A few single individuals who are rich enough and busy enough to outsource the cooking part of being an adult.

It's why I dragged myself out of Saint's bed— well, *guest* bed to come to the office. I need to look at the numbers, see how long I have until I have to restructure, downsize or, worse, close up shop.

My stomach hurts at the thought. Anxiety fists and squeezes the poor organ.

I walk through the tiny reception area and go straight into the hallway. A small meeting room is at the front of the space, next to my office. Past these two square rooms, the large cooking area takes eighty percent of the unit I rent.

Everything is white and stainless steel. Pristine and orderly. It isn't about getting things symmetrical or perfectly aligned, so much as wanting things to be done the right way. There is always a right way to do things, if you look hard enough.

All lights remain off as I go into my office and close the door. I keep the room pitch-dark for a second longer. The moment I turn on the light, I'll have to turn on the computer. Check my emails. Do the accounting. Cross my fingers and hope a plan reveals itself to me.

No established, long-term relationship. No secure, growing business.

"Shit," I mutter into the darkness.

It's not the time for wallowing. Not at work.

I take a deep breath and turn on the light. My office is functional and undecorated. A simple white box with no windows, and a wooden desk with a computer on top. A filing cabinet hides underneath next to my leg, and a single bookshelf sits at my back. All the color comes from the corkboard on the wall next to me, where a hundred sticky notes in bright shades of pink, orange, and green wait for my attention. Recipe tweaks I'd like to try, flavor combinations to experiment with, and ingredients I want to research for my athlete clients... One day, I'll have time to be playful and discover again. To enjoy the balance of chemistry and artistry that go into creating a meal, and sharing it with the world. Creating warmth and communion through food.

Today I have to lose myself in admin work and projections.

Two hours later, Jo finds me with my hands in a praying position, my eyes locked on the screen.

"Hey." She brings two mugs of coffee with her, and she places one on my desk. She sits in front of me.

I lift my eyes to my friend. "Hi. Thanks for the coffee."

"It's good to see you here. How long has it been? Two weeks?"

"Yeah. Thanks for keeping things going."

"The business side has never been easier with the sudden drop in deadlines. But the mood? Everyone's anxious, Ames."

Jo holds her own mug of coffee in her hand. Her long, straight black hair is always in a ponytail, and it waterfalls over one of her shoulders. Her bold eyeliner is familiar, drawing my sight to her heavy-lidded eyes.

She stares at me, unwavering.

I sigh. "I feared we only had a few months to find a new big client and after looking at the numbers today— yeah. Two months if I want to keep everyone employed. Three if we really stretch it and I'm willing to go into debt. Any longer, and I have to get loans or... well. Worse."

Jo knows it means closure.

Three months, at the end of the day. Just like Saint's timeline.

"We need to get busy, then," Jo says.

It's true. Every cell in my body recognizes it. That's why the reality of my situation comes with worry, and with small tremors everywhere.

I bite my lip. "Do you think that the smoothie video will make it harder to find clients?"

"What do you mean?"

"What I did was so immature, Jo."

My teeth go harder on the flesh of my mouth. My lack of composure that morning has kept me up at night. Aidan is known in the industry. Even if embarrassing him felt like revenge— a poor substitute to justice— it also showed my emotional side at my place of work. They could have decided I'm unprofessional, unreliable, undeserving of future contracts...

"Well, let's see." She sips from her drink. "Did you plan it?"

"What do you mean? Of course not."

"So it was a spur of the moment thing."

"It just happened. I was furious!"

And feeling absolutely embarrassed myself. Everyone at SBN knows me, and was aware I lived with Aidan. Did everyone know he'd been fooling around with someone else? When they smiled hello at me, were they secretly snickering behind my back?

My cheeks warm up. I taste my coffee, hoping Jo won't notice how flustered I am.

"Then I say you should own what you did and be proud," she says. "It might be your only chance at balancing the scales."

"But what if I'm blacklisted now? Suddenly, I lost my most likely network of clients if I aim to get another TV show to cater to. I should have controlled myself better."

"And waited until no one was there to see? But then you would have missed out on the satisfaction! I'm sure that ruining his perfect hair must have felt good."

I laugh. "Don't tell anyone, but yeah."

"And when I zoomed into the video— I'm pretty sure some of it ruined her blouse, too."

My friend may have been trying to lift my spirits, but her words land heavy on my chest. I've tried hard not to think of the woman Aiden cheated on me with. I'm angry at her, sure, but it's him who deserves my rage above all.

He had made a commitment to me. He broke that promise.

"Has he reached out to you yet?" Jo asks.

I shake my head. "And I have not gone to pick my things."

"He texted me." She purses her lips. "It said, 'please talk to her.'"

My mouth opens in a silent gasp. "What is that supposed to mean?"

"No idea. I didn't reply."

Irritation climbs up my torso, that he reached out to my right hand at work rather than to me. Saint is right— Aidan is a coward.

I shake my head. "I think he wants me to reach out. It's a power move of sorts. To show him I'm hurt, or missing him, or *something*."

To know he matters enough to me to be shattered at the breakup. Meanwhile, I spend my days worrying more about repeating my mistakes in love and trying to salvage my business, than the fact Aidan won't be a part of my future.

At times, I wonder if I was in love with him at all.

"Do you want to reach out?" Jo asks.

Through the years, there would be times when I looked at Aidan and wondered if what I felt was love. Even now, I'm not sure, but I can't see what else love could be. They say that after the honeymoon is over, love is peace, trust, and safety. I had those things with him— or I thought I did. Comfort filled our days. We were *calm*. If that isn't conducive to forever, I don't know what is.

I rub my lips together and shake my head again. "I don't know what I would tell him that I didn't already scream in his face. All I have are questions. Why did he do it? That kind of thing. But I'm not ready to hear the answers."

Maybe I didn't give the right things back. It's possible I don't know what real love is... or how to build it, or how to show it. Hearing him give me excuses may not be an answer to anything, and it might confirm things I fear about myself. And it won't be the thing that will fix my career.

I place the mug on my desk again and run my fingers over my face, then through my hair. "I don't regret what I did, I guess, and I have to stop procrastinating about getting my things. But for the next little while, this kitchen is my focus."

"Sounds good to me. I'll reach out to everyone I know in search of leads. We can ask everyone here to do the same."

I nod.

She echoes the movement. "I'm glad to see you're not devastated, my friend."

I go back to chewing my lip. I'm sure it says something that I don't miss Aidan. I miss the certainty I used to have before I knew of his betrayal. And I miss the security that came with thinking I had decoded the key to forever.

"It's very telling that I'm not," I admit, "but I'm not sure what it means."

"It's okay if you're confused. It's been only two weeks! And you were together for a long time."

"You get it. I am confused. In such a short time I went from heartbroken to deleting him from my heart. Four whole years together with one other person. I should be *crushed*."

Instead, all I think about these days is how to build a better future. One where he's not included.

I let out a deep, deep sigh.

"Whatever you're feeling, it's valid." Confidence fills her words.

"Are we sure about that?" I raise an eyebrow. "How can you say it's valid if we don't know what that is?"

She lifts a shoulder like she's not concerned in the least. "I'm biased and I think you've never done anything wrong ever. I'm okay with that."

I laugh.

"I'm not worried." She winks. "You'll figure it out. Just take the time to break the pattern. Don't jump into another relationship you'll try to make work for way too long."

I gaze at my lap. Jo and I aren't best friends, but we're close enough she sees the errors in my ways. Her words sting, but they help. She's right.

I nod.

"Now let's go outside and have a chat with everyone," she says. "Let's tell them there's a plan and that we're a team. They need to hear it from you."

With a flutter in my stomach, I do as I'm told.

# Chapter 7

## Ames

I return to Saint's place in the afternoon, more exhausted than I had realized. The leather couch calls my name, and I sit there to scroll through my emails and contacts. When no names stand out as potential business leads, I make a list of people to write emails to just in case, and let my gaze wander through the glistening landscape across the window.

Saint's condo is gorgeous, with lots of white, chrome fixtures, and the warmth of caramel-toned furniture. Colors aren't prevalent, except for a few abstract paintings on the walls. It may be a way to not distract from the real beauty of the place— the view steals the show. With large glass panes everywhere, one's eyes can get lost in Bellevue many stories below, and Lake Washington in the distance.

I've been here for about two weeks, and I still have no real plans. I'm still in a funk. All I've done is nap and wonder where I went wrong. Was I a terrible girlfriend? I didn't think I was, but whatever I did wasn't enough to make things work, despite my best efforts. Being a Perfect Girlfriend didn't affect the end results. Now I'm moping on my brother's friend's couch. Ugh.

Said sofa is incredibly comfortable. So cozy, I let myself slide sideways to lay on it.

Saint assures me it's okay and I can take as much time as I need. Pablo has echoed his friend when I chat with him. Yet I can't shake the feeling that I'm not doing enough. There are ways to do things right and, if I try really hard, I can find a way to get what I want. Whether it's about love or work. It's the same feeling in a different font.

I close my eyes and sink into the cushions. The weight of the past few weeks turns my body into concrete. A pit opens in my chest, until a few tears fall behind my closed eyelids. It's the sixth time I cry over this. Over what Aidan did, and how it turned my future upside down.

All the work I put into shaping my life into what I wanted, practically gone. No happily ever after for me. Lost it without a warning and with no explanation.

I don't know how long I cry for, and I don't realize I'm falling asleep. All I know is that, when I open my eyes again, it's dark outside, a soft light shines on the living room, and a blanket keeps me warm.

"Welcome back to the land of the living, Ames."

I angle my head to find Saint sitting on the other sofa. He wears black jeans with a printed pattern of large, semi-transparent flowers, white sneakers, and a light gray button up. One ankle rests on the other knee, and one elbow is propped on the back of that couch. He holds his phone on his lap, but casts his eyes at me.

"You wear shoes inside?" I ask.

"These are one of my indoor pairs."

"It shouldn't surprise me that someone who wears big flowers on his jeans, would wear fashionable shoes inside."

He gets up and comes closer, to end up sitting on the coffee table.

His eyes land on me. "Right? No slippers for me."

"I hadn't noticed."

I'm still laying down, cozy under the blanket Saint must have put on me. Warmth blooms inside. It's a mix of the effect of the blanket, and the receiver's gesture.

His lips pull to the side. "You've been... preoccupied."

He gazes at me with the same concerned expression he's worn whenever I surface from my room.

I rub my lips together. I already owe him a lot. His genuine concern only adds to the list. The scales may be unbalanced for the foreseeable future, and I don't know how I'm going to repay him for it.

"Thanks again for—"

"Stop thanking me. It's nothing."

"But I want you to know how much this matters—"

"Ames." He shakes his head and leans forward, resting his elbows on his knees. "It's okay. I just want to see you on your feet again. Not because I want to rush you out, but because I want to see you happy."

"I don't know when that will be."

"As long as it eventually happens. For now, why don't we focus on a simple smile?"

"Are you telling me I would look better if I smiled?" I smirk.

"Anything that I say now could get me in trouble."

"Correct."

"I have no interest in that."

"It's fine, I'd forgive you. After all, you're letting me stay here—"

He rolls his eyes.

"Hey! How dare you?" I aim for an offended tone, but there's humor in my scoff.

He smiles, unconcerned. "There, that's better. Next step, a proper laugh."

"You would have to be funny first."

"Oh, that's wounding. Would you settle for something ridiculous?"

"What do you mean, ridiculous?"

"I don't know. Would you laugh if I made a fool of myself?"

"I'd love to see that. We're in the safety of your condo. Alone. What on earth could you do that would make you look ridiculous?"

"You're right. It would be hard for me to make a fool of myself. Let's be silly instead."

"I'm not a silly person."

"Even better. Be silly with me."

"I can't."

"Look." He grabs his phone. "It's easy."

With no warning, the distinctive saxophone of a classic eighties song explodes from every corner of the room.

"Come," he says. "Dance with me."

He stands and offers his hand. His hips move to the dramatic sax notes, like his whole body is vibing to the music. The singer starts talking about messing up and hurting someone he loved, and I don't know if Saint chose the song on purpose, but it makes me snort.

I sit up, but I don't take his hand. "I'm not dancing to this song."

Instead of complaining, he jumps on the coffee table and continues to show off his moves as if this is his favorite song in the world.

"Come on, Ames. Remember how you liked to dance in college?"

"Yeah. At the club. Not on the coffee table at my friend's condo."

He jumps off and onto the hardwood, leaning forward again to look me in the eye. "Then go to the club with me. We'll dance there."

The song continues to blare from speakers I can't see. Saint gazes at me with patience, but there's a hint of a dare in his deep brown eyes.

A grin deepens the friendly dimples on his face. "Come on, Amy."

I suck an offended breath. I'm Ames. Sometimes, I'll allow an *Amelia*. The people who tried to call me Amy didn't last long in my life. It's not that I don't like the name— it's a beautiful name— but anyone who calls me Amy did not listen to how I like to be called.

"Why are you poking?" I ask.

"Because I want to see you fired up again."

"And you think I'll be *fired up* again if I go to the club with you."

"I mean, that's an option, but what I really want—"

The song ends, and he breaks himself off. The condo goes dead quiet. It stretches the moment, until all I can do is hold my breath and wonder at the law of relativity. Time isn't a constant, when Saint looks at me this way.

I raise an eyebrow and pretend I'm not a little breathless. "What do you really want, Saint?"

He gazes into my eyes. His pupils dilate. His eyes drop to my mouth.

My heart stutters.

It lasts less than a second, but I see the change, and it shifts something inside.

He opens his mouth to say something, but he reconsiders. Twice he blinks, before he chuckles.

"Ames— Amelia Guerrero. You're a warrior. You can do anything you want. This is a hiccup, but what is that old wisdom? A crisis can also be an opportunity. So aim for what *you* want. Go at it again. Do it even better."

His smile brings the gift of his dimples. They lighten the weight I carry inside these days.

The man in front of me is easy to talk to. All those years ago when I first met him, his boy-next-door energy, that easy smile, those teasing divots at the edges of his mouth... it had everyone opening up around him. He's the kind of guy who makes you feel free.

Sometimes that means people seek him out for a good time. Sometimes, they seek him out for an ear and an open mind.

I can't resist his powers. It's easy to share what's been plaguing my thoughts, when he invites them in with compliments and optimism. I lean forward, too, bringing us closer.

I sigh. "What I want is to fight for my business. On that side of things, you're right. I won't go out without fighting. I'll find a way to keep my kitchen, my employees, and cook for happiness again. But, with Aidan? I don't know what to do about the breakup. You know my parents divorced when Pablo and I were young. They went in and out of relationships my whole life. I wanted better than that. I thought I had it. How do I fix *that*, Saint? I just realized that, so far, I'm not any better than the people who raised me."

His face doesn't change much as he studies me. His look is focused, like he really wants to understand. Like it matters to him. It's one of the things that makes him so popular with friends and lovers alike.

"I have no idea how one fixes that," he finally says. "But I'll be here until we put the pieces together."

He said *we*.

Maybe he thinks of me as a friend. Maybe not. Regardless, I know the value of what he offers. He's telling me I don't have to do it alone.

A powerful feeling builds up my chest, a water level line that goes up and up and changes the density of my insides. It washes away some of my hurt, and it spreads like the first rays of sunlight on a winter morning. Warm, welcome, and wondrous.

Words of gratitude evade me, but I don't let it stop me. I reach and put a hand on his, and hope what I feel shows in my eyes.

Saint may end up helping me put my life back together. Fixing something he didn't wreck. I can only hope I do right by him, too.

# Chapter 8

## Saint

We're playing another away game this weekend. It's a travel day, and I arrive at the Thunderdome an hour before curfew with a plan.

My first stop is Evie's office. Her door is ajar, but something about the way her laugh sounds stops me. Just in case, I knock.

It takes a couple of seconds before she calls me in. I open the door to find her sitting on her chair, suspiciously busy reorganizing papers on her desk. Logan is in the process of sitting in a free chair in front of her.

"I see." I grin. "I caught you being naughty."

"You didn't catch us at all," Logan says.

"Thanks for knocking, Saint." Evie arches an eyebrow. "That's all I'll say about that."

I snort and come in. "Do you have a minute? Since I interrupted already."

"Sure." She glances at Logan. "Is this a social or work visit?"

She gives her boyfriend a pointed look. A signal to give me privacy.

I dismiss it with a hand as I sit on the chair next to him. "Please stay, Logan. I want to hear what you think. Evie, have you heard anything about the trade talk?"

"Nothing new. I only got confirmation they're looking into the different options. Williamson is the one pushing for a trade. I think he's got it in his head that it's an expensive move, but worth it in the end to make the team stronger. The good news is, they asked me for my thoughts on the fan split— you know, how many people love you and want you to stay, compared to those that... don't."

I cross my arms. "How's that good?"

"The boss cares about the fans' opinion." Logan's frown is in place as usual. "As the owner, Selena has a say in this, too."

"Keeping the fans happy keeps the cash flowing," Evie adds.

I lift a shoulder. "That might be true, but we know if Williamson wants me gone and he convinces Coach, Selena might change her mind. He is the GM, after all."

"Winning the big game will help." Logan crosses his arms. "Harder to trade the guy who managed a winning touchdown or two. You could get the league MVP, too."

I nod. It helps to hear my friend is reaching the same conclusions as me, in terms of my options. Except...

"I'm good, and have been *really* good the past year and a half, but receivers don't usually get the MVP. If I get it and we win the championship, though, chances are it makes me too expensive for a trade. Both money wise, but also the fans would hate the move. If I don't get it and we lose, on the other hand... I can see what Williamson would say. 'Trade Santiago. Make him the scapegoat. It will appease the masses. All these years and still no trophy...'"

Logan groans. "Don't talk about yourself in third person."

"Saint wants to stay." I grin and keep at it. It's fun to bug him. "That's the main thing."

Evie suppresses a smile. "Does Saint want suggestions?"

"He would love suggestions," I reply.

Logan groans again and rolls his eyes. "Have you talked to Coach Clark yet?"

I shake my head.

"I'll talk to him," he adds. "I'll tell him I don't want anyone new."

"Aww, thanks, QB1. I knew you liked me."

Logan releases a deep, annoyed sign, but doesn't otherwise respond to it. "You talk to Coach too. Let him know you want to stay."

"It can't hurt."

"This won't be news coming from me," Evie says, "but don't underestimate the power of having loving fans. The louder the ones that like you are, the more they'll drown out the naysayers. That *will* influence the bosses' decision, and it's something that you can leverage."

"Any ideas?" I ask.

"I think it's time for that baking show, Saint."

The smile that appears on her face is one of success. She's been trying to get me into a charity event like this for years.

I rub my bottom lip with a thumb as I consider. My gut instinct is to decline. Baking is something I do for me. It calms me and it benefits my friends, my family, and it makes me feel better when I break up with my companion du jour. Going to a show to be judged for my home cooking skills doesn't excite me, to be frank. I'm no chef, after all...

But Ames is.

I frown. Thoughts of her are never very far. Rather than watching the memory of her pass me by, pretending I don't want to go toward it and ask it to stay, I follow Ames through my mind.

It was a fleeting moment the other night, when I could have revealed too much. *What I really want is...*

The silence had been deafening, my words hanging from my tongue. My defenses were nowhere to be seen, and the truth almost slipped out.

*... to kiss you and see where that spark goes.*

Like a selfish jerk, getting lost in my old feelings for her, rather than giving her the support she needs at this time.

I don't blame myself too harshly for it. I'm only human, after all. My self-interest may be the first instinct, but I have gained some wisdom through the years. I don't have to act on impulse. I can make a choice about what I feel. I must, if I want to avoid hurting people.

The night I danced for Ames, the right choice was to bring back my attention to what she needs. I could make the same decision today.

"Is there a way to get Ames into that show, too?" I finally say. "She could use the opportunity, with everything going on."

Evie purses her lips. "I'll have to see what's out there first. I'll have to reach out to the media, see what I can find that would work for the two of you."

I nod. "I'd appreciate it. Let me know."

"Going back to the club could help, too," Logan adds. "A few people asked about you last time."

"Like I told Logan last year," Evie says, "showing your face and living a life here adds to your social credit in the city."

The corner of my lips pull down. "I'm taking a small break from the club."

While Ames is at my condo, I can't imagine going dancing, drinking, and seducing women. Letting women seduce me. Leaving with someone and taking them to my bed, while Ames stays quiet in her room next to mine.

No need to wonder why but, if someone asks, I'll tell them it's because it would be awkward.

Both Logan and Evie raise their eyebrows high.

I roll my eyes. "It's not that big of a deal."

"Tell that to the people asking about you," Logan says.

"I'm good." I shrug. "You don't need to explain anything to them."

"I told them you have someone at home now." A small curl at the end of his mouth betrays Logan's humor.

I narrow my eyes at him.

A sarcastic arc takes over his eyebrow. "Was I mistaken?"

Evie presses her lips tight not to laugh.

"Look at this comedian." I get up. "I'll be back at the club before you know it. Until then, brunch on Tuesday with the guys."

Barely repressed mirth covers Evie's face. "Maybe we can go out for dinner, the four of us? I'm sure Ames could use the distraction."

I pretend I don't see it. "I'll ask her."

Logan's micro smile grows a tiny bit. "Tell Ames it's not a date, if she worries about it. It worked for Evie and I."

"You think you're so funny." I take a few steps toward the door, still facing my friends. "You're wrong."

"It wasn't a joke," Logan says.

I smirk and wave at Evie. "I'll go talk to Coach. Logan, see you later."

"Close the door behind you, please," the quarterback says.

"You don't deserve this gesture." I press the lock on the handle, so the door is securely closed once I go. "But I'm a generous, good-hearted friend."

"We are too," Evie says. "We're helping!"

"I might add a bet to the Hypersquare board." Logan's eyes narrow. "Something to do with what happens next time Saint goes to the club."

His girlfriend stops pretending she's not teasing, and grins at me. "There was a bet there last year about me wearing your jersey, Logan. Maybe we could make a bet about Ames wearing Saint's jersey—"

I stop before closing the door and frown at them.

"*We* is too many people," I complain. "That board is supposed to be where players place their season's wagers. Last time I checked, you don't play football, Evie."

"We all know I get preferential treatment. I always have, and now that I'm dating Logan..."

"I'll add that bet for us," Logan says.

I glance at the ceiling and let out an exasperated sigh. "It wouldn't mean a lot if Ames wears my jersey. She's a friend. Do we tease Pen when she wears Bear's name on her back?"

"Maybe we should start," Evie argues.

I check my watch like I don't care what they do. "Fine. If you want to lose the Hypersquare crown this year, Logan, go right ahead."

"I can win it again," he says.

"We'll see." I wave again, and leave for Coach Clark's office.

They may think they're teasing me. Helping me in their own way. But anything that makes me think of Ames in a romantic light is too risky to allow.

I would much rather help my situation by talking to Coach Clark and convincing him I'm the receiver he wants.

# Chapter 9

## Saint

Our game is early that Sunday. We lose. The mood is heavy with dejection afterwards, even if it's only the first loss of the season. For a late-November contest, it's a pretty good record. Still, the plane is relatively quiet on the way home.

We return to Seattle earlier than usual, but still deep into the evening. It's almost nine by the time we're back at TD from the airport and I'm in my car on the way home. Just in case, I open the door to my condo quietly, and kick off my shoes as I peek inside.

I take a slow, deep breath.

Light. Sound. Warmth. They welcome me home. They soak through my feet and travel up my body, until they reach a part of me I hid away years ago. The part that would have dreamed of a thousand moments just like this. Coming home from a game, to find someone waiting for me.

Not that Ames is waiting for me.

A couple of lights are on in the living room but, from the looks of it, most of the action comes from the kitchen. I make my way there, leave my bag on a kitchen island chair, and study the scene.

Ames' back is to me. Music plays on the speakers, something I don't recognize. If my ears have it right, she's mumbling the lyrics to herself. She's washing a few mixing bowls and pots, while the dishwasher runs nearby. Both oven timers are on. I take a whiff of the air, and the smell of a full hearty meal makes my mouth water.

"What did you make?" I ask.

"Ah!" Ames jumps. The clank of metal fills the space. She dropped one of the bowls.

"Oops." I round the kitchen island until I'm standing next to her. "Sorry. I didn't mean to scare you."

Her hands press against her chest. "I didn't hear you come in."

A soft blush darkens her light brown skin. It's a beautiful mixture of melanin and dark pink, that I wouldn't get to see if I weren't so close. Without thinking, I lift a hand and trace a reddened cheek with a thumb.

"Cute," I say.

So adorable, I forgot myself for a second, and touched her.

I pull my hand away. Ames' family is from Uruguay, and sometimes we say hello with a kiss on the cheek like they do over there. Rarely, we hug. Otherwise, touching is not a language we speak.

She blinks a couple of times, but gives me no other response.

"Sorry." I take a step back and busy myself by shutting down the faucet. Water had been running the whole time, and neither of us had done anything about it.

"No, I'm sorry," she says, "but my heart is still trying to recover."

"Why are you apologizing? I came in with no warning."

"It's your home. I'm pretty sure you can do whatever you want. I'm the intruder."

I shake my head. "It was nice coming in and having you here."

"You're being way too sweet."

"I'm sweet." I grin, letting my dimples do my work for me.

"Sweeter than I knew. I have not earned this generosity."

"You don't have to earn anything. Don't tell me that's why you cooked? What did you cook, by the way?"

A small smile appears at the corner of her lips. "Who says it's for you?"

Not that I'm staring too closely.

"You're not going to share?" I ask. "Wow. If I were the kind to keep a score, you would have lost several points at once."

"Oh yeah? How many points?"

"Ten."

She grins. "How many points can I lose before I get the Bake and Bye treatment?"

"You can't get the Bake and Bye treatment. First, we would have to fu—"

Her eyes open wide.

"Date," I correct at the very last second.

Damn. That isn't much better, because that's not something I can ask of her.

I can't ever just fuck her. It's not in the cards. Not when she is a serial monogamist and I'm the serial dater. Not when being with her could open doors I closed a long time ago. I would start thinking about a future, an *us*. But I'm just a good-times player. Failing at love means I hurt people, and I can't do that to Ames. Ruining my relationship with her would be the biggest mistake of my life. I would lose her and her brother, too, most likely. So I can't date her, either.

What am I doing, playing with those thoughts in my mind? Using them as a joke?

"Fu-date?" She says it like one word. A fuck-date fucking portmanteau. "Is that what you call what you do? *Fu-dating*."

She laughs, treating it as simple banter. I breathe in her words, but they're a cloud of cement. They turn into concrete right there in my lungs. Heavy and gray and damp.

"I don't call it anything but simple, casual fun," I say.

"I think I'll call it fu-dating that ends in baking pies."

She grins but I don't get to reply. The beep of one of the timers breaks the conversation.

Without hesitation, Ames takes out a tray of what looks like buns with a creamy filling and glazed blueberries on top. She sets them up on a cooling tray, only to turn back to the oven and take out a large dish. Chicken and potatoes, carrots, parsnip, all bathed in herbs.

I lick my bottom lip. "Please tell me you were joking before and I will get to taste all of this."

"Of course!" She bastes the chicken. Oil and a dark liquid— balsamic vinegar, maybe— drip down the bird's skin. "I was too stressed watching the game. I thought we could both benefit from my stress-cooking."

"You watched the game?"

Those butterflies I feel? Not welcome. Especially since I fumbled the ball not once, but twice. Shameful mistakes that won't help me convince the GM to let me stay. Nothing but a ring and top-tier, MVP-level playing will keep me here.

I take off my hoodie and throw it across the island to land on top of my bag. Embarrassment heats up my insides, and I hide it by washing the couple of dishes still in the sink.

"I'm sorry about the loss." She puts the chicken back in the oven. "I have no idea how you guys do it. You were so close, too. Those last three minutes... ugh. I had to distract myself by making an emergency grocery list."

The sound prompts me to steal a glance at her. She shudders.

"Wait." I put the large metal bowls on the rack to dry, and use the kitchen towel on my hands. "Is that why you never went to watch Pablo's games in college? You get too nervous?"

Back then, Ames' attendance at a game was extremely rare. Pablo never complained, and I never asked. I assumed it was disinterest.

Ames shrugs. "I can't stand it. I hate seeing people lose."

"Meanwhile, I love winning."

"I can't fix the disappointment of today's game, but I can feed you roasted balsamic chicken and veggies, and finish it up with blueberry Vatrushka buns. I was going to make pasta frola but I couldn't find quince."

"It sounds incredible. Quite a treat."

"The least I can do. I know it's very late, and I don't know how early you need to be at training tomorrow—"

"I'd love to have dinner with you."

Half an hour goes by. We sit at my dinner table, the twinkle of the city out the window, and the warm yellow light above us. We talk about being an athlete and being a chef, and the things we want out of it all.

"It's so clear you love cooking," I say. "And that you're amazing at it. Wow. This is incredible, Ames."

"Thank you." There's no false modesty on her face. "But you have been eating my food for a long time. Hadn't you noticed?"

I chuckle. "Of course I had noticed, but this meal is particularly good."

"Because I made it to lift your spirits?"

I nod. "And because it got you back into cooking. You hadn't been doing it much."

I stuff my mouth with a bite of chicken and parsnip. It melts in my mouth, a mix of acid and sweet and herbs that could make me moan.

"Which is silly, isn't it?" She says, oblivious to the sound I bite back. "It makes me happy to cook. I love doing something like this for you. So why did I stop?"

"We both know why."

"Okay, fine." She wrinkles her nose like she doesn't want to admit it. "The important part is I'm coming back now. You won't mind if I perfect a couple recipes here in your kitchen, will you?"

I raise an eyebrow and smile. "As long as you share."

The light above us shines on her hair. The lamps behind me in the living room glint in her eyes. It wouldn't take much to imagine we're dining in the candlelight, if I let myself fantasize about it.

She grins. "All right. It's only fair. I do have a generous spirit."

"Excellent. Extra special, because I'm getting my smiles now, too, Amy. Just look at that."

Uff. Someone could read a lot into those words, or the wistful tone with which they come. Like how much I want her happiness. With a little imagination, they would predict her smile still pulls at me like day one.

She doesn't.

She laughs. "Careful asking for smiles, Gael. We already had that conversation."

"I'm just pleased you're doing better." I purse my lips. "Right? You are?"

"Slowly getting there. I'm still confused and whatever I feel in the morning might totally change by the evening. It's better, though. I think."

She casts her eyes to her plate and gets busy making precise cuts on her chicken.

I suck on my bottom lip. "Come to the TD. Remind my friends you're incredible and are accepting clients. It will help."

She doesn't look up at me but nods.

Later, as I lay down alone in my bed, I can't help but think that having Ames around is tempting me with things I taught myself not to want. Knots are getting untied, and it scares me to think of what happens next.

# Chapter 10

## Ames

It's early December and less than a month since I moved in with Saint. I have yet to find a new big catering client. My days are a mix of admin and a desperate search, and blissful cooking. Who knew that losing the most important contract I had would give me the time to lose myself creating new recipes? But it did, and now I spend a few hours coming up with new flavor profiles, and translating them into something my employees can make for our current clients. Good news, they've been praising the new recipes. It's encouraging.

A long time ago, I hoped to build a secure, established business that worked seamlessly on its own. I would grow it until I could hire a business manager and a kitchen manager. When the right time came, I would step aside and focus on cooking again, creating meals that brought people together. Some I would repurpose for my catering business. Some I would share with the world somehow.

That future seems further away today than it did when I signed the contract for my kitchen three years ago.

I sigh. At least, I'm creating new recipes, and they are the perfect marketing tools to get new clients. I arrive with a bunch of them at the Strike's training facility.

I park the van in the right spot of the TD parking lot and get an insulated food carrier out. It's a cold day. I'm close to the building's main doors, but the freezing wind prompts me to rush inside. Right as I enter the building, Evie makes it out of the elevator in the back of the hall.

"There you are!" she exclaims. "Can I help you with the carrier?"

"No, no, just lead the way!"

"I'm so happy to see you." She turns to the hallway that connects to the training area. "How are you doing?"

I've been to the Thunderdome before, but I'm thankful for her presence. She offered to meet me as soon as I reached out to ask for permission to bring a treat. I hadn't wanted to create issues of any kind by being impulsive and not only did she assure me it was a great idea, she insisted on being my bodyguard.

*They'll swarm you*, she said. *They're hungry after training.*

Images of Saint preying on me fill my head with no warning.

"I'm okay." My voice is a bit shaky. "Trying to come up with a plan."

"Did Saint tell you about the TV show yet?"

"What show?"

"Of course, I only told him what I put together this morning." She leads me through a few offices. "I'm sure he'll tell you a-sap."

From memory, I know we're close to the locker room. Laughter reaches us alongside a few raised voices.

"Rumbunctious guys." Evie stops me right before we go into the large space. "Give me a second to announce our arrival."

I nod. It's not the first time I witness this.

"Please cover the goods!" She's loud enough to break through their noise. "I'm coming in and I bring company." In a lower voice, she adds a few words for me.

"We want to preserve their mystique, right? Seeing them in all their naked glory seems like too much."

I shouldn't be surprised that the first thing I imagine is seeing Saint in all his naked glory. I've been living with him for a few weeks. It makes sense that warmth feathers through my body at the possibility. It's reasonable. Logical, really. Spending all this extra time with him, sharing the kitchen, hell, knowing what he looks like in his underwear. Of course my brain would be curious as to the little left unknown.

I'm about to fan myself with a hand when Logan appears from around the corner. Just like with Evie and most of the team, I haven't spent much time with him. He's a client and Saint's friend, and neither has given me a chance to get used to his severe frown.

The gesture doesn't change as his eyes zero in on Evie. She doesn't seem intimidated, so I refuse to let myself be.

Logan puts a hand around Evie's nape and brings her in for a short, but intense kiss. I smirk. I may not know him, but this seems on brand to what I would expect of him.

"Hello to you, too," Evie smiles.

I clear my throat. "Can I just have a handshake hello?"

Evie laughs. Logan doesn't say anything but smirks. After shaking my hand dramatically, he welcomes us to the locker room.

Soon, a few curious players approach us. I give Logan his smoothie, then put out a few trays. One of them holds sandwiches, the other is full of cookies.

"Please take your fill," I say. "If you like them, I offer catering and private chef services, including the smoothies you always see Logan and Saint drinking. I'm accepting clients at the moment."

It may not be enough to keep all my employees in the long term, but a few more small contracts with professional athletes would pay well. It may give me some breathing room. Logan, Saint, and some others on their team have been great, stable, well-paying customers.

"I may be interested." Leon comes closer, cookie in hand.

"Here, have my card, Leon," I say.

"Call me Bear." Leon winks.

"Can I have one, too?" Dom chews down a cookie of his own, and takes a card from me. "This is delicious, and Saint sings your praises."

"Speaking of." I take my roommate's smoothie from the carrier. "Where's Saint?"

"In the pool room," Dom replies. "Which, coincidentally, I have a question for you."

"Coincidentally?"

Dom shrugs, like making sense is only secondary to him. "You've known Saint for a long time, haven't you?"

I nod and he comes closer.

"I made a bet." He points to the big whiteboard hanging near the showers. "This is the year I learn who makes the Hypersquared."

I glance at it. A whiteboard with heavily decorated edges, bold and loud with colorful ribbons and patterned paper letters that read *The Seattle Strike Best of the Best Betting Board Team destroyer Builder: The B-Hypercubed*. A list of small bets is scribbled on the white surface, waging points to be counted at the end of the season. Whoever collects the most points, gets to take the crown and keep it for the offseason.

I raise my eyebrows.

"Every year," he says, "Saint comes in at the start of the season with this board. Gaudy as always. Never shares who made it."

I scratch my chin. "I have no idea, actually."

There's fake innocence in my voice. Bear and Evie laugh. I smile.

Saint has two little sisters. He doesn't talk much about them. My guess is they make the board, but I don't mention it. If the team doesn't know, then I won't reveal it. Loyalty is the most basic thing I can give in return for the friendship we've had over the years, strange as it is.

Dom's eyes narrow. "I don't believe you."

I shrug. "Oh well. Where is the pool? I'll take this smoothie to Saint."

"I'll figure it out," Dom says. "The pools are through the hall, past the weightlifting machines and treatment area. All the way to the back."

"Do you want me to take you there?" Evie asks.

I push the food carrier into a corner, to pick up later on the way back to the van.

I shake my head. "I'll find my way."

"Remind him to tell you about the show." She smiles. "We can text about it later if you like? Or, now that I know you're from Uruguay, we can get together to share a yerba mate drink sometime."

Evie and I have texted a bit over the past month. It's tentative, as we're just getting to know each other, but she's been incredibly kind. Gently asking me if I'm okay, and if I need anything.

I give her a sincere smile. "I'll take you up on the mate sometime, and I'll text you later regardless. Thanks, Evie."

She smiles, gives me a quick hug, and I leave in search of Saint.

# Chapter 11

## Ames

I have to cross most of the first floor of the building to find Saint. The smell of chlorine hits me as soon as I open the door to the pool room. It's a smallish, warm space, compared to the weight room behind me or the expanse of the field outside. Fully tiled, it holds five metal tubs and three small pools. One of them looks like an underwater treadmill, wide enough to reach from side to side, and with metal rods and handles fixed to the edges. A larger one, quietly waiting at a corner, seems to have underwater handrails. From my place, they look like the kind of implements gymnasts train on. Saint is in the last one. It's a much more traditional-looking one, with a sitting ledge all around.

Even through the water, I can see him relaxing in only shorts. By the time I realize I'm licking my lips, it's too late to stop it. His thick thighs are out to play again, like when I first came to his place unannounced and I caught him in his underwear. Just like back then, his chain shines around his neck. His sculpted everything is a sight to behold, including the hills of his wide shoulders and arms, stretched out on the edge of the pool.

He looks like this is his favorite vacation spot. His eyes remain closed. My heart skips a beat.

"I'll be out soon." His voice is placating. "But no club for me tonight either."

"Why not?" I ask. I may have blushed from the sight alone. "It's been a while. You used to be there every week…"

Like maybe I'm catching him in a private moment… or he could catch me getting flustered.

Saint's eyes snap open. "This is a surprise."

He tracks my movements as I take a folded stool leaning against the wall. I open it, one handed, then sit on it. Affecting a casual mood, I lean back on the wall, using a few towels hanging from hooks for cushioning.

I'm in his line of sight.

I shake the smoothie in my hand. "I brought you something."

He nods and stretches a long arm in my direction. I mirror him and give him his drink. He goes right back to relaxing against the pool side wall.

He takes a sip. "Thanks. Wonderful service. Five stars."

"Now you only need a splash of something alcoholic, and you could fully pretend you're in a seaside resort."

"Hey, this is basic self care. Taking care of my body is important in this job."

"I'm sure it is. And now that you have someone at home interrupting your recreational activities, you have to take your chance at self care whenever you can, right?"

He sips from his smoothie again and rolls his eyes. "Stop with that already. If I wanted to, I'd find a way."

"Sooo… you don't want to…?"

He runs his fingers through his hair, his eyes fixed on me. It's an effortlessly sexy move. Added to the way he studies me, like he's figuring out exactly what I'm asking… It makes me a little breathless.

"Mh," he utters. "I don't remember you ever asking about my dating life."

And I definitely shouldn't be. My four-year relationship ended only a month ago. The breakup is proving I didn't have as good a relationship as I thought. That I may not have been as in love as I believed. But I need to process all of that, be sure I'm doing things right this time. Discover what 'doing things right' means. Letting myself develop a crush on my brother's friend, the one who's opened the doors of his home to me— that's not in the picture.

I haven't even gathered the courage to go get my things from Aidan's place. Which I absolutely must do. Soon. No time to develop a crush, when I have important things like that to do.

"I've known you for a long time," I say. "I don't think it's a coincidence that you suddenly stopped going out and doing your thing the same day I asked you to let me stay."

And I have feelings about it. They tingle at the top of my stomach, and travel up my chest like sparks from a fire at night.

*Ames— pretend they're just curiosity.*

Saint cocks his head and inspects me for a moment longer. I let him, and tell myself it doesn't affect me too much. If I focus on how Saint has traditionally looked everywhere else but me when dating, I'll squash those budding feelings inside me.

He stands. Water cascades down his torso, and several drops trail slowly behind. They are a caress on his skin, and yet I'm the one shivering.

Casually, like he's holding a cocktail at a pool in some sunny destination, he comes close to me. With him still in the water, we're at eye level.

"Doing my thing?" he asks. "What do you think my thing is?"

"*Fu-dating*, remember? But I'm not judging. You get to date as much as you want. All I care about is to make sure I'm not in your way."

He places his smoothie on the tile at my feet. With the ease of someone comfortable with themselves, who has a body this world was built for, he gets out of the pool.

Six recessed lights shine from the ceiling, creating stars on every swell of muscle, and sharp shadows on every chiseled dip of his body. He glistens. I can't help but to catalog the view, until my eyes catch the patch of wet fabric at his hips, sticking to his skin. An impressive bulge distends the navy shorts.

I bite back a gasp and cast my eyes to the floor. His eyes were on me. He knows exactly what I was looking at.

I need to feign disinterest.

With my heart beating in my ears, I grab my phone from my pocket and play with it in my hands. I have a few texts but I don't open the notifications. I wouldn't be able to process anything anyway.

The image of Saint standing wet and shiny in front of me is burned in my brain. I desperately review what little I could see, because maybe that bulge was more than a play of light and shadows. He might have been hard.

Fuck. I'm sure it's obvious my sudden interest in the tiled floor and the device in my hands is only a performance. But he doesn't say anything yet, and I don't know how to break the ice. I limit myself to hiding the tremors running down my spine.

"Ames."

My name on his lips is a dare.

I lift my eyes to his. Damn, he knows what he's doing. He knows he's hot and is challenging me to acknowledge it.

He runs a finger under his chain, putting it in its place. "Have you thought about what doing my thing would entail? You in your room, and someone screaming my name across the wall? Would you be okay with that?"

All I can think about is hooking a finger through the chain and using it to pull him to—

My phone vibrates in my hand. It's distracting enough that I don't finish the thought.

I clear my throat. "It doesn't matter if I'm okay with that."

My phone vibrates again, but I continue to ignore it. I keep my eyes on Saint, as he puts himself on display for me.

"It matters." He takes a step closer. "A lot."

My phone vibrates once more, and still I ignore it. I can't look away from Saint now. Whoever gives this up first— whatever it is— loses.

"I don't want to go out seeking another mindless sexcapade." Saint lifts a hand and my heart jumps to a gallop, because it looks like he's going to caress my face. "Not when— if you're right there next door from me."

If his hand connects with my skin, I might not give this moment between us up, but I might give in.

I don't know what to make of it. Of his words. Of my reaction. You wouldn't know my life fell apart a month ago, from the way I'm obsessed over small moments like this with my brother's friend. The guy who didn't have to welcome me into his home, but did anyway, no questions asked.

The wide receiver, catching me in my moment of trouble... triggering moments of weakness.

My heart drums deep in my chest. Its vibration travels with low frequencies through my flesh. His chest is close to me, and I would only need to lean forward and steal a taste.

I'm flustered. I shouldn't be feeling any of this. It shouldn't be this intense. Why is it even happening?

If he touches me again, I might—

Except his fingers only tease my cheek. It would be easy to deny any intention to caress my face. Especially as his hand moves past me, and grabs a towel hanging behind me.

All I can come up with in response is a complaint. I *want* him to touch me.

My phone rings. I jump. Only a few select people can get through when calling, as I always keep it silenced, and I suspect— I forgot to take Aidan's number off the list of exceptions.

I check the screen. I have five texts from him, and now he's calling me.

Shame washes over me. It kills everything else I had been feeling, acting like a guillotine on the way down. Like my ex caught me flirting with my brother's friend.

I glance at Saint. The towel hangs from his hand. His eyes are on my phone, then they lock with mine.

My lungs struggle to keep up with my racing heart.

"It's him." He presses his lips together. "What do you want to do?"

# Chapter 12

## Ames

I panic. I tell him I don't know what I want to do about the call and run for the exit. It will only buy me a short time, but I will gladly take it. Now I'm back in the condo, the weight of the last few hours chained to my ankle. The heavy, dark metal ball drags behind me as I make my way to the kitchen. It's the only room with a light on that I can see, and the sweet smell in the air hints that Saint has been busy baking.

I don't know what will happen next. I need a deep, calming breath, before I face Saint again. All I can manage is a shallow puff of air. It's enough to get Saint's eyes on me... and Pablo's.

Time stands still. My brother leans against the kitchen counter, a glass in his hand with ice and an inch of an amber liquid.

His life in Canada means I don't see him as often as I'd like, and I make a photograph of him in my mind. This moment— straight to my heart.

His visit is unexpected. A little disorienting but so, so welcome.

I drink in his presence. His short dark hair, thick eyebrows, and straight nose that's a tiny bit too long. He's trim around the torso and long-limbed. His brown eyes are as warm as always, too. They never fail to make me feel safe.

I don't notice the tears that fill my eyes until one falls down my face. "We texted two hours ago. You didn't say anything!"

The memory of him standing in Saint's kitchen will be with me for a long time. Him and Saint, gazing at me with expectant eyes and soft smiles.

Pablo chuckles, leaves his glass on the stone countertop, and comes to me with open arms. "It wouldn't be a surprise if I told you, right?"

I step into his hug and squeeze. He squeezes me right back. My brother is one of my favorite people. Often, he's the only person I think of as family. When our parents divorced, we clung to each other. It has tied us together, and having him here only strengthens the bond.

"Did you know?" I ask in Saint's direction from Pablo's arms.

The football player shakes his head. "I heard less than an hour ago."

"You make it sound like I did something bad." Pablo lets me go and we sit at the kitchen island. He takes his glass back in his hand, and talks to Saint. "First of all, I didn't know I'd be able to make it until two hours ago myself. I crossed my fingers that whatever you had planned, it could be rescheduled, but you know I offered to get the code and let myself in so I could surprise Ames."

"You bribed me with dinner, too." Saint points a thumb to the oven behind him. "We were keeping it warm, and I baked us dessert while we waited."

"Should we have dinner?" Pablo rubs my shoulder. "The three of us, like we used to in college sometimes?"

It doesn't take us long to whip up a quick salad to go with the lasagna in the oven. Saint puts a tray full of his baked goods on the table as well. He promises the cinnamon sugar muffins are filled with a hazelnut-chocolate paste that I will love.

At first, Pablo jokes with us about the adventure he went through trying to make it here to see me— see Saint and I. I'm smiling more than I have in a long time. But some of this conversation will be hard, and I'm proven right when my brother gives me a long, thoughtful stare.

"I'm glad you're not doing as poorly as I imagined," he says.

I glance at Saint. "Gael has been a great friend and that has helped, but... well. I'm not as devastated as I thought I'd be."

The words pull an embarrassed feeling from deep in my belly. The warm wave builds and crashes on my face, until I'm sure I've blushed.

"What do you mean?" Pablo asks.

A big gulp of water serves as my escape. Saint's gaze is locked on me. He's taken a break from eating, it seems. Like he's had enough for now, or he finds it too distracting when he doesn't want to miss a single word.

I cast my eyes down again. They land on delicious, creamy lasagna, but the need to eat is subdued. I don't want to hide from my brother, and Saint deserves to know, too.

I sigh. "I was with Aidan for years. We planned a future together. I should be crying in the corners for him every day but, no. I've only cried eight times. In a month. And my mind is on my business more than anything and— I'm very aware I'm being self-centered. Saint is going through a lot— not only did I parachute into his life and interrupt it, but with the possible trade and everything, I haven't even asked about any of it—"

Belatedly, I see Pablo staring at Saint in shock.

"Shit." I bite my lip. "I thought he would know. I'm sorry, Saint."

"I'm not publicizing it," he says, "since I'm hoping to stay. But I should have told you, Pablo."

"One big change at a time, please," Pablo says. He points at Saint with a finger. "What the hell is happening?"

Saint nods. "We're talking about Ames' situation." He turns to me. "You get to be self-centered when your life changes so much."

"Wouldn't your life change, too?" Pablo arches an eyebrow at Saint. "A trade means moving, starting over with a new team, redefining your career... with new contract negotiations, new rankings, new team and front office dynamics..."

"You would have to move?" I ask.

The ball and chain tied to my ankle had almost disappeared, but now doubles in size. It pulls from my insides, too, somehow. Saint had told me he would have answers after the championship game, which gives us a couple more months, but I hadn't realized what it truly meant until this moment.

Saint might end up somewhere else. He might move away, just like Pablo did. Another person I might lose.

An ache takes hold of my breastbone. It latches on and constricts my airways for good measure.

This is more in line with the kind of pain I expected to feel over Aidan.

Saint nods. "I could retire if I wanted to and stay here. Money isn't the problem, but I'm not ready to give up on my career. I want rings, what can I say? Just know, Ames, if you still need a place to stay, I plan to keep this condo. You won't be left without a home."

"I'm not asking because I'm worried about where I'll stay. Which isn't to say I'm not—"

"You can stay here," Saint repeats.

"— but I didn't realize you might have to leave. Ridiculous, I know."

The last few words come out quiet. Shame weighs them down, trapping them in my lungs and tempering with my vocal cords.

I take a slow breath, trying to tame the discomfort. Not to placate him or pretend I haven't made mistakes, but to see the lessons clearly.

The situation with Aidan is teaching me I may not know how to make relationships work. That being the Perfect Girlfriend is not only insufficient, but it's unrealistic. I supported all of his career moves, didn't make a fuss about how distant we felt at times, and I took every chance I had to show him I wanted him to be happy. It didn't help. Meanwhile, I'm also learning things from living with Saint. Attempting to be the Perfect Roommate, whatever that is, has to be just as unrealistic, but I should give *something* to him as a friend. Friendships are relationships, too.

"I'm sorry, Saint."

He shakes his head. "No need. I get it. You're in a shitty situation. With me, at least I know what I can do about it. Got to play better than ever and get that MVP. For you it's not so clear."

"Shouldn't it be clear?" My voice is critical of myself. "Shouldn't I know what to do about my business? And with Aidan, well, I—"

Losing my train of thought isn't out of confusion in that regard. It's more about the way my thoughts stumble together. My feelings for Aidan trip me up. What he did makes me feel like I regressed a decade in knowing what I want out of my life. And I hate that his actions have that power over me.

"What about Aidan?" Saint gazes at me with renewed intensity.

Of course he's wondering. Aidan just called me, and Saint watched me panic. Not to mention how my things are still in my ex's condo. Saint called him a coward once, and I hope he never ends up thinking the same of me.

Pablo studies me with a frown. He's jumping to conclusions, while the thoughts and ideas multiply in my mind. I'm slow to react.

"You're thinking of fixing it with Aidan?" Pablo takes turns gazing from me to Saint. "You two. In how many ways do you plan to surprise me tonight?"

"You did it first." Saint's dimples pop. "Surprising us, that is."

I hadn't realized it's been a while since I last saw those cute smiling dips.

Am I making him unhappy? Ugh. He keeps reassuring me, telling me he's fine with me being here, but moments like this make me worry he's not being totally honest.

I have so much work to do. Until then, I'll find ways to be a better friend.

I press my lips together. "I'm focused on fixing my business. That way I can get out of Saint's hair and find my own place."

Saint shakes his head, in a convincing show of irritation that I made another reference to being in his way.

Before I can respond to it, Pablo looks seriously at me.

"But what about Aidan? Are you... going back? I know it's not the most modern thing, but I wouldn't judge you. Repairing a relationship is such a brave thing that not everyone does. You've been together for a long time, and if you wanted to do it..."

He lets the thought fade. I know he's trying to be supportive, telling me he would accept whatever I want. Somewhere inside, I suspect his question comes from the hurt each of us carries from when our parents divorced. Fixing things can be the bravest thing, sometimes.

But making things better with someone who wronged you isn't how I'm trying to be different from my parents.

I take a deep breath. "He called me today. I couldn't face talking to him, because I was afraid of what I would do. What if he only wants to give me excuses? What if he wants me to forgive him?"

Pablo and Saint pay such close attention, I doubt they're breathing.

I shake my head. "I've blamed our parents for so long, for not at least trying to fix things. For being more focused on their lost love than on what us kids needed to hear. And I don't want to judge anyone who stays after an affair. There are so many reasons someone might choose the repair, including love."

"But do you want to fix it?" Saint's voice is tight.

"Part of me thinks I should want to." I rub my lips together. "If I want to be different from my parents I need to commit to forever, right? Push for it. I have to know what I need to make it happen. So of course I had a list of things I looked for. Things I believed were needed to have a true happily ever after."

Pablo nods. Saint doesn't move.

I shake my head. "I had those things with Aidan. I was at peace. Content. He was an artist who knew how to weave words into magic. He had this gentle, unassuming way about him. Never cocky or self-agrandizing. Humble and sensitive. Such a perfect match for me and everything I've ever wanted."

I rub my lips with stiff fingers. A wave of pain could break like a wave on the shore, right on my chest, but I don't let it.

I gulp some water down and drown the feeling. "Shouldn't I be full of misery that he ruined what we had? I've given it a month, and the suffering isn't there. I've been angry, and sad, and scared... I thought that I'd feel desolated when I heard from him and you know what I felt?"

Two pairs of focused, deep brown eyes watch me carefully.

"Annoyed," I say.

Saint gazes down at his plate.

Pablo gives me a slow, understanding nod. "I see."

"I don't want to go back with him." I take a breath. "I want to understand why it failed, so I can choose better next time. I want to figure out if I ever loved him— if what I felt was love at all— because there's a reason I'm irritated and not heartbroken. I want to take my time and figure out what I need to change in me so this doesn't happen again. I want to make a plan to rescue my things from his condo. I want to come up with a solution so I don't have to fire people from my kitchen."

"Fuck Aidan," Pablo says. "You're amazing, Ames."

There's power in saying things out loud. My voice agitates the particles in my chest. They rearrange inside of me, until they find a new home between my cells.

I gaze at Pablo. "Thanks, hermanito."

He rubs my shoulder and smiles at me.

Saint's eyes are steady on me, his face unreadable for once.

I hold his gaze. In the month I've been here, I've learned to care about his opinion. I want his thoughts, too, and he gets it.

"My parents are still together." He sighs. "They married right out of high school. Had me less than a year later. As a teenager, I knew they were unhappy. I heard the fights. I saw the cold looks. But they stayed together. Having a kid in sports is expensive, and they couldn't do that and maintain separate households at the same time. So they stuck to it. For me. For years, I was the only reason they wore a ring and shared a room."

He stares out the window at the city below us, and those dark swatches of shadow where the lake waits for the sun to show up again. Saint is an expressive person. Even when all I can see is his profile, it's clear he's lost in the past.

"I don't remember seeing things change." A wrinkle shows up at the top of his nose. "I just know that for my prom night, I saw them kiss again. When we heard about my college football scholarship, they hugged and I just knew— they were better. Only a couple months later, they were pregnant with my little twin sisters."

He shakes his head. It's his turn to have all of our attention.

"When I see them now," he continues, "I think they're happy. I see them being affectionate. My sisters are going to have such different memories but, me? I can only wonder at whatever helped them fall in love a second time. How did they end up choosing each other again? Despite having seen things in each other they disliked. Maybe even hurt one other. What does it take?"

He turns to me again. That rare frown that showed up at his brow stays, making his eyes heavy as he gazes at me.

"Your parents divorced," he says. "Mine didn't. What I've learned from all of it is that it's hard to make love last. Most people can't... or won't. It's not only finding the right person who wants you back. It's both of them having the persistence, the emotional resilience to push through, the *desire* to make it work. To do every single thing they can to avoid wounding the other. No single person can make it happen— it has to be both choosing each other every day. Doing the right thing at the right time, even if that means letting them go. But if they want to try, I don't know. I don't think you should force it. You can't make someone love you, after all."

Every beat of my heart takes a word and blends it with my blood. I don't exactly know why this seems so important, but I don't hesitate. I carry his comments in my red cells, right alongside the oxygen that keeps me alive.

"If you don't want him back," he adds, "then don't do it. I'll text the guys. You'll have your own entourage when you go back to Aidan's place to collect your things. You know how big we all are? We're going to intimidate Aidan into making things easier for you."

"Thank you," I hear myself say.

Next thing I know, Saint texts with his friend group and I have a date to go get my things from Aidan's place.

# Chapter 13

## Saint

Pablo has to leave early the next day, and insists he would rather pick up breakfast on the way to the airport. Ames won't have it, and she refuses to let him leave without at least a home made sandwich and a coffee.

She gets busy in the kitchen, and Pablo rolls his eyes.

"Fine," he says. "Saint, come with me to get my carry-on? It's still in the room."

He slept on the small sofa bed in front of Ames' bed. Last night, she and Pablo bickered about who would sleep on the bed, and the sound reminded me of my ten-year-old twin sisters. At the end, he won and took the smaller piece of furniture. Ames may have pretended to be upset, but I knew better. The way her face softened while looking at her brother, she harbored no annoyance. All I could see was affection and gratitude to have him there.

It softened my heart to see it, too. I still can see it.

Ames butters lightly toasted bread. "Go. Grab your things. I need five more minutes."

I follow Pablo to the guest room. I'm not sure what his plan is, but I doubt he needs a bodyguard to get his things.

"Hey." He stands next to the small suitcase. "I wanted to thank you."

I was right. I don't say anything, but cross my arms and lift an eyebrow.

"You know how much Ames means to me," he says. "When I left town, you promised to keep an eye on her. I never thought it would come to something like this, but... thank you. Thanks for taking care of my sister."

I shake my head. I haven't been as good as he thinks. Just the night before, I let myself believe Ames' interest in me had been piqued. The way she looked at me, talking about my recreational activities with a hint of jealousy in her eyes— not that she said as much. Not that that's what she felt. But for those minutes I entertained the thought, my cock had happily betrayed my denial. Those feelings I thought I'd crushed under my heel aren't truly gone.

"No need to thank me," I say.

"That shithead. Aidan." He stares at me with a gesture that clearly means he'd like my validation.

I'm only happy to give it and I scowl at the man's name. Aidan called her trying to weasel his way into her life. Good thing she's decided she's fully done with him.

I only have to be careful not to get my head in the clouds again. She's given me no sign of looking for something new. Imagining myself as a knight in shining armor who offers to take over and give her forever is a mere fantasy. She's never seen *me* that way. Why would she? Last night she listed what she wants in love. Not a single item would be used to describe me.

I have to find a way to incinerate these feelings, these questions, these hopes.

Pablo continues to vent. "I always got the feeling he was way too full of himself but, you know. I can't go telling my sister that." He snorts. "I'm glad she's not going back to him, but you were right last night. She's not out of trouble. She'll need some time to get on her feet again."

"Please, don't you start with that, too. I don't know what I need to tell Ames so she believes I'm happy to have her here. She can take as long as she needs."

"We're all adults. I know having her here kills your style with the ladies—"

"Oh my fucking—" I roll my eyes. "You two are definitely related. I'm *fine*."

"I remember how you were in college, okay? And from what I hear, that only got worse when you got signed."

"Worse, better, it's all relative but, last time I checked, my dick is still attached. It has not shriveled and fallen off for lack of use yet. I think I'll be fine."

He laughs. "I wasn't asking about your dick!"

"We're talking about Gael's dick?" Ames leans against the doorframe.

A blush blooms on her cheeks, but she smiles through it. The grin is brazen.

My cock likes the combination, and it perks up that Ames is thinking of him. I gulp, and try my hardest— ahem— to calm him down.

"Argh." Pablo closes his eyes. His whole face wrinkles into a tight gesture. "I do not need to think about Saint's prick, ever, and I definitely don't need to think about how much he likes to use it. Especially when we're talking about my sister, and while you two are living together."

The distaste on his face acts like freeze spray on my nerves. It cools me down, and my cock unhappily retreats. Guilt anchors itself in my guts, that I was so ready to get Ames' attention on me that way. While right in front of my friend, who clearly dislikes the idea of us.

"I wasn't the one to bring up my dick." I try for a playful smile.

For the millionth time, I'm grateful for my dimples and the amount of trouble they save me from.

Huh. A few memories float into my mind of my dad giving my mom a dimpled smile to flirt with her in the past decade. Could it be he used them to convince her to give him another chance?

Not that I should be using them to flirt with Ames.

"All dicks aside," she says, "your food is ready, Pablo."

"And I *have* to leave now," he responds.

At the door of my condo, Pablo thanks me again, and Ames thanks him for the visit. Hugs last long.

"She needs a soft place to land for a while." Pablo slaps my shoulder. "I'm glad at least she has you."

It's a tease, but it needles me anyway.

———

Pablo's gone. Ames' sigh comes from deep within her, drawing her shoulders inwards. It makes sense. She will miss him.

For a few heartbeats, I do nothing but watch her. The way the morning light is so subtle through the windows that it tints all shadows in blue. How her skin and glossy hair take hints of purple, wherever the warm yellow of the lamp doesn't reach.

"Do you have time for a proper breakfast?" She turns to me, her smile somewhat sad. "I can make food for you before you go for training."

I nod, go into my room to shower, and come back out to find a gorgeous spread on the table. We eat together, like breakfast in the early morning before work is our routine. It's a thread of awareness that stays with me, stitching into each of my breaths as I tell her about the TV show Evie got for us. With so much going on at the pool the night before and with Pablo's visit, we haven't had the time to talk about it. It's prime material to keep our conversation casual, regardless of the feelings swimming in my blood.

"It's a Christmas episode for a limited series they're trying out." I put slices of tomatoes and queso fresco on half a bun. "They're the largest streaming company, right? They want to expand their catalog of food shows, and they want to do it with holiday specials."

"And the vibe?"

"Friends spending a holiday together. Evie and Logan will be there, too. To the cameras, you'll be the primary chef and I'll help you. They included a charity component, to go with showcasing your food. It will be great PR for all of us."

She takes a long sip of her coffee, eyes searching mine. Her lips take on an excited slant.

"It could help me network." Her voice barely contains her enthusiasm. "I could talk to the producers about who is catering for them, or if they know of any business opportunities. And if someone watching needs catering services, and knowing that I exist thanks to the show..."

I take my mug and clink it with hers as a toast. "Exactly."

This time, her sigh is light with relief.

"Thank you, Saint. You've done so much for me. How can I ever repay you?"

"I'll invoice you one day, remember? We'll negotiate every item."

"Right." Her lips pull to the side. "The invoice."

I give her a solemn look. It's part of the joke.

She chuckles. "For now, can I invite the guys over for dinner afterwards, at least?"

"Great idea. We can feed them here at home."

"I just hope you know I don't take your generosity for granted."

Her serious gaze lands heavy on me, throwing gravel down my chest. Each pebble is a time she's *appreciated my generosity*. Like I haven't yearned to be the one she comes to for help. Like helping her has been an inconvenience, rather than what I simply must do for her because I care.

I smirk. "Ames. Please. Maybe it's time you accept help without weighing things in a balance. We all want to do it, okay? So let me change the subject and I'll tell you more about the show."

She lets me distract her, but I know the wheels are turning in her mind. I distract her and explain that during the week before Christmas, there will be one episode released per day with famous people and a few of their guests. The idea is to present the show as if the famous person is preparing dinner with their friends. While folk cook and have fun, they will chat about a charity of their choice, and viewers will be gently encouraged to donate.

Eventually, she matches my energy and we fall back into giddy conversation. We brainstorm meal ideas for the TV show, and we make a plan to get her things from Aidan's place. It's like we're playing pretend. As if we're a team. Perhaps

91

a couple, overcoming the small frictions of everyday life. Living joint lives and planning what comes next.

I take the moment, with its quiet dreams weaved into it, and place it in a tiny box. I close it with twine, because this box can't open. I've known that for a while. Even more now, when I can see Pablo's displeased face in my mind, when he imagined Ames and I together.

# Chapter 14

## Saint

We get a driver to take the group to Aidan's place. It didn't take much convincing and Logan, Dom, Bear, and Damián have joined us for the trip. The latter offered to drive separately in a small rented moving truck, to have a vehicle where to pack Ames' things. The rest of the guys, Ames, and I ride in a large SUV.

"Tell us the plan again," Dom says. "Whose ass are we kicking?"

"No one is kicking Aidan—" Ames tries, but I interrupt her.

"— without notice from Ames herself. But if someone is going to kick him, it should be Damián. His specialty is in punting balls, after all."

"Saint—" Ames starts to scold me, but I'm not intimidated. She's not successful at hiding her delight at my comment. "We're not here to be mean to Aidan. We're here to pick up the things I still have in his condo, and to make sure my piano makes it to Saint's place with no scratches."

She gives me a worried look. As we planned for this trip, she told me of this heirloom piece. It once belonged to her grandmother and, when she moved in with Aidan, Ames brought it with her. She offered to put it in a storage unit, not to have it getting in the way in my place. I said it was nonsense and that we couldn't risk it getting damaged in a random glorified locker room without humidity control. As usual, she didn't fully believe me when I said I didn't mind.

"Wait." Dom frowns. "You play piano?"

"I don't," Ames says, "but my grandmother did. I didn't spend enough time with her to learn, as she lived in Uruguay, but she left it to me. It's a connection to my roots, you know?"

"And are we sure we're not maiming Aidan?" Bear asks. "Not at all?"

"Not unless he refuses to release my stuff," she says. "In which case we're only intimidating him."

"We're perfectly set up," I explain. "Logan, you focus on scaring him with your murderous frown. Bear, you intimidate him with your size. Dom..."

I study the man who's a tight end. He's tall and muscled but has a friendly face, and I'm not sure he can play a fearsome role.

He stares at me like he takes offense at my hesitation.

"Dom, you do your best," I say. "At the very least, you can look pretty and challenge him that way."

Bear chuckles. Logan smirks. Ames laughs.

"Hey!" Dom complains. "I thought you're here to be the pretty one. Show Aidan you're a threat and you're living with his ex. Intimidate him that way. Who knows what you two get up to alone at night, right?"

I grin and gaze at Ames. "Should we put ideas in his head?"

She bites her lip, but there's a hint of humor and nerves in the gesture.

She settles for a nod. "That might be fun, if it comes to that. After throwing that smoothie in his hair, we all know I'm not above a little petty revenge."

"Then we'll see if it comes to that," I say.

Like I'm not neatly split in half, wondering if I should push it while in front of Aidan, or if I should be good and simply follow her lead.

We get to Aidan's building and wait until Damián arrives with the truck. Once he has parked in the right spot, the group goes up to the musician's condo. All of us carry armfuls of moving supplies, a few boxes and moving blankets included.

Aidan's condo is one of the larger ones on the top floor. We stop at his door.

I motion Ames forward with a wave of my hand, and give her a little bow. "Do you want to do the honors?"

She nods and rings the doorbell. "He'll be waiting."

Her eyes are locked on the door, and she doesn't notice how the guys and I fall into formation behind her.

The door opens. A shift in Ames' posture betrays the tension she feels, and I put a comforting hand on her back. The handsome Irishman finds her first, mouth set in a meek smile. It curls into a tense, fake version when he sees the five of us standing around Ames.

"Oh— hi," he says. "I didn't realize..."

We didn't plan it, but my friends square up their shoulders in unison. It makes them look bigger, taller, stronger. The moving supplies turn into shields. I don't take my hand off Ames.

"I brought help," Ames says.

We are her guard.

Aidan moves aside and lets us all in. We spring into action at once. The guys wrap the piano in the blankets, while I shape up a box and follow Ames.

Aidan follows us as well. "Ames... can we talk?"

"You can talk." She leads me to the bedroom and I can't lie, I'm not comfortable. "I make no promises that I will respond."

This is the place where they slept together. Where he read poetry or whatever to her. This room knows the sounds she makes while I don't.

I feel sick, but I hide it. I'm in no position to feel a burning distaste in my stomach. Still, I follow her.

"I get it," Aidan says. "You're hurt."

We move into the walk-in closet, where I help her grab her clothes and put them in the box.

Ames scoffs. "You could say that. You cheated, Aidan."

"It was only a kiss."

95

I snort but keep to my task. Even without looking, I can sense Aidan bristling at my presence.

"Can we talk in private?" He asks.

"Saint," she says. "Do you think kissing counts as cheating?"

I nod. "Of course, if you were monogamous. You?"

"Yeah. I can understand attraction to someone else. A crush you have on a friend for example. But the moment you take action to make something else happen, that's too much."

I glance at her. I shouldn't make much of the tone with which she said *crush on a friend*, so I fold a sweater and put it in the box.

I nod again. "You're supposed to choose each other, always."

"Ames—" Aidan runs his fingers through his curls. His accent comes out stronger. "Please. I wasn't going to risk what we had but—"

Ames stops putting clothes in the box and faces her ex.

Her mouth is pursed with anger. "But you did, Aidan. You did. Whether it was a kiss or more it was *something* that broke the trust I had in you."

"We were so in love, Ames—" Aidan tries again. "I broke up with her. I choose you."

Ames shakes her head. "It's too late."

"It's been a month. Your things were still here. I thought it meant you needed some time..." He straightens and stands up taller to look me in the eye. "Let us speak in private, please."

"I'm not leaving unless she asks me to," I say. "And even then, I'll fight it. I don't trust you, Aidan."

Ames grabs my sleeve and pulls me closer, even if her eyes stay on her ex. "I didn't want to confront you. Have to look at your face and say goodbye. I'm here now. I'm taking my things— especially Abuela Meche's piano."

Aidan's eyes land on the point where Ames touches me. "I wrote my album on that piano— Ames— we can fix this."

By instinct, I step closer to her. Aidan's eyes narrow on me.

"You know how important that piano is to me." Ames glares at her ex. "I brought it here so high with the hope it was meant to be. I don't know how to play the piano, but the man who promised me forever did. How special, I thought. How meant to be. Then you went and decided to, what? Give it a go with someone else? Kiss her and see if she would be there to catch you after you grew the balls to break up with me? What was it, Aidan?"

I keep a short distance from her— use the momentum to stand even closer. I'm only happy to be her bodyguard, if she needs one.

"Come on, luv." Aidan palms come close in a pious pose. "Is a kiss really enough to break us up?"

"Yes, it is," she says. "A kiss can ruin everything. Just seeing you come out of that room with her— Aidan, I simply don't trust you anymore."

"Ames..."

"Just tell me why. Where did we fail?"

The guys come into the walk-in closet, unconcerned by the tight quarters. We're all about the same height, just about the same as Aidan, but packing twice as much muscle mass.

"Bloody hell." Aidan takes a step back.

Logan's frown is severe on the musician. "The piano is safe in the truck."

"The piano bench, too?" Aidan asks.

Ames rolls her eyes. Bear and Logan glare at him. No one responds to his question.

"Let's help you with anything else you need," Bear adds in Ames' direction.

"What these gentlemen want to know," I say, "is what else can they pack for you."

"Fuck it," she says. "I don't need things to be neatly packed. Please bring boxes and we'll go from room to room grabbing my things."

"We're at your service," Dom says.

They leave to bring boxes.

"Why did you feel the need to come with an entourage?" Aidan complains. "I'm not a scary bloke. All I want is a chance to explain."

My friends return and we make good work of putting Ames' stuff in boxes. First here in the closet, then in the room. Ames doesn't leave our side, giving easy directions.

She never responded to Aidan, but he follows us anyway, asking for privacy to talk to Ames.

Twenty minutes later, all but two boxes are waiting for us in the truck. Five football players and one angry woman make one hell of a team.

"Ames." Aidan tries one more time. "Please. After four years I think I deserve to be heard."

"Then have your say," she responds.

The guys and I close lines around her.

Aidan tsks. "Not in front of them."

"Then we'll see if and when I feel like hearing you speak."

"Anything else you need?" I ask, ready to escort Ames back to our condo.

"I think I'm good," she says.

Without saying a thing, Logan breaks the rounded wall we keep around Ames. He moves slowly, unworriedly, toward the remotes that lay on the coffee table in front of the TV. In full view of everyone in the room, he proceeds to remove all the batteries.

"Just in case you need these too, Ames." With full aplomb, Logan puts the batteries in his pocket, picks up one of the remaining boxes, and leaves without saying goodbye.

"Hey!" Aidan frowns his way.

Bear chuckles, picks up the other box, and leaves. He doesn't say goodbye either.

"At least tell me where you're staying," Aidan says. "Jo didn't reply to my text and I don't want to worry..."

I can't help it and roll my eyes. The way he phrased that was about him feeling well, not taking care of Ames.

"Do you have a problem, mate?" He asks me.

"A few problems, actually," I reply. "Should I list them?"

"Don't bother," Ames says and puts a hand on my arm.

Aidan sees the gesture and his eyes narrow further.

I smile. "She moved in with me, actually."

He pales. "What?"

My grin is full of the thrill I feel, that I can affect him this way. Ames gets a delighted face so I keep going.

"Yeah. It's been wonderful. We're having the time of our lives. I have people at home right now making room for the piano. I love having Ames with me."

"You do?" Ames asks. "The piano, I mean—"

I nod. "All of it is true. I even have an expert booked to come in later today to do maintenance. Make sure everything is taken care of."

"That's sweet," she says. "Let me make dinner for you tonight—"

Dom clears his throat.

Aidan crosses his arms. "I'm right here."

"— for you all tonight," she amends, ignoring her ex. "It will be lovely."

"Please." Aidan scoffs. "Don't try to make me jealous. Saint can't stick to only one woman."

The comment is a blade to my chest but ignore it.

"And you could?" I challenge. "Because we're here for a reason. At least I would never cheat."

"It was barely—"

"'Barely' *nothing*, Aidan," Ames says. "It was a betrayal. A kiss or sex is only part of the issue. The real problem is that you didn't respect me or our relationship enough to do things right."

I surround her waist with an arm and give her a small squeeze. It's a reminder that she's not alone. If I'm honest with myself, it feels better like this to me, too.

"That's right, Ames." I kiss her temple. "You tell him."

Ames gives me the most beautiful smile I've ever seen. I bring her a little closer. The soft curves of her body come in contact with the hard planes of me. Her eyes sparkle, and I could fall to my knees if this means she enjoys being so near to me.

"Really?" Aidan's voice is more than skeptical. It's acidic. "You and Saint? You think I'm going to believe that?"

"Why wouldn't you?" I act as if I am at her feet— in my mind, I am. "I can't imagine a better fate."

I take her free hand and kiss her knuckles. It lingers. I never break eye contact with her.

She gasps. There's a true reaction in her eyes— heat I hadn't seen there before. That sweet, sweet pink tints her face again.

I drop my head closer, until I can see the subtle changes in the shade of brown in her eyes. Her pupils dilate.

I'm pushing it, but it's a chance to show Aidan what he lost. Even if it torments me with what I wish could be mine.

"Who knows what will happen now that you're staying with me," I tell Ames.

"If you start... flirting with me..." she breathes.

"I'll flirt with you," I say. "See what happens next."

A whirlpool shows up in my chest. My cock twitches. Is she interested, or is this pretend? She would have to be one hell of an actress.

The thought that this could be real wrecks through every reason I've listed for why this would be a bad idea. Right now, I don't remember a single one.

Damián is the one to clear his throat. Like we need to be reminded we're in public.

Aidan's words come at the wake of the sound. "I get it, Ames. You're angry. No need to make a spectacle—"

She stills in my arms. She stays close, but she glares at Aidan. "It's not up for debate. Whatever happens between Saint and me, it's for us to know. What I do with my life is none of your concern anymore."

100

"Okay, I apologize." Aidan lifts his hands as if claiming innocence. "I'm sorry you're angry. Let's talk. I just need a chance."

She shrugs. "You lost your chance when you kissed someone else."

She grabs my hand like we do this everyday, and we leave. It seems natural when she lets go of my hand as we get in the car. My hand cools fast without her warmth. It's a visceral loss.

I think about it all the way home, and while we put her boxes away the condo. She starts to make dinner for us, and the memory latches to my ribs and weave a net on it, until I wonder if it will ever go away.

Something tells me it won't.

# Chapter 15

## Ames

"You should go to a game wearing Saint's jersey." Bear takes a swig of his beer. "That will really get Aidan thinking."

Dom pops a cheese cube into his mouth. "We don't want him thinking. We want him fuming!"

While Saint stands near me, taking small tasks off my hands like the most enthusiastic, best trained sous chef, the guys sit across from us at the other side of the kitchen island. We prepared a quick charcuterie board, served drinks, and I got busy preparing a hearty meal.

Now we debrief the events of the day, and my heart hasn't stopped drumming loudly against my breastbone. It's a slow, deep, persistent rhythm. Warmth underscores every beat, because these guys barely know me, and yet they're so clearly in my corner.

"Calling it a spectacle." Dom snorts. "He had to be jealous."

"Agreed," Damián says. "You guys were on point. It looked like you were just about ready to jump each other. He had to have seen it."

On low heat, I toast the nuts I plan to add to my favorite pesto recipe. It will wake up the oils in each seed, and it allows me some privacy. If I focus on the stove, they can't look at my face.

I'm sure I'm blushing. Again. I can still feel the spot where Saint's hand brought me close to him, and the memory alone is enough to speed up my blood.

The way he gazed at me like he wanted me. The way his hard body became a pillar to support my softness. His promise to flirt with me.

He kissed my temple, then my hand, until all my skin tingled from his touch. When we held hands, with the warmth of his large palm against mine, and those thick, long fingers that just... they could...

Aaahhh.

I clear my throat, drink some water, and take the basil out of the fridge to use as decoration. If I stick my head in and let the appliance cool me down, they might not notice what the memories are doing to me.

"No, seriously." Dom nods as if to assert his point. "Come to a game, Ames. I'll get you a jersey with Saint's last name in big, bold letters on the back."

I steal a glance at the piano. Movers I didn't know about made room for it at the corner of the condo. It was all set up before we arrived. The living room area itself is a bit tighter now, and a couple of armchairs are gone, but the instrument looks incredible. Like it was always meant to be there. A maintenance person left only twenty minutes ago, too. I don't know enough about it to discern if they did a good job, but I'm learning Saint doesn't do things halfway.

"Maybe I should go to a game after all," I say.

"Don't pressure her." Saint leans on the kitchen island in a sexy and relaxed pose.

Mischief dances in his eyes. I do my best to hide the smile that wants to take over my face, just because he looks playful. Like my brain immediately wants to match him.

He gazes at me, though he talks to his friends. "I don't even think that she likes football."

I smirk. "All I will say is that the extent of my sport watching is *rugby* clips on social media."

They all groan, except for Damián who laughs.

I give him a conspiratorial look and I fake whisper, "It's the thighs."

"I've been told I have great thighs," Saint says.

"We all do," Logan adds.

"Respectfully," I insist, "rugby players are something else. But if I can watch one of your games with Evie and your other guests, maybe I can manage the anxiety and watch you all play."

Saint is about to respond when his phone rings. To everyone's surprise, Logan's ring tone goes off as well.

Logan frowns. "It's Evie."

Without much else but a nod, he steps out onto the terrace.

"It's my agent." Saint makes an apologetic gesture with a hand. "I have to take this."

He jogs to his room, and I finish dinner with Dom, Damián, and Bear keeping me company. Logan comes back first, just as we finish setting up the dinner table. His brows are wrinkled and heavy. It quiets us down.

He must be able to feel the effect his frown has on us, because it doesn't disappear, but it softens.

"Mmh," he utters. "We should wait for Saint. It's about the TV show."

"Does everyone know about the show?" I ask.

Damián nods. "We've been bugging Saint about it."

I return to the kitchen and get busy chopping cherry tomatoes. "Bugging him? Why?"

"Evie's been trying to get him on a baking show for a while," Dom says. "He's resisted it for as long."

But he said yes this time, and something tells me it was because of me.

Two, three, four cherry tomatoes go into a bowl with lettuce and cucumbers. I count them the way I count my heartbeats. In five insistent thumps, my heart tells me to be careful, that I shouldn't take all of this as evidence that he truly cares about me. Because that crush looming in the distance is closer than I thought— it's just around the corner— and my feelings and his care could blend into dreams I can't afford. Lead my heart down the wrong path, and make it do things it's not meant to do. Not when the object of my affections objects to long-term affection.

Saint comes out of his room. Something about the slant of his mouth betrays it wasn't an easy call. A switch flips and I forget about my confused emotions. All I want is to ask him what worries him, but I say nothing yet.

He notices our attention is on him and his expression changes. It takes a friendlier form. Even the ghost of his dimples show.

"It's going to be fine," he says, though no one has asked anything yet. "There is news, but also... My agent heard the GM has been calling a couple of people. Testing the waters for a trade."

A chorus of complaints fill the room. Saint comes to the kitchen and grabs the salad bowl, as if nothing is amiss and he's ready to take it to the table. I don't say anything, but put a hand on his arm. He stills, and lets out a small breath.

Our eyes cross for a second. I see the worry he doesn't share. I squeeze his forearm and hope it tells him I care.

The show news can wait. This matters so much more.

"All I can do is win." His lips press into a thin line. "Get the MVP trophy if I can. That way they won't need a sacrificial lamb. They might feel justified to keep the best in the league."

"Good thing we're on your side. We'll win with you." Bear lifts his glass, punctuating his words with a toast.

"You're not going to get traded," Dom says. "That's the bet I'm going to win this season. It will be the biggest bet in Hypersquare history, too. It's going to get me the crown."

"You can get the crown if I get to stay." Saint shakes his head. "But you can't put that on the board."

"I don't need to," Dom replies. "I have witnesses. I'll figure something out."

Logan adds a simple-but-severe nod. "A sealed envelope with our signatures will do."

"In that case, I appreciate the trust," Saint says. "I don't mind if you take the crown for the off season, if it means I stay."

"You'll stay," Logan insists. "And you'll be the MVP and get a ring out of it, too."

Saint sighs. His eyes land on me. He gazes across the group, the line of his shoulders relaxing somewhat.

"Thank you," he simply says.

With a small smile now softening his lips, he takes the salad to the table. He gets everyone to sit, including me, and he brings the big dish full of pasta and chicken bathed in basil, nuts, and spices. Soon, our plates are full and compliments in deep voices fill the room.

"This is incredible." Logan's tone isn't very expressive, but the words hold his admiration anyway. "I'm glad I stayed."

This time, Saint's smile is genuine. "I'm glad you still want me around, Logan, despite how disappointed you must be that you're not going on the TV show anymore."

I perk up. "Something happened with the show?"

I hadn't forgotten, but the trade took priority for a bit.

Logan doesn't react to Saint's sarcasm, but answers me. "I will let him explain, but some plans have changed. Evie just told me she and I are not going to the show anymore."

"Oh?" I turn to Saint. "What happened?"

"My agent let me know the TV show producers decided to change the direction of the show," he explains. "It will just be you and me, now, Ames."

I bite the inside of my cheek. This TV show is such a big opportunity I'm still trying to wrap my head around it. I've avoided thinking too hard about it, or the nerves and hope will take over, and I will be an anxious mess.

A show like this could open doors to new business opportunities, yes. It's also a gift. The chance to cook and share my food with people, bring my traditions and teachings with me, and build community through them.

"So you and I," I say. "Next Monday. Cooking together while the cameras roll."

Saint and I, together, spending a few hours doing my favorite thing in the world. Perhaps finding the magic of synchronicity, when two people fall into a harmony that needs no melody. While surrounded by a production team and a few cameras.

I lick my lips. Saint keeps on smiling, unaware.

"I'm happy to be your sous chef again." His dimples pop. "I will say 'Yes, chef!' as often as you want me to."

"Wait." Dom studies us. "That means you're missing the gala."

Logan nods. "And now Evie and I get to go. Good."

"Really?" Bear arches an eyebrow at the quarterback. "I wasn't sure you enjoyed the party last year."

"Oh, I did," he says. "She says I have to go, I go. She says plans have changed, I say it's all good. And I can't wait to spend time with my girlfriend while we're both dressed to impress, again."

"Should we dress to impress?" Saint asks me.

He's sitting to my side. His eyes sparkle. We share a long look that has enough warmth in it, enough playfulness, he might be flirting.

My heart skips a beat. Shyness threatens to come to life, because of the thoughts I'm having and because I'm at the receiving end of his attention. Despite the way it prickles up my backbone, I manage a smile.

"It's supposed to be like a holiday dinner party, right?" I ask. "We can dress up."

"I'll dress up for you." His grin stretches wide, deepening the notches on his cheeks. "Will you dress up, too?"

He doesn't say it in as many words, and I may be imagining things, but I can hear a different question hidden in his words.

*Will you dress up for me?*

Butterflies explode in my stomach. Back at Aidan's place, I told Saint to flirt with me. Does this mean he's going to do it? And that he wants to see where it goes?

Yeah, that crush is imminent.

"I like dressing up," I say.

"And when you come to our next home game," Dom adds, "you get to wear Saint's jersey."

"I'm going to that game now?" I stare at the tight end.

"I think you should," Dom says. "Our Christmas game will be here."

"Would you mind?" I ask Saint.

He puts an arm around me, over the back of my chair. With a smile on his face, and those sweet dimples working overtime to make him look innocent, he leans close.

He gazes deep into my eyes. "First, the TV show. Then, you with my name on your back. I would love to have you there."

I believe him.

And just like that, my crush on my brother's friend, the popular jock who dates as easily as he breathes, who's a well-known flirt, takes root deep between my lungs.

# Chapter 16

## Saint

"Okay, let's do this." Mark, the show's producer, rolls up his sleeves as if he's ready to get his hands dirty.

He directs us to stand behind a large kitchen island. The set is beautiful. The countertops are all white marble, with sleek white cabinets and copper hardware. A few open shelves showcase cooking appliances and fancy enameled cast iron pots and pans in bright colors. Three ovens and an industrial-sized fridge set the backdrop, framed by open displays of rustic baskets overflowing with fresh produce. It's the perfect mix of modern and homey, with a touch of professional, and a little too close to the kitchen of my dreams. The kind I would have built for myself and a partner I planned to grow old with. Someone I might cook breakfast for, and then seduce on the dinner table. Only to do it all over again for the next meal, and the next.

I sigh and glance at Ames.

*Yeah, keep on wishing, man.*

Five cameras point their large, dark eyes our way. They temper my excitement to cook in this space. I'm not a professional at all. It helps that Ames stands next to me, a smile on her face. She looks confident. It's no surprise, since she has every reason to be. She's in her element. All I have to do is reflect the light she emits so effortlessly.

Her beauty only adds to her shine. She wears a green dress that plays with the set lights in such a way, a subtle, glimmering blue appears only when hit at the right angle. It gives a sense of ice and winter and warmth all at the same time. She pinned her curls at her temples, opening her face and inviting us all to admire her gorgeous brown eyes. Her lips are painted a bright red, too, of course.

I tap at my stomach. It's a reflex— one that aims to fix my shirt even if there's nothing to fix. The geometric silver pattern on my dark green shirt seems like a poor match for her splendor. I might as well take it off and throw it in the deep fryer.

Mark checks something on his phone. I purse my lips.

Ames gazes at me and mutes her mic. "You look handsome."

I lift both eyebrows and do the same. "I was just thinking that you look so beautiful, I shouldn't have bothered trying to dress up to cook. I might as well have shown up naked."

She blushes. "That would have been quite the Christmas episode."

"Yeah?" I smile and bring a hand to my chest. "There's still time to reconsider."

Several buttons are already undone, and I let my fingers hover at the first closed one.

"Shirt?" I ask. "No shirt? Do you have a preference?"

"Saint."

My name on her lips is an admonishment. I like it enough that I respond to it by undoing one more button.

"Oh my God." She puts a hand over my fingers to stop me. "Don't. You're making me blush right before we start recording."

"Yeah?" I grin, grab her fingers in mine, and press her hand to my chest. "The idea of me naked makes you bashful?"

Our fingers casually interlock over my skin, and I hold on so she can't easily pull away. It's my natural instinct taking over. Whatever part of me loves to flirt and seduce sees how delightful she is and takes action, no matter the consequences. That part doesn't care that my heart is involved, desperate to blow oxygen to the flames because it's *her*. Neither cares that I'm playing with fire, just to have her close a little longer.

"Shirtless isn't the same as naked—" She blinks a few times. Her blush deepens. "And it's such a safety concern in the kitchen—"

"It would be worth it. You look lovely when you blush."

"Saint..."

"Okay, then." Mark puts away his phone. "We're good to go."

Ames takes her hand away. I put mine in my pockets. We pull back, like two teens caught in a compromising position and unmute our mics. Mark gazes from Ames to me and back to Ames.

"Great. Listen." He smiles. "The vibe for this show is to make viewers feel like they're in your kitchen with you. Like they're your guests. Like you're the *it* couple, so happy to be hosting for your first Christmas as, say, newlyweds. The same kind of interaction you were up to just now— maybe tone it down a notch to keep it family-friendly— but that general energy. Yeah?"

Ames steals a glance at me, but talks to the producer. "Uhm, we're not together."

"Oh— okay. Could have fooled me but— that's fine. Viewers won't know that, right? The point is *the vibe*. That they can believe the fantasy for an hour."

Ames and I exchange a look. Her deep, brown eyes tell me she's worried. Disappointment feathers through me, that the moment is over and already something she can't fathom with me.

Mark catches the shift in *the vibe* between us and lifts his hands in a calming gesture. "You don't have to force anything. Just be yourselves and have fun. All I'm saying is show you've known each other for years. Let yourselves be swept up by the magic of the season. It will be great."

Eventually, we nod.

Mark points at the oven, the fridge, the pantry. "We did all the prep you requested, Amelia. Otherwise, just cook, chat, be friendly. We will film until you're done cooking, then pretend to sit and eat. This will likely be three to five hours, which will be edited down to one hour. Any questions?"

We shake our heads.

"The director and I may give small notes here and there," he says. "Cues to talk about the charity, other content we're looking for. Our directions will be edited out of course, so act like no one else can hear what I'm saying, and ignore the cameras."

"Sounds good," I say.

"Great. Let's get started, shall we?"

Mark steps behind the cameras. The director tells us to get comfortable and start cooking, and reminds us to talk about the food we're making.

I start by making a simple sheet cake with eggs, flour, sugar, and honey. Ames prepares a dish she calls lechón. She puts it in one oven while I put the cake in another.

"Now what, chef?" I ask.

"You don't have to call me chef." She smiles. "Let's make the picada now. That's what we call a charcuterie board in Uruguay."

We cut cured meats, cheese, and fruit.

"What do you call these in Colombia?" Ames asks.

"Picadera. They're a bit different. They have arepas, for example. I should make some for you one day."

"I'd love that."

"One day I'll make you arepas con queso for breakfast, too. Lots of butter. Maybe even a fried egg." I moan just thinking about it. "I could make it for you on a Tuesday— that's our day off— or during the off season."

I place the picada to the side, deeming it ready. I steal a grape and smile at Ames. She smiles back. "You're going to make me breakfast?"

"Brunch. It's my favorite meal of the day."

"Deal. Now help me prepare the ingredients for a pionono. The cake will be done soon, and I want to be able to roll it while it's still warm."

We collect and prepare the fillings for the savory cake roll. Lettuce, cheese, tomato, hearts of palm, and boiled egg cut into slices. We set them on their own dish, and line them up at the front of the kitchen island, closer to the cameras.

The cake is ready and I take it out from the oven and onto a cooling rack. "Why is it better to roll it while it's warm?"

"It makes it easier, as the proteins are still flexible. We're going to use a clean dishcloth as well to help."

"Yes, chef."

"Stop," she laughs. "This isn't a professional kitchen and I'm not your boss."

"But I like getting instructions. Should I say, 'Yes, ma'am' instead?"

She stares at me like I'm suspicious.

"I'm just trying to be a good student." I grin, letting my flirty side take full control again. "I love winning, and I love praise."

I'll give in to that side for only a minute. No harm done.

"I'll remember that," she says.

Color blooms on her face. She licks her bottom lip.

I wave a metal sheet on top of the cake to make it cool a bit faster. "You'll praise me, then?"

"If you do well."

"I'll earn it."

She fans her face with a hand at the same speed I use to cool down the bake. She stops after only a couple of times, like she just remembered we're being filmed.

"We'll see." She clears her throat. "Now pass me that cake, and we'll get going with the pionono."

"Give us instructions while you do it, please," Mark says.

She takes the cake out of the pan and onto a clean dishcloth, talking us through it. We put layers of ingredients on top, and she adds little tips and pieces of history to the dish. She tells me this cake has many names across Latin America, and each country has its own recipes. A preference for sweet or savory versions. Without missing a beat, she rolls the sheet cake carefully, keeping all layers intact.

"The rolling looks difficult," I say.

"The dishcloth helps support the process." She smiles. "Just make sure to do it when it's still warm to the touch, but not burning. Do you want to finish the last bit?"

She helps me. With her hands on mine, she guides me through the right motion. I'm caught on how her hands look on mine— just a smidge lighter tone, and appearing small against my large ones. Long lines that look delicate against my thick fingers. They're designed for gentle and confident touches. The kind that I would welcome all over my skin, letting her explore my body to her heart's content, melting me to an aching puddle of want.

If I'm not careful, just the fantasy will liquify me. The way my blood warms up, it's a real possibility. Yet I need her hands on mine, and this is as good an excuse as any.

"Yeah, like that," she says. "It's a little fragile. Soft hands and firm fingers, now."

"Yes, ma'am."

She laughs. "Don't get distracted."

"Too late."

"Right, well, you're doing a good job." She takes her hands away. "Why don't you finish that up? This is the perfect time for some yerba mate."

I mourn the loss of her touch, but she acts like this is all part of the show. She finds a kettle and fills it with water. I glance at her, mostly because I can't help myself.

"This is great," Mark pipes up. "Keep it up."

I take a slow, deep breath, and busy myself organizing and cleaning up. We're being recorded and I keep forgetting. Good thing she keeps me in line. I need her to remind me where those are, or I'll start coloring all over the page.

She comes back to the cooking station with a jar full of chopped dry leaves and small wooden pieces. In her other hand, she carries a small gourd rimmed in silver, and what looks like a metal straw with a flattened, sealed end.

She opens the jar and offers it to me. "Have you ever had mate? Notice the smell."

It's like dried grass and tea and something unique.

"Mhh." I give it back to her. "No, I haven't."

She pours some of the yerba in the gourd, angling it to create a hill against the side. "It's one of my favorite traditions from back home. It carries lore and customs— things you need to do to drink it right, like this."

She places the metal straw in the gourd at an angle.

"This is the bombilla," she says. "It has tens of little holes at the end. It sieves the yerba, so you only drink the liquid."

"Smart," I say.

"Love how you're talking to people at home," Mark interjects. "Keep it up."

We ignore him. The water starts bubbling up.

"Turn the heater off, please, Saint. We don't want the water to boil. Right now when the bubbles start to appear is the best temperature. Eighty celsius or around one-seventy Fahrenheit."

She adds water to the gourd very slowly, letting the liquid settle on the yerba.

"This is a shared drink," she says. "People sit around a table or around a fire and share a mate. Talk. Bond. If you prepare it right, you keep adding water and can make it last for hours."

"Most things you do right, you can make last."

My heart beats fast, and my voice is husky, but I don't have the time to figure out why.

She smiles. "That's exactly it."

Maybe it's how intimate this moment feels, even when a team of people watch us, and cameras point at us. Or maybe it's because if I knew how to do it right, there are things I would like to make last.

117

Ames sips from the straw. "Perfect. You want to try?"

I take the gourd and drink some. The flavor is strong and bitter and it wakes me up. "Wow."

"We usually share the straw, but people at home don't have to, of course. You can add sugar as well, maybe lemon rinds. Some people add peppermint. Did you like it?"

"It's strong."

"It has caffeine."

I sip some more. "It's really good."

She takes the mate from me and sips. "Let's keep going. What are you making for dessert?"

I grab flour and other ingredients. "A white chocolate cheesecake with cranberry sauce and shortbread crust."

"Sounds amazing. I'll check the lechón."

We get busy again. She checks the meat and braises it, and I get my hands dirty making the dough. We each describe what we're doing, to each other and to the cameras. Ames puts the dish back in the oven and starts on a side dish.

"Why did you become a chef?" I press the dough onto a dish.

I know the answer, but I want everyone to see her shine. The producers think I'm the draw for the show. I'm a well-known athlete. The guy that's on TV and ads and media on the regular. Fans will be curious to watch me cook... but I know better.

She's the star. Everyone else just needs to catch up.

"I chose to be a chef because food is community," she says. "For millenia, celebration was a reason to eat, and abundance was a reason to celebrate. When people come together, sharing a table means you're family. Feeding someone is an ancient way— maybe a sacred way— to tell someone you care about them."

"I love that." I gaze at Ames.

I'm pretty sure I'm broadcasting my feelings, but I don't hide it. I can pass it off as friendly admiration, because she glows.

Ames gazes back at me and a grin breaks on her face.

"Thank you." She steps right next to me. "It's the truth. Food is more than energy and nutrition. It's survival, yes, always. And it's a love letter to our bodies and to each other. It's a way to be close."

And she's close. Awe shines in her eyes— because of her love for food or because of me, I don't know. My heart misses a beat, still, because there's a chance this is a feeling for me. Oh, how I would beg for that feeling to be for me.

She caresses my face and I can't breathe. I want a million moments like this. Times when every second stretches for an eon, because in it the space between us disappears. All that exists is this joy glittering inside. The belief that it could be real, lasting, and mutual. That she could feel the same for me, too.

"You had flour on your face," she explains.

Something in me breaks. A clean snap of a cord, deep inside my chest.

*Silly me.*

Of course she wasn't suddenly taken by our proximity like I was.

"I see." I study my hands, with flour all over and dough on my palms. "I'm making a fool of myself."

"You couldn't," she says.

I raise an eyebrow and let myself hide in some playfulness. Moving slowly, I pass the back of my hand over her cheek. It's a thank you for her words, comforting as they were. It's the deprivation, too. The touch itself soothes the pang of my foolishness.

"Oops." I study the smattering of flour I left on her skin. "Let me fix that."

I'm certain everyone knows I'm doing it all on purpose, but I couldn't care less. Everyone's welcome to jump to conclusions. They will think I'm an opportunist taking a chance to flirt and seduce. It's fine. I've built my fame as a playboy brick by brick, but I know the truth. I need to be close to Ames again.

The heat that flickers in her eyes tells me she is into it, too. Her lips part. I step close and use the dishcloth I hang from my shoulder to gently clean her face.

A corner of my lips lift as I stare deeply into her eyes.

"Good?" I ask.

She nods. My heart drums against my ribcage.

I step away and we gaze at each other for a few moments.

"Love the vibes, keep it up," Mark says. "You can talk about the charity now."

We turn to the kitchen island and all the half-prepped food. I share about the charity and Ames asks all the right questions to make it seem like we're chatting while working together at home.

"All right." Mark claps after a while. "If you need a break this is the time. Amelia, can I talk to you for a second?"

She nods and approaches him. I drink more of the mate and sit on a nearby set chair. I kill time checking my phone, until Ames is free and sits next to me.

"Everything okay?" I ask.

"I think so. Mark wanted to ask about my last catering job." She frowns. "He also asked about Aidan."

"That's... strange."

She nods. "He said it was to make sure to prepare any kind of PR response that might be needed."

I frown. "Did he seem worried?"

"No, which threw me off." She smirks. "He seemed very business-like."

"That's good."

"Two minutes," another producer announces.

"This is going great, Ames." I nod. "You should connect with him again later on to ask for leads."

"I will. Thanks, Saint. I know you're doing this for me."

I smirk. "What makes you think that?"

"I heard you have avoided doing something like this for a while."

"I never had a good reason before." I shrug.

"But this is a good reason?"

I smile, say nothing, and lift a shoulder in a dismissive move.

She leans close and gives me a kiss on the cheek. "How will I ever pay you back?"

"Okay, let's keep rolling!" Mark calls.

I stand and offer her my hand. She stands close to me.

I cock my head. "You don't have to pay me back."

"I agreed to an invoice afterwards."

"Right." I laugh, take her hand, and lead her back to the kitchen island. "For now, I'll settle for you wearing my jersey at a game."

We finish cooking and sit down at a big table on a set right next to the kitchen. We pretend to eat, then the whole production team shares our food with us and celebrates our work. They praise her cooking skills and the ease with which she carried the show. I smile away her attempt at saying I had something to do with that.

It feels like we're the *it* couple that hosted a holiday meal. Right before she attends my Christmas game as my guest, wearing a jersey with my name on it.

My poor heart— it had ropes around it before. The snap I felt earlier was one of them tearing apart. I need to be careful, or every bit of cord will give way until I forget why I put them there in the first place.

# Chapter 17

## Ames

The Strike's stadium is huge. Hordes of people move towards the different doors, in a sea of blue for the Strike and red for the opposing team. Instead of following them, I show my phone to a guard and I'm allowed past a corded-off section. As if she knew I'd be intimidated, Evie offered to meet me at the staff's entrance. She prepared everything, and now I'm on my way to a special entry.

She sees me as soon as I go into the building, and flashes her badge to the guards to let me in.

"Benefits of the job." She gives me a quick hug. "Come. I have a surprise waiting for you."

Evie guides me through the massive building like she owns the place. We pass people with badges and reporters waiting for their chance, until we reach an elevator that takes us up several floors.

She smiles. "When was the last time you came to a game?"

The elevator is covered in mirrors. She wears a pencil skirt and a jersey with Logan's last name on the back. I wear jeans with mine. I French tucked my shirt, but my eyes are stuck on the word printed across my shoulders. SANTIAGO.

I bite the inside of my lip. "I'm pretty sure the last time I was at a game was in college when my brother still played."

"Your brother used to play football?"

I nod. "That's how we met Saint."

The doors open and I follow Evie through a long, wide hallway. On the outside wall, large windows let the light in and provide a lovely view of fans pouring into the building, and the city around us. On the side facing the field, shiny white walls are decorated with SEATTLE STRIKE painted in the team's blue, in big blocky letters. Numbered doors mimic the look, blending into the wall.

"But do you like the sport?" Evie asks. "Not that I can judge too hard if you don't. I never cared for football, until I got an internship with the Strike."

"No, I can't say I like it. Too stressful. I hate that there's always a loser, you know?"

"Yeah, I hate seeing them feeling bad when they lose." She sighs. "Okay, we're here."

She opens the door to the suite. It's smaller than I imagined, with a couple of rows of seats by the windows, where up to fifteen people could hang out and watch the field below. A small buffet table waits tucked into the corner, brimming with drinks and food. A high table with chairs stands near the other wall, in sight of the large TV broadcasting the game.

"Have you met the rest of the gang yet?" Evie takes me all the way to the chairs at the front, where two people wait for us.

Nerves pop in my gut like my stomach is a bubbling pot. I've never considered myself to have a gang. Jo and I are friends who work together. Coworkers who are friends. We don't really spend much time together outside of that. I have my brother and Saint, of course but, looking back, I think I made the mistake of focusing too much on Aidan in recent years. The handful of exes before him.

It's weird to realize that I was so narrowly focused on making romance work, to prove I'm different from my parents, that I forgot about me as a person. I lost myself. The idea of friends faded into a distant background.

Texting with Evie over the past few weeks has expanded my mind. My heart. If I'm right, Evie and I are slowly becoming friends. Friendship with her is a set of timid sprouts, branching out to create a full, dense crown on the tree of my life. Connecting with the group at large could only add depth and warmth to my dream of a happily ever after, and make my life richer.

It's another gift that comes from the unexpected breakup, and the life Saint has invited me into. The friendships I'm making are showing me who I am in wholly new ways.

It's yet another reason to hope he doesn't get traded. My friendship with him has deepened, too.

A pang seizes my heart at the idea he might have to leave. Crush aside, a piece of me would break with him gone.

I shake my head. I can't afford to think about that. Better to leave it for when I can't sleep in the middle of the night.

I clear my throat and smile. "I've met Nat and Pen before, at the post-season party last year."

Nat and Pen return my grin, and the gesture reaches their eyes. Nat with her gorgeous lavender hair is the first one to hug me. Pen follows right after. The light of the window glints on her nose ring.

"Yeah, I remember you." Nat sits again.

"Me, too," Pen adds. "Happy to see you here! And wearing a jersey, I see?"

I sit next to Pen, and Evie next to me.

"It was part of the deal," I say.

"Look what I brought." Evie gets a thermos, a mate gourd, and a container full of yerba from a small cubby under the window. "I bought a few bombillas and mates, just in case you don't want to share."

I keep my smile in place. "I'm good with doing it the right way."

"Excellent!" Evie adds some yerba to the mate. "I've been imagining this moment since I learned your family is from Uruguay."

"Look, the guys are coming out," Nat says.

I lean forward and watch the show. Playing at home means the Strike get the diva treatment. A smoke screen reveals one athlete after the other, encouraged onto the turf by five cheerleaders on each side. Each of the players has a personality as they enter the field. Logan runs and waves in a sober manner, while Bear charges forward in an imposing way. Dom and Saint dance, of course.

As much as I'd like to pretend I can admire both equally, I'll admit the truth in the quiet of my mind. I only have eyes for my roommate.

After the coin toss, it's clear The Strike will start on defense. In football, offense and defense are different parts of the team. They take turns depending on how the game progresses. All our favorite players, the ones we're here for, play on offense. They'll stay on the sidelines for the first drive. We sit back and focus on each other for a while.

I sip from the mate. "Do any of you love the sport?"

Pen's lips turn down at the corners. "I think we're all here mostly to support the guys."

"I think it's fun." Nat shrugs. "I like it. And I love getting together here, chatting, watching them win."

"Which reminds me..." Evie grabs her phone. "Did you hear about the latest bet?"

Pen chuckles. "What are they up to this time?"

"It's Bear, Saint, and Logan. It's an edit. They let me record them while working out, and I mixed it with their outfits coming into the game today. The one to get the most likes wins. Want to see?"

We huddle together and stare at her phone screen. Logan's video is first, with a series of overlapping images that first show his arrival to the stadium earlier today, wearing a tailored, casual blue suit, and his usual frown. It's mixed with images of him wearing only shorts, and doing the classic crossfit battle rope workout... in slow mo. His arms and shoulders pop, while still showing off his abs and well-defined torso.

"In my eyes, he's got to win," Evie says.

"Who would have guessed you would feel that way, huh?" Nat laughs.

"I cannot be blamed," she responds.

Next up is Bear. His arrival shows him in fashionable black pants and t-shirt, covered by a tan, dressy overshirt. He also works out in only shorts, letting us admire the intricate tattoos covering the generous expanses of muscles and plush padding... and how he does hip thrusts with impressively heavy barbells.

"He should win, clearly," Pen says. "I know he's my best friend but... wow."

"We're going to be biased, right?" Evie asks. "We all have our own favorite."

"But can you imagine?" Pen insists. "We're all big girls and the way he handles heavy weight..."

Nat, Evie, and I gaze at her with curiosity.

"Never mind," she says. "Show us Saint."

The two previous videos were set to the same song, and Saint's is no different. They're all edited with the same effects and, at the bottom in the description, they make it clear it's a friendly bet. They tag one another in each video.

Despite the similarities, the sexiness level is exponentially higher in Saint's post. His arrival outfit is a stunning black moto jacket printed full of blooming pink and red flowers. The shirt he wears underneath is dusty pink, and the neckline is low enough to show his chain. He winks to the camera like he's flirting with every single fan at once.

"I love how he dresses," I confess.

"It's definitely fashion forward," Nat adds.

The workout video manages to impress regardless. Like Logan and Bear, Saint wears only shorts and nothing else except his chain, a backwards baseball hat, and a cheeky smile. Unlike Logan and Bear, Saint jumps the rope.

I have never paid such close attention to a jumping rope video before. Saint does tricks with it, his muscles engaged and tight as he moves. His smile never falters, and those sweet dimples look fiendish this time.

It's all about stamina and fine motor skills. Cardio endurance. Finely tuned body.

I die a little inside. Thirst is to blame.

"Brave wearing only shorts for this," Nat says. "See how his chain moves with each jump?"

Yeah, I noticed. And those thighs— they should be criminalized for how they're making me feel.

I gulp.

Pen chuckles. "Or maybe it was on purpose."

"Logan was there while I recorded," Evie says. "He scowled and told Saint he should invest in compression shorts stock. You know, because he's proving they can hold *everything* in place."

We laugh. I hold back from fanning myself with a hand.

"I was trying hard not to look," Nat adds. "It seemed intrusive. He's had dinner at home with Damián and me. I don't want to stare at his crotch!"

I can't say I'm as strong as Nat is. The video is still playing, and I study the area in question. It is not an obscene view, but there's enough there that you want to look closer. Make sure you're seeing what you think you're seeing. Worse for me, because I remember how he looked when he came out of the pool.

I shiver, lean back in my chair, and steal more mate.

"So who's winning?" Pen asks.

"Saint, but we'll see." Evie adds hot water to the gourd and sips from it. "There's still time to go."

Of course he's winning. It's almost unfair.

"You have to be objective," I tease. "You may live with one of them, but fans know what they're doing."

Evie purses her lips in humor. "You live with one of them, too."

Pen jumps out of her seat and saves me from having to find a good answer. Something better than, *it's different.*

"Oh!" Pen exclaims. "They're playing now. We missed the switch, oops."

We stand near the window and watch. Whatever play they made, it's good. Saint sprints with the ball toward the end zone. Nerves instantly sprout in my belly.

I grab Evie's arm. "I don't think I can watch."

"Yes, you can," Evie says. "If they score, you need to see what they do."

Before I know it, Saint crosses the final yard, throws the ball hard into the grass, and it bounces off and away. He dances in place and, when Dom joins him, they do a series of coordinated moves.

I'm still frozen in place. I cling to Evie.

She rubs my hand in a comforting manner. "Ugh, I love it when they do stuff like this. See them dancing? I bet they practiced that."

"And look at the crowd," Nat adds. "The energy is immaculate."

Bold silver words appear in the megascreen, reading *HEAR THE THUNDER*. The whole stadium seems to break into a roar. For a second or two, the bass of it makes my chest vibrate.

"Wow. Yeah." I release Evie's arm. "That is pretty sweet."

Pen's eyes glint. "Not as sweet as when the guys dare Logan to make a heart with his hands in Evie's direction."

"He'll do one for me at the end of the game today." My friend grins. "Because he knows I like them, not because of a bet."

"Aw, that's nice." Pen sits and we all imitate her. "It must be love."

"Right?" Evie tracks Logan on the field on his walk back to the bench. "We love a man who will show his feelings freely."

The Strike's defensive team takes the field, and we all relax into our conversation again.

"Talking about showing things freely." Nat smirks in my direction. "You're wearing Saint's jersey."

"It was Dom's idea." I chew on my lip. "And I wanted to show I support Saint."

"What did your roommate say?" Evie asks.

"Not much. He gave me the jersey this morning and told me he looked forward to seeing me in it."

He said it with a smile I couldn't decipher. His eyes lingered on me, too. Butterflies invaded my stomach at the time, for some reason.

I frown. "But if it's anything like it was in college, that means something, right? At least in their mind."

Evie sips from the mate and nods. "They compete over everything, including how many people choose to support them. At least that's my theory."

"Yeah, it's a possessive thing, too," Pen says. "They go a little caveman over having their inner circle wear their jersey."

"Especially their partner," Nat says.

"Or best friend, like me." Pen smirks. "Bear would hate seeing me wearing someone else's name, even if we're not together. That's why I said 'inner circle.'"

"How many people have worn Saint's jersey?" I ask.

Evie gives me the mate and I take a sip. The three women next to me gaze at each other.

"No one has worn his jersey before," Nat eventually says.

My chest stirs. Air seems scarce, all of a sudden. Those butterflies come back to life for good measure.

I do my best to tame them with a deep breath, and by paying attention to these golden nuggets of information. I'm not sure why, but they matter.

"In fact," Nat adds, "I think I've heard Saint say he doesn't let his dates wear his jersey on purpose."

"That makes sense." Evie takes the mate from me. "He's told me he's very careful about letting dates believe there's a future with them and, somehow, the jersey is part of that."

I rub my lips and pretend the comments haven't made me dizzy. So much meaning could be garnered from them, but I'm not ready to face them.

"So how are things going since the breakup?" Pen asks.

I mask another deep breath in a long sigh. "They're okay. The biggest issue is still my business. We filmed that episode with Saint for the streaming service that I'm really hoping will help bring in cash and opportunities. It's coming out tomorrow if you want to watch it."

"We'll watch it!" Nat says, and Pen and Evie agree.

"I appreciate it." I smile. "I have this fantasy that if the episode does well, I'll get to ask the producer for leads and options. Otherwise I really need to start thinking about loans."

"Did you like recording it?" Evie asks. "I can always find other shows like that for Saint. I'm sure he'd invite you each time."

I chew the inside of my mouth. "I really enjoyed it, actually. It felt like I was cooking with Saint for friends that were about to arrive. Even having to talk to the cameras. It was like sharing my thoughts and feelings about cooking and food and community... It was great. But let's not push Saint. Let's see what happens with this show first. My focus should be on my business, anyway."

A lot of it is going into managing this raging crush on my brother's friend instead. No matter what my feelings are and the number of fantasies they plant in my mind, a relationship with him is not one of those branches I'm hoping for.

He dates plenty, current break notwithstanding. Jersey with his name aside. He's never been known to date long-term, and I won't have anything less.

Except Saint is a feast himself, and there's nothing *less* about him.

The true problem here is that I'm nowhere near ready for another long-term relationship. I need to figure out who I am first.

"How's your ex behaving?" Nat asks. "When Damián and I got together, my ex said some pretty horrid things, from what I heard afterwards."

"Saint and I are not together—" I feel the need to clarify— "but Aidan got jealous when he learned I'm staying with Saint."

"That's good, right?" Pen asks. "Fun, at least. He's a well-known musician I think? It has to have hurt his ego that you moved in with someone with so much to offer like a pro-athlete. And Saint is cute."

More than cute, but all I do is nod.

The Strike intercept and we jump to the window again. My hands latch in front of my chest, and I squeeze hard enough to rub my bones together, watching the scramble on the field.

"How do you do this all the time?" I cry. "My stomach is twisting!"

But when the cornerback manages to score the touchdown, Saint celebrates on the sidelines and dances with his friends, and the warmth it evokes could make me melt.

Until he turns toward the suite and points at us. He keeps on moving to music only he can hear, and even from this distance I know he smiles. *Melting* is too soft a word for what I feel now. Whether he pointed at the group or at me, the heat at every nerve ending can't be any less than ignition.

# Chapter 18

## Saint

Two of the touchdowns are mine. It's a good performance, but a voice deep within my skull nags me that I need to push for more. Nothing less than exceptional sportsmanship will convince the team to keep me. I better break a couple of records or I won't get a chance at the MVP award, and that's a risk I can't take.

I don't let myself worry too much about it tonight. With this win, we're basically guaranteed to make the playoffs. I let myself celebrate it with everyone in the locker room, before heading up to the suite.

Ames will be there, and I can ignore my fears of a trade for a bit longer, if I can focus on her.

I follow the guys to the top-most floor, and I enter the room last. Bear and Pen already laugh over a joke I didn't hear, and he takes her face in his hands and kisses her forehead. For a quick second I assume they're about to kiss, but no. It's a sweet, tender moment, and I look away. Logan and Evie embrace and do in fact kiss, but I skip over them too. I seek the sight of Ames.

She stands near the TV, gazing at me with nerves and expectation. The voice in my head disappears. Warmth infuses my blood. My chest opens, ready to welcome her into me.

I take slow steps toward her, our eyes locked. I gaze at her, thankful she's here, and hungry for a reaction— anything— from her. Eventually, I stop less than a stride away. It gives her room to decide the next move.

It's a good move. She takes a step closer to me. Like she assessed our distance and deemed it immense. Like she wants to fix it, only I'm not sure what that entails. I cock my head and smirk, watching her make up her mind.

Her eyes glint. "Congratulations, Gael."

She gives me a slow kiss on the cheek. It lingers.

I take a deep breath. The simple praise grabs me by the heart and adds a few extra pumps to my system. It's the kiss, of course, but also...

"Stop using my first name," I rasp.

"But I like using it."

I like it as well. Too much. I give her a dubious look because I can't encourage her to use my name if it's going to make me weak for her like this.

I've always preferred people to call me Saint. It's the easiest pronunciation and it goes with my brand. But my name on her lips... fuck.

"I love that I'm the only one who uses it," she adds. "And I feel like I deserve the special treatment, after I put myself through the stress of watching you play."

"Uhm, I played wonderfully, thank you very much. Did you see me score two touchdowns?"

"Uhm, yeah," she mocks. "I also noticed the tackles."

"Oh, Amy. Were you looking very closely?"

*Tell me you were watching me closely.*

"Don't call me Amy," she complains.

It only makes me want to tease her harder.

I step closer to her. "Amelia. How closely were you looking at me?"

"Very close." She blinks twice. Slowly. "I didn't look at anyone else."

It's a bigger win than getting the team into the playoffs. The need to jump and fist bump the air invigorates my limbs, but I pull back. I give her one of my boy-next-door smiles.

"I like that," I say.

"I was worried about you. Are you okay? That last tackle looked awful."

"Everything is very okay now."

Her phone rings and she takes a step back.

"Yeah?" She retrieves her phone from her pocket.

She gets a half-worried, half-annoyed look, and groans. I steal a glance. It's Aidan.

"I might have a bruise on the left side of my chest," I add. "It hurts a bit at the moment."

And my heart, too, but I don't mention that. I know her attention is half on the call already.

"Sorry," she says. "I just— there are a few questions I've been meaning to ask him."

My stomach drops to the bottom of my belly. It's an icky feeling. I nod.

She scurries to a corner and answers the call. Joy isn't anywhere to be seen, which comforts me. She looks anxious at first, then royally irritated.

I purse my lips and keep track from afar.

"You okay there?" Evie shows up by my side.

"Why wouldn't I be?" I steal a glance at my friend, but return to Ames right away.

She's still on the phone. She rubs her eyebrows, and the gesture broadcasts her anger.

"You had a great game." Logan stands next to Evie, holding her hand. "But your face looks more like mine at the moment."

I stare at him. It takes me a second to first notice I frown, and to belatedly smooth my brow.

"I'm fine," I say.

135

Bear and Pen join us. I check on Ames. Yep, still angry.

"Clearly," Pen smirks. "You're okay."

"How are you enjoying your living situation?" Evie studies me closely. "It's a big change, getting a roommate so suddenly."

"It's great."

"Are you ready to go back to the club?" Bear asks.

I know what he's implying. Dating has been my way of life for a long time, and I stopped all at once. It's got to be confusing for them.

To me it hasn't been a problem in the least. Any sexual frustration I feel has to do with having Ames on the other side of a wall every night, and not being able to do anything about it. I haven't spared a thought for other women.

Maybe there's a world where I can please every one of my friends, and get to enjoy myself, too.

"I'll see if Ames wants to go to the club," I say. "We'll join you tomorrow."

"She might," Pen says. "We were talking about the club earlier. When it was clear you guys would win the game, we told her we should go celebrate."

"Let's do it, then."

"So back to normal... but not really." Bear grins. The scar on his top lip goes white and stark against his dark beard.

"Things are normal," I argue.

Ames finishes her call. I perk up and watch her come to us.

"Absolutely the same," Evie teases.

I pretend like I didn't hear it.

"Everything okay?" Pen asks.

"I'm getting Aidan off my list before I forget again." She taps on her phone several times. "So annoying. Someone from the late night show recognized me on TV during the game and told him I was here. I didn't even know we'd end up on the screen!"

"Sorry," Evie says. "They started doing that last year when they realized we're fun to watch. Our reactions, the gossip, et cetera."

"It's all the show around the game," Logan explains.

"Well, it pissed Aidan off." Ames puts her phone in her pocket and crosses her arms. "Good. All I wanted to know was why he cheated, which he never explained last time, remember?"

Bear, Logan, and I nod.

She continues with her justified rant. "He couldn't answer a single question this time either. I still didn't get an explanation why he did it. All he did was tell me I should forgive him. As if."

"Do you want to go to the club with us?" I ask. "It would piss him off more."

"We have to go." She smirks. "I told him I was going with you guys. Pen mentioned you all like going, often on a Monday since Tuesdays are your day off. Please don't let me look bad. I made a hundred assumptions."

"Of course we'll go tomorrow," Bear says. "It'll be fun. Like old times."

"Ready to go home now?" Evie asks Logan.

He nods and Evie busies herself saying goodbye, and chatting with Ames about the mate and their next get-together. Logan gives them his back to talk to me inconspicuously.

"Last year you said you'd place a bet on Evie and I," he says. "You said we'd be together within a month."

I narrow my eyes at him. "What are you up to?"

"Nothing. Just thinking I get it now."

"Get what?"

"You make this face when you look at Ames. I bet I looked at Evie the same way."

"Would I have won that bet?" I purse my lips.

"We started things that same night."

"I'm not starting anything with Ames." I shake my head. "Definitely not tonight."

"You respected it when I said not to put your bet on the Hypersquare, so I won't either." He raises an eyebrow. "But a month sounds about right."

"That would put us near the big game. I don't think she's into me that way, and I don't date. This is wishful thinking, my friend."

"Maybe," he says. "But you know I'm calling it."

"Okay," Evie takes Logan's hand again. "Let's go."

"Good night," I tell her. "And blessings. You deal with a lot, being with this guy."

"Oh, I love dealing with him." She smiles and they leave.

"Let's go home?" Ames asks.

She does not take my hand, but we leave together. Twenty-two year old me would be confused that it's happening, and overall thrilled regardless.

I focus on that on the way home.

Standing right outside her bedroom door, we say goodnight.

She smiles. "I'm looking forward to going out dancing with you tomorrow."

Despite myself, I am too.

# Chapter 19

## Ames

Last time I was at this club, it was when Saint invited Aidan and I to the post-season party last year. The place looks the same, with its dark cushioned benches and booths in the VIP section, tinted by the purple recessed lights hidden behind the furniture. A few scattered armchairs are strategically placed to create different sitting areas, with side tables flanking them to hold drinks and food. It's classy and luxurious and, the way the team is treated here, it's clear why they have made it their favorite place to gather.

Last year, I remember feeling like Aidan and I fit right in. Him in his suit and me in a pretty dress, with these athletes and their people all dressed to the nines. Tonight, I wear one of my favorite outfits, but my emotions don't play nice. My soft gold satin blouse drapes low on my chest, and a matte black pencil mini skirt shows off my thick thighs, yet I don't feel as confident as I usually do.

"Everything okay?" Saint leans closer to me. "You look too serious for a night out."

He sits next to me, an arm around me on the back of the booth. He wears tailored pants in a dark sage tone, and a shirt that calls for my hands. It's a darker, less saturated color than his pants, but the texture is some sort of brushed velvet, and the neck looks more like a stylish version of a robe collar, than a shirt per se.

He looks delectable. Somewhere in my body, a decision has been made to increase my core temperature. It must be why I'm slowly heating up.

He's so damn fashionable. I've always known it. I noticed it last year, too, when Aidan and I came here. It hits differently tonight, somehow. No joke, my mouth is watering.

"Yeah, I'm okay." I gulp. "Just thinking of the last time I was here, and how things have changed."

"Why would you think about last year? Why do that to yourself?"

I laugh. Several of Saint's friends came to the club tonight. Dom is to the side with a beautiful someone in his arms, while Bear and Pen sit on a side bench near us, enthralled with each other. Next to Saint and I, Logan and Evie complete the group. They all look amazing, making me glad I chose this outfit and didn't hold back.

Scattered through the VIP section, other friend groups sit around, twice as many people with faces I don't know, conversing and enjoying the evening. The music is loud up here, but not so loud the group we're in can't hear each other.

It doesn't stop Saint from leaning close and talking to my ear.

"You look beautiful," he says.

I turn to him and smile. "Thank you. We all do, right?"

"So I look good, too?" His grin is a devastating mix of sexy and cute. "Do you think that's why I won the social media likes bet yesterday?"

He's unapologetic about fishing for compliments, and I find it endearing. It makes me playful, but I don't directly engage. I lift my eyes to the ceiling and shake my head, like I can't believe I walked straight into that.

There's something vulnerable about admitting to him tonight how good he looks. It's a slippery slope. Like I'll end up confessing he always looks incredible, and that I admire his fashion sense. That it kidnaps my attention, and it makes me crave the touch of the textures of his clothes, and the softness of the skin underneath.

I don't manage to say anything at all.

"Fine," he says. "Don't tell me I look good. But will you dance with me? We should have fun."

That I can do.

We go down to the dance floor. The music is louder here. Deep, insistent bass resounds in my chest.

He grabs me by the waist and brings me close.

"This okay?" He asks close to my ear.

I nod, put my hands on his shoulders, and move to the beat of the music. One, two songs, and my body has learned to follow Saint's guidance. His lead is confident, telling me what to expect from him with subtle but clear pressure of his hands. At times, the swaying of our bodies echo waves in the ocean, then flags billowing in the air. Melodies entwine us together, until I don't know where he ends and I begin.

Through it all, we keep our steps small, maintaining our proximity. Whenever his hands invite me to create any distance— just enough that he can lead me through a turn or half a spin— he brings me back and we end up plastered against each other. Maybe that's why our legs interweave. We're dancing bachata to every song.

I'm in a trance. The heat of our movements release his pheromones into the air, and they put me under a spell. One of my arms goes over his shoulder, my hand at his nape. The other lands on his chest. The velvety fabric is soft under my fingertips, and his heartbeat follows the bass around us. It echoes the drumming inside my chest. It's been years since I danced like this.

One of his hands splays on my back. The other is anchored to my hip. His chain rests on his clavicles and, in my heated mind, I realize I could close my mouth over his skin, and clamp the metal links between my teeth.

I think it means I'm going feral.

"Saint?"

It's not me who's calling his name. The only reason I know that is because the voice isn't laced with the yearning simmering in my veins. It startles me.

I don't realize I had been dancing with my eyes closed, lost in his arms, until I open them to find a stunning blonde inspecting us.

Saint keeps me close, but gazes at her. "Hello, Victoria. It's been a while."

A smirk curls her lips, and the gesture is somehow alluring on her perfect face. She studies me, from head to toe.

I swallow back the distaste in my mouth. A green little leprechaun dances in my stomach. It's an unfamiliar, unwelcome creature.

She smiles at me. "Can I cut in?"

*Oh, no. She didn't.*

The damn leprechaun turns into an imposing, angry green monster. Mutant muscles and torn clothes. The kind that could flip cars and take out an army on his own.

"Not tonight," Saint starts, but I've spoken at the same time.

"No." The syllable is sharp on my tongue.

"I'll give him back at some point," she insists, her eyes calculating on me. "I promise. We only get three dates or so before he moves on. Right, Saint?"

Victoria gives Saint a flirting smile. Saint purses his lips in a calculating gesture.

"I'm just wondering if I can get a second round," Victoria says.

The green monster goes into full rage. It roars inside. I want to pull Saint closer and claim him and, dammit, I have no rights to him. It takes five shots of tranquilizer to calm the monster down. From the bitterness on my tongue, the main ingredient is shame.

My chest caves in. Fuck. What a reminder that Saint and I are only friends. That I'm getting in the way of Saint's options.

I'm about to offer to go back to the VIP section when Saint pulls me closer.

"I'm delighted with the partner I have tonight, Victoria," he says. "Besides, you know I never do that."

Victoria shrugs, taking the rejection in stride.

"Worth shooting my shot. Enjoy." She smiles and winks at me. "He's for sure fun. Just don't get attached. He's not built for anything real."

She kisses Saint on the cheek. It's an innocent move, from the looks of it, and Saint knows it. He doesn't react, except for a subtle flinch no one can see or feel but me. I'm the one he keeps close and tight in his arms.

I can't question the soft way his body jerks. I'm too busy managing the jealous mutant inside of me, when it makes an attempt at waking up. It's tempting. A kiss on the cheek is what I do with Saint, and no one else is allowed to use my move. Rage feels better than the embarrassment of forgetting myself and the role I have in Saint's life. I cling, but it escapes me. I'm the roommate that begged for shelter when her ex betrayed her. I am not one of Saint's dates, no matter how powerful the spell of dancing with him was.

Victoria leaves. I gulp a few times. Bitterness still coats my mouth.

"I'm sorry about that." Saint releases me somewhat. "Is everything okay?"

No. Possessiveness like I didn't know drums deep in my bones.

I close my eyes for a beat. His hand rubs my back in long, soothing arches, and I take a deep breath.

The warmth of him against me is an easier, better feeling. I want to keep following the beat while he holds me close. I want to get lost in the fantasy of it again. Pretend that Saint and I danced like this back in college and one thing led to another, and we've been together since.

The thing is, it didn't happen like that. He dated a hundred Victorias back then, and just as many in the years after. We're adults looking for different things. I may not know yet how to turn a long-term relationship to death-do-us-part, and I'm far from being ready to try again, but I know it starts with partners who want the same thing. I just need to figure out a way to not lose myself in the process.

It's a sad realization. I won't get any of that with him. It doesn't serve me to hope Saint will one day change his mind and look at me that way. I know what my role is, what the right path is, and I need to remember that.

He watches me closely.

"I think I need a break," I say.

He nods. "Let's get a drink."

I don't react when he takes my hand and leads me toward the stairs leading up to the VIP section.

A club staff member is opening the velvet rope to let us up, when someone calls from behind us.

"Saint?"

We turn by instinct. It's a brunette this time, but she gazes at my... friend... with less cheek than Victoria and more longing. She looks familiar, somehow, but I can't place her.

"Rebecca?" Saint asks.

He steals a glance at me. I study her face again, hoping it will click. I've seen her before but I don't know...

"Hi—" Rebecca stares at our hands. "I'm sorry. I didn't mean to interrupt. It's only that I haven't seen you at the club in a while..."

It hits me all at once. She was leaving his place when I arrived. She was the last Bake and Bye victim.

This time, rather than jealousy, I feel a hint of heartbreak. For Rebecca, and for the brief moment I believed I could face a different ending.

He smiles at her. "I hope you're well."

Saint unobtrusively guides me up a few steps.

"I am, thanks." Her eyes follow us. "Have a lovely night."

She turns and walks into the crowd. Saint and I start our way up the stairs.

"I'm sorry." He gazes at me. "Again. It's not always like this, I promise."

"You didn't do anything but be polite." I suck on my bottom lip. "It's okay."

"Still. I'm sorry. I wish I could stop it. I don't mean to... but it's inevitable, really, since I come here so often and, well..."

He shakes his head and lets the sentence die, but I can hear what he meant anyway.

*Since I've slept with so many people.*

"I'm sorry, Ames."

I don't mind the fact per se, but how it reminds me yet again how different we are. One day, I'll try for my happily ever after again. Eventually, Saint will want to go back to dating. Probably as soon as I'm gone from the condo, and he can come back to the club and to his routines unencumbered.

We don't say much else until we're sitting in a booth with friends around, and we've ordered water and drinks.

"If you want to go back down and meet someone—" I start, but he shakes his head right away.

"Don't, Ames."

"If it's because of the logistics I can just... go somewhere else..."

Not that I have somewhere else. Maybe I can ask Evie to let me stay at her place, if she's staying with Logan...

"Ames. Don't you realize? If I wanted to, I could take a date to a hotel overnight."

"But you don't want to do that?"

All he does is get closer and shake his head. "I don't."

It means something. It challenges my thoughts— maybe. Maybe not, but I don't get to think it through, or let it stop the rollercoaster of emotions I'm on tonight.

"Sorry. Ames?" Evie taps my shoulder. "I don't think you've noticed who's staring at you."

"What?"

"Don't look, but over there. Near the railing, at the end of the balcony? Aidan is there."

"What?!" I harsh-whisper.

I can't help it. I glance at my ex, and he notices.

I turn to Saint. "Fuck. I think it's my turn to apologize to you."

"Don't you dare," Saint says. "This is his doing. Or did you invite him here?"

145

"Absolutely not, but I mentioned the club last night during the call. He knew where I would be. I never thought he would show up."

I steal another glance at him. He stands a few yards away, shamelessly studying us. Judging, I think. I'm not sure how to respond.

"What should I do?" I ask.

"Ignore him?"

"Probably." I bite my lip.

"He's watching us." Saint locks eyes with me. "Don't hate me for this."

He pulls me close. I forget about the questions I was asking, or his exes, or even about Aidan for a long second.

Next thing I know, I'm sitting on his lap.

# Chapter 20

## Saint

Ames squirms on me and all blood rushes south. If my heart can't handle it and I end up with angina, I would only have myself to blame.

"Oh my God," she mutters.

I don't know what to make of her expression. Is she reacting to how I brought her to me? To Aidan studying us from across the VIP section? Can she feel my hardening cock?

I can't make it out, and I don't have time to think through the options. Or the blood flow to help my brain much at the moment.

Everything else disappears, pushed into nothingness by this move that landed her on my lap. None of my exes wrecking my evening with Ames. No questions from her about who I want to take to my bed. Not the words on the tip of my tongue, that might have revealed exactly who I want. None of it exists. Nothing matters, but her on my lap.

I lean close, and speak into her ear. "Let's make him question everything, shall we?"

It's an intimate gesture. It's what I might have done with someone I'm trying to seduce. I surround her with my arms for good measure.

She shivers.

"This is evil," she says.

"They say revenge isn't nice." I smirk. "But then, why does it feel so good?"

She turns so her legs fall over the side of my thighs. She sits closer to me like this. The movement has me biting back a groan.

"You okay there, Saint?" Evie smiles at us, enjoying the show.

I clear my throat. "Very well, thank you."

I adjust Ames on my lap. It doesn't help. It makes things worse.

"I'll leave you to it, then," Evie says and turns to Logan, giving us privacy.

As if choreographed, Ames and I turn to gaze at each other. Despite the low-set lights, we're close enough I can catalog my favorite details on her face— the freckle at the end of one of her eyebrows. The burnt umber of her eyes, darkened in the soft purple glow around us. The gentle curves of her top lip.

"I'm sorry," Ames whispers to my temple. "You didn't sign up for any of this."

"Stop apologizing, please." I press my lips together. "It was my idea."

"Yes, but..." She doesn't finish the thought, but she wriggles on my lap. "This is... affecting you..."

I bite the inside of my lip. I'm fully hard now, and she has clearly noticed.

"I should be the one apologizing," I groan. "I can't help it, under the current circumstances."

She watches me closely.

I sigh. "Let's show him how much he fucked up. Otherwise, just let this... human reaction... remind you how fucking desirable you are. Or ignore it. Whatever you prefer. Please."

"It's hard— I mean— it's difficult to ignore."

"Thank you." I lean my forehead against her shoulder and burrow into the crook of her neck. "I didn't think things through when I brought you to sit on my lap."

My position hides me, and I can only hope it gives me a chance to get my act together. The fact that we must look intimate to our witness helps. The fact that it gives me access to her skin, soft and warm against my face, doesn't.

"Should I... sit back down next to you?" she asks.

"Not unless you want to. I'm sure he's fuming right now to see what he lost."

And what I can pretend to have for the next few minutes, if she stays in my arms.

"I'm petty enough to like that thought." She caresses my hair, and I could purr to it. "If you're sure? I'll do whatever you want."

Dangerous.

My cock, desperate, begs me to take her up to her word. The only reason it doesn't wave a white flag is because it's trapped under her generous thighs. As it is, we'd both beg for mercy, and happily surrender to her will. She doesn't realize that her offer is more than I've ever dreamed to have.

I'm too wretched to let this chance go.

"You could drop a few friendly kisses on me." I take a deep breath and fill my lungs with her perfume. "He'll think it's part of our foreplay."

"Like this?" She kisses the crown of my head.

"Too innocent." I angle my face so my temple is on her cheek. "You might want to try again."

"Like this?" She kisses my temple. My cheekbone. "Or this?"

"Warmer," I mutter, my eyes closed. "Getting hotter by the second."

"You like it, huh?" She kisses the other cheekbone, then my cheek.

*Like it* is too simple an expression. My blood is heating up, and my muscles are liquifying, and if she wanted me back, I'd become her willing servant.

"I'm easy," I finally say. "You give me a few kisses and tell me I'm a good boy and I'll kneel at your feet."

She chuckles. "Don't tell me all your secrets. What if I'm tempted to see if you're telling me the truth?"

"I'm telling you the truth." I kiss her cheek now. "You can test it if you like. I'll be good for you."

I kiss her jaw. She takes in a shaky breath. My lungs echo her.

"How far do you want me to go?" I ask.

"What are you thinking?"

"I'll start with your neck." I gulp. "It will piss him off."

"Right. Aidan." She chews on her bottom lip. "He's watching."

"We don't have to do anything you don't want to do."

"So is this up to me?"

"Always."

"What about what you want?"

"I think it's clear what I want, Ames."

She knows how this is affecting me. I squeeze her lush form to me, filling my arms and my hands with her body. So generous, so giving, so tempting.

I'm transparent. If she wants to look, she'll see my chest has turned to glass, and my heart beating fast is the only organ keeping me alive. My cock? It's killing me, because it's still bound to feeling her weight, her movements, her warmth. My cock and I are not allowed to do more.

If she wants to look, she'll figure out how gone I am for her. It must be written all over my face, too.

I lick my lips. My heart could explode, and I can only take deep shallow breaths in anticipation.

She nods and tips her head back. I dip my head to the crook of her neck. My mouth parts... only to close in a lazy kiss on her warm skin.

I frown in abject focus. She shivers in my arms. I take a deep breath and open my mouth again. My lungs are full of her perfume now, and I swear I can feel her heartbeat against my lips. Should I nip? Lick a path up to her jaw? I don't make a decision— my lips close on her again, the tip of my tongue connecting with her skin—

"Guys." Evie elbows me.

Her voice shocks me out of my dazed state. It takes an inhumane amount of effort to glance at my friend. For a moment, she even looks blurry to me.

She points to the space in front of Ames and I.

Aidan stands a couple steps away from us, staring.

"Hi, Ames." Aidan digs his hands into his pockets.

"Hey." She surrounds my shoulders with an arm. "Didn't think I'd see you here tonight... or ever, really."

The glass over my chest— it cracks.

For a moment, I forgot this is for show. To provoke Ames' ex. That I have a part to play in this charade.

I muster a smile. "Hello, Aidan. Are you having a nice evening so far?"

Internally, I'm barely back to my senses. I gather whatever I can and use it for a stint.

He frowns. "I see things have... evolved."

"Yeah?" I say. "What gives you that impression?"

Ames laughs. It feels like a gift, so I thank her with a kiss on the cheek.

She doesn't react to my kiss, but stares up at her ex. "Maybe things have changed, maybe they haven't. I don't see how that's any of your business, Aidan."

"So if I go out there and date other people—" his Irish accent comes out stronger, the more he talks. "If I go down there and dance with someone else... it's not a big deal?"

"It's not a bigger deal than you cheating on me," she replies.

"Atta, girl." I grin and accommodate her on my lap, making a show of it.

Disdain takes over the line of the musician's mouth.

"I don't recognize this side of you," Aidan says.

She shrugs. "I don't remember asking for your opinion."

"What we have—" he tries.

She shakes her head. "I don't owe you anything but basic respect as a fellow human being."

I chuckle.

"We're over," she insists.

"Right." He studies her, then me.

"Good night, Aidan." Ames rests her head on mine.

"Toodaloo, mate," I echo.

I'm obnoxious and I know it. My words are nettle leaves thrown at him.

He ignores me. His face saddens as he looks at the woman in my arms. "I... miss you. I never meant to hurt you like this."

Ames shakes her head. "Enough, Aidan. Go."

She stares up at him and waits.

The tall singer shakes his head and gazes at her for a long minute. He ignores everyone else. Ames gazes back, but her face is inescrutable.

Eventually, he gets the message and nods. He turns to leave, but stops himself at the last second.

I squeeze Ames to me again. Just in case.

He scoffs. "My first single. It's coming out next week. It's one of the songs I wrote for you."

In my arms, it's easy to sense the way she stills.

"I'll take it as your goodbye," she says.

"It can never be," he says. "Music is forever. Every time that song plays, it will be for you."

He leaves, going straight for the stairs down to the dance floor.

I take a deep breath. At least, my cock is dormant again, in the face of what just happened.

"Wow," Evie says. "That was a lot."

"How are you doing?" I ask Ames.

"I'm okay." She sighs. "I think this was a better goodbye than last time I saw him."

"So should we celebrate?" Evie asks.

"I'll buy you drinks," Logan says.

"Yeah." She sits next to me and smiles at our friends. "Let's enjoy the night. Maybe we'll get to dance some more later?"

Her eyes land on me. The need to surrender overtakes me again.

"I'll dance with you for as long as you want," I say.

# Chapter 21

## Saint

We dance until late into the night. We don't talk much. Ames looks like she wants to lose herself to the music, moving close to me no matter the song, and I am only happy to oblige.

Just like earlier in the evening, she keeps on touching me. At one point, her fingertips run over my chain and I don't know what to make of it, but I come close to combustion. I fall deeper and deeper into my feelings, until they wrap me in silk and steel and my nerve endings become livewire. Even the gentlest of touches set my body aflame.

Next time we need a break, we decide to call it a night and come home.

Again, she kisses me on the cheek goodnight. "Thank you for everything, Saint."

I watch her go into her room, my feet nailed in place. The rope I tie at my ankles is made of every ounce of will I still have left. My whole body is begging me to follow her, but I know it's a selfish wish. Dancing together and a little convenient payback on her ex are no evidence I am the Mister Right she's looking for.

It's dark in my room, when I finally make myself lay down in bed. I'm too wired from the night to fall asleep. I stare at the dark ceiling, replaying the night. How she reacted when I brought her to my lap. How she kissed me. How she touched me.

The fact she didn't complain or move away when she realized how hard I was. *It's difficult to ignore.*

But does that mean she would have wanted me to make a move?

If this were anyone else, I would have taken it as a sign that she wants me, too.

I'm so turned on my brain is tormenting me with the possibility. A movie plays in my mind with all the things I want to do with her. All the things I told myself a long time ago I couldn't risk wanting with Ames, when she's looking for everything I'm not good for.

She wants a happily ever after and I don't fit with that archetype.

But, fuck, I'm one hell of a Mister Right Now.

Before I know it, I stand outside her room again. I'm hard as a rock, and dithering on the edge of a decision I can't come back from. Knocking on her door could change everything.

I place my hands on the doorframe, head hanging low, despairing but holding back, because this isn't as simple as jumping in and seeing where we land.

That's when I hear the moan. The buzzing of what I can only assume is a vibrator.

Lust is a waterfall down my back, pooling at my core, filling up my belly. My lungs.

Another moan reaches me. It's low. I shut my eyes and beg my ears to become superhuman. The sounds are subtle, and there's no way I'd hear it if I weren't standing right outside her door. Before I know it, the hum disappears altogether, and a single, throaty gasp takes its place. Somehow, I know she pushed the vibe inside her.

My breathing hiccups. My heart stutters.

I place one hand on the door. The other lands on my cock— my boxers can barely contain it. Singlehandedly, I push the fabric low and free my erection, wrapping it hard in my hand. I don't move. The way I'm feeling, it wouldn't take more than a pump or two before I make a mess.

Fingers splay over the door and I push, like my subconscious is seriously considering tearing down the barrier and joining Ames.

She moans again. My hand forms a fist against painted wood and, because I'm weak, I pump on my cock once with the other one.

If I'm going to do this, now is the time.

If I do this, I have to make her understand it will not last. That I'm not built for it. Like I've done every time, with everyone else. Ames may be the only one I would have risked everything for, but she deserves better than an untested guy who doesn't fit what she's looking for. Especially when it could result in pain. Worse, when it would be layered hurt on top of her recent breakup, except I would be the one to cause it this time.

I pull the hand back from the door. Could she ever...

She moans again. I give myself another pump. A drop leaks. I shiver.

If she says no and I've taken this risk I could...

Another moan. I don't know if it's hers or mine.

"Shit," I whisper.

I take a step back. Another. I don't know what I'm doing, or why, but I go back to my room. I make it all the way to my bathroom, slap the light on, and pump fast on my cock. I can still hear her moans resounding in my head. Sounds make it out of my throat and, fuck, it doesn't take a whole minute. My balls seize and I come so hard I forget where I am. All I know is my hands catch some of it, and my lungs can't keep up, and it's a miracle I haven't collapsed to the floor.

I've been holding back this climax for too long.

Some time later, my eyes open of their own accord. The countertop is white stone and far too bright for my poor brain. I blink a few times, barely aware that my cock is still half hard in my hand.

"Fuck."

I flip the faucet on and put my hand under water, only to find cum dripping from three wet lines on the mirror.

"Damn."

Still catching up with my breathing, I grab a towel and clean the mess I made. My image mocks me on the reflection, with its torn, anguished face and muscular body that won't get me closer to Ames.

It doesn't serve me to be at the top of my game, when that only makes me a jock, and not the kind of artistic man Ames is known to be drawn to.

At some level I understand that. I have to have known it, because I stepped away from that door for a reason. While I despaired over joining her in bed, asking if she'll have me for a little while, my subconscious had my back. Ames has always been clear in what she wants. If I want to fool myself that I could be that for her in the short term, I'd be the one to blame. The resulting heartbreak would be for me to live with.

A couple more passes of the towel on the mirror and it's clean, but my reflection's face looks just as forlorn. All these muscles that make fans and dates fawn over me, and all the skill that is setting me up to a win this season— they don't cut it in Ames' eyes.

Even if she was aroused today like I was, and even if that's what had her moaning in her room tonight, it doesn't mean she'd choose me over what she really wants.

Why would she? Ames doesn't deserve anything but the best. She should never conform and settle for a guy who can't give her the future she has a claim to. And I can't be the guy that goes into it knowing that it could all result in pain, and I'd be the cause of it.

Hell, I'm not an option. I haven't proven myself yet. We have to make it to the final game first, and make ourselves the best. As for relationships, my adult life is all the evidence she needs.

In love, my existence is no more than just a habit, and a collection of desirable traits with an expiration date.

# Chapter 22

### Ames

On Friday, Saint says goodbye with a hint of sadness and restraint hidden behind his eyes. The start of the playoffs is in two days in another city, and his Thunderdome curfew approaches fast. I choose not to question the heaviness that envelops him. I ask if I can give him a hug, and we hold each other for a long minute, before I kiss his cheek and he leaves.

Restlessness prickles my chest. It doesn't go away after I close the door behind him, or when I wake up the next morning, or after I clean up the remnants of my lunch. I'm already nervous about the game they will play in less than twenty-four hours.

Alone in Saint's condo, I putter about mindlessly. I end up doing admin for my business, and shop around for potential loans if it comes to that. The distraction doesn't last long. Later that night, I sit on the sofa and set out to deal with these nerves in the only way I can imagine.

> **Ames**: Please don't respond if you can't. This isn't a priority. But do you mind if I invite the girls over for a watch party tomorrow? I don't think I can do it alone

It doesn't take him long to answer. I can imagine him in his hotel room, laying in bed. Maybe smiling after getting my message.

> **Saint**: Invite them. Have fun. Watch us win. It's your home, too, Ames.

It helps the nerves somewhat.

> **Ames**: I know you will be amazing but I also know the stakes are high. I already get anxious during games

> **Saint**: I love that you're making it into an event.

> **Ames**: It helps when Evie and Pen and Nat are there to calm me down

> **Saint**: my sports psych would call that intellectualization, Amy. It's okay. You don't need to keep explaining. Do what makes you happy and have fun

> **Ames**: I'm sorry. I should be a cheerleader. I have total trust in your skills!

> **Saint**: You're good. Don't apologize for this. I like that you care. Trust me, I'll play better now that I got to text with you. If you're watching I'll want to show off.

I welcome the change in topic. Teasing is so much easier than having my self doubts pointed out to me.

> **Ames**: Oh, yeah? But you're such a showman it's like you're always peacocking, on and off the field. How will I know this time you're showing off because I'm watching? Tell me what kind of signs to look for

**Saint**: peacocking? Excuse me. I dance because I enjoy it.

**Ames**: And because you want to show off. You like the edits your fans make online, be honest

**Saint**: Have you been checking out those edits, Amy? Be honest.

I snort. Of course I have. Before bed sometimes, just to check what people say about him. Alone in the dark, I can watch Evie's video of him jumping the rope and study it in detail, unafraid of what my face might show despite my best intentions. If the algorithm starts feeding me more and more videos of him dancing, or collections of him in his best outfits, I cannot be blamed.

**Ames**: I think the app geolocated me somehow and thinks I'm a fan.

He sends me a picture of him grinning. It triggers a small heart malfunction that I ignore.

**Saint**: You're funny. I know how those algos work. Your eyes linger, don't they?

**Ames**: Only because I'm trying to figure out if that's what it looks like when you're showing off.

**Saint**: Tell me you like it and I'll send you a selfie of what I'm wearing right now. As a reward.

**Ames**: So cocky. You can't help yourself, can you?

**Saint**: I cannot. Now tell me

**Ames**: I will not

**Saint**: Are you sure? I'm shirtless.

**Ames**: Gael, stop.

I send the two words before I know what I'm doing. My breathing has picked up.

**Saint**: But you wanted to know the signs! This is me showing off.

**Ames**: I thought it was something like… I don't know. Logan and Bear headbutt their helmets together and make power poses. You and Dom dance. Anything else I've missed?

**Saint**: Logan makes a heart toward Evie.

**Ames**: I didn't think that was showing off

**Saint**: he's showing off his feelings.

I lick my lips. Texting can be like walking on an icefield. You miss out on all the tone cues. Assuming he meant that in a wistful way could crack the white surface and drop me into freezing dark waters.

A few words appear on the screen anyway. I'm typing them myself, but I hesitate. It's a question I shouldn't ask.

*How would you show off your feelings for someone you love? I'd like to keep track for no reason at all.*

The full sentences glare at me on the screen, the cursor blinking patiently until I make up my mind.

A call comes through from an unknown number.

*Fuck it*, I mutter as I press send on the text.

I answer the phone to distract myself.

It's Mark, the producer from the streaming network.

"I'll keep this short," he says after a few niceties. "We liked your presence— your energy while recording the Christmas special. We want to produce a pilot for a cooking show with you. We're in a rush. TV is always in a rush, but we'd like to get the conversation started on Monday with your agent and our team. Get the vibes right, pick a few tentative dates, all of it. Are you on board?"

I'm not altogether sure a tremor didn't hit the city, and reached me up here in Saint's condo alone. I say yes, like this isn't the kind of news to shake up my system.

The call ends and I leave my phone screen-down next to me. I'm shivering, despite the perfect temperature in the room. It's an internal source of cold and shock. I need to recover before I go back to my texts, but I stare at the device with little shakes at the tips of my fingers.

In the quiet of the space, the ceiling lights glint on the black mirror of the phone lenses, and the symbol at the back stares right back at me. Saint is busy, and I shouldn't text him again and get in the way of his concentration. He needs to win, so he can stay in the city. But we were already messaging and having mindless fun. I asked him a daring question I hope he doesn't read too much into. I might have a reply from him that might give me clues of his interpretation.

All I want to do is tell him about the call. Hear what he has to say. See his encouraging smile.

When I finally break and get on my phone again, I see Saint responded within one minute of my last.

> **Saint**: You'll know because I will tap my chest twice, three times in a row, with my right hand. Tap tap. Tap tap. Tap tap. Like a heartbeat.

A few minutes later, he sent another. Then another.

**Saint**: everything okay? Did I lose you

**Saint**: text me later if you like. Or whenever. If you send me a few encouraging words during the game, they'll make me smile after, no matter what happens. I may not always be able to get to my phone when I'm away, but I like getting a notification with your name on it. I will always get to them as soon as I can.

**Ames**: Thanks for that. I actually needed it. Something big happened and I wanted to tell you.

Dots appear on the screen right away. Like he'd kept an eye on his phone.

**Saint**: I'm always happy to hear what you have to say. What happened?

**Ames**: Mark called. He wants me to record a pilot for a cooking show

Typing it sows anxiety seeds in my diaphragm, and roots sprout as I wait for Saint's response. This show could solve my business problems in a way I can't yet comprehend. It's the kind of thing I can't dare to dream about, until every step has taken place, all paperwork is signed, and I'm in front of the cameras again.

Is it a good idea, or am I being terribly foolish? I don't know, and it's too soon to predict.

**Saint**: What?! That's incredible! Of course they would see you and want to give you your own show. You were amazing. You'd be great on TV

**Ames**: So you think I should do it?

**Saint**: Please tell me you'll do it. We'll figure it out. We'll celebrate both our wins tomorrow night.

For the next thirty hours, I focus on preparing the watch party, having fun, and managing my nerves. I get Evie to take up as a temporary agent for me, and we make a toast to celebrate the opportunity and the incredible game the guys are playing. If I get a few extra drinks while entertaining my friends, I tell myself it's not a big deal. It's preparation for my celebration with Saint.

# Chapter 23

## Saint

I have almost thirty texts from Ames by the time I check my phone after winning the game. The celebration is still going on strong in the locker room, but I take my time re-reading my favorite ones.

At my cubbie, I sit down and smile.

> **Ames**: the TV zoomed in on you dancing to that touch-down. You're such a great showman

> **Ames**: are you okay? Damn tackles.

> **Ames**: am I jinxing it if I say I think you guys are soooo going to win this game?

> **Ames**: I've had a couple of drinks, which is only partly why I feel bold enough to tell you that play was HOT

**Ames**: another drink, and now I can't find a way to delete that text. Oh well, you did look HOT

**Ames**: you know what they say about peiple who dance well right? Hahaaha I bet you do

**Ames**: I can't wait for you to come home. Ill wait for you. You said we'd celebrte

**Ames**: Ignote the typso. CONGRATUELATIONS ON THE WIN AAAH YOU'RE AMAZNG

**Ames**: the way theyre replayijng your touchsdowns on TV they wuld have to be FOOLS to let you go. Evie agrees with meeee

"Who's the one sexting now?" Logan's voice has the same serious tone as usual, but I know him well enough to know he's teasing.

Saint: Can't wait to see you tonight.

I don't text anything else in response. When I choose my words this time, I want to do it while looking her in the eyes.

"I am not sexting." I put my phone away in my bag and prep my things for the shower. "Why would you say that?"

"I'm really enjoying getting back at you for the grief you caused me last year when I was falling for Evie."

"Did I tease you about sexting with the love of your life? I would never."

We mirror each other as we get ready for the shower, with towels at hand and our change of clothes hanging in the cubbie. The ruckus around us has started to calm down, as we all get antsy to go answer press questions and finally take the bus to the airport.

"You told me I looked like I was sexting when I wasn't." He frowns. "Then you told me you'd set me up with someone else. Shameful."

"I'm sure you took it with the same equanimity I am. I'm not sexting with Ames, and I don't need you to set me up with anyone else, either."

He raises an eyebrow. "Huh. You looked like that when talking to Ames? What could this possibly mean?"

I narrow my eyes. A gratified, tiny smile takes over his mouth as he grabs his phone. His eyes scroll down the screen, and his face changes in slow motion.

I chuckle. "Is Evie texting you, too?"

"Mhh. Let's make sure we're all on the plane on time," is all he says.

Several hours later, I open the door to my condo with curiosity bubbling in my stomach. Ames' guests should have left, as far as I know, but I'm not sure what to expect.

The living room lamps are on. Music plays from the speakers. A few piano notes ring in the air. They're random, and not part of a melody. They clash with the Latin Pop song filling up the space.

I close the door behind me. A quiet click is all it takes. Ames hears it and jumps off the piano bench.

"Gael!" She turns and wobbles. Her hands and ample ass press on the keys, and several dissonant notes clang in the air. "Oops. I'm okay."

I drop my bag and run to her. "Are you sure?"

I kick the bench aside and bring her into my arms, just in case she loses stability again.

Her hands land on my chest. She lifts bright eyes at me. A soft smile tilts her lips.

Ames is stunning, soft against me, willingly held in my arms.

My whole system stutters. My heart beats faster than it does when I score a touchdown. I pull her tight, pretending she's still unsteady, but it's only an excuse. This is as close as I might ever get, and I'm too weak to resist. I may be offering myself as her support, but I'm the one in need of a backbone.

It's just a taste. With my name on her lips, and the warmth of her body against mine, it's a morsel I can't resist.

Her fingers curl and she fists a handful of my shirt. The drumming in my chest intensifies.

"I'm really good." She blinks slowly. "Ready to celebrate with you, if you are. Your win and the call about the show..."

"Tell me everything," I whisper.

<hr />

She makes me a drink she says has no name yet, but was a success during the watch party. It has rum, lime, mint, and pomegranate, and it's fresh on my tongue after we toast to the win and this offer that fell in her lap.

"Never in a million years did I think I might end up on TV." She sips from her drink. "Not that it's a sure thing at all, but the ladies told me I should act like the show's already mine."

We sit on the sofa. Soft music plays around us. The city outside twinkles against a dark backdrop, and the light of the lamps are a mellow honey in the room and on her skin.

"So you want the opportunity?" I ask. "Can you see yourself hosting a TV cooking show?"

"Fuck yeah!" she laughs.

I chuckle. I've dreamed of evenings like this. It's late in the night, I just played a brutally demanding sport for hours, and I'm sore and bruised, but nothing is further from my mind than rest. Not when Ames sits next to me at home, grinning every time she gazes at me.

"I loved recording the holiday special with you." She smiles beatifically at me. "If it's anything like that, I could share recipes and that togetherness I love so much about food."

"I can see it. A cozy show where you cook meals that bring people close."

"It's all about celebrating. Friendships and family and love... you know, all the important things. Love in all capitals! Maybe you and Pablo could be my guests one day, and I could have a special about those things. The two of you representing all of it. Can you imagine? Would you be my guest?"

A soft blush reddens her beautiful face. Her eyes shine with mirth, and the big waves of her hair look windblown and wild. The gestures she makes are bolder than usual, and her voice is a little raspy. She's uninhibited, still a little tipsy from the earlier festivities. I can only hope the sight will never leave my mind.

"I'll go every time you invite me." I smile. "What would you want to do with your catering business?"

"Those dimples." She sighs.

I smile harder, so my dimples pop more. Her eyes journey over my face, down my chest, before she covers her face with her hands.

"I'd keep my business," she finally replies. "Focus on private events. I'd let Jo run all of that. A TV show would be great publicity, right? And with that cash, I bet I could keep everyone employed until things pick up."

"I bet. I'm excited for you."

In a clumsy series of movements, she kneels on the sofa and leans closer. I raise my eyebrows. The change is the physical equivalent of a non sequitur.

"I'm excited for you, too!" she exclaims. "You keep winning. They *have* to keep you. You can't leave."

"I'm doing everything I can to stay."

"Evie said the fans adore you. What's not to love? Everyone's got to see it. You score in every game, you have the flirtiest smile always, even when there are no cameras around. Those social media posts? Hot. And you're so warm and friendly with people around you..."

Warmth and longing and this feeling I've always had in my chest— they pulse, taking turns in different colors, creating a kaleidoscopic effect all over my inner world.

She glances at me. Her eyes twinkle.

She laughs.

"What?" I ask.

Her arm is close to me, resting on the back of the sofa. I can't stop it. I run my fingers over her skin in long, gentle caresses of my fingertips.

Her mirth softens into a chuckle. "I thought I kept myself on the right side of tipsy all evening, but I just said you're hot and I don't mind a whole lot. I must be more intoxicated than I thought."

Her eyes follow the movement of my fingers on her.

I smile. "You don't have to be drunk to admit I'm hot."

She laughs again. "And soooo cocky. And always flirting. You're flirting, right? I think you're always flirting."

"I can't help myself."

My voice comes out rueful, confessing truths I'm not ready to share about my feelings for her. How even when I know I shouldn't flirt with her, all I want to do is flirt with her.

I don't think she notices it.

"How did I not realize it before? The cockiness. The flirting I would have noticed years ago. If you ever directed it at me, that is."

"You must not have been paying close attention."

"I have paid att— attention. Too much, at times."

She's not slurring her words, and that wasn't quite a hiccup either, but I inspect her with curiosity. I have never really seen Ames under the influence.

"Is there such a thing?" I ask.

She frowns. "I shouldn't."

"Go right ahead, Amy. Pay close attention. I'll love every second of it."

She chuckles, thinking I'm making fun of things.

"Let's take it easy, then." I make a long pass of my fingers on her arm. "We said we would celebrate."

"You have work tomorrow."

174

"We're celebrating." I clink our glasses and we drink some more. "I'll sleep another time."

"We'll go to bed soon. Each to our own room!" She giggles. "They were teasing me earlier about us living together."

"Evie and them?"

"Yep." She takes a big gulp of her drink. "I was teasing Pen about Bear. She keep— keeps making comments about him so we teased her. Then she teased me about my comments about you and she gave back as hard as she got."

"Wait. Were you making comments about me to them?"

I'm vain enough to love the thought. Greedy enough to be thankful she's been drinking and some filters have come off.

"You can't blame me." She points an accusing finger at me. "I have eyes. I live with you. I danced with you. I am a warm blooded human who likes sex and who hasn't had a mind-blowing night in years and years..."

The air in the room turns to fog, dense as it comes into my lungs and stays there. It's harder to breathe, to know this about her. I want to tell her it's a terrible injustice, that she deserves better. That if she only lets me, I could give her what she needs. That I could set the standard for what she should expect.

She only needs to give up on the happily ever after bit.

Fuck.

She laughs. "Oh my god. I shouldn't have said that. Will you forget I said that?"

"I can't forget it."

"Oh, well, then— fuck it. It's true, and you can do the math."

"What math?"

Because all my brain is doing is trying to argue that maybe, just maybe, Ames is thinking of flings and mind-blowing sex more than she is about long-term relationships that lead to forever.

This plus that, minus him, multiplied by me...

"Did you figure it out, yet, Sherlock?" She drinks the rest of her drink and goes to the kitchen, where she starts making herself another one. "Actually, don't bother. I'll tell you. One, you're unfairly sexy. Two, Aidan was boring in bed. Element—aril—ly."

She laughs like it's the funniest thing she has ever said.

I finish my drink and meet her in the kitchen. I lean on the island and watch her carefully. She takes my glass and makes me another drink, too.

She's frowning now, shaking her head.

"You okay, Ames? Let's switch to water for a bit."

"I hate him, Saint." She keeps working on the drink. "I mean, not really. But I hate him!"

"Me too."

The man got to have her for years by his side. He got to hold her, tell her beautiful things, have her think about him as worthy of her love and attention and warmth.

Aidan should have treasured her. He should have counted his lucky stars and held her close.

Instead he hurt her. He was a selfish jerk who chose what he wanted even if it would cause her pain. The worst kind of self-serving jackass.

She thinks my response is a joke and she snorts. "I tried to spice things up, too. I got a couple's vibrator— there are these vibes you can use together, I don't know if you know—"

"I know about them." I gulp.

I'm getting intoxicated too, but not because of alcohol. The conversation itself is a rollercoaster, getting me dizzy. The thoughts and feelings it's winding up has a lot to do with it as well, if I'm honest.

"Aidan was so offended." She pushes my drink closer to me, but I don't touch it. "He never let me use it. I bet you'd be okay using it."

"I would be okay," I croak.

I would be so eager. No point in lying.

But there may be a point in hiding how this conversation is affecting me. I dig my hands in my pockets, and fists my hands to create some extra room.

"I knew it!" She pumps the air. "I bet you're not boring in bed."

"I try not to be."

The words taste like flirting on my tongue. My body has decided that this is foreplay, ignoring the way my brain screams for me to return to my senses. The fact that I remember the way she moans, that I know she still has that vibrator, and that she's asking my opinion— it's all that matters right now.

She watches me with unwavering eyes. I can hear the thoughts in her mind, because I'm having them too. The heat sparking under her lashes is an echo of what I'm feeling deep in my gut.

Dangerous.

"I'll get us some water," I say in a low voice. "Maybe we should go to sleep..."

She licks her bottom lip and takes a step closer to me. Her hand comes to my chest, where a single finger makes it between the panels of my shirt. Her fingertip burns on my skin.

"Or just go to bed," she whispers.

Her touch is a spell. Lava replaces every drop of blood in my veins in an instant. It's a miracle my clothes don't simply combust.

It's a magical moment. Time itself is affected, uncaring of the laws of physics.

Right now, she wants me.

But it's not fully *right*.

What's happening is powerful enough to veil the answers. I hold myself still, until I can remember what the issue is.

I glance at my watch like I can process what it says. I immediately forget.

"It's getting late..." The terrible excuse embitters my mouth.

She steps closer. "I've never seen your room."

I gaze at her. No answer makes it through my lips. I don't know what to say.

Before I can figure it out, she grabs me by the waist, puts herself between me and the island, and brings me close.

"Fuck. Ames—"

My heart beats as fast as the wings on a hummingbird. Her fingers hook me from my pockets, and her nails scrape against my skin through the thin material, and I could perish from the sensation.

I cage her. It's not a conscious decision, but a needy, needy one. Her body is warm and lush against me. The stone is cold under my hands, and it's a poor respite for the fire burning in me.

"You said you were easy." One of her hands travels up my torso.

I lick my lips. I did say that. Followed by, *you tell me I'm a good boy and I'll kneel at your feet.*

I could end on my knees any moment now.

Several buttons are undone already. She finds the first closed one, and plays with it like she might undo it.

Dead. I'll be dead any minute now.

*He died from an unrelenting erection, an all-encompassing fever, and high blood pressure resulting from holding back when his friend's sister tried to seduce him.*

"I meant—" I stutter. "What I meant was—"

But I've forgotten. She stares at my mouth, and the one hand leaves my chest so she can run a fingertip over the bottom lip. I shiver. A strangled sound makes it out of my throat.

"The other day, when you got hard..." Her voice is breathy. "Was that just..."

"Nothing... just... about it."

She frowns. Licks her lips. My chest works like I'm sprinting. I'm harder than I've been in my entire life.

It takes inhumane effort not to push my erection against her. Not to take her mouth and do what I so desperately need to do.

She pulls at me from my shirt. "Maybe... since we're living together... you could show me your room..."

I resist. She lifts herself to her toes. Her lips come close and I feel her breath on my skin— it's an invitation to kiss her.

I'm overtaken by my need for her.

Through the haze, a high-pitched screech breaks through my mind. It's a message. It's sharp. Nails down a blackboard. Relentless.

All the things I felt the other night when I gave in and used my hand are still true.

Truest of all is that she's half-drunk.

"Ames," I whimper. "You've been drinking."

"I'm not drunk."

"You're not sober, either."

The words sever through the moment. A machete, the cold metal of its blade cleaving the moment, because I can't take what she offers when I don't know if she means it.

I take a step back. She lets me go. Pain fills her face, but she masks it and aims for a brave front.

"No. Fuck." I put my hands on her shoulders. "I'm sorry. I don't mean to hurt you—"

My heart still mirrors that hummingbird, even if the rest of me has frosted over.

A small bird, meant to skip from bright flower to bright flower, trying to survive the frozen tundra.

She shakes her head, eyes closed. "No. Of course. You're right. We shouldn't. This is no way—"

"I won't do this. I can't. With alcohol involved, and knowing what I know— you deserve better than this."

"That's really the right way. I just... I wish I didn't..."

She puts the mostly-full glasses in the sink. It's an attempt to clean up. To appear normal.

"This is important," I say. "We should wait until we're both clear-headed to talk about this."

"Of course. Thank you. This is so sweet. You're right, I'm not clear-headed."

The look on her face tells me that no matter if she believes the words, she's feeling the rejection.

"Shit. Ames. I'm sorry. Let's talk tomorrow after training."

She takes a few steps back and out of the kitchen. "We're going to the club tomorrow night. I was meant to tell you and I forgot. I'm sorry!"

I follow her, but she creates more distance between us. I stay in place, while she places a hand on her door's handle.

"Anyway." Her tone is airy and overly cheery. "We'll talk about it. I promise. If not tomorrow, then on Tuesday. I'll make us breakfast and we'll... debrief."

I have a heart, but I can't feel it. It's disappeared somewhere. It's gone, down into the Earth's crust, finding its way through dirt and rock.

"I'm so fucking sorry." It hurts to talk. "It's what I have to do."

If my dating life is a track record that shows I'll never be Mister Right, accepting her seduction would make me wholly wrong. I could never take advantage of her.

The way my chest crumbles and my heart collapses under the pressure of its hiding place— those matter none at all.

"I get it." She nods a little too vehemently. "It's the right thing to do. I should be thankful. I am! We're good, I promise."

She goes into her room.

"Good night, Saint."

The door closes softly.

I'm nothing but a ghost working the machinery of my body, until I fall into a fitful sleep.

# Chapter 24

## Ames

*Oh my god.*

The words appear fully formed in my mind before I can fully wake up. Memories crash against my skull and I hiss—

Saint's face as he tells me he won't *show me his room*. The way the ground seemed to give out from under me, when I finally understood that I had shown my cards, my *feelings*, to have them given back to me like that. Gently, wisely, and still so painful I had to make a quick exit and hide behind closed doors.

Embarrassment follows me all day. Its sticky, cold, wet voice whispers into my ear. It tells me I should act like nothing happened, because it would be easier that way. Then it tells me I have to apologize. That I have caused Saint enough trouble, to now add the tangled byproducts of my poor attempt at seduction.

Except I told him we'd talk soon. An explanation is the least I can do. To reassure him he doesn't have to worry about me making things too complicated again.

A text is my overture.

**Ames**: everything going well today? What's the best plan for the club tonight?

**Saint**: I'll come home after training and we can go to the club together, if you like

He didn't say anything about things being okay, and only answered the second question. He might have been busy, but damn. I needed reassurance.

I cringe. Worse, when he later has to change our plans.

**Saint**: I'm sorry, but Coach is keeping us a bit longer. I'm hearing we'll meet you there. Is that okay?

**Ames**: Of course, I'll see you there.

Evie, Nat, Pen, and I text and make different plans. A few hours later, I'm wearing my sexiest outfit in an effort to gather confidence— a black, tight pencil skirt with a subtle silver sheen to it, and a loose striped blouse. It's a beautiful piece that mixes soft, matte velvet, and sheer black gauze in a large chevron pattern. The transparent bits allow for my black longline bra to peek through as I move, but it's no more than clues and a hint at what's underneath.

We chat away in the VIP section of the usual club, and though most of them order a cocktail and water on the side, I choose only the latter.

"What's that about?" Pen asks.

"I overdid it last night," I say.

"We all overdid it yesterday." Nat stares at her glass with suspicion.

Pen nods vehemently and, though she has a drink, it goes untouched. "We'll take it easy tonight."

I gaze at them, surrounding me in one of the lux sitting areas. They all look amazing in their club attire, and not an ounce of embarrassment shows on their face. Why would it? If it weren't for what I did later in the night, I would be a bit hungover but content over the watch party, and happy about how close it seemed to bring us as friends. My humbled, bruised ego has nothing to do with that.

I sigh. "Let's just say I kept overdoing it."

Evie raises an eyebrow my way. "What do you mean?"

"I said more than I should have to Saint."

They all stare at me, waiting for more information.

I take in the moment, warmth spreading through me despite the topic. When I said I want to add depth to my life with good friends around me, this is what I meant. Times when I can open up and ask for an ear and maybe some advice, from people who care about me.

I make myself speak. "I tried to make things happen with him. They did not happen."

"Things... of a sexy nature?" Pen asks.

I scrunch my face. "He said no."

Everyone gasps.

"Are you okay?" Evie asks.

I make a weird motion with my head, somewhere between a shake and a nod. "He was sweet about it. And he was right to say no! He said I had drunk too much, which I had."

"Good," Pen says. "It was the right thing to do but, if I were you, I'd probably still be hurt."

"Especially coming from someone who says yes so often, right?" Nat frowns. "It's been a while since I saw him with anyone. Not that I'm keeping close track, but you would think he's pent up."

I may not have all the pieces, and some of them look like they belong to a whole different puzzle set, but this hasn't escaped my mind. I don't think he wants me like this, and that should be fine.

When we finally talk and he finds a kind way to explain why, I will keep myself together and accept it gracefully.

"He was right to do it, of course," Nat adds, "but..."

I nod. "But I'm embarrassed."

"No need to be embarrassed!" Pen rubs my knee. "Ask for what you want, always."

"We were teasing you about living with him and resisting temptation, right?" Nat chuckles. "We may have put the thoughts in your head."

"I bet that in your alcohol-soaked brain," Evie says, "it was perfectly logical."

It was. In my mind, we were two adults currently not involved with anyone else. I thought maybe he would want to take me up on my offer, since I was right there. I told myself that he's a modern man who wouldn't let his friendship with Pablo get in the way of some fun with me.

The fantasy titillated me, with promises of incredible sex with someone I already like so much.

*I won't*, he said. *It's what I have to do.*

Because of my drinking, or because he knows that nothing but forever will satisfy me and he doesn't date, or maybe because of Pablo, after all. Probably, it was a mix of all of it. Regardless, he hasn't shown interest in years. Living together might not be enough to change his mind.

Pen stares at me. "You need a rebound."

"From Saint?" I startle. "Nothing happened!"

"From Aidan!" Evie laughed.

"I *tried*!"

Nat points a questioning finger my way. "So you want a rebound?!"

My mouth opens but nothing comes out. I blink a few times.

I frown. "I suppose... maybe I do."

At this point, I don't think I'll ever know why Aidan did what he did. A couple of times when he reached out, I asked but he didn't answer. Now I don't expect to see him again, and I won't get to demand answers one last time. Maybe a rebound is the closure I need. The final nail to hammer that coffin closed. A way to say, *hey, look, I'm fine. Forever can wait.*

Evie is about to respond when four large shadows approach. We turn to them in unison, to find Logan, Damián, Bear, and Dom.

I look past them in search of Saint, but he's not there.

The group says hi and we all shift to make space for the newcomers. After getting drinks, Dom's guest arrives and they start chatting nearby. I keep stealing glances at the stairs, waiting for Saint.

"Ames," Bear says. "Did Saint text you? He said he would. He had to stay to talk to Coach about the potential trade."

"Oh! Let me see."

I check my phone.

> **Saint**: Coach wants to meet with me to discuss strategies to get me the MVP award. I don't know how long I'll be, but I'll go to the club asap. I'm sorry. I'll be there soon. If we end up not having time to talk tonight, we'll talk tomorrow morning. Looking forward to breakfast with you

"There are a hundred people dancing downstairs." Pen leans close to me. "Do you want to go meet someone?"

I gaze back at her and consider the stirred up emotions still swirling in my gut.

"I guess I should at least try," is all I say.

# Chapter 25

## Ames

I'm dancing with someone I don't know, and I'm not having a lot of fun. I close my eyes and try to lose myself to the music. The rhythm is deep and sexy, and I can follow it easily, letting my body perform to it... but it's an act. I don't feel it in my bones.

It's all fake. It's hard to connect with my current dancing partner, and I move on to find someone else. I catch myself comparing him to Saint, and how natural it felt to sway with him. How much I fed off being close to him that night, dancing in his arms.

I tell the guy in front of me that I need to use the washroom. Cold water on my neck might help calm my confused feelings, and let me figure out what I truly want.

When I'm done, a new dancing partner doesn't fix things. His hands feel wrong when he tries to pull me closer, and discomfort takes a hold of my stomach.

This is not working.

I should give up and go back upstairs. Ask my friends to set me up on a few dates if that will help me break this pattern of jumping from one long-term relationship to the next, without taking a breath or figuring out what I truly want out of my happily ever after.

"I'm Brad," my dance partner whispers into my ear.

His breath has my skin crawling. He keeps talking but I can't make out what he says. I can't look him in the face either. I push away.

"Thanks for the dance," I say. "I'll go to my friends now."

He doesn't let me go. "One more dance."

I push away again. He still doesn't let me go.

"I'm going to my friends," I insist.

"Can I get your number?"

"It's not going to work."

"How do you know?"

"She knows."

I whip my face to Saint. His look is menacing on Brad, and his voice hard.

"Let her go," Saint demands.

My mouth hangs open.

"You're—" Brad frowns in surprise. "You play for the Strike—"

"Let. Her. Go." Saint steps closer to us.

I'm free.

Brad lifts his hands like saying, *no harm done.*

Saint keeps his eyes on the blond man in front of us, and shifts his body until he stands between Brad and I.

"All good," Brad turns and mutters something I can barely make out, but sounds like, *you better win us the championship, you dick.*

Saint faces me. "Everything okay?"

My heart is beating a hundred beats a minute, but it's mostly the shock of Saint's sudden appearance. Brad is already less than an afterthought.

The fact Saint looks amazing in tailored black pants and a blue-gray satin shirt, printed with large tropical flowers in shades of burgundy and pale yellow, only adds to my body's response.

I have to tear my eyes away from his chest, and the patch of skin calling for my lips in front of me.

"I— yes," I say. "Thank you."

"May I?" He offers me a hand.

I take it and he brings me close. Gently, he guides my body to move slow.

"Did you want to dance?" he asks.

I put my hands on his shoulders and smile. "I would love to."

This. *This* feels good.

Saint holds me, one hand on the round of my hip and the other one on my back. He gazes at me and we start swaying to the music.

We're transported to that first night when we danced together. Except he studies me like he's checking if I'm doing alright.

"Thank you," I say.

"What a piece of shit. He wasn't letting you go."

"You were watching?"

"I saw you when I arrived. Stayed. Paid attention to what was going on."

He looks like something sour landed on his tongue.

Beats and music surround us, but we don't follow their instructions. While everyone around us moves at a fast pace, Saint and I slow dance.

"I wanted to make sure they were treating you right," he adds. "Looking for a sign that you wanted what you were getting."

"It didn't go as planned."

"What did you plan?"

I hesitate.

The satin of his shirt is soft under my fingers, and I trace patterns on it with a nail. My eyes land on his chain.

I study each link as I speak. "You date a lot. You make sleeping with people look easy. Do you think I need a rebound?"

He slows down further. We're mostly immobile on the dance floor as he inspects me. The way he licks his lips, his dimples come out to play.

I lose track of them when he speaks to my ear.

"Do you want a rebound?" he asks.

I take a deep breath to soothe my haywire pulse. It's a mistake. Now my nose, my lungs, my brain is full of his cologne.

"What do you want?" His breath plays with my tender skin. "That's all that matters."

I close my eyes and breathe in his scent again. "I don't know what I want, but I'm trying to figure out what I need. I spent years investing in a relationship that fell apart for reasons I may never understand. Every relationship I've had, I've gone all in. They have all failed."

"So you're thinking you might want to try something different."

It's not a question.

"Before you ask," I say, "I have not had a single drop of alcohol since last night."

He doesn't say anything.

"You're an expert at this," I try again. "It's all you do, right? Casual relationships only. Bake and Bye, three dates in. Teach me."

"Ames..."

I pull away, only enough to see his eyes. Intensity fills his dark irises, punctuated by a rare frown.

"Teach me to seduce someone," I say. "How to have mind-blowing sex with them for a short while just for the fun of it. I want to learn how to end it when things are not meant to last forever. Because I was settling with Aidan and fuck me if I will ever settle again. One day I'll go for forever again, with someone who wants it with me too. Until then, I want to be myself and have easy, casual fun, then walk away. Like you do."

We're not dancing at all anymore. I'm in his arms, he scrutinizes me, and determination beats in my chest.

"You have no idea what you're asking me," he says.

I lift my hands up his chest, channeling the soft fabric at his neck between index and middle finger. It lets me touch his skin, just a bit, just one pad on the warmth of him. A nail grazes against his chain, and I repeat the motion a couple of times.

His fingers clench on their spot on my body.

"There's no one I trust more to show me how to do this." I lick my lips. "You won't lead me astray. You're so... warm, and incredible, and last night— you were so good to me last night, rejecting me softly for the right reasons—"

"I didn't reject you. Please. Ames—"

"You've been so good to me. So generous. Last night you were genuinely kind. Can I ask you for this, too? Please, Saint? It's the last thing I'll ever ask."

The wrinkle between his brows intensifies, and the inner corners pull up in an unhappy gesture.

"It won't take much." I make a gesture to the people dancing around us. "Help me pick. Then tell me what you would want from someone trying to seduce you. What would turn you on, if I were someone else?"

"You have no idea, do you?"

His voice is gravelly, clear to my ears despite the loud music around us.

"I have no idea what I'm doing." I shake my head. "That's why I need your help."

He watches me for a long minute.

He smirks. "Don't ask me to help you pick someone else when I'm right here."

I blink a few times. "What?"

He guides me back, his step certain, slipping past a velvet rope telling us we shouldn't go where he leads me. He doesn't let it stop us, like such rules are not meant for him.

The light on the dance floor is already low, but in the nook under the stairs it's almost nonexistent.

He pushes me against the wall. I gasp.

"Next thing," he says, "you'll tell me I can add it to the rent invoice as consulting services."

He lets out a humorless chuckle. The barest hint of irritation weighs down his voice, in a tone I had never heard coming from him.

He rests his forearms by my side on the wall, hands under my shoulders. It brings him right next to me, and it cages me.

"Saint— I—"

"I won't help you pick. If this is what you want, then I don't trust anyone else to do it. This is what I'm good at, isn't it? What I'm good for."

"What do you mean—"

"I'll show you what I do." He presses on me. "Do you want fun sex? Mind-blowing sex? Short-term sex with no strings attached, so you can walk away when you're done with me? I'll be that for you. I'll be your rebound."

He's hard against me and, with a roll of his hips, he makes sure I know it.

I gasp. I cling to his shoulders. I'm sure my nails must be hurting him, but I can't stop it, and he doesn't complain.

"I'll be such a good boy for you, Ames, you're going to thank me at the end. I'm a ride you won't forget."

I forget how to breathe. His confidence and his promise, and the shock drumming in my chest at his suggestion— an electric current runs through my skin, and every tiny hair in my body stands at attention.

"Is this a good idea?" I finally gasp.

"I doubt it," he rasps, "but isn't that partly why you want this?"

"Do you mean it?" I fist my hands on his satin shirt. "I thought you didn't— want me—"

He lets out a pained, unbelieving laugh, and kisses me.

# Chapter 26

## Ames

My lungs go out of commission. My heart tumbles into somersaults. All because Saint is kissing me, and nothing matters more than the press of his mouth on mine. The push and dance of his tongue on mine.

A deep, all-consuming hunger takes over. It's rooted in my core, lapping at my belly with flames. I hook my arms around his neck and clinch to him. I pull him closer with all my might, lifting myself to the tip of my feet, because I can't fathom anything else but *more*.

He lets out a sound of approval, and it's fuel to the fire taking over my system. His hands travel over my waist, my hips. Every few inches, the journey stops and his fingers grab onto my flesh, like he needs to test the edges of my body, and the lush hills of my skin.

He tries to stop the kiss, but I miss his mouth already, and I go for seconds.

He makes the same sound again and I echo it this time. I push my hips against him, seeking friction, and he gets the message. One of his hands trails down my body and latches on my thigh. He pulls up and I'm only too happy to follow the instruction. With my leg up by his narrow hips, he presses against me.

"Amelia." His forehead drops to mine.

My skirt rolls up to the crease of my thigh and lower belly, exposing me to him. I don't care that a crowd of people dance just outside our nook, and someone could see us at any point if they only squint and find the right angle. The flimsy fabric of my underwear and his trousers doesn't prevent me from feeling the length of him, and how it finds its way to my clit somehow. It's enough to drive me wild with need.

"Gael." I moan.

His eyes close in concentration, but the roll of his body doesn't stop, and he rubs against me in an insistent pattern. I could melt. The one leg keeping me up falters, and Saint grabs me by the waist for extra support.

I can barely react. All I do is take in the relief of him pressing his body against mine, how he holds me up, rubs against me. I pepper kisses on his face.

"I thought—" kiss. "You didn't want any—" kiss. "Of this."

"From the moment we met, Ames." His hand touches my skin under my shirt. "I've been thinking about this since the first time you looked my way."

"You... have?" I kiss him again. One corner of his mouth, then the other.

I can feel his words on my lips.

"I have. Now you want me to teach you things, and I will oblige. Rule number one— you demand what you deserve or you walk away, Ames. Anyone who gets to have you in his arms has to know what a privilege it is."

"Oh my God."

His hips become more insistent. He doesn't seem to care that we're in a semi-public place either.

He groans. "He better be a fucking *simp* the moment he learns of your existence."

My breathing struggles to keep up with my heart. I unbutton his shirt and run my hands down his chest. His skin is as hot as I feel.

"Will you let me show you, Ames? Will you let me be your servant and show you the kind of total devotion you're entitled to?"

194

"Only if you tell me what you want, too." I bite back another moan. "It should be a give and take."

"All I want is your permission. Please. Let me touch you. All I need is a chance to get lost in your taste, in your warmth, in the sounds you make when I have you coming again and again with my tongue. My fingers. My cock. Your vibrator... or mine."

My heart flips again. "Holy shit."

"Use me. If you want a rebound, then that's what I'll be. Take what you need then walk away. I'll be anything. I'll do anything."

I grab his shoulders like I'm hanging on for dear life. My throat is raspy with the force of my breathing, and my chest hammers with his words, and I can't seem to get close enough to him. In a haze, I put my lips to his neck and buck against him. I need him to do more. He responds in kind, and I find myself nibbling on the corded muscles of his neck.

When my lips graze his chain, I moan and take it between my lips.

"Fuck," he growls. "Stop, or I'll do what I want to do right here, all these people be damned."

We're half-way to exhibitionism. The only reason I'm not exposed to hundreds of people is because the stairs protect us somewhat, and he blocks the view with his rolling hips. Anyone taking a good look would get a show, regardless.

I've never been this overtaken. It muddles my brain. All I care about is this white-hot heat coursing through my veins, and the need to have Saint against me for hours. To know what he's really like in bed. Have him touch me and letting me touch him back.

I breathe hard. "Maybe I want you to be wild and take me here under the stairs."

His hands leave me to handle his belt buckle. I'm so shocked I forget every curse word I know.

"I wasn't serious!" I hold his hands in place.

"Rule number two. You demand everything and anything you want. If they can't or won't do it, then they're not for you."

"The standards you are setting are too high."

"I'm just getting started."

# Chapter 27

## Saint

I get her on my lap in the car. She comes to me willingly, undoing me. Her kiss tells me she really wants this— she really wants *me*.

If being her rebound is a mistake, it's the best mistake I'll ever make.

I kiss her like what we're doing is meant to be.

Things could get heated again, but there's no privacy window between us and the driver. We keep things cool, caressing safe spots softly, speaking into each other's ears. Our conversation includes words of doctor check ups and contraception. They could be dry and cold, but they sound like poetry to my ears. We kiss as we realize we could skip the condoms if we wanted, but we decide we'll do it only if and when it feels right to both of us.

By the time we make it to my door, I'm so desperate to touch her that I consider kicking it down. The only reason I don't is because I can't manage a good strike with Ames in my arms.

"Do me a favor and take the keys out of my pocket," I mutter into her neck.

She gives me a delighted giggle. "I have my own keys, remember?"

She turns in my arms and handles the lock.

"Maybe all I wanted was to get your hand in my pants." I kiss the spot where her neck meets her shoulder. "You might have liked what you found there."

We make it inside. She laughs. I kick the door closed, then guide her deeper into the condo, still kissing her neck.

I try to get her in her room. She resists, making for my door. We stare at each other in a brief standstill.

"You don't sleep with your dates in the guestroom, do you?" she asks.

"Never, but your vibrator is in your room."

"Oh. Oh," she repeats in a different tone.

I lead her to her room. "Besides, tomorrow I'll have a new bed delivered. You don't have to wonder about anyone else. You can help me break in the mattress."

"That's... overdoing it, right? I shouldn't make a fuss."

"Make a fuss. Nothing would make me happier." I stop a few steps from her bed. "Nothing is too little or too big. Anything you want— I want it for you."

"Saint—" She doesn't finish the sentence, and jumps to me again.

I catch her. I kiss her. I moan into her mouth, and she must like it, because her hands get greedy. She trails hard fingers down my body, until she can grab handfuls of my ass.

Those sparks I felt all those years ago crackle and explode like fireworks under my skin. They burst and blast from my chest, a bomb without a sound, because right now, for a little while, Ames wants me.

I'll make it worth her while.

"Tell me your wildest dreams," I whisper.

It takes her a second, but she speaks against my skin.

"I don't have any," she admits.

It doesn't make sense and, for a moment, I blame those sparks. They're making me clumsy. They latch onto my heart and the mirage of the moment, and push me to envision a future with nights like this between us.

But this isn't about my delusions. It's about her desire.

I create distance between us and stare into her eyes. She looks dazed.

"Ames. When you fantasize about the things you crave in bed. What do you think of?"

She blinks a few times. "I didn't... use to think much about that."

Her admission tears at me. I want to curse every lover she's ever had, for not falling to their knees in gratitude to share her bed, and because they had her at all. I would be embarrassed at my sudden jealousy, but I like the idea of atonement via making her dreams a reality.

"Rule number three." My voice is rough. "Ames, your fantasies matter. All of them."

"But if they don't fit with my partner's—"

"The right partner will at least care, no matter how little time you have together."

"That's the fantasy," she mutters.

"Hey." I interrupt the thought with a brief kiss. "We'll start small. Any fantasies at all?"

She stares at me for a while. "Lately... lately I've been fantasizing about you."

My mind blanks. Her words, spoken quietly, burrow into the core of me. The spot turns soft and white.

It puts a small smile on my face. I step away, creating some distance between us. I open my arms like I'm ready to be crucified.

"Then take me," I say. "Do with me as you will."

She gazes at me like she's gauging my sincerity.

"Go ahead." My voice deepens. "Test me."

She continues to study me, but heat shimmers in her eyes now.

Her eyes travel down my body. Two, three steps, and she's next to me again. Her breasts and belly brush my torso, but I don't move. With calm composure, she starts to slowly undo my shirt buttons.

"Don't move." She stares into my eyes, then her gaze latches on my lips.

Shivers run down my spine at the sudden confidence in her voice. My arms fall somewhat but I keep straight, leaving my chest open as she pulls the panels of my shirt to the side. With exploring fingertips, she traces my torso. My necklace, my earring, my neck. I gulp.

"Huh." Her fingers touch my Adam's apple, then stop at my pulse. "Is this affecting you?"

My heart has taken on a fast thrum.

I bring her hand to my chest. "Do you feel that?"

She nods.

It takes a deep breath to manage a confession. "I've thought about this since I met you."

I have also thought about more than simply getting her in my bed, but I keep that in. That part is *my* fantasy, and not one I can bet on. Not with my track record, and the one time I tried it ended in mocking laughter and sticky failure. I will not hurt her with my unchecked hopes. With not being able to make it work, bringing about an ending I did not want or choose.

Not when Ames only wants me for a short while, too.

She frowns. "But you never tried to sleep with me."

A corner of my lip curls. "I'm taking my chance now, Amelia."

If this won't last, I'll make the best out of this wild offer I put at her feet. I'll leave her with memories, so she carries this time together with her just like I will.

It's as much pride as I'll allow myself.

"Tell me how you want me." I grab the edges of my shirt and slide it off my arms. "You're in control."

"I thought I told you not to move."

I freeze. My shirt hangs from my wrists, trapping me.

"That's better." She grabs me by my chain and pulls me. "Kiss me."

The hammering in my chest continues, but I don't move. I don't touch her, except for our lips and tongues in a languid, exploring kiss. Her thumb makes circles on my pulse, as her free hand makes a path down my chest and around my waist.

A chill runs down my spine. She digs her nails softly into my skin.

"You have goosebumps." Her voice is quiet, barely more than a breath.

The hand at my neck travels down. She teases my tight nipple with a nail.

I moan. "I want to touch you."

"Not yet."

"Is this how you test me? I'll be so good."

"You said I can do anything?"

"Anything."

"I can focus on me? What I want? Be who I am, and being that in bed too?"

"Yes. A thousand times. Yes."

With a little smile curling her lips, she undoes my belt buckle.

"Fuck," I mutter.

"I've seen you in your underwear," she muses. "I've seen you wet out of the pool."

She lets my pants fall to my ankles. My cock strains against my boxers. My heart beats faster than when I'm running for a touchdown.

The silk of my shirt turns to handcuffs on my wrists. I keep still as she runs her hands down my torso again, studying my body, killing me softly. Her eyes follow the path of her fingers, as they caress the ridges and valleys down.

Without hesitation, she runs a single finger leisurely up the length of my erection.

I make a deep sound.

"That day at the pool," she says, "I thought you might be hard. The way this looks right now? You weren't fully hard then."

"I think..." My voice is gravelly. I clear my throat, but it doesn't help. "I think that's a compliment."

Her fingernail makes a path on the head of my cock and I whimper.

"Do you like praise, Saint?"

"I'll earn it." I gulp. "Please. Let me earn it."

There's nothing dignified about how I sound. Desperation isn't my style. Usually I'm fun in bed. Laughter, teasing, and multiple orgasms are my brand. I'm confident and eager and I drink their compliments like nectar.

But this is Ames. With her, I am more than eager. I am hungry. Pining, even as she stands within reach.

She enjoys it, from the blush spreading over her face.

"Take off everything but your underwear," she commands.

She steps back to give me the room. I obey.

I stand, hands fisted by my side.

"Do you want me to strip for you?" She asks.

"Let me do it." I tense my muscles until my chest and shoulders pop. It's the only way I manage to remain still. "Can I touch you?"

"I can see the strain that holding back is causing you. Makes me feel sexy."

"You're so sexy, Ames. Let me show you."

"You already are."

"More. I'll show you more."

She bites her lip and pulls her striped blouse up.

"No!" I shake my head. "Please. Let me do it. I've waited too long to do it."

"Tell me more." She drops her blouse back to place.

I lick my lips, and tell her what I'm ready to confess.

"The other night. After the club. I almost knocked at your door afterwards."

Her chest rises and falls, and my breathing matches hers. "Having you here with me. Next door to me. It's torment, Ames."

She comes close again, her eyes locked to mine.

"Can I undress you?" I ask.

"Tell me more about that night."

"Having you on my lap. Squirming. Showing you how much I wanted you and letting you believe it was just nature. For show. I ended up at your door, my hand on my cock, desperate for you."

Her blush deepens and I feel it in my dick. I bite my bottom lip, hard, because I'm about to lose myself to this agony building inside.

She puts her hand on my hard length, and I'm closer to my breaking point than I've ever been.

"Oh, *fuck*," I breathe.

She rubs slowly. Her mouth opens. Shallow, fast breathing moves her chest, as if she's trying to control herself, too. Her breasts push against the neckline of her blouse, and the bra that tantalizes me through the transparent bits of fabric.

"Ames. God. I can't get your moans out of my head."

"You... heard me."

"Please. Let me hear them again. I was there only for a few minutes. I promise. I walked away. Please, let me hear you moan again. I need to make you moan. I need your moans to be mine."

"They were, that night. They will be yours tonight, too."

I'm the one moaning now.

"What rule of dating casually is this?" She asks.

The universe is set to break me tonight. It makes a caricature of my heart and the times I fantasized about commitment.

I should be happy she expects this to end in the near future. It should make things easier. It's what I wanted, when I heard her in her room. For her to understand it wouldn't go anywhere. Now she's the one not wanting this to last. I should be content with taking what I can and making a few life-changing memories.

I should be happy, but I'm not. I'm resigned. She'll move on, and I'll have to find my way back to dating casually.

"Rule number four," I growl. "He better be fucking devout. Pleasing you has to be all he cares about. You deserve nothing less."

I clench my jaw. My cock pulses in her hand.

Our eyes lock and I beg for mercy.

# Chapter 28

## Ames

Saint stands in front of me, tension straining his shoulders and arms. Chest and abs. Fisted hands. He's holding on by a thread, while giving me total control. The power of it runs through me with white-hot electricity, and it's lightning coursing through my nerves, crackling and demanding that I give in.

If this is what he makes everyone feel— if this is how he offers himself to the people he has sex with— then it's no wonder he can have anyone he wants and they all would do anything to be with him.

I'm giving all of myself to him, too, like everyone else.

"How many people have you slept with?" I ask as I stroke his cock.

He moans. "Why are you thinking of them? I— God— I am not."

"Did you lose count, Saint?"

Jealousy flares up in the pit of my stomach. It tints my blood green. Again, a part of me forgets that Saint has every right to date a million people if he so wishes, and I have no right to covet his attention. His choice. His affection.

"Ames. Please."

His throat wobbles again and I wrap my free hand around his neck.

If I'm going to be possessive, I'll give in to it for tonight. This moment with Saint could be pure ecstasy, and I won't let anything get in the way.

"All my life," I say. "I did everything right in love. I prioritized my relationships with these men who I thought were so sensitive they had to be emotionally mature. I thought I was doing so much better than my parents. All I did was settle."

I slide my hand to his collarbones, and run a thumb over his chain.

"I don't want to settle again." I frown. "Never."

"Never settle, Ames." His voice is hoarse. "The moment you're not happy, you walk away."

He's earnest. Tremors flutter over his chest.

One of my hands still rubs his erection. I set a faster pace and he closes his eyes.

"If you—" he tries. "Fuck. If you are in any— any way unfulfilled—"

"Is my hand distracting you, Gael?"

"I'm trying to— have this conversation with you—"

"Why?" I close my fingers around the shaft as well as I can, and stroke the head with a firm thumb.

Because I can, and Saint offered himself to me, and seeing him struggle makes me feel powerful.

He's giving himself to me. It's all about me tonight.

He groans. "You're— saying something important and— fuck. You're going to make me come in my underwear if you keep this up."

I'm a queen, with the king at her command.

"Open your eyes," I whisper.

He obeys slowly.

I raise an eyebrow. "What makes you think I wouldn't enjoy that?"

"I need to... earn... it..."

I smirk, drop to my knees, and close my mouth over the length of his cock, still trapped under fabric.

"Ames— shit!"

"Such a good boy."

A deep sound makes it out of his throat as he comes. His hips buckle, just once, like in the height of his climax he forgot himself. A wet spot spreads through his underwear.

Pride feathers down my chest as I stand. A cocky smile takes my lips, because I made him lose it. Even now, he restrains himself and keeps himself as still as he can.

"Damn." He breathes fast. Rose colors his cheeks for once. "Fuck. Sorry."

"Don't apologize."

"But I haven't even touched you and I'm not eighteen anymore and—"

"Saint. Don't apologize."

He stops himself.

"How often do you let other women take control like this?"

"Ames. Don't think of them."

"But I am, so tell me. How often?"

It takes him a second to answer. "Never."

Power rushes through me all over again.

I take a step closer to him. "Do you know how amazing it feels disarming you like this? That you only let me do this to you?"

Despite his orgasm, he's fully alert. His breathing is deeper now, but fast.

He studies my face, my eyes. "I told you I'm at your mercy."

"And you want to show me?"

"Yes. Please. I can still be so good for you. It won't take me long to recover, I promise."

"Oh, I'm not done with you." I hook a finger through his chain and pull again.

He's docile and leans closer. "Tell me what you want."

"Show me what I've been missing out on."

"Can I touch you?"

"Touch me."

"Thank God," he says and, in a swift, assertive move, brings me to him.

I'm enveloped in his arms as he kisses me. Deeply. Desperately. Without missing a beat, he touches me over my clothes first, learning my body again like he did back in the club. He tests the edges of my clothes and pulls at them slowly. My skirt comes up before it goes down and to my ankles. I step away from the black puddle, and he follows me closer to the bed.

His fingers play with the loose fabric of my blouse. "Be careful the next time you wear this."

He kisses my neck, his hands caressing my skin and exploring the structured lines of the bottom half of my bra.

"Why? Jealous of what others get to see?"

I run my fingers through his hair. I want him to be jealous.

"Show off what you have," he says. "Let everyone know just how gorgeous you are."

I feel his words on my skin and I shiver.

"But if I see you in this shirt again, wearing a bra like this again, I will remember how you feel in my hands. Your softness and the texture of your clothes. The taste of your mouth. And I may not be able to help myself."

I moan. "If I don't wear it, you won't remember?"

He takes off my shirt, a small smile on his lips. "I'll remember. This shirt might just break me for a second time."

"I think I like breaking you."

His smile stretches somewhat. He guides me next to the bed, and drops a kiss on my lips.

"Keep breaking me, Ames. As much as you want to."

His hands go around my ribcage and he undoes the hooks of my bra. His hands are gentle as he removes the piece of clothing from me.

"You already have," he says, before he kisses me, hard.

His hands splay and grab me by my waist, only to throw me on the bed. I fly for less than a second, but it feels like freefall. By the end, my feet are dangling off the bed. His lips trail over my jaw, back to my mouth, down my neck, as his hands massage me and his thumbs tease my nipples. Energy still courses through me, but it has changed. Now it's the thrill of knowing he wants me.

He licks the swell of my breast, then swirls his tongue on a tip. I moan and let my fingers swim in his hair.

"You're everything," he mutters against my skin.

His words cascade down my skin, a caress that stirs something inside of me. Ease and power entwine and cut through me. My heart skips a beat and gooseflesh appears all over. Such a simple statement. Exactly what I crave.

I may have lost myself in recent years but, in this moment with Saint, he sees me whole.

I get to be me, take what I want, and he wants me to do it.

His hair is silky between my fingers. I pull at it. He groans.

"Let me show you," he whispers.

I want to feel how he sees me. Do as I need to do. Take all he offers.

"Show me," I say.

He licks— kisses— licks down my belly. Closes his mouth on my mound, over the fabric of my underwear. I buckle, and he chuckles.

"Yes, Amelia." He stands between my legs. He pulls down my last piece of clothing, his eyes locked on mine. "Let's see what your body can do."

"Are you that good with your mouth, Gael?"

"Yes." His smile is feline. He lifts a hand in a scouts-honor gesture. "A receiver's hand does a good job at helping, too."

His fingers look long and thick, now that I'm paying attention. I gulp.

He takes a few steps back and takes off his underwear. I sit up on the bed, breathing fast, feasting on the sight of his naked body.

I don't ask him to let me study him but he does anyway. He stands still.

His earring and chain contrast beautifully on the golden tan of his skin, and his deep brown eyes shine with the heat of his gaze. His generous shoulders and the long lines of his muscles call for my lips and my tongue. He's trim, but just the right amount to know I would touch flesh rather than stone, and I could bite and get a nice chunk of him between my teeth.

I lick my lips. I have never cared about using my mouth quite this way, quite this much before.

"You want me, Gael?"

The muscles low on his waist are developed, creating a tantalizing handle for my fingers, and a V pointing to a glorious, proud erection.

I want my mouth all over there, too.

"I've wanted you for years," he replies.

My lungs work fast, yet I'm breathless. He's dropping revelations like rain on me, little endearments and praise, and I want more. Craving is too simple a word for what I feel. It's a thirst, an ache, true lust. And in the middle of it, he tells me he's wanted me like this for a long time.

Anything but him and me like this has been a waste.

I'm mending it all tonight.

"Then get on your knees," I command.

I rest the weight of my torso on my hands. I'm so turned on that I fist the bed covers to ground myself.

He falls to his knees. Heat crackles in my veins.

I open my legs further, and devour the way his eyes study my pussy.

"How much do you want to taste me?" I ask. "Beg again."

"Amelia. Please. You're killing me. Let me use my tongue on you. My lips. I beg."

Fire breaks over my skin, burning slow and steady in my lungs. My muscles squeeze on nothing.

"Crawl to me," I moan.

"Amelia."

He goes on all fours.

I gasp, the sound making it through my sandpaper throat. "You are such a good boy."

I'm so turned on I'm getting dizzy.

I don't recognize myself. I've never acted like this before. Never talked like this before. Saint brings out parts of me I never knew. I don't think they can go back to the shadows again after tonight.

His movements are slow, like a panther on the floor, as he shows me the lengths he'll go to do my bidding.

"Fuck. Please." He moans. "Let me taste you. I'll worship you. I will make your pussy into my altar."

He stops with his face within an inch of me. "I beg you. I need my mouth on you. Please."

"You're so confident." I lick my lips. "And on your knees."

Grooves and dips mark the muscles on his shoulders and arms. His heated gaze doesn't waver.

He may not be touching me, but my body is about to combust anyway.

"Gael—" His name sounds like a moan on my lips. "Show me."

He whines. The sound sends shivers down my spine. A tremor wants to take over my body, but it doesn't get to. With an open mouthed kiss, he takes my pussy with lips and a hungry tongue. I fall back to the bed. My veins turn to tinder. My skin combusts.

"Addicting, Amelia." He swirls his tongue on my clit. "I knew you would be."

He pushes a finger in as he sucks on my flesh. I buckle. Two fingers now, and the stretching makes me see white.

"I'm the luckiest man on earth." He takes the fingers out. "Can you take three?"

"Do it," I heave.

He pushes in with a third finger. "Ah, yes. Like this. See how you take my fingers? You're perfect."

"Saint." I buckle.

"Come on. Give me one." He does something with his tongue that brings stars to the back of my eyelids. "Please. I need to see you."

His mouth returns to me. He's ferocious and eager, and one of his fingers pushes up against a sensitive place, and I'm— done.

I come. My belly tightens. My pussy spasms. My whole body goes taut, until my breath dies in my throat.

"That's right, yes." He pumps his fingers through my orgasm. "You're so good."

Air comes back into the room, and a guttural sound I'm sure I've never made before leaves my throat.

"Holy shit, Saint."

"Mmh, yes."

He tries to keep using his mouth but I stop him with firm fingers on his hair. I pull. "It's too much."

He obeys, just like he's done all night.

He gets up, only to trail kisses up my body. "Your body can do so much more."

"Ah, Saint." I shiver as he licks my neck, then blows on it.

"Next time you'll come first. And second. And third."

"Maybe... maybe I should tell you now that I don't really come more than once."

He nibbles on my earlobe. I half-expect him to settle between my legs and fuck me now, but he holds himself away instead. His focus is on my jaw, my chin, my cheek.

He doesn't speak right away. After a few seconds, he locks eyes with me.

"Let us test that," he says. "Together. See what you're truly capable of."

"Is this another rule of dating casually? To push the limits?"

"No. This is just for us."

In my post-climax haze, his words gain meaning I don't think he intends. *I want to be the only one.*

It doesn't matter that my body has mostly calmed down after my orgasm. The afterglow in my chest brightens, and it turns the most beautiful sunset gold, carrying words I don't know what to do with.

*I'd like you to be the only one.*

But these aren't the words Saint said, and mine have nowhere to go. He offered to be my rebound, not my forever. The rules he's given me don't include keeping my heart under wraps, but they should.

"How are you going to do that?" I whisper.

It's a question for him, but also for myself. He only does casual, and that's what I told him I want. I can't fail at this so quickly. Nor can I pull the rug from under him with my stubborn dreams.

He rescues me without knowing. I lose myself in his easy smile, and those dimples, and the sweet kiss he gives me.

"Is your vibrator charged?" he asks.

"You still want to use it?"

"Of course. We'll use mine another time."

"So you really have your own?"

My heart stutters. It may be a complaint that I'm so ruthlessly ignoring it. Or it might be the heat coursing through my veins once more, at the promise in his words.

He gets off me in a swift move. "Where is yours?"

"In its pouch under the pillow."

Kneeling on the mattress next to me, he gives me a long look.

"It's your fault!" I chuckle. "I've had to use it a lot more than expected recently."

He moves to find it. "I think I'll take that as a compliment too."

"You should."

"Now sit up, Amelia."

The vibrator lands next to my hip. Just as I lift my torso, he finds a place behind me. He guides me to lean on him.

His hands caress my thighs, the rolls of my hips and belly, and up to my breasts. I sigh and melt against his chest.

"Like that." He kisses the spot under my ear. "Let's wake up your skin again."

He plays with my nipples. Tiny flames erupt all over my body. My breath quickens.

"It's working," I whisper. "You're so good at this."

"Is it, now?" One of his hands makes a path down to my pussy. "Am I, now."

Two fingers find my clit and make teasing circles on it.

"It is... you... are. What are words?"

"Mmh, lose your words some more, will you, Ames?" He does something with his fingers that has me shivering against him. "And tell me everything going through your mind. Every word, every fantasy, every single thing. I want it all."

"Saint, I... I..."

"Say it. Tell me all of it."

"I... I want you to do the things you promised. I want you to show me what my body can do. For the next week... or two... ah..."

His hands turn more confident. With a thick fingertip, he circles my entrance a few times. At my breast, a thumb rubs my nipple.

"Keep going." He speaks into the shell of my ear. "Please."

"Gael. You gave me control tonight but, right now? It feels like you have as much power as I do." The last word turns into a moan halfway. "I'm losing my words. My sense. My composure."

He slides his calves under my knees, to hook my legs over his. It opens me up further, while keeping me in place.

I whine. "We've been at this for— for— a while. And we're taking our time, and we're doing things in a way I never have and I'm already so far beyond anything I've ever done—"

"Ames."

His words echo a prayer. My cheeks burn with a furious blush, but I'm not embarrassed. I'm impossibly aroused.

"Saint. You've already shown me more than I thought I'd have. My body is already feeling things I didn't know were possible. I think I can come again... And if this is how you touch everyone I will just— I may just— Ah!"

He pushes two fingers into me again, and they make an indecent wet sound.

"You hear that?" he asks low into my ear. "You're soaked because of what we've done tonight. But if it's because of how I've touched you, I need you to know something."

He kisses my neck, gently rolls my nipple between two fingers, while three tease my entrance. I moan and roll my hips, getting his fingers just a bit deeper into me, pressing his hard cock between us at my back.

"Tell me. Gael. Please."

"Don't you know? I'm touching you like I've touched no one else."

"No one?" I ask despite myself.

"So if I've been a good boy for you—" The hand in my pussy leaves me, only to turn on the vibe— "Will you do this with me?"

"What? I..."

His hands take mine. His arms keep me in place, caging me against him. Between our fingers, the vibe.

"That night outside of your room," he whispers. "I imagined you touching yourself like this."

He presses the vibrator against my clit. I moan.

"Does this feel good, Amelia?"

"Yes. So much."

This vibe is a tight c-shape, and he pushes one of the ends into me. Just a tiny bit.

"Oh— I— Saint."

"Yeah. Do you feel that, Ames? Is that good?"

"Yes! Oh my God. More."

"Then help me push it in. Just like I imagined that night. Please. Do this with me."

With interlocking fingers, we play. We tease. We push the vibe inside, slowly, in and out. My hips roll of their own accord. My breath is quick and raspy on my throat. His hard cock is hot against my back.

I come. It's different— longer rather than explosive. Waves of contraction out of my control, each spasm yearning for more.

Usually, I become oversensitized when I orgasm. I'm done afterwards. A second orgasm is difficult to achieve.

This orgasm is different. I'm still aroused. I could come again— easy.

"Saint. Ah!"

"You see?" He keeps helping me press the vibe against my tender, oversensitized flesh. "It's so good. You're so good."

"You're incredible."

"Is this what you need? I'll give it to you. It will always be about you."

"But— you— I should—"

"You *should* nothing. Just letting me do this, I... ah."

His hands shift, only enough that he can hold my arms between his. In this new angle, with his large hands, he pushes two thick fingertips inside. They add to the vibe pulsing inside.

"Fuck! Gael!"

"The way you move... the way you sound... it's all I need."

He forces the vibe against my g-spot and my clit at the same time, and I'm so aroused I must be glowing with the heat of it.

"But when you're ready," he adds. "When you're ready, Ames, I'll add my cock to the mix. If you want it. I'll do it only if you want me to."

I'm so lost in these relentless waves of pleasure that I'm sobbing. It's full-on despair for more, as if I'm not already coming.

Sex like this— it's new. It's powerful. I'm so beyond anything I've felt before, and it's made me greedy.

Feral.

I don't make a conscious decision, but I change positions with swift, determined moves.

I push him to the bed and straddle one of his thighs. "I want you to."

My hands grab his cock. I ride his thigh, using his long leg muscles to press the vibe against me. I pump him. Hard. Insistently. Possessively, dammit.

"Jesus Christ," he moans.

"Can I— would you—"

"Yes, Ames. Yes, a thousand times over. I'm yours. Do as you will."

"You don't know... what I'm saying..."

"Do it. Use me. There's nothing you could do—"

His words die in a deep groan when I sit on him.

Cock and vibe together. Stretching me in ways I didn't know I could be. Adding fuel to the all-consuming heat inside.

He moans. Maybe I do too. I roll my hips back and forth, and the spasms intensify. They haven't really stopped in who knows how long, and now they reach into my lower belly.

It's an orgasm and a promise that I can do it again, harder.

"It's never been like this," he whispers.

I have never done something like this before, either.

Saint is giving me one hell of a gift, letting me know him this way. Letting me know myself this way.

"Ames. Please. Tell me this feels good."

"So good. You're so fucking good."

He whimpers.

"Such a good boy, letting me use your cock this way."

"Fuck. Come again. I can't come until you do. Please, give me another."

"You want to prove yourself that badly?"

Words come out of my mouth, escaping from some hidden corner of my mind. I don't choose them as they spill out of me.

"You want me ruined?" I ask. "Forever chasing this high again?"

I ride him, up and down, just barely, enough to drive us wild with the vibrations and friction and sensation.

"Yes. Fuck! Amelia."

"You want praise, don't you?"

"Anything you'll give me. Please."

"No one will compare, Gael."

He whimpers. "Yes, just like that. Tell me again I'll ruin you."

"I've never had better than you, and you may leave me corrupted and entitled to things I didn't know possible—"

"Amelia!"

A deep groan leaves his chest. He jerks against the mattress, breaking my rhythm and changing the angle somehow. The liquid warmth of his release fills me up.

"I'll never forget..." he mutters. "You're... the only one to..."

The end of the sentence disappears between his lips. It doesn't get processed and I can't guess at it— I'm coming again. This time, the white glow inside of me takes over and turns my skin transparent. My whole body spasms, and everything shines white. For a moment nothing else exists. I'm a supernova, testing the limits of light itself.

I come back to myself in stages. It takes time before I notice how my fingernails dig into Saint's chest, leaving deep half moons in his flesh. His hands cling to the rolls of my hips, and his face is a mix of pleasure and pain.

"Fuck, that vibrator is— Damn," he complains.

I scoff-chuckle. My brain isn't fully back online yet, and my body is still shaking, but I manage to get off him and fall onto the mattress with my dignity intact.

The vibrator is covered in the results of the past hour. I put it on a tissue on the side table and turn to Saint.

He gazes at me with sleepy eyes. "I feel like I didn't do enough. I promise next time—"

He stops when I laugh.

"Are you serious?" I ask.

"I am. I said I would impress you."

"You did, Saint. Wilder than my dreams. I didn't know what to expect and yet... this was better than I imagined."

"Now imagine when I get to show you what my body can really do to yours."

"There's more?"

"I'm sure there is. We'll do this for a bit, right? In fact, we should continue the discovery process to really get started—"

He makes as if he's going to keep going for another hour or two.

I laugh.

He gives me a sleepy, dimpled smile, and brings me close. We kiss, but I keep it soft and gentle.

I put a hand on his chest. "Tomorrow."

He sighs. "All right."

Tomorrow I'll wonder how long *a bit* means. Tomorrow I'll wonder what happens next.

# Chapter 29

## Ames

Waking up on my side is a normal occurrence. Opening my eyes to find a glorious, golden brown body next to mine isn't.

The onslaught of memories it brings is a welcome adrenaline shot. His perfectly round ass, a revelation among buttery sheets, makes me wish I woke up like this every morning. With a view of his thick thighs. The gentle hills of his back muscles. His face is half hidden in his pillow, and the sweet curl on his lips is something I'd like to see first thing every day, too.

I'm high from the aftermath of the night before.

I had never had sex that was so unscripted, so liberating, so generous before. My abs are sore from my orgasms. A smile rests on my lips, too, and I have to wonder if it was there while I slept.

Man, Saint loves to please a woman. It didn't feel like a performance. He loved pleasing me. I felt *adored*. And from the way we're holding hands, it was special to him, too.

In the sunlight that filters through the thick curtains, a deep inner warmth blooms.

He deserves to brag... and a good meal to nourish us, recover, and prepare for more.

I carefully get out of bed so as not to wake him up. The tank top I use as a pajama shirt lays on the floor, forgotten after falling off my bed the night before. Wearing nothing but that and my underwear, I grab my phone and tip toe out of the room. My last sight as I close the door is Saint's ass.

With a grin on my face, I collect ingredients and prep everything on the kitchen island. It's late in the morning and brunch is his favorite meal, so I put some effort into it. A mushroom omelette, some julienne-cut veggies, cheese, fruit... if I make some arepas as well, it might prompt those dimples to show up first thing in my day as well.

Damn, I still feel like I'm glowing. Cutting through a red pepper and smiling like I am one with nature. Cleaning the insides lovingly like I will gently wash the seeds to plant in my beloved garden.

Last night, Saint said he'd been thinking about it for a long time. The way he treated me, I believe him. He must have been so used to getting whoever he wanted that waiting for this chance with me had him pent up. Making him lose it and come in his boxers? It will surely make it to the highlight reel of my life when I die. However long this lasts, I will remember this night above all. Even if it all leads to Saint teaching me how to end things earlier than I ever have.

The last thought falls on me like a cold mist. It dampens my shine. But I can't forget we're doing this for a short while. This is not the happily ever after I seek. Saint doesn't see romance through the same lens I do. He's already always himself, and that includes having no interest in permanent attachments. I can't forget it.

Red strips fill a bowl. I take one and munch on it mindlessly. With my free hand, I put a few strawberries to soak in water and a bit of white vinegar.

It's *good* that this thing with Saint won't last. This way, I won't be tempted to lose myself in him, and I won't lose him. Being with Saint for a short while will teach me all the lessons I've been missing out on. With his kindness, with those revelations he called rules... In just one night, a new philosophy is taking shape.

Boredom isn't the price of comfort. Monotony isn't the price of security. And predictable sex isn't the price of being with someone forever.

I sigh and leave the strawberries to their bath. I pick up my phone. Last night, I wrote something quick to Evie to let everyone know I was leaving and not to worry. I didn't explain much, and I fully expect to have a small interrogation waiting for me in my texting app.

Evie didn't disappoint. She sent several messages asking to know who I left with and wanting to hear all of the details, asking me to text her in the morning with proof of life. I smile. Her concern is sweet and brings happy bubbles to my stomach.

Her last text, sent an hour earlier, doesn't.

> **Evie**: Hey! I haven't heard from you yet, so I'm keeping an eye out for your message, but I'm sending this new one anyway because if I were you, I'd want to know. News about Aidan came up during my general media check this morning. He's been out and about with a few different dates. People online are commenting on it because it's new, and it may be promo for his album, but his fans are speculating because they know about the breakup. Let me know if you want to talk about it <3

Without much thought, I look up his name. I ignore the bio at the top of the results, and find several pictures of him with three different gorgeous femmes. They all have long, straight hair. They're all thin and elegantly dressed, too. Their make up game is on point.

The disgust in my stomach doesn't make me proud. It's not about his dates. As far as I know, they did nothing wrong. But the fact Aidan is out there showing off his new single status— now that he finally accepted it— it feels childish, somehow. Like he lost his favorite toy and now shows up to the playground with three new ones.

Ufff. I'm not proud of those feelings, but they're real. I can only hope he's not toying with those three dates the way he toyed with me.

I go back to Evie's text a few times, unsure of what to tell her. I keep flipping back between my browser and my texting app, biting the inside of my lips the whole time. That's why I see my brother's text right away.

> **Pablo**: any news about the TV show? Maybe I should visit again, or maybe you can come see me

Right. I should also spare a thought to my brother, and what last night with Saint does to the relationship among us three.

I didn't want to confront that so soon, but here we are. Still, I find a way to delay things another few seconds. I send a quick note to Evie to tell her I'm okay and I'll write more later, then turn to the conversation with Pablo.

> **Ames**: Hey! No big news since we last talked. My friend Evie is helping me negotiate a contract while I sign with an agent. I have two calls on Monday, and by next week I may have everything sorted

> **Pablo**: sounds like I should fly again for another visit. Time for another celebration?

I bite my lip. If Pablo visits, Saint and I will have to either pretend nothing is going on, or explain nothing is *really* going on. My brother may not be entitled to know I hooked up with his friend, but I'm not bold enough to tell him I asked Saint to teach me to have flings anyway. Besides, once upon a time, Pablo told me to think hard about ever getting involved with Saint. Even back then, Pablo knew I wanted forever and Saint doesn't do that.

I take a deep breath and rub my lips together. Stalling is the only thing I can think of for the time being.

**Ames**: I would love to see you! Things are so chaotic right now with the playoffs and the contract negotiation and pilot filming plans... Let us know in advance, okay? No surprises this time. Let's plan something!

**Pablo**: No surprises. I'll let you know!

My phone clanks as it hits the stone of the island, but I ignore it. The masa for the arepas should be ready now. I wash my hands and start shaping the simple bread. Should we tell Pablo anything? I don't know if he would understand that Saint and I have the perfect set up— for a little bit. As long as I can prevent feelings from showing up. My brother knows me too well.

"Morning." Saint smiles at me, dimples full force. "Give me a sec."

I startle, but the view fixes everything. Still naked, ass still glorious, he goes into his bedroom. Soon he comes out again, wearing only his jewelry and a new pair of bold underwear. This time, it's a neon pink, tight strip of fabric, with a navy waistband. His hair is messy, he looks happy and sleepy, and it softens all the worries swirling inside my mind.

I leave the arepa on the tray and grab more mix in my hands.

I lean on the kitchen island. "Morning."

He kisses me with complete disregard for the fact my hands are full of white cornmeal mix. I melt, my hands listless in the air next to us.

"You weren't in bed when I woke up," he says. "I didn't expect heartbreak first thing in the day."

I laugh.

"You think I'm joking?" He kisses me more.

Sweet, exploring kisses that turn me to goo.

"I promised you breakfast," I manage.

I did. What feels like ages ago, when I thought he was going to turn me down gently after I propositioned him. Ha.

His lips trail down my neck, the sensitive skin under the shell of my ear. "I promised I'd show you what my body can do."

I shiver.

*I could get used to this. All of this.*

And that scary thought is enough to show me just how careful I have to be.

"And you're going to do that while fasting?" I ask.

It's as much as I can do to temper the situation. My best attempt at teasing him.

"Would that impress you?" Saint runs his hands down my naked thighs.

He's locked-in on feeling me up. My offer of food may not be as foolproof as I hoped.

I take a slow breath, this time to calm myself. "Not if the arepas on the grill get burnt."

It doesn't work either. My skin remembers last night, and wants flames igniting my nerve endings again, and a new series of multiple orgasms.

So greedy already. But I'm not the only one, it seems.

"I'll turn it off—" he turns to the stove, only to find nothing there yet.

"Pablo texted," I blurt.

That cools him down. He stares at me for a moment, to finally nod.

"Right." He washes his hands at the sink. "Everything okay?"

Without drying his hands, he takes over shaping the arepas. I wash my hands, set a cast iron pan to warm up, and work on the rest.

"He wants to visit," I say. "I stalled. I told him to give us a warning as we're pretty busy."

"That's true. We are. Things will only get more intense as we get closer to the final game, and with your show on the table as well..."

"I wouldn't want him walking in on us having sex on the couch, you know."

I steal a glance at him. His mouth tilts in a smile.

"As long as I get to fuck you on the couch," he says.

I laugh. "I don't want my brother walking in on me! Or us— ever."

"But do I get to fuck you on the sofa? What about the kitchen island?"

I fake a shocked gasp. "Do you really mean the kitchen island?"

I'm smiling again as I put a few arepas to cook. Like we're talking about what movie we might watch tonight. He continues to work, almost done with the masa, and shaping the last couple pieces of cornmeal bread.

"What I'm hearing is yes on the sofa." A beatific look takes over his face. "And that I'll have to seduce you to let me do things here."

He caresses the stone like it's a cushion and he's inviting me on it.

I hold back a chuckle. "I'm serious. We need to talk about this. What would happen if he shows up out of the blue?"

"I'm serious too." Still, there's no tension visible on him. He puts the last of the arepas on the tray, and washes his hands and the metal bowl in which I prepared the masa. "Pablo doesn't have keys to my place. We'll be fine."

"Okay— fine. But do we even want him to know about last night and the next— little while— whenever this ends? Or do we wait until after so we can pretend nothing happened?"

He studies me closely. "What do you want?"

He leans on the kitchen island, arms crossed now, waiting for my answer. I set up a steel pan to warm up as well, to finish preparing our breakfast.

I shake my head.

"You know, when we met," I say, "Pablo told me you don't do relationships."

"He warned you off me?" His voice is knowing, with a sad despondency to it. "I can see why."

I gaze up at him. "He told me he just didn't want us to get hurt."

"It's funny." There's no humor in his voice. "He talked to me, too. He told me that if I wanted to keep dating the way I do that was all good. But to not try to date you, if I was going to treat you like everyone else. That it would hurt you, because it's not what you want."

He frowns, dimples nowhere in sight.

"You've never hidden what you do." I keep my eyes on him. "This is temporary. I know. Short and fun is what I'm looking for."

"Right. Yeah. Well..."

He doesn't look as relieved as I expected.

"It's like we said last night," I say. "You can teach me. I need what you know. Ending things nice and early. And I trust you. I can't imagine anyone better. With you... after last night... I don't think I'll lose myself. You won't let me. You're amazing like that."

Wherever this adventure with Saint leads us, I need it to help me break my patterns. I don't want it to be another time I throw myself at a relationship, as if I can make it into my happily ever after with the strength of my will.

"I'm not as good as you think." He frowns. "But I will never ask you to be someone you're not."

I take a step closer to him. "Saint... this— you— I think you're who I need right now. We can make sure we keep things good for both of us. So go ahead and be with me like you are with your dates. I won't be offended. Flirt with me but keep me at a distance if that's what you do. Sex me up until I forget how I used to date. Bake me a pie when we're done so we can laugh about it and be close afterwards. I don't want to lose the friends I'm making thanks to the past couple of months and— and I don't want to lose you."

Saint places a hand on my face. His thumb caresses my cheek. "I don't want to lose you either."

"We can do this. In two or three weeks... maybe right before or right after the end of the season. We can come out of this with a handshake and pie. Maybe we'll share it to celebrate."

"Are you really asking for pie?"

"Yes. I want to learn from you. I want the whole Saint experience." I take another step. "Fu-dating, remember? Bake and Bye included. Especially once you start to really feel the need to start dating like you used to. Just give me a small warning. I really don't want to get in your way and I don't want anything that feels like cheating either—"

Aidan's to blame for that thought as well.

The way Saint turns into a statue next to me, I forget about it in the next instant.

"I don't cheat." He stares at me with hardened eyes. "Ever. I may date quickly, but even if they're seeing other people, I only see one person at a time."

Cold, controlled irritation exudes off him. It leaves me motionless for a second. I watch him closely, rearranging a few things in my brain, making room for this new piece of information.

"I never meant to imply otherwise." I put a hand on his chest. "I'm sorry."

His heart beats fast. Rather than worry over his anger, or feel guilty for my words, his reaction turns to reassurance. It helps, that he responds this way to the idea of cheating.

"If this is what we're doing," he says. "If this is what you need, I'll be who you need. It's what I offered last night. Just tell me there won't be other men. No other practicing. We will do this and we will do it right. You and I, in a daze of feeling where no one else exists. High on sex and proximity. On smiles and touch. See me for who I am and I'll do the same for you, until we learn who we need to be."

"Yes." I try for a smile. "Exactly. I didn't think you and I would do something like this. This... I want to enjoy this. Enjoy *you*."

For as long as it makes sense. For as long as he lets me.

When I first came to Saint's condo and he made me chocolate with cheese, we talked about three months before we knew if he'd get to stay and if I'd get to save my business. Now three months living together can mark the end of this short relationship, too. Give or take.

His chest works in long, deep swells. His eyes never leave mine.

I wait, letting him work through whatever weighs in his mind.

"All right." A corner of his lips curls. "I said I would be your rebound. I said I'd teach you to walk away from relationships when they're not right for you. If that's what you need, I'll be true to my word. That way no one gets hurt. Clear expectations."

I smile. "I knew you'd be reliable like that."

"Sure. Let's call it that."

"What would you call it?"

"We may need to discover that together, too." He kisses me.

"Well, now you have me curious. What else could it be?"

"Not altruism, in any case. I'm getting fresh arepas from the deal." He grabs handfuls of my ass. "And the most delicious dough I've ever had within my reach."

I chortle. "Okay, Casanova."

"Hey. Don't undervalue the power of this ass."

"Who says I am?"

"Because no other ass has the power to make me walk away from homemade, just-cooked arepas."

One of his hands remains anchored to my butt, while the other turns off the stove.

"Excuse me?" I raise an eyebrow.

"I'd rather break my fast by eating your pussy right now, is all."

"Wow. Okay."

"Right here."

Without warning, he lifts me to sit on the kitchen island.

"Woah! Saint—"

He kneels. "And I'm pretty sure that, later, you're going to let me sex you up on the couch, too."

"Oh, yeah?"

He nibbles on me through my underwear. Shivers run down my spine. My nipples harden to pinpoints through my tanktop, too.

"And later than that, when my new bed arrives—" he adds.

"You got that new bed?"

"Ordered before coming out of your room. When it gets here—" he uses a finger to move the patch of fabric covering me to the side— "We'll have an inaugural ride on my new mattress. You said I need to sex you up until you forget about everyone else. I'll fuck you until you forget your own name."

"Is that what I said?"

He licks me. "It's what I heard."

My breath hiccups.

"Will there—" I try. "That is— the arepas will get dry and cold. I promised I would... feed you..."

"You are." He licks me again. Caresses my thighs. "Something tells me I can live on your orgasms alone."

I moan. "Saint..."

I'm still processing the words, overtaken by the fire in his eyes, when he stares at me and dips his tongue between my labia.

"Rule number five, Amelia. Everything else can wait."

And he shows me just what he means, by eating me out on the kitchen island until I forget my name, too.

# Chapter 30

## Saint

It's been a week and a half since I made myself into a sacrificial lamb and offered myself as Ames' rebound. I'm sore from training and from how much sex she and I are having, but I do my best to keep myself focused.

Ames has been vocal about what she wants. I agreed to the guidelines. No matter what my heart cries for when I hold her close at night. Even if I wanted to beg for something different from the moment we talked the morning after. She and I have an understanding, it's what I wanted before I knew she wanted me, and I'm supposed to be on cloud nine.

And I am. I really am. I've never devoted myself to someone like I am with Ames. I've thrown myself into this time together, taking as much as she'll trust me with. It may be my poor yearning heart, seeing things it wants to see, but I swear she's giving me everything. I see it in her eyes. In the way she touches me, the things she whispers to me in the throes of passion, or in the quiet times before we sleep. Surrender. Abdication. Pleading.

It's bringing me to my knees.

*She* wants me.

She *wants* me.

She wants *me.*

The guy she's known for years. A man she's had a hundred platonic meals with. The friend she came to when she was in need.

But I'm dreading how quickly the days are adding up. I don't want to think of the moment Ames realizes I'm not rushing to end things. That despite accepting the role she wants me to play— the womanizer who will be happy to walk away from this fling— someone who can teach her how to give up on long term when things are not right for her— I am not ready to press the brakes on whatever this is we're doing.

We said right before or right after the big game.

The truth is, short of it slapping me in the face and pushing me out of the way, I'm aiming to buy us extra time. Even if it terrifies me to try.

Try what? I don't know. The teacher has no idea what he's doing.

Balancing our days and nights with the promises I made is always on my mind. Even while I'm on the phone with my sisters.

I sit on the terrace couch and watch the sun set behind Lake Washington. At ten years old, Aixa and Maribel are a hoot. They talk over me, too excited to let me properly respond, beyond a few chuckles here and there and a few rushed words.

They tell me about their school projects and anything else that crosses their mind, etching a persistent smile onto my face.

"We started collecting materials for the new board!" Aixa says. "You promised next year we could make it pink."

"I did say that," I concede.

Maribel speaks before I've finished. "Are you getting your ring this time?"

"Of course he is!" Aixa responds for me. "We talked about this, Mari."

She's exactly two hundred seventy four seconds older than Maribel, and takes her older sister role seriously.

"I'm not pressuring him!" Mari complains. "I'm just doing the math for his first visit."

Typically, I go spend time with them right after the season ends, and once more after they finish their school year. Pre-season schedule permitting, I try to take them somewhere fun, too.

My time with them is precious. I've never lived with them, since they were born right after I started college. The relationship we have is the result of a lot of effort on my part. I try to be present from far away, reminding them I'm their older brother, and that I love them very much.

Time is flying past so fast, their eagerness to spend time with me may not last much longer. I'm making the most of it. I'll deal with the heartbreak later.

Funny, that this philosophy applies to what's between Ames and I as well.

Except with the twins, I know they can't actually get rid of me. With Ames, she could, and I'm facing an end I worry about. Planning to deal with that pain afterwards, somehow.

I shake my head and I take a chance during a small silent window in Aixa and Maribel's conversation.

"I'll let you know as soon as I have a date," I interject. "I'm not sure what I may have to do after the season ends."

"What do you mean?" Aixa asks.

The twins are highly sensitive, and read my tone easily.

I sigh. I'm not ready to talk to my sisters about the risk of a trade, but it's time.

I mull over my words for a second. In the space between my thoughts, I take comfort in the way Ames shows up on the terrace and asks to sit close.

I nod at her and let a few words fall from my lips. "Mom and Dad know this, so you can talk to them about it. Don't talk about it with anyone else, okay?"

"Of course," Maribel says. "We never talk about our famous brother with anyone."

"If they guess, it's not our fault," Aixa adds.

Ames cuddles next to me. My chest glows with the same tones of bronze and orange tinting the sky.

I smile. "It's never your fault, mis divinas."

235

"Tan divino!" The twins respond in unison and laugh.

It's a Colombian expression of love and admiration for beautiful and amazing things. Calling someone or something *divine*. Every time I call them that, they respond the same way. It's a little joke we have with each other.

I gaze at Ames. I don't know if she knows what it means. The way she looks at me with tenderness makes me want to call her mi divina, anyway. I lean closer and nuzzle her hair. Herbal scents fill my lungs, and I sigh.

*"Okay if I stay?"* she whispers.

I nod, a pinch in my chest, because I'd say *forever* otherwise.

It's been exactly ten days since I offered myself as a rebound, making this thing with Ames my second longest relationship ever. The longest one was the time I tested myself to see if I was relationship material. That one lasted two weeks.

Any other time, I would have made a pie already. Now I refuse to even come close to my baking ingredients. Just in case it gives Ames any ideas.

I'm so, so done for.

"Hello?" Aixa says. "Are you there?"

"You have to tell us!" Maribel exclaims.

"Right." I clear my throat. "There's a chance I might get traded. If that happens, I'll have to move after the season."

Ames caresses my arm. The light of the setting sun paints her skin a bright amber. Her smile, until then free and summery in winter, cools down.

I grab the remote from the coffee table in front of us, and put the outside heater temp up a few degrees. The winter evening needs it, and so does she. And I.

"What?!" my sisters reply at the same time.

"Where would you have to go?" Maribel asks.

"Obviously he doesn't know!" Aixa's tone is severe.

"But maybe he knows what teams are interested!"

"Do you know what teams are interested, Saint?"

"I do." I have a blanket with me as well, and I wrap Ames and I in it. "Coach Clark told me last week."

Under the knitted cover, Ames finds my hand and squeezes once. Twice. Leaves our fingers interlocked, tight.

"The Pythons have shown interest." I stare at the horizon. "The Brawlers, too."

"Both of those are across the country!" Aixa complains.

Maribel's tone, on the other hand, has a clear tinge of worry to it. "Does that mean you're moving even further away?"

"Not if I can help it." I infuse my words with confidence— for all our sakes. "My agent knows I'd rather stay here, and so does Coach Clark. It's the GM I have to convince."

"How are you going to do that?" Maribel asks.

"Winning is my best chance," I say. "Being named the MVP."

This game is so competitive, I have to be practically perfect to get the award. *Breaking records* kind of amazing. Otherwise they'll just give it to a QB.

The ring protects me from the fans' disappointment and their need for a scape-goat. Winning the season and the title combined can protect me from a trade. Why release a player who was pivotal to the biggest prize there is in our industry? But it's not enough to aim for it. I have to get it... or else. It's a razor-sharp line between success and failure. Not getting the award but having an MVP-style season makes me desirable to other teams. It's a powerful card for a GM to play during the trading season. Other teams would want a player that performed at that level. Right now, I'm performing at the right level... for either path to materialize before me.

I *need* the MVP award. And my first ring.

"You promised you'd invite us to the game if you made it to the final." Aixa's voice through the phone is clear and assertive.

"I need to talk to Mom and Dad about it. You're still so young."

So innocent. So free with their love. So trusting.

"We know!" Aixa says. "You don't want people following us or whatever."

"Or whatever, exactly," I say.

And growing up fast. I don't think my life will give me children, but the way I want to protect my sisters, I know I'd be an overbearing dad.

"But we're older now!" Aixa says. "And we want to be there."

"You promised, Saint," Maribel adds.

I sigh. "I did. I guess I have no choice now."

"You can talk to Mom and Dad..." Aixa leaves me in suspense for a second. "To plan the dates we're flying into the city the big game is at, and the hotel we're staying at, and how we're going to get to the game."

"Let me win the conference first, okay? Plans will lead us nowhere if the Strike loses that game. One and out, remember?"

"We know how football works." I can hear the way Aixa rolls her eyes.

"You'll totally win the conference game!" Maribel exclaims. "And we'll make pompoms! They'll be blue and purple."

"You can make pompoms in whatever color you want," I say. "I'll keep my word. You'll be there every time I go to the big game. Now it's time for dinner. I can hear Mom calling in the background."

They protest, but eventually we say goodbye. I throw my phone between Ames and I on the sofa, and turn to her with a questioning smile. I've never let anyone hear me chatting with Aixa and Maribel.

She comes closer to me under the blanket. With no words, she asks to lean on my chest. I welcome her, wrapping her shoulders with an arm. Our fingers still interlock over my thigh, in the warmth of our cocoon. I sigh.

She nestles against me. "You're extremely sweet with them."

"They're my favorite people."

"So they're the ones making the hypersquare board?"

I nod. "They're very proud of it."

"Not many people know, do they?"

"I've only told you."

She burrows into me. "I'll keep your secret safe."

The sun approaches the skyline, full of shadowed trees, hills, homes, and faraway stretches of land and water. Everything is tinged in honey and ochre, including the clouds rolling in.

"Only thing is," she says, "if the twins are going to watch the final game, it will be hard to hide the fact. You know Dom bet this is the year he learns who makes the board, right?"

"Yep. It's okay. You heard them— they're growing up. Or so they think. They're just babies in my eyes."

She chuckles. "They're not. Aren't they technically pre-teens?"

"Don't break my heart like that, Ames."

"Just think of the memories they'll make. And wouldn't you love having them there, too?"

"Yeah. I'd love having them there. And my parents. And if you wanted to..."

I don't finish the sentence. She's been at games before, she watches my games when she's not able to come, but attending the most important game of my career as my guest might be too big an ask.

She sighs. "I'm waiting to hear from the show's producer. They want to film the pilot soon, and I'll have to fly to their studio for it. But if I'm still here, maybe I could..."

I squeeze her close. "I'd love that."

"No matter what happens," she adds, "I want to be there. Especially now that I know about the Pythons and the Brawlers. To think you might end up on the other side of the country... but if I don't get to go because of the pilot..."

If nothing else, distance has the power to end things between Ames and I. But it also means I have three more weeks of this bliss. At least.

"Let's not think much about that yet," I say. "One game at a time. We need to win the conference first this weekend."

The one we lost last year.

"It's not fair," Ames says. "I want to be at the final game, but might not get to go because of the TV show. I could definitely go to the conference game, but we're not going because of Coach Clark's new rule about not allowing guests on the field until the championship game."

I caress her hair and stare into the horizon. The conference game is the last step before a chance at a ring. If we win that trophy, we'll make Strike history.

Coach wants the chance at both as much as we do. It's made him strict. More than usual. Keeping us tight. He's watching us like a hawk, and reminding us of the importance of discipline and concentration every chance he gets. All of the coaching staff is on board, and we're hearing the message. Still, just in case we don't, they're taking extreme measures.

Winning next weekend's game makes us champions of our conference. It means a big party afterwards. We celebrate the trophy we just got, and the chance at a ring. For years I've watched the winning team welcome their guests into the field, to watch them receive the prize and rejoice together.

If we win the conference, Coach is letting us have a small party, but no guests on the field until the big game. So we're disciplined about curfew and training. So we keep our concentration. If partners and family and friends want to attend they can, we just won't see them. The guys and I never ask our people to fly for away games since we can't spend time with them, and we've decided it's up to the girls if they want to go. They decided to stay home this time, too.

It's not ideal, but we agreed. We'll compensate for it afterwards. I'd be thrilled anyway, if Ames could make it to the field on the most important event of my career.

"I get it." I sigh. "I want you at the game— all of them, if it was up to me. But I know you have to put your everything into that pilot. That show is your breakthrough."

"Yeah. It's all so up in the air, but I have to stick it out. I'm still betting my business on it. If I get the show, I get to cook for fun again and get the cash flow and interest I need to save my kitchen. If I don't... if I don't, it may be too late to save it. I may need to get loans I don't want to get, and fire people in the process."

"We'll figure it out." I kiss her temple. "We'll see what the producer says."

"And we'll see what happens after the final game. If you have to go..."

I take a deep breath. "Let's wait. There's not much to be done tonight."

"Saint... I would miss you so much. If you have to go..."

She says my name like I matter. Like she still wants me close.

My chest caves in, the weight of my feelings is so high.

"You won't have to miss me," I whisper. "As long as you want me around, I'll be here. Somehow."

Even if I end up at the other end of the country. No matter if that involves this situationship or not. I want her in my life.

"Then let's stick together for a bit longer, yeah?" I add in the same tone.

"Yeah. A bit longer sounds great."

We watch the sun set, many questions hanging in the air, but holding on to each other. For a little longer.

I'm not sure how I'm supposed to teach her to end things, when I don't think I can.

# Chapter 31

## Saint

We're in my room, in my new bed. It's the night before I have to fly to the conference game.

I'm fucking her hard. The bed covers and sheets are strewn on the floor. They fell as a result of our mutual exploration, and neither of us seem to care. We're too busy enjoying this thing we have.

Every night, we pretend we have countless evenings just like this.

"Saint— ahhh."

"Tell me." I pump my hips harder. "Talk to me."

The bedframe rocks back and forth with the force of my movements. I hold myself high above her, so I can see her tits rock, too.

"I... you..." Her eyes are closed, her mouth slack with pleasure. "You're so good. This feels so good."

"I can make it feel better," I groan.

I have my cock ring on, tight around my shaft and balls. It has a knob that can vibrate and tease her clit— but with my thrusts, it doesn't do its job as well as it could.

I can't have that.

"Ames." I twist us in bed. I come out of her but, with firm hands, guide her to straddle me. "Take me back."

"I've never... ahh."

She takes a second to adjust to the new position, deep as I am in her.

"Holy shit," she mutters.

"Stay like this." I dig my fingertips into the plush rolls of her hips. "Just like this. Don't move."

"Saint— I—"

With a single hand, I accommodate the vibe head to fit between her labia and right on her clit. Reaching without seeing, I search for the remote and up the intensity of vibration.

"Saint!"

"Do you like this?"

She doesn't respond except for a quick nod. Her head drops back. A flutter of her inner muscles steals a groan from me.

"Don't move," I repeat, the words ground through my teeth. "Please."

"I want to." Her voice is raspy.

"Not yet. I need— I beg— let me feel you like this."

The warmth of her body sheathes me. Her thick thighs bracket me. Her nails dig into my chest.

"Nothing feels as good as this," I confess.

My bedroom is a sanctuary. Walls and furniture fill the space in moody coffee shades— cappuccino, mocha, espresso everywhere. Except for my bed and curtains, draped in rich, light cream tones. All metals are a brushed, muted gold. The lights are subtly tinted to add depth and emotion.

"Take it easy," I moan. "Take it slow. Let me feel you."

The walls of her pussy ripple again around me and I push my head against the pillow.

"Yes, just like that," I say. "To feel these vibrations and what they do to you. Just like this. Please."

She whimpers and collapses on top of me, like the sensations are too much. I wrap my arms around her as she kisses my neck. Moans again.

I echo her. "Tell me it feels good. Tell me you feel the vibe and my cock and it feels good."

"I've never felt this good." She rolls her hips— once.

I squeeze my eyes shut, and hold on to her right.

She rocks again. "I need to move. Please. Please."

A strangled noise makes it out of my throat. I trace the mountains of her body until I can grab her hips hard again. I guide her movements. In this angle, she presses onto my vibe. I bite my lip.

"Gael!"

She comes with my name on her lips. It's a long orgasm, waves of pressure around my cock making me see white.

"Amelia."

I roll us in bed again so she's under me. I press my hips into her, forcing the vibe to intensify her climax. When the spasms slow down, I roll my hips gently, going as deep as I can and staying there, pushing, letting the vibrator do its thing.

She whimpers. "It's too much."

"Tell me you'll take it. For me. Please."

"You like this?"

"I'm inside you. Feeling you. There's nothing better. I beg you."

"Only if you're a good boy."

"I am. So good. Right? Do you like this?"

I move in and out, only an inch at a time. The way she squeezes me now, I know she's doing it on purpose. I groan.

"Will you make me come again?" she asks.

"I need to. Be good and give me another one. I can't come until you come again."

"You want me to come again that badly?"

"Yes. Always. Yes."

She takes the remote I threw onto the mattress and changes the vibration pattern. The sensation travels through my cock and deep into my lower belly. I moan. The change makes everything hypersensitive again.

"Do you like this, Gael?"

"So much. Do you like it? Tell me you like it. I need you— I need—"

I keep rolling my hips in small circular motions, making sure to push into her flesh.

"Tell me you want me to come again," she whimpers.

"I need you to come again. I need to feel your body give in to me. Over and over."

"Do you love knowing you're the only one who can make me feel this way?"

"Fuck. Yes."

"Do you want to hear that I'll never stop thinking of you and what you can do to me?"

I whimper.

"Is that what will make you— make you— come and fill me with—"

She sobs as she comes. The sounds coming out of her throat, her fingertips digging into my shoulders, her thighs squeezing me tight. Fragmented awareness that makes me spill myself in her.

"Ames. Holy shit. Holy fuck. Amelia."

I'm halfway through my climax when the words rasp through my lips. I stay still, focusing on the fading jolts and outbursts of her body, and the intense sensation the cock ring, her movements, and my orgasm put me through.

I'm still trying to recover as we decouple. At my side, she finds the remote and has enough presence of mind to turn off the vibe.

"I can give you another," I complain.

"Saint," she says.

My name is half-scolding.

This is officially the longest relationship I've ever had, at just over two weeks. We've had sex often enough that she knows I always offer more, and for me to learn she accepts my offer only sometimes.

I never want to stop asking.

"Come here," I say instead.

I open my arm in an inviting gesture, leaving my poor cock to deal with the rings of silicone still keeping it hard. I'll need to wait to take them off.

Ames sighs and snuggles up to me.

"I would have never guessed how much you love to cuddle," she whispers next to my chest.

I caress her arm with lazy fingers. "Don't ask anyone about it. You'd be shocked."

"What do you mean?" She chuckles.

"I've received complaints in the past that I don't cuddle enough."

"Nonsense. You're always asking me to be close!"

She doesn't know she's the first one.

"Of course I do," is all I say.

It's those sparks I felt for her a long time ago. It's the way those have grown into something deeper, brighter, and enduring.

They used to flicker. Now they emit a steady, bright glow.

I lick my lips and breathe through the sudden tightness in my chest. I'm in trouble. So much trouble.

"Saint... are we... fu-dating?" She chuckles. "Remember that? From when I had just gotten here."

"I remember." I keep my breathing even.

"It's hard to believe. I always wondered why you never tried to have sex with me and now here we are."

"You were always in a long term relationship. I couldn't get in the middle of that."

"Meanwhile, you were always *fu-dating*."

247

I sigh. "I can't say you're wrong."

We stay quiet for a second. The patches of skin where we touch are warm, but goosebumps appear like rivers on her flesh. Her fingers are motionless on me and, while I can't study her face to know what she's thinking, I know she's thinking hard.

I should get up and get the blankets. Cover us and coax her into sleeping just like this with me. See if she'll let me make up for time lost by making her come once more.

But I don't say anything. Before she can ask for more, her phone rings.

She gets up. Her body jiggles from her movements. It's a glorious sight.

I sigh. "The fucked right look is good on you."

I want to be the one getting her hair messy like this. The one making her climax over and over again. And the one kissing her good morning. Always.

Ending this would wreck me.

I'm not sure she processed what I said. No way she knows what it meant to me.

She stares at her phone, then at me.

She bites her lip. "It's Pablo."

I nod. She might as well get distracted. It will give me time to recover and figure out where the hell to go from here.

"Hey!" She says to the phone.

She stands naked, mild consternation on her features. She glances at my cock, still half-hard and tied in silicone rings, and shuts her eyes close. Tight.

I bite back a sad chuckle. She evidently isn't ready to think of us as more than fuck buddies. Talking to her brother while I'm on display like this is weirding her out.

"Dear sister of mine. You texted?"

The room is quiet enough that I can hear Pablo's words clearly. I rub my face with both hands and vaguely realize I should say something.

"I did?" Her voice is high-pitched.

Or maybe I should walk away. Or let her know I can hear it. Would that make her panic more?

To be fair, even if we'd been together for three decades, she might not want to talk to Pablo while I'm naked and wearing a cock ring.

"You forgot?" he asks.

"I— I'm sure I did. Text, that is. Yeah. I have news."

I raise my eyebrows.

"So you said in your message," Pablo says from the speaker. "What's up?"

"Uhm... right."

"Is everything okay? You sound weird."

*I'll go out*, I mouth to her.

She shakes her head. "I'm okay."

"Wait. Can you talk right now?" Pablo asks. "You can text me later if you can't. If Saint is there with a date and things are awkward—"

"There's no date." I say the words without thinking.

Ames' eyes open in renewed panic.

*Fuck*, I mutter, even if I want to rebel with a laugh as well.

We're both naked. I still have my cock ring on. Ames and I are on the phone with someone who would never expect us to do what we just did.

And all I want to do is say, *hey, remember that warning you gave me about Amelia all those years ago? Yeah, I really needed a reminder, now you're too late.*

"Saint?" Pablo chuckles. "Shit, it's still weird to get you on the phone when calling my sister. Funnily enough, I texted *you* earlier."

Ames puts the call on speakerphone, throws the device on the bed close to me, and gets busy putting on her pajamas.

"Sorry," I say. "I haven't checked my phone in a while."

Ames throws my boxers at me with force. I chuckle.

Fully unaware, Pablo continues. "I was going to ask you about the game this weekend, how you're doing."

I remove my cock ring like it's the most natural thing in the world. "We keep on going, preparing to win, assuming we will."

This is my mutiny. Pretending none of this is embarrassing is as close to defying the agreement Ames and I have as I can get.

Not that we were explicit about not telling anyone.

"Can't believe it." Pablo laughs. "Wow, Saint. Remember in college? We dreamed of this. Now you're almost there— again."

Fully dressed, Ames goes as far as to comb her hair with her fingers. Even if Pablo can't see anything.

"You should come to the big one," I say to Pablo. "It's in San José this year. We're inviting our closest friends and family. My parents and my sisters are going to be there, too. And Ames, of course. I think. Maybe."

I smile in a tease, seeking a smile back.

It doesn't come.

The frantic energy buzzing around her dies. Her movements slow down. She wrings her hands together as she sits on the bed, avoiding my gaze at first.

She bites her lip. "Remember how I said I was waiting to hear from the producer?"

I nod.

"Yeah? You heard from them?" Pablo asks.

She sighs. "This is the news I had. They emailed my agent and me. I'm recording the pilot in ten days. I'm flying that Thursday, we have a few meetings through Saturday, then we record on Monday."

"Wait," Pablo says. "So you're going to be in LA the whole weekend and miss the big game?"

I get up and put on my underwear, like it will help.

Yeah. She's not attending as my guest.

I look away to buy myself some time. My stomach is on the floor, quickly finding its way to the cold lake waters. My heart follows behind, hoping to disappear into its depths.

It's hard to breathe, the way my chest is heavy with the news.

But I knew this could happen. If I imagined she'd be in the suite to meet my family, to watch me play, to find me on the field afterwards... that was all my doing. None of it is part of our agreement.

This is too big an opportunity for her, for me to be selfish and ask her to support me instead.

"For the pilot only," she adds behind me. "My agent is negotiating that the proper show filming happens here, but the pilot has to happen there. Budget reasons, they said."

I turn and run my fingers through my hair.

"You hadn't said anything." I keep my voice neutral.

"I was... distracted." She points to the bed a few times. "I'm sorry."

"If I can be a poor substitute..." Pablo speaks from the phone.

"Of course." I clear my throat. "Please come! I'd love to have you there."

Though Ames' presence can't be replaced.

"And we are so excited about this chance for you, Ames," Pablo says.

"We are. It's such an opportunity," I manage.

"They're saying that if the execs like the pilot— and if the tests do well— they would start with ordering ten episodes. Depending how those do, we'd film a second season." She gives me a tenuous smile. "Can you imagine?"

"I can imagine." I pull a smile from somewhere in my guts. "Excellent news."

"That's the dream," Pablo says.

"It is." Ames takes a deep breath. "I hope I can carry an episode on my own."

"Of course you can, Ames." I put a hand on her knee. "You will dazzle them. You'll see. We will be pursuing big career goals at the same time. That's kind of cool, isn't it?"

It is, even if her absence will be a big splinter in my side.

# Chapter 32

## Ames

"Explain to me again why we're not at that stadium?" I ask.

We're at Evie and Logan's place. It's a nice house, airy and light. Everything is in shades of a very, very pale yellow and warm honey. It looks straight out of a fancy furniture store quarterly magazine, in a minimalist sort of way.

Technically, I know why we're watching the conference game here and we're not there huddled in a suite. My question is mostly a complaint. Evie knows this, but she still explains.

She brings me a new drink and sits next to me on the sofa. "Apparently the guys asked Coach Clark to change his mind but he didn't. He insisted he wanted no distractions. Logan was grumbling about it before they traveled."

An impressive cream sectional surrounds a large TV, and we gather close, right in front of the screen. Pen sits while doing and undoing a braid. Nat stares at the screen with a focused face. The Strike is currently winning, but there's a lot of time left.

"Grumbling because of the morale?" I sip from my drink.

Saint didn't grumble while saying goodbye, but he hugged me and spoke to my ear instead.

*I wish you could be there.*

That's what he said. While holding me close by his door, right before he went to the Thunderdome in time for curfew, and I attempted to work at what's left of my catering business for a few hours.

It was hard to concentrate. Competing feelings clashed and warred inside. Warmth, because everything Saint and I have done in the past couple of weeks has settled in my heart with feelings of candles, blankets, and my favorite tea. Anxiety, because I was meant to stop myself from feeling these things at all.

"They love it when we're there," Nat says, "but it's not always practical. They can't really spend time with us after a game when they play away. That's why we typically only go to local games. No point in flying if they have to stay at the hotel and never see us, right? The conference game is one of the exceptions, though."

"If they win and we're not there for the party..." Evie sighs. "That is what's hurting morale."

"Bear said he plays better when I'm there," Pen mutters to herself. "I wish I was there."

Evie and I exchange a look. It's like Pen doesn't realize she's thinking out loud, and that half the time, her words verge on not-purely-friends territory.

Pen sighs and shakes her head. "Apparently Coach Clark promised a party if they win, but it will only be for the team and at the hotel afterwards. They will celebrate on the field if they get the trophy, but the rest will be at the presidential suite. The big game in two weeks will be different, of course. If they make it, we're all going."

There's a break between plays and other coverage fills the screen. They show the Strike players arriving at the stadium. The third to arrive is Saint, wearing another fashion-forward outfit. Chocolate pants and a white shirt with block letters I can't read, plus a striking blazer. It's covered in paint blobs that could have been born from Dalí's imagination.

I sigh. "It sucks I won't be there if they make it to the final game."

All three faces turn to stare at me in shock.

Guilt spikes inside. It pierces my heart. I've been trying to tell myself it's better this way, that it will give me some sorely needed time and space. Distance might be what I need to unknot my heart. But the truth is, I don't want separation from him. I want to celebrate with him or to hug him close if they lose. To come to bed with him in the middle of the night, still smiling from dancing together, ready to talk about the next day. And the next, and the next.

I squeeze my eyes closed. Ugh.

"It's because of the cooking show." My voice is apologetic. "We're filming the pilot. I'll be in Los Angeles."

Fuck, I really, really need this TV show. Scratch that. I *want* that TV show. It's the closest, realest way to get what I need— the exposure, the business, the cash to keep my personal business afloat. Not to say anything about getting to enjoy the process of cooking again, like I did when Saint and I did the Christmas special. But who knows. I need to say the right things at those meetings, excel at the pilot, and cross my fingers everyone likes the results.

"But you were planning to go with us?" Evie asks. "To support our guys? It's only..."

"Six hours away by car." Nat's face shows the disappointment I feel. "On a weekend where everything stops to a standstill. Including the roads."

I stare forward. The TV occupying half a wall is invisible to me.

Yeah. If I could, I would be at this game and the next. It may not be an easy time for me, watching him play and worrying about his success and the chance of injury, but I care about him. The team. I would want to be there for Saint and our friends.

I remain quiet, unsure what to say at first. "It's a moot point, isn't it? I can't be there."

Because I will be in LA, and because I am way past confused. I should cling to whatever lines I can find, or I won't prevent devastation when Saint bakes me a pie. Even better, I should ask Saint again how to recognize the signs for when he's ready to end things, so I'm emotionally prepared. Keeping track of his cooking ingredients isn't cutting it. Knowing it will likely happen within two or three weeks isn't cracking it.

"Does Saint know you won't be there?" Pen asks.

"He does." I frown. "He didn't seem happy, but my brother is going, so it should be okay, right? His family will be there, too. He won't be alone."

Nat and Pen gaze at each other, while Evie stares at me.

"I think he would rather *you* were there too, Ames," my friend says.

I bite my lip. The comfort I wanted to feel that he might not miss me is nowhere to be found. I want him to miss me, dammit. In a world where this thing between us didn't end, I would move mountains to be there with him.

"You've caught his eye." Pen cocks her head my way. "For a while now, he's only been to the club with you. He stopped dating."

"He went cold-turkey, from what we could see," Nat adds.

And even though they don't know it, we've been sleeping together. He's put his attention, his care on me. In return... I asked him to end it. And I said I would do everything differently this time, including anything that requires putting someone else first.

Besides, not even a chameleon like me has enough colors to mimic a thousand different women. I never want to be the kind that tries to shape herself to what their partner wants. Not anymore. Especially when I may never find a way to twist myself into the right shape for someone like Saint.

"I don't know how long that's going to last," I whisper.

I shake my head, unsure of where to go from here. What I want and what I should want don't align. I don't know how to make it all fit together.

The game starts again. My friends let me think as we watch the Strike go on offense. The camera focuses on Logan at first, studying the quarterback's play. He throws the ball and the feed switches to a large pan of the field. Tension builds among us, watching with baited breath to discover where it lands.

Saint catches the ball mid air. He grabs it tight against his ribcage, turns and twists a few times, and manages to evade defensive players from the other team. Moving with the grace and speed of a superhero, he jumps into a sprint.

A gasp escapes me. Evie's hand squeezes my forearm. Saint leaves everyone behind.

It's been only a couple of seconds, but it feels like an eternity. My lungs refuse to work. Saint runs and runs, eating yards and sprinkling loose turf under his cleats. Only to slow down and stop three steps away from the goal line.

He knows he has the touchdown. Ever the showman, he turns toward the crowd and asks for applause. The crowd goes wild. Walking backwards, he crosses the line— dancing.

Nat and Pen laugh. Evie watches me. Saint throws the ball to the ground as his teammates reach him. He goes into an elaborate choreography with Dom.

I sigh. "Do you think he'll be the MVP?"

What I'm really asking is if he'll have to move to another city. Of all the reasons I've been clutching to my chest not to let myself fall for Saint, I haven't thought about this one enough. If I don't know what to make of all these feelings when we're sharing a bed, I don't know how I'll survive what we're doing together when distance is in the mix.

"His stats are good." Evie's voice is factual, but there's a hint of challenge in it. "He's broken a couple of records. He has a good chance at it."

I didn't know that. Another way in which I'm not showing up for him. And I'm entertaining feelings he doesn't expect? If I let myself imagine a romantic future with Saint, the least I could do is show him the kind of girlfriend I would be. Wanting to act differently from old relationships shouldn't mean Saint gets nothing but company at night.

Except he's never welcomed feelings like this in the past, and showing up like a Good Girlfriend is what I did in every single relationship before. It was never enough on its own. It didn't work. I still don't know what to do differently. I promised to do differently. Shit.

I'm trying to be a lover, but I'm really just a fool.

I don't recognize myself. I'm setting myself up for the worst heartbreak of my life, and I have no idea how to stop it.

"You're going to figure it out," Evie says by my side. "I know you will."

I smile. "Thanks, Evie. You're the best."

"I'm here when you're ready to talk."

"I know."

They all are. Pen watches me with a small smile, while Nat nods. Their patience falls on my shoulders like a cloak. It's warmth all around, protection from the rain if the skies were to break.

"Thank you," I say.

"For now, let's watch them win." Evie grins. "What do you say?"

"Who's ready for another drink?" Pen asks. "We won't be at their party... but we'll make our own."

# Chapter 33

## Saint

Several camera lights point in my direction, making the lenses and journalists no more than a shadow around me. Microphones, recorders, and cellphones hover near me, and I smile.

My grin is powered by sunlight and winning. The stadium floodlights shine on me, throngs of people on the field celebrating the win. Lightning runs through my veins.

I'm a few steps away from the top of the world, and as high as I've ever been. I scored half the touchdowns that got us the win in the conference championship. It's been weeks of this thing with Ames, and we're going on strong.

I may not be a singer crooning to thirty thousand people, but I know a thing or two about craving adoring eyes. In moments like this, I'm closer than ever to seeing myself as a catch. A real one. The kind that Ames could gaze at with hopes of forever. The kind of Mister Right she deserves.

"This is the strongest the Strike has ever been." A reporter gets themselves heard above the noise. "After losing this game last year, what do you have to tell the fans?"

"We've worked hard this season to get here." I lick my bottom lip. "We'll give it all in the final game. Our fans will get what they deserve."

"The Strike has never made it past this point," another reporter says. "What does it feel like to be so close to your first big win?"

"It's everything I've wanted, since the first time I stepped foot on the field. I'm doing this for the team, the fans, for my family. The Strike means a lot, to a lot of us. Being here for those who support us is our why."

"You're in line for an MVP award. Do you think you'll get it?"

"I'll keep working real hard for it." I put on a big smile that I hope looks confident. "I want it. For myself and for the team. Aiming for it is partly how I'll show everyone how much the Strike means to me."

Including the GM, the owner, and Coach Clark. I'll show them all I want to stay, and why they should keep me.

I need to stay. The ring and trophies aside, my people are here. Including Ames. If I dare ask for a future with her, one where the love they write about is ours, I don't want to shoot myself in the foot by telling her I have to leave in the same breath.

Scary, the way I'm thinking about us like there's a future in the making.

"Your performance this season has been exceptional. Which skill are you most proud of?" someone else asks.

Deep somewhere in my mind, I know they mean on the field. Still, Ames takes precedence. She fills my mind, and it stops me in my tracks.

The things I want. The things we've done. Knowing her sounds now. The way she looks when I pull a third orgasm from her. The time I got six out of her. Yes, I keep track.

Giving her multiple climaxes may not be something others may consider my best skill, but it's certainly something I'm grateful for these days.

I don't know what my face shows, but the people surrounding me must get a feeling of what kind of thoughts clash in my mind.

A cheeky smile takes over my face, and I let it. I play the game with them.

"We know your fame, Santiago," the reporter says. "But don't get naughty on national television."

"I haven't been naughty." I raise my eyebrows in an innocent gesture. "But I can't say you're wrong to imply... you know."

They snicker.

"You don't have to worry." I grin harder. "I'll show you what I pack—game-wise. I promise you'll like what you see regardless."

They laugh this time, and I make my way to the showers.

In a little while, we'll come back to the field to receive the conference trophy. Afterwards, we'll get together in the hotel penthouse to celebrate. Somehow, I'm sure I'll continue to entwine the high of the win, with the high of my feelings for Ames.

If we win the biggest sports trophy in the country, maybe I'll get to stay... and have a fighting chance with Ames, too.

<hr />

The team and half the coaches fill the presidential suite at the hotel. The space is grand, almost to the point of stuffy, with its ornate golden frames and heavy leather furniture. It's fine. It all fades to the background, when we're celebrating the Strike has won its first conference title.

The main suite is large, with several rooms no one occupies, a large bar, and an imposing dining table for twenty people. Big people of mixed ethnicities and boisterous voices fill the space, drink, and make merry. My closest friends and I, plus Rafael, sit on the couches. It's a rare occurrence to have the quiet defensive tackle with us. He's in the chat group, he's part of the group, but he lets himself fade into the background. Quite the feat for a man nearly as big as Bear, but we don't push him. We let him be. He's dealt with plenty already, and we're celebrating.

I sigh. It's a good moment. Hope and joy drift in the air like a gentle breeze of our own making.

"This is it," Damián says. "This is what we've worked for all these years."

"Now our first ring." Logan lifts his drink in a mock toast.

"The only thing missing today is those we love here with us," Bear says.

Damián and Logan agree. I hold back. It's a touchy subject.

"And those we don't love, but could have fun with, right?" Dom adds my way.

He's asking for complicity. I would have given it freely in the past. Dom and I have been the playboys in the group for years.

They don't know I'm the furthest from a serial casual dater I've ever been.

I sip from my beer. The hoppy liquid and its million bubbles are all I have to drown the voice in my head. The one telling me I don't need to label it as a relationship for it to exist. That it's real, and I'm deeper in it than I thought, nevermind my fears about it.

Whether I crush and burn, it doesn't change what I already feel.

Music of all sorts plays loud in the background. A new song comes on, and I pretend it's exactly what I need to quiet the mind. It's smooth and romantic, despite the faster beat someone added to it. Like a remix of a love song you might dance to at the club, and move to slowly at night, once the melody and you and someone special are stripped down to the basics.

I would make lov— I would seduce Ames to this song, in its original form.

Or so I think, until a word gets pronounced in an unexpected way. The voice sounds familiar and yet...

I frown.

Logan stares at me with a similar gesture. "Evie played this for me, I think. Do you recognize it?"

The lyrics are easy to follow.

*Persistence through the years*
*Tenderness at these keys*

*Love, dry your tears*
*We're settled*
*It's settled*

"Fuck," I mutter.

"Is that what I think it is?" Bear asks.

A dance remix of Aidan's ballad. The one he wrote for Ames.

Disgust washes over my torso, cold and sticky as if I'd spilled my drink.

"Change that!" I yell to Amir, an edge rusher currently leading the music selection.

"It's a good song!" He screams back.

"I don't want to hear it," I insist. "That singer is an asshole."

"Change it, Amir." Dom complains. "We're celebrating, but not with that song."

"Fine!" Amir complains, but skips the song to something I don't recognize.

"That was a downer," Damián says.

"Is he still acting like a vulture?" Logan sips from his drink.

Disdain pools in my stomach, condensing into a sickening feeling. I put my beer on a nearby table and cross my arms.

The corners of my lips turn down. "Not for a while. Not since Ames told him to get lost at the club."

"And how are *you* acting around her, these days?" Logan asks.

I rub my left temple and mostly ignore his question, though I steal a glance.

He raises a challenging eyebrow. "I'm only returning the favor. Remember the interventions you put me through last year?"

"And what makes you think I need an intervention?" I ask.

I reach back for my beer, mostly to have something to do with my hands.

"You have all the signs." His tone is wise, like he's an expert at these things now. "Even if you haven't admitted to anything."

"Is there something to admit?" Dom asks, a worried wrinkle on his brow. "Am I the only one who's going to be single now?"

Bear frowns. "I'm single, too."

"Except you and Pen—" Damián starts, but Bear does a good impression of his nickname and interrupts.

He grows three sizes, his powerful wall-like shoulders turning to iron. "Don't suggest we are in love."

"Look, I get it." Damián makes a placating gesture with his hands. "I spent a lot of time trying not to dwell on my feelings for Nat when we were friends. Not that you're doing the same or just pretending you're not in love—"

He adds the last bit quickly, once Leon's chin drops and his eyes turn menacing. The scar that splits his top lip looks dangerous in its halo of black, thick beard.

"I'm not pretending anything," Bear says. "Pen and I are friends. That's what I'm making clear."

"Fair," Damián says. "All I'm trying to explain is that you two seem like an item and it's easy to forget you're friends."

"Well, don't." Leon growls. "I don't."

"Message received," Dom adds. "You're single, too. Good. I don't want to be the only one choosing the unattached life."

"We're getting distracted." Logan frowns. "This is an intervention for Saint."

"I have to insist," I say. "There's no need for an intervention. I'm giving off no signs."

From the sound Logan makes, and the gestures everyone else gets on their face, I'm wrong.

"Are you going to deny you have feelings for Ames?" Logan challenges.

I grind my teeth and put the damn beer away again. I can't deny it. As much as I've tried, I know I'm in the middle of feeling a lot for her. I may go to great lengths to avoid labeling it, but denying it out loud seems like a betrayal. A disrespect of what we have.

But does that mean I'm ready to talk about love?

What a risky thought. The question I have not let myself ask comes closer. I'm prey to its hunger.

Should I try what I've never dared? Should I try for a relationship with Ames?

"Don't trap me like that," I eventually say. "If I feel something, she should be the first to know. Not you lot."

"So you feel something." Rafa stares at me with his dark, sage eyes. "But she doesn't know."

I gaze back at the big man. As a defensive tackle, he's muscled and padded, though less than Bear is. Still fuller than the rest of us and, with his grounded, private energy, he gives wise father vibes.

Not surprising, since he has a young child.

His quiet presence anchors me.

I shake my head. "I don't do relationships, remember?"

"Why the hell not?" Logan asks. "I have reason to believe you've felt things for Ames for a long time. Even before the whole Aidan debacle."

"Even if that's the case." I smirk, trying to infuse some humor to it. Keeping it light, because I'm a pro at that. "Doesn't mean I should get a diamond ring and down on one knee."

"Never thought I'd hear Gael Santiago talking about marriage." Dom's voice is heavy with resignation.

"I am *not*," I try.

"I'll be your best man," Logan says. "Unless you think it should be her brother. I won't be offended."

"You've been part of the team for eighteen months." I put on a defiant smile, responding to his humor. "You didn't make it into the group chat until a year ago. How dare you sass me like this?"

His mouth remains in an amused angle. He's enjoying this thing a little too much.

"I'm not sassing you," he says. "I'm trying to do for you what you all did for me. You told me to not let Evie go. I'm telling you the same. Don't let Ames go."

I don't want to let her go. I haven't had enough time with her.

It's hard to believe it's been less than a month since I brought her to my lap and she let me hold her close. The fabric of reality itself changed after that night, stretching and deepening and carrying knowledge I never held before. Sex and life look different from this edge I'm so stubbornly clinging to. One where I'm teetering at the face of jumping into the unknown.

I shake my head. "You don't understand."

"Then explain," he insists.

I cross my arms, my chin on my chest as I think. None of my friends speak. Their eyes are fixed on me, tracking me as they wait for my response.

"I am not relationship material." The words rasp out of my mouth. "I'm a good time. I have fun. Always short term, never making any promises. They love it for a little while, then I let them go. Everyone knows that."

Logan frowns. "Bullshit."

I raise an eyebrow at him, like I take offense at his language.

"What our beloved quarterback means," Rafa says with full aplomb, "is that while that's true, it doesn't mean you can't have long-term romance, too."

"I've never sought long-term." I stare at him and rub my lips together. "Except once. A long time ago, I wanted to know if I could make one work regardless. Suffice to say, it didn't end well, and I learned my lesson."

"Of course it didn't end well." Bear is the one to frown this time. "I've never heard of a break up that went truly well. Even people who say they're going to be friends after— it never happens."

I shake my head. "It wasn't about that. I didn't go into it wanting to stay friends afterwards. It's more that... well. She knew me enough to know I can't make relationships last."

"What did she say?" Rafael asks.

I close my eyes. The look on her face is clear in my mind, like it happened yesterday.

Kylie was a pretty girl of light skin and lustrous brown hair. We'd known each other since my first day on campus, and had a casual on-and-off thing going. She knew me well enough, I thought, and I liked her a lot. Who better to try to fall in love with? To go the distance with?

But when I tried to make it official, she laughed.

I had just shown up with homemade pie to one of her classes, to walk with her back to her dorm. As soon as we were inside and I left dessert on her desk, she gazed at me with playful eyes and a dismissive curl to her lips.

*Why are you doing all of this? Do you even know what it takes to be with somebody for a long time? You don't, the way you've always dated. Why would anyone risk their heart for someone like that? You're not Mister Right. Long term is not what you do. Why fake something else? It's only going to hurt people.*

I stood there, frozen and eyes wide open. She was right. I had never sought love until then. I had never learned how to make it work. How to make sparks happen. Why would anyone choose someone like that for a real relationship?

Back then, she had placed a gentle hand on my face and smiled.

*Don't hurt people, Saint. Not being an asshole is the best thing you have going for you. That and that sweet body, too, I guess.*

Just like all those years ago, she laughs again in my memory. Like it did then, the ghost of it shocks me.

I echo her last words. "'Don't ruin the fun we're having with promises you can't keep.' She thought I was being ridiculous."

With no sparks and no affection, it never would have worked. It would have ended in hurt. On the other hand, no one would choose to go for it just in case. With a guy who's never proven to have what it takes, when it counts.

If Kylie was right at all, I can't go around wielding my hope like a weapon, offering forever when all I have is a dream and no guarantees. When pain is the most likely result.

I sigh. "I can't tell Ames how I feel. I don't want to hurt her, knowing I'll eventually disappoint her. She deserves so much more than that. Someone who can recite poetry and give her a happily ever after guaranteed."

That's why even asking the question in my mind is throwing me into a minefield, and pulling Amelia to walk through it with me.

Damián and Bear study me closely. Dom frowns. Logan continues to smirk.

"I know someone who could give her that," Logan says. "He can tell her beautiful things and work on forever with her."

His words poke at a sleeping warrior inside. He wakes up, instantly furious, filled with jealousy. I can't believe my friend is implying there's someone better than me for her. It may be true, but it's hurtful, and not the kind of thing I want to hear at the moment. I may not be able to write poetry for her, but to tell her pretty things all I have to do is be honest about my feelings. I may not be relationship material, but working on forever with her may be... may be exactly what I want...

*Oh.*

My heartbeat changes pace. It goes steady, deep, and strong. I gaze at Logan, then at my friends.

I want to be that person. I'm afraid I won't be, but I want to. Desperately.

"I mean you, in case it's not clear," Logan adds. "You can do those things."

I purse my lips. "What if I end up hurting her?"

"What if you're hurting her by not telling her?" Rafa asks. "What if you're missing out on something beautiful?"

"What if I'm being delusional?" I argue. "What if I lose her because she can't go back to being friends after knowing how I feel?"

"That's always the fear, isn't it?" Damián asks. "But you need to understand that not telling her is deceiving her, too."

Bear glances at Damián for a long time, but the kicker's gaze stays on me.

The narrative I held onto for so long dissolves into faraway memories. Whirlpools form in my veins, swirling into tiny currents in the middle of my chest. It's a dizzying sensation.

"Let her choose, too." Rafa gives me a small smile. "Tell her the truth of what you feel. What you want. See if she wants the same thing."

Dom's eyes are sad, revisiting things in his mind I'm not privy to. "It's the right thing to do."

The torrents around my heart turn into a riptide.

A new story unfolds. It takes shape right in front of my eyes, words re-arranging themselves into new prose.

"Fuck," I mutter.

The question I've avoided asking is not the right one. It's not a matter of whether I dare try for a relationship with her, despite the hurt it might bring her—us. It's whether I'll do the right thing and ask if she wants one, too.

It's not about pulling her into the minefield with me. It's simply asking if she wants to walk into it with me.

Not asking her means fulfilling a prophecy of my own making.

"Fuck," I repeat.

"The playboy catcher has been caught," Dom adds. "Stranger things have happened."

I smirk. He's using the wrong term on purpose to bug me. Whoever used it wrong the first time would have never guessed at her impact all these years later.

"Careful." I close my eyes, trying hard to pacify the swirling sensations behind my sternum. "You're a playboy catcher, too."

"Nah." He shrugs. "Lightning doesn't strike twice, and I'm fine with that."

In the haze of my discovery, I'm not sure what he means, but I know it's true for me. Ames is still the only one I've felt sparks for. In the past few weeks, they've turned into roaring flames.

I will not be a coward and let them die. At least not until I offer them to Ames in a jewel case made of crystal and welded with the gold of my hope.

If it gets smashed in the process, then I'll pick up the pieces from the floor.

And offer them to Ames once more.

They have called me a catch in the media. Some went as far as to call me a catcher— of women. If any of that is true, it's ironic I have to catch Ames now instead.

# Chapter 34

## Saint

I thank my friends and promise I'll ask for help if I need it. My chest feels raw after the recent revelations, but I tell myself it's good. It's progress. It's life-changing. All I need to figure out next is what to tell Ames when our loose deadline comes.

I take the glass to the bar and ask for a water bottle. More than a drink, I need breathing room. No wonder that my steps take me to the terrace.

The night is dry and cold. No one is out here but me. I sit on one of the terrace couches and gaze at the twinkling lights of the city. I sigh. The next two weeks are going to be extremely busy with training and media. I don't know how the hell I'm supposed to find the time to fling myself into the abyss, and tell Ames how I feel.

As long as Ames doesn't push me off the cliff herself somehow, chances are I'll have to wait until after the game to tell her everything. See where that leads. If it means finding a way to go back to the friendship we used to have before she moved in, then coming to terms with that. If it doesn't, happiness will shield me when convincing Pablo that dating Ames won't follow my tired old scripts.

It's ok. I can still be with her without revealing my whole heart just yet. Seeds can be planted. Dreams entangled. I don't have to wait to chat with her the way I want to for the rest of my life.

> **Saint**: Are you still at Evie's?

I leave my water bottle next to me on the cushion and hold my phone in both hands. Three dots have appeared on my screen, and they put a smile on my face.

> **Ames**: No, I'm at home now. How's the party?

> **Saint**: It's okay. Smaller than it could have been

> **Ames**: I bet. I wish I had been there to celebrate with you. I complained about it profusely to my friends.

> **Saint**: Yeah?

> **Ames**: Every time you showed up on TV. This was the game I could go to, and I didn't get to?

I still grin when I call her. She answers right away.

"Even though you get too nervous watching games?" I ask.

"Yeah. Seemed... important."

"Aw. You care about me, at least a little."

"Of course I do. Don't tell me it surprises you?"

"Maybe it does, maybe it doesn't. The important part is I got to hear you saying you care about me."

I want her to care. Everything could change if she cares. Even if all she wanted me for was a fun hookup. Caring means she might consider more with me.

"You're important to me, Saint," she repeats. "Everyone was upset we couldn't be there to celebrate with you all. I was upset the most, because I won't be there for the next one."

A cool breeze moves through the terrace and I shiver. I keep my voice quiet, letting this conversation be only for us.

"I wish you could come."

"Now, with everything..." She gives me a long sigh. "Me, too."

Her voice, with softly spoken words and a lingering warmth... They blanket me.

"The fact you want to go means a lot," I say.

"I'll be thinking of you while I'm in LA. Maybe I can watch the game on TV that Sunday. I don't have any meetings that day. I'll get a chance to send you a hundred messages again."

"I would welcome a thousand. I love getting to read your reactions after the game."

"I will. A thousand and ten texts at the very least."

"Maybe we can make it into a tradition. If I have to go play for another team..."

I don't know what makes me say that. Once upon a time, weeks before I sacrificed myself as her rebound and just after her breakup, we talked about what would happen if I end up leaving. In a few words, I told her she could keep living in my condo for as long as she needed to.

That's still true, even as it takes a new shape inside of me.

Whether I stay or go, I want her to live with me.

That won't happen if she doesn't want to do this new thing with me, or if I end up on the other end of the country.

Fuck.

"I don't like to think about you leaving," she whispers.

"I don't like to think about it, either."

This is scary. How to tell her I offered to teach her how to end things, and now I want to try for forever with her. How to tell her that even if I have to leave, I don't want to leave this thing between us. How to find a way to tell Pablo I'm possibly in love with Ames.

"Then let's not think about it," she says. "Evie told me you might get MVP. They will *have* to keep you, right? No way they can give away the MVP."

"That's the hope."

"Ugh. Saint. Lie to me if you have to, why don't you? Tell me you'll stay here in this city."

"I can't lie to you," I say. "And I can't make promises I don't know if I can keep."

I need to be careful. So careful, to promise things I know I can do.

I can promise I'll give it my all.

"Winning isn't entirely in my power," I add. "But we'll make it work."

"I know you'll do everything you can," she whispers.

"I will. So hard."

Could I commute? Sure. Some players do... when they have a family that needs to stay put, for the kids' school or the spouse's job. I'd be willing, for a relationship with Ames and for my friends. But it would take a toll, and maybe blacklist me with my new team. I wouldn't be spending much quality time with them, after all.

I can live with that, if it means living with Ames and our future. Staying in my friends' lives.

Another cold gust of air envelops me, but it doesn't affect me much. A source of heat has taken hold of my chest. It feels like determination.

"You never do things halfway." Her tone is wistful. "I know you'll be here if you say you will."

"Rule number seventy seven. You deserve their whole effort. I'll give you full effort."

"Saint." She laughs. "How many numbers did you skip there? I'm pretty sure you haven't given me more than ten rules. What were those again?"

If she's forgetting the things I told her about keeping things casual, I can't say that I'm upset. If I can start planting thoughts in her head about what I'd want to give her, that's a pretty good use of the rules game.

"Rule number one hundred twelve." I smile into the phone, even though she can't see it. "Forget about the rules, and go for what you want. I'll do the same."

"Yeah? What do you want?"

I gaze out to the city again. A million tiny lights flicker in the dark of the night. The kinetic energy of my quick-beating heart could power a million more.

"You," I say.

She stays silent for a second, two, five, and I hold my breath through it. Until she chuckles.

"I guess winning *excites* you, huh?"

I smirk, even if she can't see it. "Yeah, we can say that."

"I want you too, Saint."

I don't move. She thinks I was talking about sex. That I meant it as a seduction. I'm too flirty to assume anything else, and my fame still precedes me. She has good reason to come to that conclusion.

"Right here, next to me in bed," she adds in a whisper.

Fuck me all over again. Not that she's wrong. I want her that way, too. All the time. The way my cock is already responding to her suggestion is proof enough.

In the face of not knowing what to do to show her what I mean in love, I go for what I know the best.

"Yeah?" My voice has gone deeper. "Ready to sleep, or..."

"Or." She takes a deep breath. "Have I told you how amazing you look in that tight football uniform? And those clothes you wear..."

"What about when I'm not wearing any clothes? Do you like that, too?"

"Always. I think I like you always."

My heart stops.

"Fuck." I close my eyes and rub my face. "When I met you, you came to dinner in jeans and a loose white blouse. I've never seen anything sexier. You made it sexy. The look you gave me— I've never forgotten."

"And when I'm wearing no clothes?"

I shift forward on the couch until my head rests on the edge of the back cushion. My cock finds room in the tight confines of my pants, but I ignore it. I keep my hand away and fist my water bottle instead.

"You naked on my bed is my favorite sight," I rasp.

She moans. I squeeze the bottle in my hand, begging the cold to keep me in control. Where's another breeze when you need one?

I lick my bottom lip. "You have no idea the sight you are. All those indulgent curves, all that flesh I can touch and make mine. Decadent and fucking plump. Melting into my sheets. I want to get lost in your body. Over and over again."

"Gael..."

"Touch yourself like I would. You know how I would touch you, Amelia. Caress your skin, explore the dips and hills. Give me those sounds again."

"I want it to be you."

"I'll do it again. Again and again for as long as you let me."

"Gael—"

"Get the vibe. Yours. So you can imagine I'm inside you and playing with your clit at the same time."

"I'm already close, just with my fingers."

"Let it be the vibe. Please. So I can control it from my phone. Let it be me. I need it to be me. Please."

For a little while, all I can hear is her fast breathing, a few escaped sounds from her throat, and my own blood rushing in my ears. Precum builds and if I move even a little, it will leak into my underwear.

I keep myself still, except for my hand. The bottle was cold enough to create condensation on the plastic, wetting my hand. I slide my palm under the bottom of my shirt, up my abs and to my chest. The cold air chills the watery path. It doesn't help as much as I thought it would.

She moans. The water might as well have been lava.

"Are you pressing it into your clit, Ames? Did you push it inside?"

"I'm imagining it's you."

I jerk my hips once, despite trying not to. The friction of my clothes is enough to make my eyes roll up.

Fuck. I'm going to come in my pants again at this pace.

"Make it go faster, Saint."

"I'll do more than that."

I check my surroundings. I'm still alone, but I'm outside. It's fine for now. I tap on my phone until I'm on the vibrator's app. Without fully thinking of it, I choose a faster setting and a different pattern.

She whines.

"Yes, Ames." I keep my voice low, only for us, gravelly with my feelings. "Let the vibe touch you but know I would do much more. I'd be kissing you. I'd be talking you through it, just like now. I'd be inside you letting that vibe drive us wild."

I change the pattern again. The ghost of a hiccup resounds on the line when I get the phone back up to my ear.

"In my mind," I say, "I'd touch you like we were naked together in my bed. I'd make love to you all night. I'd give you so many orgasms we both lose count. And when the sun comes out again, you'd be so soft and unbound, I'd keep you close in my arms. I'd move slow and deep inside of you. Lento, mi divina. Bailaremos lento."

My heart wants to jump out of my chest. It's running out of my mouth, too, but it's not enough. She can't truly understand the many ways in which I mean my words, and I can't explain. I'm too wound up, my brain hazy with the need to be with her to do as I promised. My cock is back to my favorite type of torment, the one where I want Ames desperately and she doesn't know it. The kind where a few words from her and a single touch would have me finishing before I meant to.

"Saint... I... want you, too."

Her feelings are entwined with her breath, unnamed as they are. Compacted and hidden in her want. I'd ask more, but I have no plan. No idea how to say things right. And if this is working for her and it's half as good as I want it to be for her, then this isn't the time, anyway.

"Fuck," I mutter, and let the curse carry all of my frustrations. The climax I can't allow myself, and all the ones I won't get to give her tonight.

I change the pattern again and set it to the hardest setting. Laughter reaches me from the suite behind me and I curse again.

The bottle lays abandoned next to me and I steal a glance at it. In the blur of my feelings, I consider uncapping it and emptying it on my head. Except that would welcome a hundred questions, and it's unlikely to solve the problem. Only one thing will.

I stand slowly, to prevent much precum from escaping onto my boxers. My brown pants would show even a single drop.

"Ames. Keep touching yourself."

"I am. I can't stop."

"Shit. Yeah. Like that."

Crossing my fingers that I'm safe from leakage, I dart for the bedroom sliding doors at the other end of the terrace. I choose one of the darkened ones, hoping the lights off mean no one is there.

"One day soon—" I try the door. It's blissfully unlocked and I get in— "I'll tell you everything I can't say when I'm miles away and surrounded by my team. I'll find every word, Ames. But now I want you to touch yourself, okay? Make yourself come with the vibe and my voice in your ear."

"I'm close. If only I just..."

"No. Wait for me. Soon. We'll do it soon."

I cross the bedroom without paying attention to a single detail. I'm fully focused on the bathroom, and I don't stop until I make it inside and lock the door behind me. I slap the light on.

"Are you touching yourself?" she asks.

"I'm touching myself now."

I undo my belt and yank at the layers of fabric covering me. I free my cock, and let out a long, strangled groan when I fist it in my hand.

"What can I say... to help you..." she tries.

An unexpected scoff escapes my throat. "You don't have to say anything, Ames, don't you see? Everything you do is what I want. I just need the little noises you make, and to know you want me too."

I stroke myself once. Twice. I close my eyes and focus on the sensation, on the call, on us.

I frown in concentration. "If you want to say something, say it. If you feel something, give it to me. I'll take all of you. I'll make it all mine."

"Saint—" my name is strangled on the phone.

I'm pumping faster now. "Bella, sólo tú. Only you can get me hiding in a random room like this when I want to be there with you. Speaking into the phone when I should be saying sweet nothings to your ear. Touching myself when I want to be inside you for hours."

"I'm going to come. Saint!"

"Come for me, bella. Eso, así." I swallow her moans and grip myself harder. "Tan divina. I'm seeing you breaking in my arms, Ames. Giving into this climax that's for me, even if I'm miles away. I can see your face, you know? It's seared behind my eyes. I know how you look, and I need more of it."

Her breathing is broken by the spasms I can't see, but I know rake her body. My lungs match her, because my own orgasm races behind her.

"One day soon," I groan, "I'll love you unhurriedly, fully, thoroughly. Until I lose myself in you, and you don't want to be anywhere else."

"Gael..."

I come. I say things but I don't know what. It's dangerous to forget myself like this, but it's not in my control, and all I can do is let my climax take over. I've already been saying things I probably shouldn't, and it didn't stop me. My feelings overflow and I can't stop them, either. My brain is empty, and my body is pulsing and trembling, and my senses are on overload. The yellow lights above the mirror shine like suns, and they're the stars by which I find my way to the present moment again.

I open my eyes slowly. My lungs still work hard, but I'm recovering. Ames seems to be back to herself as well, from the slowing breaths I can hear on the phone.

"What did you say?" she asks.

I wince. "Errr.. when, exactly?"

"Just then. Not the Spanish— well, I guess it could have been Spanish then at the end, too."

"Damn." I take a deep breath and open my eyes. "I guess we'll never know."

"Did I blank out your mind, then, Gael?"

I smirk. "Everything is empty, I think."

She chuckles. I grab toilet paper to clean up after myself.

"What about you?" I ask. "All nice and liquified?"

"Yeah. Good job, sir."

"Ma'am. At your service."

"I'll just say *you* called *me*, Saint."

"I'm a proactive servant, what can I say?"

I get myself back in order, turn off the light, and go out into the darkened bedroom. With a smile on my face, I sit on the bed.

She laughs. "Five stars. Though the Spanish should get a special mention. Is that your secret weapon? You hadn't used it like that before."

"Never used it like that before. I can't say that I planned it."

"Really?"

"But if you liked it, I'll call you bella as much as you want."

"Divina was my favorite."

I grin. "Noted."

The word isn't fully out of my mouth when the door opens.

"There you are." Dom gives me a quizzical look. "I thought you were getting a drink."

"I left it outside." I chew on the inside of my cheek. "I'm on the phone with Ames."

"Oh. Right." He arches an eyebrow. "Anyhoo. Coach wants to talk to us."

"Five minutes," I say.

"Say hi to Ames." Dom smirks. "Don't dilly dally."

"Dilly dally?" I laugh.

"Yeah. Chop chop." He chuckles. "You know what I mean. Pedal to the metal. We have a lot to do and we want it all, don't we?"

"You're obnoxious." I grab a decorative pillow from behind me and throw it his way.

He catches it no problem, throws it back to me, and leaves.

"He's gone," I say to Ames. "Finally."

She chuckles. "That was a close call. But you have to leave now?"

"Yeah, I should."

"So what happens next? The big game is in two weeks, right?"

"Yeah. This week will be heavy training and media. I don't know the exact dates yet, but we're flying to San José several days before the big game. More media. More training. We'll be busy."

"When do you hear about the MVP?"

"Usually the awards are announced on the Thursday before we play."

She sighs. "You're amazing. How do you handle the pressure?"

"I've been training for this my whole life." I smile. "I can't let the pressure distract me. All I can see is the prize."

And in my head, that includes a life with Ames.

"Okay, then," she says. "We'll come up with something, right? We'll prepare. You for the game, me for the show. And then, when you're back... we'll figure out the rest when we're both back."

"We'll know more. We'll talk."

"Let's try to make the most out of what's coming our way. Yeah?"

"Yeah. Good night, Ames."

We end the call with the words I can't say stuck in my tongue. I'm lost in lust, maybe lost in love, and lost on how to make this last with Ames... but I won't let that stop me, either. At all.

# Chapter 35

## Ames

Saint is being pulled in a hundred directions, as the team prepares for the big event. I've barely seen him. The little moments we have, he holds me close and kisses me. Sometimes that leads to sex— sweet and tender, or hurried and urgent. Sometimes, he lays his head on me. It can be my shoulder, or my tummy, or my thigh. Then he falls asleep with me as his pillow, long sighs escaping his lips.

Despite these short stolen hours, I miss him. It's terrifying to feel as much as I do for him. I'm barreling down to an epic love story that's doomed to end, and I'm helpless at stopping myself.

In fact, I'm eagerly doing more. Including little things I know will put a smile on his face, like brunch food in the middle of the day. He's leaving in a few hours. There's no reason why I can't make his favorite meal when it's too late for lunch but too early for dinner.

That's why I march down the sidewalk, trotting back to the condo after a shopping trip. I carry a few brown bags in my arms, full of his favorite food. I have about an hour to cook before he comes home, we eat, and he leaves for curfew. If I time this right, he'll go to San José with a grin on his face.

The smile I had of my own weakens— one of the paper bags breaks right as I take a step up the stairs to his building. Three oranges roll away, and the berries I just bought crash on the floor. The eggs remain close to my chest, luckily, shielded by an arm and a box of cornmeal. I'm making my own version of chocolate con queso, and I'm not sure where the chocolate is.

My cheeks warm up but I return to the curb and start picking things up. I get the berries but a few things are missing. The chocolate is still MIA, as is another orange. I get up and search around me. The single fruit magically appears in my field of vision.

"I think you're missing this," Aidan says.

I freeze. Nothing moves, except for my eyes. I'm stiff, but Aidan isn't. He's relaxed, standing in one of his signature casual poses.

A small smile tilts his lips. "Hi, Ames."

"What are you doing here?" I manage.

"Helping you pick up the mess, it seems."

"Don't try to be funny. It's not welcome."

"Alright, alright." He lifts his hands in an innocent gesture.

There's an orange in one large palm, and the chocolate container in the other.

"What are you doing here?" I demand.

I can barely hold the things I carry in my arms. I cling to them like they're lifesavers.

"I think you have my music book." The smile on his lips intensifies. "The one where I wrote my album and some of my poetry."

"Bullshit."

He shakes his head and drops his hands. "I bet it's still inside the piano bench."

Shock dissipates, to be replaced by the clear punch his presence knocks into my stomach.

"Have you ever lifted the cushion?" He gives me a smug look. "It has a small storage space there."

I purse my lips. It's a gesture I know well, but used to think was endlessly cute. I'm fully annoyed now. Especially because I didn't know that the bench had a small storage box.

"That's the last place I saw my things," he adds. "I promise. They're not anywhere else. You have to believe me."

"Why not text me?" I frown. "I could have left it with the concierge."

"And who would have helped you take these things up to the condo?" He shakes the ingredients he's holding hostage.

"What did I say about trying to be funny?" I pretend I'm going to walk past him and leave him with my food.

He can keep them prisoner. I'll make do with what I have.

"Ames— no. Please. Wait a second."

I don't know what stops me. I don't turn around.

"Look," he says. "That book is important to me, and I thought you maybe had me blocked. I know I made you angry enough to deserve it."

I turn. "So you came here and fancied yourself on a stakeout?"

"Tell me everything you still need to say to me, yeah? You can mutter to yourself all the way up the elevator, like you used to do when we were together. Remember?"

"You're not going upstairs with me."

"But— Have you heard the song I wrote for you? The radio version. I could play it for you up on the piano—"

I scoff. "No and no—"

"Listen." He takes his phone out and, before I know what's happening, a song plays between us.

The piano notes— those he composed in my abuela's keys. I remember them like a distant memory. The kind that's as solid as a cloud, and just as hard to grab a hold of.

I don't want to grab it, but it grabs *me*. It surrounds me and I'm forced to breathe it in. It imbues me with those feelings I used to have, when I thought all I had to do was push for it and bend for him and we'd be happy.

Ever since his album was released, I've avoided this song. Both in my mind or the radio, I've not allowed it near me. Now it's slow dancing in my ears, and stomping on my heart.

*Love, dry your tears*
*We're settled*
*It's settled*

I gave myself into loving someone I didn't truly love, and who couldn't love me the way I needed. Not with the respect and generosity I gave.

My shoulders come up into my ears. I'm hypertense, holding back my tears, hoping my body will shield me from all of this if I pull myself in harder. The song keeps playing, but I'm not following the lyrics anymore.

It's terrifying to think I would have kept going, oblivious, making myself believe I was with the right person. If he hadn't cheated, I would still be telling myself I had found my happily ever after. But the cheating was a symptom of how bad things were.

Should I thank him for freeing me? Never. There were better ways to realize the mess I was in.

But I still want to learn from it.

"Why did you cheat, Aidan?" I cling to the bags in my arms.

"I regret it," he says. "Everyday. I've been dating and I hate it. I miss you—"

"Stop. Don't. That's not an answer. You've never told me why you did it. That's the only reason I'm still here."

"You have to miss me too. That's why you want to know, right? I didn't mean to break your heart. I was immature and selfish..."

"I do not miss you, Aidan. I want to know why you did it so I can— I don't know. Prevent it next time. Do my part. Do better than you next time. A time when it's *not* with you. And you keep on not answering!"

"I was lonely, okay? We were busy and in a rut and we didn't— you disappeared on me. I didn't know what to do."

"Are you kidding me? I did everything to make you happy. If you were lonely, you should have told me. What does it mean, I disappeared on you?"

"We were so happy when we met. We wanted the same things, right? Or so you said. But the longer we were together, the harder it was to believe. You stopped having opinions. You never asked for anything. Did you even need me? Fuck, day in and day out, we went through the motions, but you were never there. I couldn't find you. I thought you were going to look for someone else and not even tell me."

"So you did it first? How childish! What about fucking talking to me?!"

"Alright, yeah, I went about it wrong. But we're talking now, aren't we, love? We can come back from this. I don't even care that you've done who knows what with Saint—"

"Don't you dare."

I try to take a step away but he stops me with a hand on my arm. I pull away, but it's too late. He's already talking.

"You're going to regret not listening to me. Whatever you've done with him, it will end right here with you outside of his building again. Did you think I wouldn't realize you jumped into his arms? You moved in with him like you did with me. You're changing to be more like him— jumping from one relationship to the next like he does. Even faster than before. Because he chased you, didn't he? And now you're into sports? Don't make me laugh."

"You have no idea what you're talking about."

"I saw those clips of you at the stadium. Wearing his jersey. Please. You've never had a jersey in your life. Now I bet you're watching his games and tracking points. You told me you hated sports. But he's an athlete, so of course now you're into American Football, too. Because he is."

That shuts me up. I have been engaging with sports a whole lot more. For Saint.

"The way he flirted with you in the club— and the way you let him. Like you were one of his— Shit. He flirted with you every second of that bloody TV show," he adds. "Now you're not happy to have your catering business anymore. Did he suggest the TV show? Is that why you're doing that? Maybe when you said you were happy with your small business that was another lie you told yourself. Maybe it's only what you thought I wanted to hear. Now you're doing what you think he wants."

"That's not..." I manage.

But it is. He's talking about how I lost myself in relationships.

He keeps on going, my feelings invisible to him. "I bet he loves oranges, too. You're making his favorite food, I just know it."

It's such a petty, ridiculous accusation, but I flinch. Because it's true.

I don't know what to do with that, but I know I will not let him see how he's affected me.

"Feeling better now?" I find balance where there's none, and I steal the chocolate from his hand without dropping anything. "Did you finally say everything you wanted to say?"

"No. I'm sorry. I'm angry and venting, but I really don't mind what you've done with him—"

"You're making a spectacle, Aidan."

He stops.

"You ruined what we had. If you had told me we had a problem, we could have done something about it. Back then, I would have. Not now. You're four years too late to be who I needed."

"You're not going to give me another chance?"

"No. We've been over since the moment I caught you. You have to hear it, this time. Don't show up again."

"Do you love him?"

It's my turn to halt.

I think I might. If not, I'm just a few steps away from falling for him.

I haven't felt like this in... ever.

I feel more than I thought possible.

But I'm not telling Aidan that.

I try to leave, but he follows.

"Ames. Come on. You know you're just going to make the same mistakes with Saint. You're walking right into a new thing without figuring out who you need to be."

I face him again. "How dare you point the finger at me like that? *Who I need to be?* What about who *you* needed to be? What about what you should have done differently?"

"We'll talk it out. Please, love."

"Do not call me love. We will not figure it out. I made mistakes, but that's as true as how wrong you were for me. I just never realized until you showed me."

"I fucked up," he admits. "I'm sorry."

"You did. I hope you are sorry. Maybe you'll learn a thing or two from how things happened between us. I am sure as hell trying to learn my part."

"Fuck." He shakes his head. "This can't be the end."

"It is. We've been done for a long time, but what you did shot a hundred extra bullets into what was left of our relationship. You showing up here like this? It's just the last one."

He closes his eyes, pain marring his brow.

"Bye, Aidan."

I don't wait to see how he reacts, but his final nod puts an end to us.

My head held high, I go up the stairs to the entry hall and into the elevator. As soon as I enter the condo, my eyes fill with tears.

I leave the food on the kitchen island in a heap. My heart is in my throat. Without a conscious decision, I make for the piano. Aidan was probably lying, but I check the bench anyway. I pull at one edge of the seating cushion and it opens on its hinges.

The booklet is there. It's blue like his eyes, with nothing written on the front. It's worn, and memories of him writing on it come up until my eyes blur. I sit on my knees and flip through it. The song he wrote is there, right in the middle. The bridge enrages me all over again. Settled, my ass.

We weren't settled. I settled.

I don't know what to make of Aidan and his excuse. Loneliness is a word I didn't know I could use for what he and I had, but it fits. Being with the wrong person leaves you alone.

I deflate. Knowing why he did it doesn't fix anything. It doesn't explain where he and I failed. How I didn't realize that the rhythm we had was really a rut, or why he chose to betray my trust instead of fucking talking to me and telling me he wasn't happy. Beyond being a self-centered, egotistical coward, that is.

It doesn't explain how I didn't realize I was changing myself to be right for him.

Worse, I may be doing the same with Saint. Am I?

I throw the booklet into its house in the bench and close the lid on top. It's easy to let myself crumble on top of it. With my arms for a pillow, I cry.

Tears stream down my face. They wet my arms. It's the last time I weep because of Aidan, but it's not because of his cheating. It's a release of the unresolved pieces I still carried inside. I'm forced to see the thoughts and feelings pass me by. They're threads out of my mind, heart, and soul, showing me where we were, and how far I am from that these days. They entwine into a braid of hopes I used to carry with me, when I believed I had found a way to make things work no matter what. When I thought I had cracked the code and outdone my parents in one fell swoop.

Now I don't believe either.

Fuck. Could Aidan have a point? I have done things for Saint I had never done before. I found ways to be into football. His favorite foods are the real staple of the home and our cooking. Hell, they're in a small mountain on the kitchen island right now. All my friends are his friends. My clients are his teammates. The TV show is in the works thanks to what he did.

I'm afraid I'm repeating the patterns even when I told myself I wouldn't.

Failure is everywhere. Everything I set out to do in relationships escapes me. Including what I hoped to do with Saint. I'm feeling more than I planned to, and I've changed more than I thought, and the realization adds drops of acid to my blood.

I promised it would be different this time.

It's scary.

It's a mess.

Because if this is love, then I'm in real trouble.

# Chapter 36

## Saint

The peak of my career is brighter than I thought. I'm building to the biggest game in the sport. I'm busier than I've ever been, going for gold with training and the media. Cortisol runs in my veins, pushing me to go harder, making me fly through this time so I can land in Ames' arms at the end of it.

I've never been closer to my dreams than I am right now. That's why I smile as I ride the elevator to the condo. My heart drums against my breastbone, because while the quick meal Ames promised me is a brief goodbye, I know what awaits me on the other side.

When I come back from San José and she comes back from LA, our schedules will open up for a short while. I'll make the most of that time. I'll ask her on a date and make it special. Words I haven't chosen yet will ask her to give me a chance. If she wants to, she'll take my hand. I'll hold on to it, and never let go.

I grin just thinking about it.

The door closes behind me with an energetic click. "Honey, I'm hooooome."

I expect laughter. Maybe some music in the air. Instead, there's only silence.

I stop in my tracks. My smile cools down. I scan the condo from my spot in the entrance, searching for clues. All is still, almost with a museum quality to it, except for the piano bench. It's open, for some reason. I didn't know it did that.

"Saint?"

Ames' voice comes from the kitchen, hidden around the corner.

I find her behind the island. The line of her shoulders pulls down, weighed by invisible anchors. Her brow wrinkles. Her lids are red.

She hasn't looked like this in weeks.

I take a few steps to her and jolt to a stop. "What happened?"

She blinks a few times, like she's trying to make up her mind.

"Ames. Please. Something happened. Tell me what it is so I can make it better."

"But you have to leave soon, and I don't want to wreck your concentration. And the food— it's going to go cold—"

I briefly glance behind her. A beautiful spread waits on the counter.

The way my stomach twists, I don't think I can do the meal justice.

"What's going on?" I insist.

I don't move, beyond grabbing the edge of the stool in front of me.

Ames shakes her head. "It should wait. We can talk after."

"Please. Nothing is more important than finding out why you look like you've been crying."

She holds herself up with hands firmly planted on the counter stone. My knuckles go white.

She sighs. "Aidan showed up outside of the building a while ago."

"What?!"

Sudden anger resounds in my voice. Buzzing fills my ears and power bolts through my limbs, as if I have to fight a wild animal. It's the rage that Aidan could wreck our bliss once more, and the sudden urge to protect Ames from whatever he caused her.

She shakes her head. "He wanted the notebook where he wrote his songs and a few poems. He left it inside the piano bench."

294

She makes a small gesture to the instrument behind me.

I keep my eyes on her. "Did you burn it and tell him to go to hell?"

She smirks. "No. I got some anger out and told him to get lost. Again."

"So... we get to burn the notebook together when I'm back?"

"Undecided, but you tempt me."

I purse my lips. Clench my jaw. He probably planned the whole thing. I can see it— Aidan leaving the notebook in the bench, biding his time. He didn't seem to believe Ames the first time... or the second time. This gave him one last chance.

Not what matters now.

"Are you okay?" is all I ask.

She nods. "I'll be okay. It just got me thinking."

Anger turns into fear. My stomach turns once more.

"What's going on?" I ask. "Talk to me."

"This time with you has been great in so many ways..."

Something inside me cracks. I sit on an island stool. Things are caving in.

"It's been so good, in fact," she continues, "that I'm forgetting we were meant to end it soon."

I'm too worried to feel happy.

"Maybe..." I lick my bottom lip. "Maybe that's a good thing."

"Is it, though? Our casual deadline isn't too far away. How long can we do this before things get too conf— complicated?"

"Infinite. We'll uncomplicate it."

I never understood the idea of forever until it took root in my heart. Until I got her out of her room and into mine. Now it escapes my lips and it's easy. I want it more than ever.

"It doesn't have to be complicated or confusing," I add. "We can make it what we want."

"What do we want? Saint, I'm afraid what we have is a relationship and not a rebound thing."

My heart beats fast. My lungs only pull shallow pants. Everything blurs but Ames standing still across the kitchen island.

"Is that so bad?" I ask.

"We didn't mean to make it into a relationship but we fell into it anyway. It's too soon. I don't want to make the same mistakes."

"Then we... don't. We keep each other in check. Whatever mistakes you think we might make. We'll tackle them."

"Are you trying to tell me you're okay with this?"

I had never had tunnel vision like this before. It makes everything look like crystal. Things look so fragile, I hesitate.

Her brow pulls up high in the center. Wrinkles draw lines on her forehead. Her shoulders pull up.

She expects a no.

I'm not ready to tell her everything and do it right. It has to be okay. I'll have to find my way in the dark.

"Yes, Ames. More than okay. I was going to wait until I was back. Until our deadline, so we had time—"

"What?"

"I was going to ask you to go on a date with me. A real one. The kind where we talk about us and the future and I was going to..."

Something in her face stops me.

"Why?" she asks.

I keep my movements slow, lest I spook her. Rounding the island, I come close to her.

She lifts her eyes up at me. I give her a tenuous smile.

"Why do you think?"

I say it like it's obvious. It hangs in the air with finality.

She studies me, mouth opening bit by bit. Her gasp comes after.

"But—" she stalls. "But we said... and you never... you're not looking for the same... thing..."

"Ames..."

"I relied on you being strong!"

"Was I weak for falling for you all those years ago? This time around, all over again, despite telling you this would be temporary? Maybe. But to me it feels like I've never been more invincible. I've always felt this way for you, Ames. From the moment I met you. I felt something I knew was different, and important, and it scared me. Even then, I tried to do something about it, but I didn't figure out the full truth until you showed up at my door, and I couldn't help my heart."

"The truth?"

"There's no way to test myself or have a guaranteed future but, if I'm going to try with anyone, I want it to be you."

"Oh, God."

"I can't think of anyone else. I don't want anyone else. Have you wondered why I stopped dating as soon as you made it through that door? Now ask why it was so easy, and I'll tell you it's because there's never been anyone else but you."

She covers her mouth with both of her shaky hands. Tears fill her wide-open eyes.

I take one last step toward her.

She speaks through her fingers. "Wanting isn't enough. If it was, I would still be with every ex. I wanted each one of those relationships to last. It wasn't enough."

"But did they want the same thing? If Aidan wanted it, he had a terrible way of showing it."

"The way he keeps— kept trying to get me to give him another chance means he did. He wanted to, and he screwed up. Can we be any better than that? I can't lose you if we wreck this. I still don't know how to make things work—"

"Fuck yes, we can be better. I'll promise it to you. Right here. I will not give up on us. I'll keep showing up and asking you what's wrong, then fixing it. And I'll tell you when I'm struggling, so you can do the same with me."

"It can't be that simple." A tear falls down her face.

I cradle her face and dry the tear with my thumb. The drumming in my chest is insistent, hammering so hard against my breastbone it's at risk of breaking.

"But it is, Ames. It has to be. We can make it be that simple for us. If you feel like I do, then we'll have a million good weeks, like we've had since I told you I'd be your rebound. Hell, since you came to me when you were hurting. I just need you to want the same thing. I crave you to want the same thing. To want me like that."

"Saint..."

"I want you to go for love with me. For your— our— happily ever after. There will be rough times. I want you to get angry with me when I mess up. And I still want you to come to me every time you need something. Give me your every doubt. All the love in your heart. Of course I'll get angry at you at times. Other times I'll ask for a lot, just like I am right now. But we'll do it together."

"I don't know." More tears overflow. "What if I'm not what you need? Because this isn't— I'm not me. I have not fully found myself yet. And what if I end up bending myself backwards? I didn't even realize how much I've done... and if that's not how you make a relationship work, then I have no idea how to... how to..."

"Then let's not know together." I bring my forehead to hers. "Let us figure it out together, bella."

"We should be scared."

"I'm terrified. Who knows what waits for us."

"Then, what? What if you get traded? How do we figure this out long distance? When we're lonely and all we have are texts. Will you feel the same way?"

"I will."

She shakes her head. "You can't know that."

"But I do. You deserve to be loved exactly how you want. And I want to love you that way. That's not going to stop if I'm away. All I need is that you want the same thing."

She doesn't answer.

I frown. "I was going to tell you how I feel after the game. I hoped I'd find a romantic way to show you what's in my heart. I thought I could tell you something... I don't know. Something that would convince you. I guess blurting it all out will have to do."

"I have to think."

"Can you feel, too? Thoughts can get so tangled up. But I'll trust what's in your heart every time."

She stares at me. Motionless. Big beautiful brown eyes, with reddened lids and blushing cheeks.

"If you feel half the things I feel," I add, "you'll want to try with me. And if you don't..."

She nods.

"You know," I whisper, "I used to think I couldn't ask you to do this with me. That it would be unfair, because I couldn't promise I wouldn't hurt you. I thought it made me selfish to ask for more. Then I realized that no one can make that promise. We all walk into the maze hoping we will find our way out. All I can ask is if you'll hold my hand so we can walk through the twists and turns of life together. That's what you need to decide, mi divina."

Her eyes close in a renewed gesture of pain. More tears fall down her face.

"I'll give you time." I kiss her forehead, then each wet cheek.

I step away.

"What do you mean?" she asks in a thin voice.

"It works out, if you think about it. We both have to be in different places in the next little while. I'd rather do this with you. Keep talking and working through it but, since we will be apart... maybe it's what you need to make up your mind."

"Saint." She shakes her head and looks down to the floor.

I check my watch. "I can grab some food on the way to the Thunderdome. I'll get a few points with Coach Clark if I'm there early."

"Right. Yeah. I'm sorry. I know..."

"Don't apologize."

"I was going to give you food. We were going to have a nice meal."

"We'll have a chance when we're back. We can talk again. We'll know if I have to leave. You'll know about your show."

"What if I'm not meant to figure this out alone?"

"We're not meant to do it alone. Until we're back together, talk to your friends. Tell them everything. I'm not embarrassed."

"I'm going to give it my all, Gael."

"Then maybe this is another shred of proof I can give you. Let's get through this. I'm not going to give up just because of this... discussion. Or because we'll be apart for a bit. What matters is we'll come together again to give it another go."

"And if all I want is friendship?"

"Then I'll love you as a friend. Don't you know?"

# Chapter 37

## Saint

San José is a whirlwind of media, training, and mental preparation. I'm the player I need to be. The entertainer people expect.

No one sees the ache warping my breastbone. The way it stretches my chest in all the wrong places, until my skin feels taut around my body and a little too thin.

When I offered myself as a rebound, we agreed we'd break up. For years I told myself it had to be that way with everyone, including Ames. That I didn't know how to do anything else. I seared the belief into my brain, that I shouldn't be so selfish I'd be willing to hurt people.

Now Ames and I are the closest we could be to ending things... without having ended them. It hurts like a motherfucker.

I answer every reporter's questions while keeping my feelings contained. I smile even if it doesn't reach my eyes. When I'm eating a meal with my friends, I chat with them even as the food turns to chalk on my tongue.

She could say no.

She could say she won't let anything else matter, and choose the future we can't see. Just because it's with me.

I've worked to this point in my career for fifteen years, but this is it. This could be the start of the most important journey of my life. Or the end, before it even began.

# Chapter 38

## Ames

I'm in LA. For nearly three days, I've had meetings where I smile while my heart drowns. I've been as charming and smart as I can manage, when all I want to do is get in bed and forget about the world.

I crawl back to my hotel after another long day, only to climb into bed and cover myself with the duvet. It's starting to get dark outside and I haven't turned on any lights. A good fort-like feeling is precisely what I want.

Maybe it's more like a cave. It seems like the ideal place to hide and push away the embarrassment. The one born from how I keep messing up.

I didn't handle the conversation with Saint as well as I should have. Part of that was the shock of his words, when I was so sure he didn't feel half of it. Part of that was worrying that I feel too much to see things clearly. Part of that was the fumes of the fight with Aidan. Regardless, I didn't carry my share of the conversation.

Saint deserves better than that. Especially since I care about him so much.

I hug myself under the covers. My stomach rumbles, but I ignore it. Again, Saint gave me all the power. It's on me to choose what happens to us in the future.

In the past, I dreamt of this kind of agency. Now that I have it, it's too much responsibility.

My roommate-could-be-boyfriend and I haven't talked much since he left for San José. The ceremony for MVP was on Thursday. He won. Of course he did. He received the award while I was having dinner with my agent.

Pride washed over me for him. Relief flooded my chest, because it got him one step closer to his goal. Still, I hesitated to reach out. It took me a couple of hours to break, but eventually I did.

> **Ames**: Congratulations. So close now

> **Saint**: Thank you. Yeah, it's good news.

> **Ames**: Are you okay?

> **Saint**: I have been better, but I'm trying to focus on the game on Sunday. You?

> **Ames**: Same, but trying to focus on my meetings.

> **Saint**: Good luck to us both.

> **Ames**: I miss you. I promise I'm thinking hard about us. Feeling hard, too.

> **Saint**: I miss you too. Very much. I would have loved to have you on the field with me.

That was it.

He's extra busy, and knows I am too. He said he'd give me distance, and he's keeping to his word. We're taking some time to process, and I'm doing as I promised. Yet only after a few days since we said goodbye for a bit, my heart's already on a strike and working at half capacity. It refuses to carry on as usual, because I miss him. Oh, how I miss him. But I didn't show him how much I actually feel for him.

Every missing beat digs a little deeper into my chest, because something fundamental is missing when we're not in sync.

I shake my head at myself and push the covers down to my waist. I turn the TV on. The voices and sounds fill in the space enough for a little while. If I pick a sports channel and they talk about football, that can only help get me a little bit closer to Saint somehow. Yeah, it means I will still be submerged in a world I never planned to be in, but it's the only way to have a little bit more of him.

I settle on some sort of pre-game show. I leave it on, while I get on my phone to look up news about Saint on social media. I get lost in new clips and edits his fans have made of him.

There's an edit of different clips of him dancing on the field, made to match the beat of a popular song. A few others focus on his answers to reporters, and his professional career. Another one collects several shots of him smiling at the camera, fans, and players. The description on that one simply read, *DIMPLES*.

I sigh. My heartbeats echo the efforts of an old steam engine, burning through coal harder than it shows, all to push things into motion. They may seem slow, but there's depth to them. An incredible amount of energy is being put into it.

Missing him means I care about him. It shows me how much I want him in my life. How I want him to hold me close as we talk through this time in our relationship. I would cling to him, so we never have to do this apart again. All I need is a little push and I'll be the one begging, asking him to convince me it's not too soon, that we're going to make it, and we're never going to give up on each other.

I'm not processing anything that shows up on my phone screen anymore. I throw the device on the bed and stare at the TV.

I've been talking to my friends. I haven't shared every single detail, but they didn't need the particulars to support me through this. They were appropriately excited when I told them things had happened between Saint and I, and indignant when they heard Aidan had visited one last time.

> **Pen**: would you have responded the same way to Saint if Aidan hadn't shown up?

I still don't know the answer to that. The most likely turn of events if Aidan hadn't shown up, is that I would still be alone in my hotel while Saint prepared for his game. I wouldn't know how he feels, but my own feelings might have had me thinking of forever with him. At least I'd be happier, because we wouldn't have left it the way we did.

*We'll wait and talk again.*

Ugh. I should at least have kissed him.

Or maybe not? Do I want to hold his hand and walk into the maze with him? Yeah. I just don't know if it's the right thing to do. It may not be the best for us. Going unprepared may wreck everything.

None of that matters, the moment his face fills the TV screen.

They show a clip of him where someone asks him about the award. I press pause on everything else, especially my torn emotions. All I care about is getting this small piece of him.

He wears a bold shirt with a few open buttons. The design is some sort of paint splattering that resembles animal print. In shades of cream, sage, and golden hues, it shows off the deep bronze of his skin. With his earring shining and his hair nicely done, the smile curling his lips looks stunning.

I would be stunned, for sure, if it weren't for the hint of sadness in his eyes.

"You went from a few seasons where you never made it to the playoffs," a reporter asks, "to making it to the big game in just two years. How are you handling it?"

"I'm handling it like a pro, what can I say?" He grins and those sweet dimples show up again.

His chain peeks through the open panels of his shirt. Those times I actually bit the metal links come back to me, or when I pulled him from it and he so willingly followed instructions.

Desire pools so swiftly, I can't deny just how deeply into him I am. Not that I'm trying, anymore. If nothing else, lust is clear. The way we fit in sex and intimacy is immaculate. That part has never been an issue. What I need to define is if what our hearts bring to the picture is the right thing for us.

People laugh around him on the TV. His diamond earring glints at the lights shining on him.

"I've trained for this my whole life." His hand lands on his chest, like he's speaking from the heart. "I've worked for this. The changes we made when Logan came to the team have set us up for this. We're the team we need to be. We'll do this again and again. For us and for the fans. As long as we're together, we can keep the Strike on top."

I smile. He's hinting at wanting to stay, without revealing much.

The main reporter nods. "And now you got the league's MVP for the season. It usually goes to QBs but you've had such a great season. You broke those records, including most receiving yards. It's like you could read King's mind—"

"Exactly." Saint nods and makes a gesture like asking for more praise. "Keep going."

He gets more laughter at that.

His eyes still hold dejection, but he has them all in a trance. He plays the game. They fall for it. No one sees what I see.

My throat gets a little tight. I happen to know how much he likes to be told he's good. I want to tell him how good he is more than anyone. And I want to hold him and tell him he doesn't have to feel despondent anymore.

The interviewer responds to Saint's smile with one of his own. "How did you overcome those dry years to get here in only two seasons?"

"Like with everything else." Saint taps his chest, deep in thought. "Anything you want to excel at, you need to work hard to get it. Find the discipline to get through the days when you can't imagine you can keep going. Doing the hard things you know will get you closer to what you've committed to."

His words scratch my mind. I sit up on the bed.

"That's a whole lot of motivation," the reporter comments.

Saint nods. "It's easy when you know why you're doing it."

"Why do you do it?"

"Why else?" He taps his chest. "Love. Isn't that always the answer?"

Tap tap. Tap tap. Tap tap.

"For the love of success?" the interviewer asks. "Of the sport?"

"All of it. Anything you love, it's worth giving your whole effort to. And I love this game. My team. The life I want deserves this kind of commitment. I'll give it my all for as long as I'm here."

Tap tap. Tap tap. Tap tap.

I gasp. The covers end up all the way to the bottom of the mattress. I sit on my knees right there on the bed. To anyone else, the way he drums on his chest could seem like an unconscious move, the kind that shows he's thinking hard.

I know better. I remember.

The rest of the interview goes ignored. I check my text chain with him. It takes several swipes, but I go back far enough to find the right message. The one where he told me that would be his sign to show his love.

I go back to videos I found of him on social media. In a few of them, he does the same gesture. Every time, he's talking about getting through the hard times by putting effort in.

Warmth imbues my face. I tear up.

He's been sending me messages. Not by text. By his sign. The one he told me about when I asked a few weeks ago.

The bed turns into a prison. I pace the room, seeking the space to process, looking for some extra air.

When I was old enough to think about romance, I told myself I would be different from my parents. I said I would work hard at relationships, because fixing them can be the bravest thing. The part I got wrong was thinking that meant I needed to bend myself into whatever shapes my partner needed from me.

Even back when I discovered Aidan's cheating and parachuted to Saint's condo, I wondered what true love felt like. What it looks like. Once upon a time, I thought I'd find it with artists. Someone creative would be in touch with their feelings, right? I would get to feel *with* them. They would have the emotional intelligence to talk about the important things in love, too. Art and love are the same at their core. They birth connection. Among people and us and life. Someone in touch with that would surely crave life-long love, right?

Wrong. I found it in an athlete who opened his heart to me and asked me to do the same. What I sought came in a different package than I expected, that's all.

I thought what I had with Aidan is what people call love. It felt good enough to be comfortable. Peaceful. I could see myself living that life until my last day. What I feel for Saint is... *fire*, compared to that.

I'm in the hotel bathroom, unaware of how I made it here. I sit on the edge of the tub. Elbows on the stone counter in front of me, I hold my head. Puzzle pieces are all up in the air, but I can see them clearly now. I pick each oddly-shaped cutout and re-arrange them to find a whole new landscape.

I met my new friends thanks to Saint, but they're my friends because I opened up to them. I'm in LA because the producer believes in me, or he wouldn't have offered a show without a mention of Saint being there as well. I follow football because it's Saint's world, but he's in my world as well. If our territories overlap, it's because we're living life together. We're more than the sum of our parts. We push each other to grow in our own right.

Now things with Saint aren't really broken, they're being... adjusted. And we're fixing it anyway. He's being clear about what he wants. He wants to discover who he'll be with me, and asks me to do the same. He said these few days could be proof of what he does when things get hard. He said he wouldn't give up.

What a show of his commitment to this with me. We're not at our best, and we're making a huge decision about our future. But we're not broken up. We're not each going our own direction. We're working through it.

Saint is showing me what he does when things get hard. He's fixing everything he didn't break, and he wants to do it with me.

I stare at myself in the mirror. My hair is wild, and my makeup mostly in place. A small black patch smears a corner of my eye, and my foundation doesn't fully hide my blush. The bright ceiling light puts heavy shadows under my eyes. Clicking the lights on immediately turns on the fan, and its burr fills the space.

Caught without warning, someone might think I'm forlorn. It couldn't be further from the truth. I straighten up. Lift my chin until all shadows disappear. Square my shoulders.

I finally know the truth. What's happening with Saint is right.

The conversation, the challenge, the process makes it right. That's why this is different from any relationship I've had before. He's in this *with* me. It's not a take it or leave it situation, where I'm the one bending backwards without help or compromise. He's not here because he likes me enough to stick around. He sticks around because he cares about me and it makes him want to work through things when we need to.

Mind blown.

In the past, I went above and beyond thinking it would do the trick and make things work. I took responsibility for things that didn't belong to me. But compromise is only fair if it's mutual.

All I have to do is be myself and meet him halfway. Doing hard things for each other, back and forth, to build something good side by side.

*Hold my hand so we can walk through the twists and turns of life together,* he said.

We will both lead the way.

I will show him. Go into the maze and find him, and hold his hand so tight he knows I will never let him go.

**Ames**: Hi friends. I need help.

**Pen**: Whatever you need

**Ames**: I need to go to San José tomorrow. Can someone sneak me into the stadium somehow?

**Evie**: this is my time to shine

# Chapter 39

## Saint

When I discovered this sport all those years ago, my first dream was one day making it to this game. Still lanky, back then, but fast. I put my everything into making this my career.

I take a step. Another, and another, until I'm sprinting out of the tunnel and onto the field. Smoke screens and cold spark machines remind me how important this all is. The roar of the fans engulfs me. I let it all wash over me, but there's a corner inside they can't reach.

I'm split, because she's not here. Her absence is a torn muscle right in the middle of my chest.

My grin is in place as I do a couple of salsa moves, alone on the turf and wearing my uniform. I let my need for her bring out my dimples. There's so much joy inside when I think of her. Pain, too, but I welcome everything. Anything to do with Ames is to be carried with me as I play one of the most important games in my career.

No matter what happens next, I don't think that's ever going to change.

———

Two decades. Practically two thirds of my life. They have built to this.

With my parents, my sisters, and my friend watching. With my teammates' guests, and millions of people glued to everything we do here on the field. There's so much adrenaline in my veins, everything happens in slow motion.

I know what play we're going to try next. Logan doesn't look at me as he sets up. If he did, it might give something away.

It doesn't matter. I know how to read his mind.

I take my position. I wait for the signs. Logan starts the drive, and I stop thinking. I am all heart, all motion. No more than fragmented pieces of awareness.

Running. The smell of clean sweat and torn grass. I evade two guys. My position— locked. I find the ball up in the air. Quick— check for defensive players. Outmaneuver them.

Leather at my fingertips. The comforting shape of the ball against my ribs.

Fuck. Yes. Caught it.

I explode into a sprint. I'm forced to run in a diagonal to avoid the men wearing the wrong colors. It lengthens the distance, but that's okay. I'll endure. I have the stamina.

The rush of hormones in my veins. The kick of fire in my muscles. The way my lungs expand and contract in a measured, steady rhythm. My body is a finely-tuned machine bringing me closer and closer to the end zone.

In just a few seconds, I'll cross the goal line. The crowd's clamor booms and rumbles. I smile. No one can stop me now. The cool air on my face welcomes me as I dive into another touchdown.

I roll on the grass like a well-trained acrobat, ending on my feet. The ball still in my hand, I lift both arms up to the sky and scream at the top of my lungs. My teammates reach me and jostle me hard enough I could lose my balance. I don't. Instead, I spike the ball and laugh. Dom joins me, and we twist and turn in place with a brand new dance move.

We're in the biggest game of our careers. I just scored the Strike's third touch-down.

It may be the high of our near win, but certainty fills me like never before. Asking Ames to take my hand was right. The promises I made to her were the ones I had to make. Opening my heart and admitting I don't know what will come our way, but I want to find out with her by my side... that's what makes me relationship material. For her. It makes me right for her, if she'll have me.

I can only hope she sees it the same way.

# Chapter 40

## Ames

I'm stuck in standstill traffic in a rented car. I don't know if there was an accident or if this should be expected within a certain radius from the stadium. Regardless, I hate it.

A rock sits squarely on my chest, making it hard to take full breaths. I cross my arms on the steering wheel and lean on it, but I end up pushing on the horn with my boobs and tummy. I jump back at the loud sound. The driver in the car next to me gets annoyed and frowns at me. They make a rude gesture with their hand and I turn away not to provoke them anymore.

I'm late. The game started long ago. While I'm listening to it on the radio and keeping track, I should be there. That was the plan. Evie would pull strings and get me inside, so I could join them in the suite. Somehow, at some point, I would show him I'm there. Saint said he would have wanted me on the field, so I would try to surprise him there. I'm trying not to think about what happens if they lose. I'd still kiss him, and I would still tell him I'm all in, but I would hug him through everything and hold him a lot more.

The way the radio just celebrated Saint's touchdown for the Strike, that's not a fear I have to concern myself with at the moment. My one worry continues to be how the hell I'm going to make it to the suite in time.

The cars move a bit, but not enough. I clench my jaw. Shake my head.

With the car stuck immobile for a few minutes and still so far away, I brave breaking the law and I get on my phone.

**Evie**: where are you? We're just about to get to the half-time show

**Ames**: I'm trapped half an hour away by car. Twenty fucking miles. I can't walk that in time, but I'm about to try. Better than traffic that doesn't move

**Pen**: Park the car somewhere. Try transit

**Ames**: I'm doing it.

The map shows I'm close to a highway exit. Some time later, I drive out to a busy, but moving road. I follow GPS directions to a transit stop.

It takes me nearly two hours to get to the stadium. I'm running. My heart hammers against my breastbone. Blood rushes in my ears, and my thoughts are a little cloudy with anxiety, but I make it to the right door. As per Evie's instructions, I show my phone to a guard. He lets me in.

Bass fills the air. They carry tremors I can only feel in my chest. A roar builds around me, heavy with anticipation. I'm trying to follow the map Evie shared of the stadium but it's not accurate— or I'm too overwhelmed to follow directions.

I get the notification as I'm typing a text.

The Strike wins.

The whole building trembles. Sound travels through metal backbones and concrete pillars. In my dazed state, I wonder if this is being registered as a small earthquake somewhere.

I choke up and die a little inside, because I missed it. Stress wants to escape through a scream and I can't let it. All I would manage is to beg someone to give me more time, but I've run out. People appear from every corner, flooding the small corridors in this section of the building.

My phone shoots several texts at me in quick succession.

**Nat**: Where are you?!

**Evie**: We're going to the field! Come find us. Do you want us to tell Saint?

**Pen**: If you don't make it on time, Bear and I will kidnap Saint to wait for you

I could cry, but it won't do me any good. I need to find my way to Saint and my friends.

**Ames**: I'm trying to get to the field

The map still makes no sense to me, but I try to follow it. Changes must have been made, but I can't keep track when hundreds of people keep going in different directions. Guards direct the chaos, and I'm forced to move with a specific group toward a large concrete arch.

Sunlight and flashing lights mix as I reach the sitting area. I'm in the lowest level, the one closest to the field... but not on the field.

*Fuck, fuck, fuck.*

I elbow my way to the fence. A different hundred people fill the field. Blue and silver explode from the sky. Cameras mill about, catching on all the happy faces and hugs and excited voices. Those around me on the grandstand cheer and jump and laugh, joining in the fun from our place away from the team and their people.

I don't let it deter me. Amir is one of my new clients and a defensive player, and he's close enough I might get his attention. He's hugging people, screaming, excited, and giving me his profile.

319

"Amir!" I yell. "Hey! Amir! Please!"

Admins and coaches nearby ignore me when I switch to calling on them.

"Hey! I need to go to Saint! Please!" Not having a response, I switch to my client again. "Amir! It's me! Amelia! Your private chef is here! Fuck's sake."

I'm not loud enough in the resounding echoes of the stadium. Confetti continues to rain on everyone. Coach Clark gets the sports drink spilled over him. No one could care about an extra voice calling for them from the bleachers.

Crumbling is a real option, but I don't let myself. Gratefulness washes over me, when it means I catch sight of Dom running across.

"Dom!" My voice is turning raspy from screaming, but I force it out as loud as I can. "You have to hear me! Dom! It's Ames!"

His head snaps my way. "Ames?"

Relief bursts deep in my stomach. I can barely hear my name out of his mouth, but he's staring firmly at me.

"Saint!" I call. "I want to get to Saint!"

He glances at the field, then back at me. Calculations run through his head as he assesses the people between us. All around us.

He points at me with one hand. With the other he tells me to hold back. Then runs away.

My heart is about to stop, but all I can do is wait. With my hands holding on to the thick metal railings for dear life, I stand and watch people part in front of Dom.

Saint stands there with his family and Pablo. My roommate-nearly-my-boyfriend kneels to hug two young people, and I hold my breath, my heart in my throat.

# Chapter 41

## Saint

I'm steps away from the peak of the world. The highest I've ever been, but not as high as I could be.

I'm on my knees, hugging my sisters. My parents stand near us. Even through the noise, I can hear my mom still sniffling in happiness. Pablo is part of the group as well. As one of my guests, he's right here with my family.

When he hugged me, he grinned big and patted me on the back. He praised me and said he knew I could do it. I couldn't say anything, because all I would have managed was to reveal how I feel about Ames.

*I'm in love with your sister. Please be okay with it. Will this make it okay?*

My sisters screech into my ear, too joyful to contain the sound. I smile and pull them closer.

My friends with their loved ones remain around us, too. In a sea of celebration, a strange undercurrent pricks at my attention. I open my eyes to see Dom running my way.

People part as my friend approaches. From the corner of my eye I see Logan holding on to Evie, his hands on her butt like there's no one else. Bear and Pen hug close, forehead to forehead, her hands around his neck in a romantic pose. He'd call me out for reading into things that way between them, but I can't spare them another thought.

I don't know what unconscious part of my brain is processing this moment. I act on instinct. I don't pay attention to Dom or anyone else— my sight seeks something past them. My eyes know where to go. Somehow, I know what I'm looking for. Who.

I find her in the crowd up on the first level of seats.

I stand.

"Saint?" Aixa says, but I can't respond to it.

I'm locked in on Ames. I start walking without realizing. I forget about Dom, my parents, or Pablo.

I'm trotting now. It turns into a sprint. I'm running to Ames.

I vaguely take note of the way she stands. Hands tight against her chest, tension on her shoulders and arms as she watches me approach. Sparkling eyes locked on mine.

It's not a decision, but an inevitable move to use the benches near the back wall to jump up the ledge. Fans scream as I hold on to the thick metal barriers for leverage. Ames closes the distance, her arms around me as I cross the thick metal rods.

For an instant or an eon, we stand in front of each other. Her hands on my shoulders, mine on her arms. I search her eyes, like I can find an explanation in them, even if I don't need the words.

I put my hands on her face, bringing her closer to me. People around us disappear. The stadium is empty. Gone from my mind, because Ames is here, and she's in my arms.

"Gael..." she manages.

I kiss her.

It's hunger. A craving for her, for this feeling. For sharing the same space again. Breathing the same air again. It's more than mouth to mouth and tongue to tongue— my whole body is in it and so is hers. My hands keep her in place, yet she's the one bringing me closer. I pour my heart into it, but it might be her bloodstream beating at my fingertips. I'm a rock and she's water shaping me through millenia, softly yet persistent, all in this instant.

She wouldn't be here if she weren't ready to be with me. She's holding on to me, kissing me with everything she has, because I'm kissing her like that too. With the intensity of this moment, we don't need words to promise forever. But I know this is the start, and it has me flying higher than when I scored the touchdown that won us the game.

The world comes back to existence in stages. It's the screams around us, the applause. The pats on my back. I fight it. I keep on kissing her for a little longer. Even when we stop, I keep my eyes closed, clinging to the feeling, searing it into my memory.

I drop my head to hers, temple to temple.

"You're here," I say.

"I have to go back to LA tonight but—"

"You're here."

"I had to be." She grabs my hand. "I get it. You're with me. I need to be with you, too. We're together. I *had* to be here."

"You will hold my hand."

"Because you're holding mine right back."

My heart. It's fuller than it's ever been, yet so light I have to wonder if her words have bent the laws of physics. Hope and yearning and trust are one and the same.

I smile. "I'm at the top of the world... because you're here with me."

"I couldn't stay away," she says. "I didn't want to be."

I kiss her again. "Take my hand and come with me, then."

# Chapter 42

## Ames

Saint climbs over the barrier again and helps me across. He jumps down to the field and helps me down to the bench first, then the grass.

I expect him to take my hand and lead me away, but he surprises me with another kiss. Another wide grin and extra glorious dimples.

Whatever anxiety I still carried inside dissipates into the air. It's mist under the noon sun. The warmth of a giant star bursts in my chest, vaporizing everything but knowing that Saint and I are in this together. Nothing else matters but this.

Happiness is too big to contain. I kiss him again. He laughs, the sound echoing my own joy. With crinkling eyes, he takes my hand and leads me to his family.

Belatedly I see the cameras pointing in our direction. Who knows how much of our moment is making the rounds on TV now, but this doesn't matter either. They can show what we feel to the world. Then everyone will know we're this kind of happy.

Some of his teammates pat us on the shoulders. More than one heavy handed congratulation has me shaking, but it's a good feeling somehow. They welcome me with big smiles and more than one joke about catching their receiver.

I would tell them he caught me first, but that's for him and us and the people we love. He squeezes my hand again and leads me deeper into the crowd. He takes me to those who know us best. I don't need him to explain who the four people in front of us are. I smile at his family and study them with the same curiosity they do me.

Saint is a blend of his parents. They all share the same complexion, but the waves in his hair are his mom's, while his dimples are his dad's. The shape of his eyes are the same as hers, while the eyebrows are a carbon copy of the older man. Both smile at me with wide grins, shifting between inspecting me and giving their son a pointed look. I think they're pushing Saint to introduce us already.

He doesn't just yet. Saint puts a hand on one of the twins' shoulders and smiles at them. The two must be identical, though they don't dress the same. One is in jeans and a graphic t-shirt, with her hair in a ponytail. The other wears leggings and a skirt, her hair in a braid. They're wiry and tall for their age, and look at me with shock more than anything else.

I press my lips together to hide a giggle. Glancing to the side is meant to give them some privacy as they pull themselves together. Locking eyes with my brother is an accident.

Pablo stands next to Saint's parents. He's staring at us with a dumbfounded look, worse than the twins'.

I bit my bottom lip. I'm pretty sure it doesn't do anything to hide my grin.

"Hey, so," I start. "I'll say hello first to Saint's family, okay?"

He doesn't respond. Saint glances at Pablo but doesn't do much else.

Saint clears his throat and turns to the twins. "Mis divinas, I'd love for you to meet Ames."

Closer to them now, I catch a few extra details. Both of them already have the marks of dimples on their face, even as they frown at us. They have streaks of blue in their hair, though they have it in different places— one has it at her left temple and up to her ponytail, while the other only shows down the braid. Silver threads mix into them, shining in the stadium lights.

I didn't expect the nerves in my stomach.

"Hi there," I smile. "It's lovely to meet you. Great job with the Hypersquare board, by the way."

"Hi. I'm Aixa," the one in the skirt says. "This is Maribel."

"Thank you." A tenuous smile appears on Maribel's face. "We love making the board. It means Saint has to think of us while he's away."

"Something tells me he would think of you even without the board," I say.

We're in a tight group, the field is so full of people. Someone walks past us and we come a little closer.

"Are you his girlfriend?" Maribel asks.

"Mari!" Aixa exclaims. "We shouldn't ask that!"

"But it's the first time we meet anyone he's kissing out in public like this!" Mari fake whispers.

I don't know what to say, so I say nothing. No one can take the grin off me, though.

Saint glances at Pablo, then his parents.

"Yep." He presses his lips together, but his dimples show deep and sweet. "Ames is my girlfriend."

Pablo's eyes grow wide, but he still says nothing.

Saint's mom opens her arms. "Can I hug you? It's the first time I meet— tú sabes. A girlfriend."

She seems flummoxed.

"Mom—" Saint tries, but I step into her arms.

"It's a pleasure to meet you." I automatically kiss her on the cheek like we do in Uruguay.

"Will you come visit us with him?" She puts her hands on my shoulders. "I have so many questions."

"Oookay." Saint calls for his dad. "We're not pressuring her into that right now. Papá? This is Ames. Ames, this is Patricio."

"Call me Pat." He shakes my hand. "I didn't know my son knew the word *girlfriend* existed."

I laugh.

"Oh, and I'm Juliana," his mom says. "You can call me Julie. And whether or not Gael is prepared to bring his girlfriend to our home, I am inviting you now. You can come without him."

"Mamá," Saint says while I laugh again.

Logan shows up with Bear on his tail. He makes a head gesture I don't understand, but Saint nods.

I gaze around us. Evie and Pen stand a few yards away. They wave at me excitedly, smiles plastered to their face and eyebrows wiggling wildly. I grin back and wave at them. With a small series of gestures, I tell them I'll find them soon.

"A sec," Saint says to Logan.

Pat and Julie continue like nothing happened.

"We waited too long for this!" Julie says. "Pat— Gael tiene novia!"

"I have to go for a bit," Saint says, "but first..."

His eyes lock on my brother. Pablo stares right back, mouth pursed.

"I have to say I'm shocked too," Pablo says in an unreadable tone. "Is this for real?"

Julie and Pat gaze at each other, then at my brother. My eyes narrow. Saint sighs.

"You guys wait here." Saint tells his family. "The stage is that way. If you see action up there, watch it. If not, you plan how else you're going to tease me now that you've met Ames. I'll come back for you guys in a bit. Pablo? Come with us?"

Saint holds my hand tight. I squeeze back. Pablo crosses his arms but follows us.

People are still packed on the field. We find a spot nearby and make our own little group. I'm not sure what Logan's sign meant or what Saint has to do next, but there's no time for that when Pablo frowns at us.

I frown back. "Please don't get toxic now at this ripe old age of ours."

"Toxic?" he says.

"Pablo..." Saint tries for conciliatory.

I stare my brother down, never mind he's taller than me. He's not *that* much taller.

Saint looks like he meant to keep talking, but I take over.

I raise an eyebrow at Pablo. "It would be a pity if you go pre-historic on me now and think you can disapprove. But if you do, you have to know it won't stop me. I am with Saint now."

Saint's eyes are on me. I'm too busy holding a defiant stare on Pablo to see it clearly, but I think he likes my reaction. I confirm it when he kisses my cheek.

Pablo raises both eyebrows high. "Look— I saw the way you looked at each other in college. I'm not a fool. But after all this time, I didn't think living together for a couple of months would change your mind. The Saint and Ames I knew wouldn't get into something like this. Saint— you've never had a relationship that lasted more than two weeks. And Ames, well..."

I clench my jaw. "Toxic. Medieval, at least."

My brother rethinks whatever he planned to say and closes his mouth.

Saint puts a hand on my back and adds his two cents. "You know why my parents teased me like that five minutes ago? Because I told them to not expect girlfriends, years ago. I told them I would never bring anyone home. That changed with Ames."

Saint gives me a small smile. Pablo studies him.

"Ames isn't just another short-term date," Saint tells my brother, while gazing at me. "I'm all in. And even though I haven't properly asked, the fact Ames is here says she is in, too."

"I just don't want to see you both hurt," Pablo says. "I thought you wanted different things. That's all. I love you both."

I shake my head. "We're not getting into this without thought— or without care for each other."

329

Saint brings me closer but gazes at my brother. "Do you need to know I agonized over this? Because I did. I've felt things for Ames since the start. Having her close these past few months showed me just how much I feel for her. I never want to hurt her, Pablo. I hope you can trust that."

I gaze at Pablo. "All you have to do is believe us. This is right for us. We're going to make this work."

My brother gazes from me to Saint. Gears turn in his brain— I see them coming up to speed behind his eyes.

I place a hand on Saint's face and make him look my way. "Kiss me again. Maybe he needs more evidence—"

"Okay!" Pablo complains. "I saw you already. I don't need to see it again."

"You better get used to it," Saint says and kisses my temple.

"Fine." Pablo stares up to the patch of sky we can see between tall gallery structures, cables, and lights. "I believe you, but please admit this is weird."

"It's not weird," Saint argues. "It's everything I wanted."

"Fuck," Pablo complains. "You look way too happy for me to fight you on this. God forbid I'm toxic now. Pre-historic, she said."

"Exactly." Saint grins. "You wouldn't want to be any of those things. But even when I thought you might be, it didn't stop me from falling for your sister."

I shrug. "I didn't even worry about it too much."

Saint laughs and steals a kiss from me.

Pablo groans. "Fine! I got it. I'll get used to it. Eventually."

"You'll have time to acclimatize," I say.

Dom appears by our side.

"We're waiting for you, lover boy," he says. "Come on. You can charm your girlfriend later."

"I have to go," Saint kisses me once more and ignores Pablo's renewed groan. "It's time to get the trophy. I'll find you later."

"I'll be with Evie and them, and your family."

"We'll deal with LA later," he says.

"We'll deal with *everything*."

# Chapter 43

## Saint

I'm on top of the world.

With the trophy in one hand, the other one goes tap tap. Tap tap. Tap tap.

# Chapter 44

## Ames

Those few hours after Saint gets his trophy go by in a blur. We celebrate and party together at the hotel, and I kiss Saint so much I lose count.

We take breaks, of course, but we never stop touching one another. We hold hands. We hug. We stand side by side, me tucked to his shoulder and his arm around me. His team, his family, our friends, and my brother surround us. It's joy all around.

They tease us. We take it in stride. When Evie announces that Saint and I are going viral, we laugh with everyone else.

This is a time when I love notoriety. It's medicine for the last time a video of me got really popular online. All doubts I ever harbored are crushed under the sole of this moment.

Eventually, Saint gets me a driver to take me back to LA, and insists on taking me to the car. The pilot for my show is still scheduled to be recorded in the morning. I have to go back to my hotel, but he can't leave with me. He's still tied to expectations until he can go back home in twelve hours.

We leave the party and walk toward the elevator at the other side of the hall.

"After you come back from LA on Monday night," he says, "we'll have a party of our own."

"Do you think it will be different?" I ask. "Sleeping together now that we're... together?"

We step into an elevator.

He kisses me. "It will be so good we'll never forget."

"Promise?"

A feral smile is the way he answers, before kissing me again. Pushing me against the mirrored wall. If there are cameras in the elevator, a few guards get a bit of a show.

"I had my time tonight," he says when we stand near the car. "You will have yours tomorrow. You will shine."

"I'll take a nap in the car, then sleep some more in the hotel. Traffic shouldn't be as bad on the way back, right?"

"That's what the map says, but text me throughout."

We do just as we planned. I go back to LA and film the pilot with a permanent smile on my face. I'm pretty sure I glow, and true joy fills my voice every second of it. The amount of praise I got after gives me hope. Their questions about production and scheduling even more.

Later in the day, when I'm up in the air, I grin realizing Saint is probably on the way back home at the same time.

He's already there when I make it back. With arms wide open, he welcomes me to the condo. I run to his arms, and we kiss in the middle of the room.

With these two big things behind us, our calendars open up. All I can do is wait for the answer about the TV show, which should take about a week. Until then? Saint makes sure to provide me with a million new memories.

We come back up for air when it's time to visit the Thunderdome. My confirmation email could arrive in my inbox any second now.

I'm waiting in the locker room with Evie. Players are counting betting points to finalize who's taking the Hypersquare crown for the off season.

Saint and Logan's cubbies live side by side. Evie sits on Logan's chair while I sit on my boyfriend's. Logan stands with his friends nearby. He frowns while they rib him about losing the crown, after winning it his first year, when he proved Evie wanted to date him and got a few extra points for it.

We're waiting because Dom and Bear are vying for the prize. Dom won the bet about who makes the board, after the very chatty twins revealed the secret at the after party. It's not enough to win. But Saint is up with management at the moment, discussing his future with the team. When he comes back, he'll know if he stays. If he does, Dom will steal the crown.

The gossip mill runs on a healthy current of news and whispered updates among players, their agents, and everyone else. People have heard rumors about Saint possibly leaving. The consensus is that now that they won the season, it won't happen. Still, they won't celebrate until Saint comes back with confirmation.

Besides, fans seem to be enamored with our love story. It made the rounds of social media, where it got picked up by fans and connected to my video throwing a smoothie over Aidan's hair.

"I'm telling you," Evie says. "Strike fans are eating it up. Everyone knew Saint's fame as a playboy. Then he goes and makes his feelings for you public for millions and millions of people. *Globally.*"

"Not that I'm upset by what you're saying," I reply. "But he must have kissed someone on record before?"

"From what I'm seeing, you're the first."

"Not even when going in and out of the club?"

"Not even. I'm serious. Everyone understands what that kiss really means. The owner and all of the front office would be silly to ignore the power of that kind of PR. Fans would hate to lose Saint. That kiss was too good."

I mellow for the millionth time. That kiss was really, really good. Just thinking about it brings back the roar of ten thousand people into my chest.

Saint shows up from the side and kisses my cheek. "It's because everyone can see you're my last first kiss."

I turn to gaze at him.

He kisses me again, this time on the lips. "And the first kiss I want to last."

"Oh, okay." I smile. "This is how it feels to melt inside. Once upon a time, I would have thought that line to be cheesy."

"It's cheesy when you're not already in your feelings," Evie says sagely.

"Uhm, excuse you both." Saint raises an eyebrow. "It's not cheesy if it's true—"

"Saint!" I stand. "What are we doing talking about cheese?!"

"Cheese has so much umami—" he keeps going like he needs to defend one of his favorite foods, or let his reputation be ruined.

"How did the meeting go?!" I ask.

He stops. He smiles. He grabs my face and gives me another kiss.

"I'm staying, divina," he says.

I screech and jump into his arms. People around us get what that means.

"Get me that crowwwwwwwwwwwn!" Dom roars.

Saint holds me close, not caring about how everyone else has turned their attention to the Hypersquare board. Evie joins the group dealing with the casual crowning ceremony. They give Dom his prize.

Saint only has eyes for me. I grin, thankful he's staying, and that his arms keep me grounded. I might have flown away in elation, otherwise. If he'd had to go, we would have made it work, but this is what we wanted. The life we're ready to have is here with our friends and our careers.

"Did you check your email?" he asks.

His thoughts have followed a similar path to mine. Hearing about my show is the last item in our checklist.

"Not yet," I reply. "What if they haven't responded? What if they did, and I learn they don't want to order the episodes?"

"What if they want ten episodes because they see you as the new face of their food entertainment department?"

I shake my head. "Don't. The disappointment will be too much if I let myself imagine."

"But I must." He kisses me. "Who else but me to put these thoughts in your head? You have a built-in cheerleader at home now."

When he talks about home now, it sounds different than it used to.

He shamelessly snakes a hand to my butt— to steal my phone from my back pocket.

I fake sigh. "We did talk about you wearing a skirt. And now that your sisters are making pompoms for us..."

"Ready?"

I nod. He brings me closer and guides me to tuck my head on his shoulder. He holds out my phone behind me and checks my emails. I take in his smell.

In such a short time, he already feels like home. These three months have changed everything.

I don't need a set of rules anymore. I don't need to prevent things from going awry. I don't need to change myself for the future I want.

He cares about me not for what I do, but because of who I am, and he wants it all.

I close my eyes. For several seconds, all I can hear is his heartbeat and the sounds thirty people make around us. The conversation, the laughter, the promises.

He kisses my temple. "Congratulations, mi bella."

"What?!"

I go rigid in his arms, jumping back enough to study him. I'm breathless.

He kisses me on the lips and grins at me. Dimples pop. Earring shines. Chain peeks.

Why would he be congratulating me, unless... unless he read the email and they did... and I'm going to...

He jumps to a bench in the middle of the room. "Attention, everyone! May I get a big whoop to celebrate Amelia Guerrero, the new host of 'Food For The Heart'!"

He points at me with a hand, while inviting me over to stand on the bench with him. People around us start clapping and hollering. In a daze, I take his hand and let him bring me up next to him.

He gives me a smacking kiss. "Congrats, Ames. Your ten-episode season is planned to release in early winter."

The next bit of celebration goes by in a blur, too. Saint jumps down the bench and helps me down. Shoulder pats are heavy on me again. Evie grins.

She hugs me. "Congratulations. I'll binge the season and replay it a few times."

"I'll set up a watch party," Saint says.

Logan stands near Evie and puts a hand on her back. "Damián is saying we should go to his house for a barbecue."

Food brings me back to my senses.

"Oh! I have the perfect dessert," I say. "We'll just need to stop by at home for it."

"You do? Have dessert?" Saint looks at me confused. "I didn't see you bake anything."

"That's because I didn't want you to see me baking."

He raises both eyebrows. "Should I be worried?"

"We'll see," I say with a grin.

# Chapter 45

## Saint

We make it home.

"Are you worried?" Ames asks in a playful way.

"Let's say I'm... curious."

She lets out a delighted giggle. I follow her to the kitchen. Yeah, I'm curious. And a bit suspicious.

As a well-trained chef, she marks every container she ever puts in the fridge. She takes two plastic boxes out, the kind where restaurants put ingredients and the results of food prep. It's a Tuesday, and those have been there for a couple of days. The blue marker on masking tape reads, *Wednesday Dinner Prep.*

I didn't question it. Now I wish I had.

She opens one of the white containers to reveal a... pie. Carefully, she places it on the kitchen island.

It's beautifully decorated. The sides are naked, but detailed meringue work tops it in waves and peaks. She must have used a torch, because different tones of caramel and gold brush every edge. Chocolate shavings rest in the folds, with touches of edible gold on them.

"And now for the final touch..." she says.

Ames opens another container, this one smaller. Out of it comes a chocolate sail type of decoration, which she digs into the meringue. Gold lettering work stands out on its surface.

## FUCK FU-DATING
### Breaking up with Breakup Pies

Belatedly, I realize my mouth hangs open. I snap it closed.

She laughs. "Don't think I didn't notice you stopped baking."

"I didn't want to put any ideas in your mind."

"But you love baking."

"I came close to burning every recipe, just in case."

"What about this instead?" She pushes the pie closer to me.

I cock my head. "We decided we're not fu-dating."

She nods. "We're not fu-dating. We're dating. Properly. Nothing else matters. Not that we only meant to be roommates for a few months, or that it's only been a few months since my last break up."

"Because that one was your last break up."

"I'll have you acknowledge that we had our last break up at the same time. Remember how you had broken up with someone the morning I came here?"

I laugh and round the kitchen island.

I lick my bottom lip and lift her face with a finger on her chin. "I guess you're right."

"It's only that we found what we were looking for with each other."

"Nothing matters as much as that."

She gives me a quick kiss. "So this pie is to say goodbye to breakups. It's also a ceremony of sorts, so you can go back to baking without it involving a Bake and Bye situation."

"Can we acknowledge I used to bake for my friends too?"

"Sure. But let's take this one to Damián and Nat's house now. Let us let them make fun of us for the pie—"

"We both know they will primarily be making fun of me."

"And you'll take it like the champ you are."

I drop my forehead to her. "Soon, you'll go with me to the post-season dinner where we'll officially get our rings."

"Then we'll figure out our schedule. With trips and pre-season training..."

"And your filming dates and having to restructure your business."

"We'll do it holding hands," she says.

"I'll kiss you every chance I get."

"And isn't that the perfect way to go about it?"

# Epilogue

## Ames

### Eighteen months later

I'm trying out a new recipe for the second season of my show. Saint keeps me company while practicing a simple piano melody.

I steal a glance at him and smile. He doesn't have much time to work on his piano skills, but he's been consistent. When I questioned him about it, he said he wanted to give me a thousand happy memories with the instrument. The plan, he said, was to help me forget any negative associations with my grandma's favorite possession.

"It sounds great in theory," I replied back then. "But it makes you only even more of a catch. An athlete who has such a sweet heart? Who will put it into music, too? You know there were a few of your exes that wouldn't believe you had settled down. What if one of them tried to cut in again while we dance at the club?"

"No need to be jealous, bella. We don't have to tell anybody and, even if they did, I'd reply like I always have." He kissed me.

I turn to goo just from the thought.

*I'll marry her one day. I'm happily taken*, he said every time.

He's said it so much, those exes that thought he would never commit to someone have finally caught on. It's been ages since anyone came up to us, that didn't fully understand we are an item.

Now I'm waiting for him to propose.

I thought of marriage once in a while. The world likes to think weddings are the best day of your life— the start to your happily ever after. While I always liked the idea of a big party to celebrate your love with someone else, I never pushed for it in my past relationships. Even back then I knew enough to know what you promise at a wedding doesn't guarantee forever. I cared so much more about doing things right, than having a party where I told people I had found what I was looking for.

These days, I can't think of anything sweeter than marrying Saint. It was about finding the right person, after all. The one who wants to be with me for who I am. Who wants to stick around no matter what. That was the key I was missing.

With him, I want the party and *all* the promises.

It's a good thing that Saint seems to be on the same page. I caught him checking my jewelry box recently. Evie and Pen said they caught their husbands giving Saint advice on proposals— Logan said to find something cute with significance, while Bear insisted it had to be honest and from the heart. A couple months ago, Saint asked me if I had any dreams about how my ideal proposal would go.

I said I wanted something simple, only for us. He smiled and said nothing else.

When he proposes, I know what I will say.

*What we have feels right. I want it forever. You're my happily ever after.*

I'm pretty sure it's happening soon.

Food is prepared and in the oven for the next few hours. I clean and put everything away as Saint gets the hang of the music piece. The sound grows in confidence as he repeats the motions over and over again. It's clear he's putting the same devotion and discipline into it as he does everything else.

I come close to him. "Do you want anything to drink? I thought I might make us mate."

I kiss him on the cheek. He doesn't stop playing.

"In a little bit." He smiles, dimples and all. "Sit with me?"

I cock my head but do as he asks.

"Would it ruin your practice if I play a few notes?" I ask.

"Join me, please."

He stops working on the piece, and starts on random chords. I imitate him as if he were teaching me what he's learned.

"You smell divine," I say.

"You look beautiful, mi divina."

We're in everyday clothes, but even on a random Tuesday Saint is fashionable. He wears black pants and a burgundy t-shirt. The latter has a deep V to show off his chain, and painted black details on his shoulders. They're made to resemble lace and large enough to look like the epaulettes of a military uniform.

He keeps on playing. It's not a melody, but random little pieces. I continue to echo the movements he makes. The results should be dissonant, but they're not. They fit, somehow.

We smile at each other. Playfulness blooms.

"Why are we sitting here?" I ask.

We've had a couple of squabbles. I wouldn't call them more of an argument than when Aidan showed up the last time, and Saint told me of his feelings earlier than he'd planned. Rather than making me doubt what we have, they've made me feel better. Stronger. We know how to resolve the issues. It may even be our superpower.

And I don't have to fake being someone I'm not to make things better.

"Remember when you first came here? You asked me to let you pay rent." He snorts.

"I remember. You said you'd invoice me."

"I never did."

"Don't tell me you're thinking of invoicing me now? It's a little late for that, bud."

He chuckles and shakes his head. "I thought of invoicing you, Amy, but I'm not."

"What would you even have put there?"

"Something about a lease agreement, then a discount for being cute."

"Right, right."

"But then I thought, how do I put a price on being happy with you? On the life-changing months we had back then? If you hadn't come here that morning..."

He plays a couple more notes, both hands on the left side of the piano. They're deep and ominous.

"I don't like to think about that," I say.

"Me, neither. Every time I think about what could have gone wrong..."

I put my head on his shoulder. "It's okay. We're here now."

He plays a few more notes. From left to right, they turn lighter and brighter.

"I promised I would be." While one hand keeps on playing notes, the other one reaches for a spot behind the music rack. "And now I want to promise you more."

He holds a small velvet box between us.

It doesn't matter that I thought it might be coming. I gasp.

"This can't come as a surprise." He stops playing and opens the box.

The ring is beautiful. A large diamond in an emerald cut crowns the top of a thick gold band. Ceiling lights reflect on the polished metal shank, and sparkle on the hundred internal facets of the stone.

At least some of those bursts of light come from the tears building in my eyes.

"I thought maybe..." I manage. "Saint..."

"Ames. For the longest time, I thought I couldn't commit to anyone. I never wanted that to be wrong as much as when I met you... or when you moved in

348

with me. Now all these months later, I can't imagine my life without you by my side."

I forget everything I planned to say. I'm too choked up to say anything at all. All I can do is stare at the ring in its velvet box, then at Saint, then back to the ring. Over and over again.

He gives me a soft smile. "When I met you and tried to test myself in relationships, I didn't truly understand love. I thought it was the result of choosing someone you liked, someone you fit with, and waiting for love to show up. So much so, I went about it wrong. Until you, Ames. It's with you that I learned what love is really about. That it's because you love someone that you'll choose them every day. I will always be thankful for that."

He takes the ring out of the box and holds it between two fingers.

"Ames, you came to me one morning and took my heart. I'm glad you kept it."

All I can do is nod.

"I promise I'll never stop wanting to love you," he continues. "I'll stay right here, next to you, holding your hand as we walk together. No matter what the journey throws at us."

My voice comes out thin with emotion. "I promise the same."

"Should we put that in our vows? Promise it in front of our friends and family?"

There are words I meant to say. They're nowhere to be found.

"If you say yes," he adds, "I thought we could celebrate. My group chat is waiting to hear the news. If you agree to add this promise to our lives together, they'll bring their better halves for dinner tomorrow night at our favorite restaurant. Logan with Evie, and Bear with Pen of course. Being the two happily married couples in the group, they felt very strongly about congratulating us properly. Everyone else will join. Nat and Damián, and Dom and Mariana as well. Rafa might not make it but he's invited, plus-one TBD."

He's naming our friends, the ones who will always be there for us too. Saint knows how important they all are to me as well. That in this story of him and I, friends were a gift that keeps on giving. No matter what, my friends are there for me, too.

My life is truly rich now. Everything I ever wanted, but didn't know how to recognize.

"I knew they knew," I finally say. "What about your family?"

"We'll call them later, and go out to celebrate when we visit them next."

"Aixa and Maribel are going to lose it."

"They already are. Now can you imagine my mom?"

"And Pablo? Does he know?"

"I... let him know. Did not ask for permission."

"You know me so well."

"He said he saw this coming and is happy for us. That he'll visit us soon and take us out for dinner."

"So everyone knows. And we're going to celebrate?"

He nods and offers me the ring.

"And what if I had said no?" I ask.

"You haven't said *yes*, divina."

"Oh, did I forget?" I gently grab his face and kiss him.

"Tell me yes, Ames. I beg."

"Yes, Gael. I'll marr—"

He kisses me firmly. "Fuck. You always make me work hard."

"But you love it."

"I love it." He puts the ring on my finger. "And I love you."

"I love you, too."

The ring shines on my finger. Saint takes my hand and kisses it.

One last promise, and everything I dreamed of.

The best happily ever after I could ever have... because it is with Saint.

Do you want to read about **Ames and Saint sharing big news with the twins**, while Ames is recording her cooking show? Visit the film studio when you sign up to my newsletter! Go to leonorsoliz.com/catch-2ep and get the second epilogue.

You will also get exclusive NSFW art when you sign up ;)

# Thank you

Writing this book was the result of a lot of love and patience.

Summer was a hectic, extremely busy time. I sold a house, bought a new home, moved and downsized, and visited family abroad. We went through many transitions as a family. Through it all, I kept working my day job and writing. I stressed about how long things took, and lost sleep every time I had to move the release date again. But the book is here now and I couldn't be happier.

I couldn't have done it without the help of wonderful people.

First, my little family. Without their patience and encouragement, I would still be writing and editing and trying to reach the final line. I want to thank Mr Leonor, for taking over a bunch of extra responsibilities to let me pursue this dream. Thank you for reassuring me when I need it, and for never being angry that I am yet again asking you to edit in only one week.

Next, I'd like to thank my friends. From support with plot to wonderful ideas, you nourish my stories. Thank you, Janelle, for the Bake and Bye and the smoothie on Aidan's hair idea. Thank you, Sookh Kaur, for understanding like few people really can, and for helping me shape this story to what it is today. Going on a dramatic Author Vent with you is always a highlight, too!

I also want to thank my beta readers. Your commentary helped me polish this story and fine-tune Saint and Ames' happily ever after. Thank you Cassie, Erica, Jennifer, Josie, Keshia, Lynell, Michelle, Mikayla, and Shona.

Finally, I want to thank my readers, especially those who volunteered to help me spread the word of Saint and Ames. One of the best things about being indie is that I can do whatever I want with my book, and I promised you this time I would do something fun. If you signed up to help me with a cover reveal, I would thank you here on the book. Your name printed for posterity! And wow, was that amazing.

Many thanks go to...

**... people who tagged me on social media:**

@addicting_reader92

@audiobooksmostly

@bee.in.a.book

@books.with.love.handles

@cubanareads

@dara90210

@hellopotato21

@marisolreadsbooks

@naturally.caffeinated.reader

@priri.reads

@read_with_serena

@shellbelleh

@spice.spine

@the_bookish_brewnette

@tia_birsreads

**... people who shared to stories:**

@_afterthischapter

@amberinpages

@andireadsromance

@bookishlatinajenn

@_bookish_lauren

@booksandcurls

@booksareadoorway

@bookwhimsy2

@bookworm_dre

@brennathebibliophile

@cover2covertx

@chronically_kd

@curvygirlreadsromance

@curvyliterary

@daisywrenauthor

@danislittlereadingnook

@dees.libros

@delightfullychaotickay

@fatgirlsmut

@gi_reads30

@isabel.reyes.34

@kimberlyyyreads

@kristyb_readsromance

@lahobbitcurvy_

@leyendoconc

@librosconshoutouts

@marianbooks.613

@marisolreadsbooks

@messing_with_books

@mimi_throughthepages

@naturally.caffeinated.reader

@ninafiegl.books

@rubys.biblioteca

@sarah_thebooknerd

@saritasbookshelf

@shellbelleh

@stylesaplenty

@thecurvysavante

@tightly.unraveled

@what.karla.reads

@whatsgabireading

@yarleneslibrary

**... and people who signed up to share:**

Ale

Alexandra Shaw

Alexiana Gala

Amanda

Ana Rosa Elliott

Angela

Ashley Sanchez

Audiobooksmostly

Birch Spiker

Brenna F.

@brittnnnay1

Carson Steiner

Cassie

Clarissa

Dara Wasalino Tremblay

Dara Wasalino treo

DeAnna Beeman

Dee C.

Kammie Dickerson

Karla Escutia

Karla R.

Kassy

Katie D.

Kimberly

Kimberly

Kori Matlock

Laura Gonzalez

Lauren Ashley

Lauren (@readknitcoffee)

Liz (@romancereader1)

Marisol (@marisolreadsbooks)

Mayra Young

Mercy Kay

Michele Inestroza (@bibbidibobbidibooksfairy)

Michelle Antunez

Michelle Hardy

Naila

Naturally.caffeinated.reader

Priyanshi (@priri.reads)

Robyn

Sally Nuttall

Sam Blevins

Samantha Vetting

Serena Buss

Sherry Harrison

Shyloh

Tegan Houze

Tiffany Ong

Virginia

If your name is repeated it's because you're extra awesome <3 Tags are weird on social media and they don't always work, so I wanted to make sure to thank you all for each little bit of support I saw. Without readers' encouragement and engagement, this journey wouldn't mean the same. Literally.

# Other Books by the Author

## Find everything at leonorsoliz.com

Some of these stories are available in audio format!

Check all listening options and audio news at leonorsoliz.com/audiobooks

To check all my series and plans, visit

leonorsoliz.com/upcoming

# About the Author

Leonor wrote her first Meet Cute at eight years old and never really stopped. After many years of practicing and dreaming, she took the plunge and wrote a full-length romance novel. Then she wrote some more.

Her books are cozy and fun: low conflict, slow burn books that will make you swoon... and will reward you with great spice. With a healthy dose of humor, these stories guarantee a happily ever after to her plus size and latine characters.

Leonor is a Latina author living in Canada, working as a therapist during the day and fitting as much writing to her life as she can. She's also a multi-crafter, trying her hand at watercolor, jewelry, and anything else that strikes her fancy. She illustrates and designs her own covers!

## Connect with me!

leonorsoliz.com

hello@leonorsoliz.com

Instagram: https://www.instagram.com/leonor.soliz/

TikTok: https://www.tiktok.com/@leonor.soliz.author

Facebook: https://www.facebook.com/leonorsolizz